THE HUNGRY HILLS

A poignant story of one woman's fight for the people she loves: the first in The Durham Trilogy

Janet MacLeod Trotter

THE DURHAM TRILOGY: heartrending sagas set in Durham's bygone mining communities

THE HUNGRY HILLS was shortlisted for *The Sunday Times* Young Writer of the Year Award.

Published by MacLeod Trotter Books

New edition: 2011

ISBN 978-1-908359-07-0

www.janetmacleodtrotter.com

(The photograph used on the cover is of Janet's maternal grandmother)

Janet MacLeod Trotter was brought up in the North East of England with her four brothers, by Scottish parents. She is a best-selling author of 15 novels, including the hugely popular Jarrow Trilogy, and a childhood memoir, BEATLES & CHIEFS, which was featured on BBC Radio Four. Her novel, THE HUNGRY HILLS, gained her a place on the shortlist of The Sunday Times' Young Writers' Award, and the TEA PLANTER'S LASS was longlisted for the RNA Romantic Novel Award. A graduate of Edinburgh University, she has been editor of the Clan MacLeod Magazine, a columnist on the Newcastle Journal and has had numerous short stories published in women's magazines. She lives in the North of England with her husband, daughter and son. Find out more about Janet and her other popular novels at: www.janetmacleodtrotter.com

By Janet MacLeod Trotter

Historical:

The Jarrow Trilogy
The Jarrow Lass
Child of Jarrow
Return to Jarrow

The Durham Trilogy
The Hungry Hills
The Darkening Skies
Never Stand Alone

The Tyneside Sagas
The Tea Planter's Daughter
The Suffragette
A Crimson Dawn
A Handful of Stars
Chasing the Dream
For Love & Glory

Scottish Historical Romance
The Beltane Fires

Mystery:
The Vanishing of Ruth
The Haunting of Kulah

Teenage:
Love Games

Non Fiction:
Beatles & Chiefs

In memory of our son Stanley – with love

*****

THE HUNGRY HILLS

Youth walked last night among rich meadows,
Breathing scent of Nature's bloom,
And lingered in the woodland shadows,
Where evening birds called through the gloom.

He climbed the walls on Highfell Moor,
Fringed around by noble trees;
Drank from streams of water pure,
Felt the kiss of Evening's breeze.

Youth watched the sunset spill its fire
Upon The Grange where he did dwell,
And felt again the heart's desire,
That months of war could not dispel.

He saw them playing on the lawn,
The carefree ghosts of boyhood years,
Until they vanished in the dawn,
The spangled dew their farewell tears.

Youth woke, still thirsty for his past,
Those hills that hungered for his tread,
But now the die of Fate was cast,
And he must follow Age instead.

Rupert Seward-Scott
June 1916, France

Chapter One

1924

Louie half crouched on the three-quarter bed she shared with her sister Hilda and cousin Sadie, and gazed down the back lane. The midden men, 'shit-shovellers' as her brother Davie called them, moved like shadows in the grey light, flickering between their cart and the back yards like silent jerking figures in a moving picture. They hurried to remove yesterday's refuse and filth before the July sun could cook up a sizzling stench from the middens. As the early birds began to chatter, the horse-drawn cart clip-clopped away down the back street, led by its phantom masters. Louie saw young Sadie scamper across barefoot to the outhouse.

'Hildy,' Louie hissed, 'it's time to get up. Hildy, it's the Big Meeting today!'

The Big Meeting! Today was the day every pitman in County Durham took to the road, along with his family, and marched in solidarity on the ancient citadel of Durham City, in celebration of their oneness as miners. In the downstairs rooms of the opposite terraced row, oil lamps were being turned up and their yellow glow spread up the street.

'Hilda, man!' Louie twisted her long plait impatiently and gave the younger girl a prod. Hilda carried on sleeping, whistling through her teeth like an old kettle.

They were obviously sisters, even Louie could see the resemblance; tall and long-limbed like their father, both with the round cheeks and small chin of their mother, and stubby noses that looked as if they had not been finished off properly. Like their three elder brothers, the girls had the bright-blue Kirkup eyes, arresting but too deep-set to be bonny, as Mrs Parkin often told their mother.

'Shame they don't have your brown eyes, Fanny,' Louie could picture their neighbour say to their mother as she leaned her large apron-bound bosom over the yard gate. 'Still, they're canny lasses, Fanny, and pretty faces don't get the washing done, now do they?'

At least she did not have Hilda's small mouth, overcrowded with teeth just as her head was overstuffed with fanciful ideas from all the books and magazines she read, and she still only twelve! She would grow out of it, Louie consoled herself.

Downstairs she could hear her mother moving about preparing for her husband's return from the night shift with their second son, John. Having snatched a few hours sleep in her parlour bed, she would be boiling up the water for their baths in front of the kitchen fire. The heady, salty smell of bacon already filled the house. Today they could all have a leisurely breakfast together, not like the surly, subdued meals that usually preceded the men going to the pit.

Reluctantly Louie admitted to herself she should be helping. She pulled at the curtain which separated off the girls from their brothers' half of the upstairs room. Ebenezer, the eldest, lay with his pillow over his head. Ever since his return from the war in Flanders five years ago he had slept like this; Eb was quiet and a bit odd. Of all the sandy-haired Kirkups, he was the fairest, thin wisps covering his baldness and eyebrows so pale they were only noticeable when covered in coal dust.

Eb worked day shift on the pit bank, sorting stones from the coal with the old men and boys; a war hero demoted to the screens. It annoyed Louie that such menial work did not seem to bother him. She had been so proud of her big brother when he had been a hewer of coal, elite among the pitmen and a hero from the Front. But she remembered the day they had brought him screaming out of the pit, held down by three men, crying like a bairn in front of the neighbours. So he exchanged his pick and explosives for the pit bank and a lesser wage, and spent his evenings in the allotment, content if not happy.

A snore rasped out from the figure slumped next to Eb, and Louie grinned. Davie was another matter. He was happy mad. His spiky hair grew like the yard brush, exuberant as himself; he was forever trying to damp it down with water when he went out.

'Our Davie was born smiling,' their mother would say affectionately. Life to him was a joke at the corner of the street with the other lads, a packet of Woodbines or a pint at the club; a kiss round the back of the stores' warehouse with one of the girls in drapery, or a dance at the chapel hall.

Davie was as uncomplicated and playful as a pup, at times as wild as a pit pony dragged into daylight, for ever incurring the sharp-tongued censure of their chapel-going father. Jacob Kirkup abhorred the demon drink, smoked a pipe twice a year - at Christmas and Big Meeting - was a faithful union man and a lay preacher at the Methodist chapel, known among the drinking fraternity as a ranter. He exhorted his sons to read and improve themselves, pointing with reverence to Gladstone on the wall of the parlour as their model, a God-fearing Liberal. Louie's father was one of the most avid readers at the Miners' Institute, self-taught and self-enlightened. He cried over Dickens, was wary of Marx and knew the Bible like the seams of the Eleanor and Beatrice pits which he had helped sink in the 1890s and worked ever since.

'Davie,' Louie shouted, 'it's time to get up. Mam's cooking breakfast. Haway, Davie, are you awake?'

There was a grunt from the dark side of the room but nothing stirred. Louie huffed indignantly. Why did he have to go drinking the night before the Big Meeting? She knew he had because he had come home smelling of liquorice to hide the wafts of stale beer. Their mother had not been fooled, but she never told him off now he was a working man of seventeen and bringing money into the house. Discipline was a matter between Davie and his father and as the latter was on night shift, there was no harm done.

'Parkin's pig is loose in the lane!' Louie taunted loudly. Eb jerked up in panic at the urgent voice, and Hilda's hissing-kettle breath came to the boil as she awoke, but Davie lay unmoved.

Louie stood in annoyance, pulling her bed-shawl around her. Parkin's pig usually provoked a reaction. Davie had once let it loose from their neighbour's yard out of sheer devilment and it had charged off towards the dene with delighted squeals. All the children from five rows round about had chased it down to the burn, with Mrs Parkin and her snotty-nosed son Wilfred in pursuit. Finally they had caught up with it when the fat beast had got stuck between two tubs on a railway siding, parallel to the leafy dene. PC McGuire had dealt out summary justice and given Davie an on-the-spot hiding, which was nothing to the one Parkin had given him on his return from the blacksmith's shop at the pit yard. He had muscles like forged iron and a ruddy face that panted like bellows when he shouted, and Davie had not been able to sit down for a week.

'Parkin's pig?' Hilda looked up in bleary-eyed astonishment.

'Yes, Parkin's pig.' Louie winked back. So began a chorus of 'Parkin's pig, Parkin's pig!' until a pillow came hurtling out of the gloom. Hilda hurled it back and a battle ensued.

'I'll give you bloody Parkin's pig,' Davie grunted, and felled Louie with a swipe

2

from his pillow. It burst and feathers flew up everywhere, covering his sisters in a soft, tickling shower.

'Eee, there'll be hell on.' Louie stifled a giggle. 'It's all your fault, Davie.'

'Isn't it pretty?' Hilda cried, chasing the elusive feathers round the cramped room as they swirled down behind the wooden chest of drawers and were sucked in under the beds by the draught. 'Like fairy snowflakes, they are.'

'You do talk nonsense,' Louie scoffed, taking charge. 'Push them under the mat, Hilda, we'll have to sweep them up while Mam's busy making the picnic.'

Davie laughed at their concern, and without embarrassment swung out of bed and pulled on his trousers. 'By, I'm ready for that breakfast. Haway, Eb, you cannot play the euphonium all day on an empty stomach.'

'Can I help you put out your best clothes, Davie?' Louie asked excitedly.

'Aye,' he grinned back, 'and Hildy can mend the tear in my shirt - it's just a small one, but she's canniest with a needle.'

Louie felt peeved that Davie had not asked her, but then Hilda's stitching was always neat; it was the one practical skill she seemed to have inherited from their mother.

Dawn light was now seeping in at the small window and they heard the scrape of boots in the back yard. Without looking, Louie cried, 'That's Da and John home. Come on, Hildy, we should be helping.'

The sisters pulled back the dividing curtain while they dressed hurriedly in work-a-day clothes. Later they would put on their Sunday best. Hilda had helped Louie alter the waist on her summer dress to make it more fashionable and had added some old lace from their mother's wedding gown to the collar. She would wear it with a straw boater and her fair hair gathered up at the front off her face and pinned at the back, now she was fifteen and no longer a schoolgirl.

The sisters flew downstairs, avoiding the men's shoes that they had polished last night and placed each pair to a step like orderly members of the colliery band. A pile of pit clothes lay like a spoil heap in the narrow corridor; the men's jackets and cut-off hoggers that enabled them to crawl in tunnels two feet high.

Without a word said, the girls picked up the coal-ingrained clothes, took them into the yard and beat them against the back wall. Hilda coughed at the dust clouding around them, and within seconds their starched white pinafores were grimy with black flecks.

'Fancy John being allowed to carry the banner this year.' Hilda stopped and smiled a dreamy smile.

'He's not carrying it, he's holding one of the cords,' her sister corrected, smearing her forehead as she pushed a loose strand of hair from her eyes.

'Still, that's a grand thing to do - like a Roman soldier marching into battle under the legion's eagle.'

Louie looked sharply at her sister, gangly as an overgrown runner bean, her long sandstone-coloured plaits unravelling about her plump cheeks. Hilda's blue eyes sparkled, though, when she talked her funny talk, and Louie wished her eyes could shine in such a way.

'Where do you get such notions?' she demanded incredulously.

'Books; Miss Joice lends them to me.'

'I've never seen you read them.' Louie was suspicious.

'Eb lets me keep them in the shed at the allotment,' the younger girl answered triumphantly. 'Sometimes I read to him while he gardens.'

Louie's mouth dropped open in amazement. Eb was a dark one, that was for sure.

'Don't tell Mam or Da mind, Louie, promise?' Hilda's face puckered in concern. Louie's face tightened, then relaxed.

'Hurry up with these clothes now, we'll make everyone late.'

'Promise, Louie?' Hilda put her long fingers on her sister's arm.

'All right - but it's not good for you, Hildy, learning isn't for girls, not more than a bit of readin' 'n' writin' and addin' up for the housekeeping.' Louie warmed to the advice-giving as she dashed her father's jacket against the brick. 'Lads don't like a lass with too much learning in her head; they'd think you was odd. Lasses with knowledge end up as spinsters, Hildy. Now you don't want to be a spinster, do you?' The older girl stressed the word as if it were some grave disorder.

There was too much of it around these days, as her mother said, too many men killed in the War and too few husbands to divvy up. Louie shuddered at the thought that there might be another conflict to carry off the young lads of her generation. Imagine living on at home for ever like the four Dobson sisters in Railway Terrace, looking after their ageing mother. Never, thought Louie! Her mother was already preparing her 'bottom drawer', filling it with pieces of linen, sheets and tablecloths. They would take them out from time to time, smelling of mothballs, and embroider flowers and initials on to a napkin or sew lace on to an antimacassar. Louie's nostrils would fill with the musty, spicy smell of her treasure, conjuring up in her mind the day when they would come out for good and adorn a colliery cottage of her own, or, if she was lucky, one of the more spacious council houses that were being built beside the village green.

'Miss Joice is a spinster,' Hilda countered after a minute of silent reflection.

'Exactly,' Louie replied. 'Teachers are spinsters 'cos they've got too much knowledge. That's what I've been telling you.'

Hilda picked up John's cap and gave her sister a direct look. 'So who are you going to marry, Louie?'

Louie felt herself blushing at so direct a question. 'Eee, how should I know? I'm not even courting yet,' she answered primly.

'Will it be one of John's friends or Davie's?' Hilda pursued the subject in her usual methodical way. It wasn't worth mentioning Eb; most of his friends had died in France.

'Maybes,' Louie held up a pair of trousers and inspected them. 'More likely one of John's with him being a hewer. They earn the best money. Davie's friends are just putters and drink all their wages at the pub. I'm going to marry a respectable lad like Mam did.'

'Like Sam Ritson?' her sister asked. 'His Da's a church warden at St Cuthbert's and he's been something important at the lodge, I've heard John say so.'

'Sam Ritson?' Louie scoffed. 'Da says he's a Communist and doesn't believe in God. I'll not be marrying the likes of him!' She vigorously folded up the trousers and slapped them on the neat pile. 'Anyways, he sounds boring. John says he's always talking about politics and getting back at the bosses. And our Davie says he cannot dance to save himself and he never goes to the socials. My lad will be a canny dancer, but.'

'Eb thinks Sam Ritson will be a great leader,' Hilda persisted. 'He speaks up for his marras when there's things to be said at the pit. Eb and John think he's canny.'

'Shut your mouth about Sam Ritson,' Louie answered with annoyance, and, tossing her hair over her censorious straight back, led the way into the house.

In the cosy kitchen there seemed hardly room to stand. Fanny Kirkup was warming the teapot with boiling water from the kettle that always sat snug on the hob of the black kitchen range.

'Mind that bath, Ebenezer!' she warned as her eldest lifted the zinc tub full of dirty water, narrowly missing the dark head of Sadie, his eight-year-old cousin. She squatted on the floor oblivious to the danger, twisting paper sticks for the parlour fire.

'We've dadded the clothes, Mam,' Louie announced, looking for approval. Jacob Kirkup smiled at his daughters, his scrubbed face as clean and shiny as a pitman's could be, and greeted them with a kiss on each fair head. He was tall for a miner and although he was into his fifties, his body was firm and muscle-bound from the relentless daily hewing of coal. Only his beard, completely white, and the snowy hairs among the red on his head betrayed the premature ageing of an energetic man.

'Hilda, set the table,' her mother ordered, 'we'll all eat in the front room together this morning.' She gave Davie a sharp look; he was already helping himself to a thick slice of bread and cheese from the central table. Louie reached up for the caddy on the high mantelpiece and spooned a generous amount of tea into the warmed pot.

'This is a proud day for the Kirkup family,' Jacob smiled as he settled into his seat at the parlour table. 'Our John helping to carry the lodge banner, aye, it's a grand day.' He patted his second son on the back and John grinned, his fair face shaved, and raw from scrubbing, with tiny creases of black in the lines around his eyes. The men took their seats at the table first while the girls served them with porridge and bacon.

'And Eb's playing in the band,' Hilda piped up, licking grease from her fingers.

'Aye,' her father agreed.

'Better not drink too much, our John,' Davie mumbled, his mouth full. 'Don't want Keir Hardie to fall off the banner into the gutter, now do we?'

John's temper flared at once. 'You're the one who should be told. You better stay out the gutter 'n' all.'

'That's enough, lads,' their father reprimanded sharply, 'or I'll cuff the pair of you.'

'Who's Keir Hardie?' Sadie asked shyly, hovering at her Uncle Jacob's elbow.

'He was one of our greatest leaders, pet.' He smiled at his niece allowing her to butter his bread for him. 'Not a Liberal, mind you, but a fighter for the working man.'

'Keir Hardie supported the suffering-gettes too,' Hilda added, struggling under the weight of the teapot.

'Suffragettes,' her father corrected.

Hilda splashed more tea into Eb's cup. 'Miss Joice said so. Keir Hardie said it was wicked what they did, making those ladies go to prison and making them eat up their noses.'

'Be quiet and pour the tea, Hildy,' her mother warned, bringing in another plate of bread. Louie looked warily at her father, knowing that for some reason, talk of suffragettes put him in a bad mood.

'Miss Eleanor was a suffering-gette, wasn't she, Mam?' Hilda persisted. 'You always said she was the nicest of them at the Big House. Miss Joice said Miss Eleanor went to prison too.'

'Aye and look what it did for her.' Jacob Kirkup suddenly exploded. 'She's like an old woman hobbling around with a stick, an embarrassment to the Seward-Scotts, she is. To think our pit's named after her as well. They wouldn't have named her the Eleanor if they'd known the way their eldest daughter would carry on. I don't want to hear any more talk of Eleanor Seward-Scott, Hilda, do you hear? Women like her don't know their place, that's what.'

Hilda looked up startled and spilt tea on the green baize tablecloth.

'Hilda, look what you've done!' her mother scolded. 'You're that clumsy you'll lose your own head one of these days.'

Louie rushed for a cloth to stem the spillage and Sadie looked on with wide, nervous dark eyes as Hilda's cheeks turned flame-coloured.

Eb ruffled her hair comfortingly as he pushed back his chair, his breakfast finished. 'Don't worry, lass,' he whispered quietly. 'I'll be off then,' he announced. 'The band is meeting at the pit gates in ten minutes, John.'

'Aye, I'm coming.' His brother stood up and the two of them left the room to get ready.

After that there was a rush to finish off breakfast and clear away and the girls quickly forgot their father's angry words in the excitement of preparation. With the picnic prepared, Louie revelled in the luxury of putting on her best clothes. Standing before the parlour mirror, eyeing the young girl with her bound-up hair and blue-ribboned boater, she felt almost attractive.

'Listen, there's the band coming, Hildy!' She flew to the window and peered out through the net curtains. She could hear the low thud of the big drum, the rhythmic blast of trumpets and brass, and the vibration of hundreds of feet on the march, as the colliery band and its supporters swung down Hawthorn Street.

'Come on, Sadie.' She helped the young girl into her coat and grabbed her hand firmly. Sadie could be awkward about bands, the noise and the crowds of people seemed to terrify her. But today Louie's enthusiasm seemed to make her orphaned cousin brave, and they stepped out into the street together.

In the fresh early light the family tagged on to the stream of villagers following the band. Louie's chest contracted with pride to see Eb up front, music clamped to his instrument, a frown of concentration on his face. Then she spotted John bearing one of the front banner cords, Keir Hardie's bearded face nodding approval from the massive flag swaying above him. Fluttering beside the miners' hero, the image of a strong-jawed pitman grasped a pick in an aggressive salute.

The banner passed and they fell in behind, beckoned on by the large flapping picture of a distressed woman and her sorrowing children on the back of the banner. 'We Succour the Widows and Orphans' it promised, a kindly union official offering a sympathetic hand to the woman in black. The picture always made Louie want to cry for the poor, sad children, and she glanced at Sadie, wondering if it would upset her 'too. But the child was humming tunelessly under her breath and making a tentative skip as she gripped Louie's hand. Louie decided that Sadie probably could not remember her parents. After all, she was only two when her father was killed in France and four when her mother, Louie's auntie, died of influenza.

The miners of Whitton Grange and their families walked the half-mile to Whitton Station and boarded the special trains for Durham City that ran all morning. It was only when they arrived in Durham that Louie realised Davie was nowhere to be seen. She was momentarily annoyed by his disappearance; she wanted to parade through the narrow medieval streets with Davie making jokes at her side. There had not been a Big Meeting for three years because of the lockout in 1921, and Davie had promised he would dance through the town with her; but then it was typical of her favourite, wayward brother to make promises he forgot to keep. So she allowed the raised voices and laughter around her to sweep all thoughts of Davie to the back of her mind.

To Louie, Durham was the 'city on a hill' to which her father would exhort the congregation to aspire when he thumped the pulpit on a Sunday. She always marvelled at the tall houses with glimpses of secluded ornate gardens, and the wealth in the shops: jewellers with chiming carriage clocks, men's outfitters and ladies' haberdashers with hats suspended in the windows like exotic stuffed birds. She longed to work in such a shop, for some kind, wealthy lady who would let her try on all the silliest fashions. But today many of the shop fronts were boarded up, their treasures hidden from the pit folk while the traders cowered at home.

Louie knew there was no escaping Whitton Grange for any fancy shop; since leaving the strictures of the classroom, life had been a relentless round of house-hold chores, and the euphoria of leaving school had evaporated like froth on a washing pot. But on Gala Day she could dream of something better.

'Are you going to see Minnie?' Hilda latched on to her other arm as they were jostled down the hill from the station.

'If she can get away,' Louie answered. Her best friend Minnie Slattery was in service in a boarding house, part of a large private school in the town. Her parish priest had given her a good reference and she had been hired as a lowly laundry maid, but being a Catholic she was lucky to be hired at all. Service or home; that was the dreary choice until they found husbands, Louie thought. She had not heard from her friend since she went away, and she longed to hear all Minnie's news.

'Hold on to Hildy,' Jacob Kirkup instructed Louie, 'and keep next to your mother.' He lifted Sadie's skinny body on to his shoulders in one easy swing so she could look out over the crowds and avoid being trampled underfoot. She clung on to the brim of his hard hat, delighted to ride so high.

Louie and Hilda skipped arm in arm, nearly whipped off their feet by the tide of bodies that moved relentlessly onwards. The tunes of bands clashed and mixed together as one phalanx of miners merged with another. As they swept on down the North Road and past the former Miners' Hall with its impressive octagonal clock tower, Louie could see an endless wave of caps and dark suits moving ahead of them across Framwellgate Bridge, their brightly coloured banners proudly held high. The girls sang as they paraded past the bystanders and Louie felt she would burst with pride.

'Mam, look at the people who've come to watch us. I bet they wish they were us,' Louie smiled at her mother. For a moment, looking at the older woman's pasty face with the dark-ringed eyes, she thought her mother was going to cry. She was dressed in her best blouse and purple skirt with matching brimmed hat; Louie was always proud of her mother's neatness and beauty. But now her face was glistening with sweat and her usual liveliness was subdued. She looks tired, Louie thought, and vowed she would help out more tomorrow.

About the time the last of the bands reached the racecourse by the riverside and the banners were arrayed around the platform of prestigious speakers, Davie was beginning his third pint of beer in the Market Inn. Disappearing from his father's watchful eye had been ridiculously simple, and he half suspected his father had allowed him to slip the leash. Whatever, he was happy in the fug of human bodies and ale, with his drinking partner Tadger Brown.

'Here's to the union,' toasted Tadger.

'The union of lads and lasses,' they chorused together, laughed and downed half a pint.

'Your John's a lodge man now, Davie. Must be proud of him, but.' Tadger pulled a solemn face, knowing how the brothers sparked.

'Proud as a lion, Tadger.' Davie nodded seriously. 'It makes me happy just thinking of him stuck in the Temperance tent celebrating with a cup of tea.' Davie grinned.

'The cup that cheers but doesn't inebriate,' they cried in unison, raising their glasses again. Davie finished his beer first and wiped his mouth on his sleeve. He half turned as someone nudged his shoulder on their way to the back sitting room.

'Watch yourself,' a girl shouted at him crossly, her tray of drinks wobbling precariously.

'Sorry, pet,' Davie smiled, and then looked again with interest. She was about his own age, slight, with auburn hair hanging in loose curls about her shoulders. Her face was made up; hazel eyes highlighted and lips reddened, and he was immediately attracted by the look of disdain she bestowed on him.

7

'We'll have a couple of pints when you're finished,' Tadger said, slurping off his dregs.

'I'm serving in the back room,' she answered with a curl of her lip.

'Then we'll sit in the back.' Davie turned and followed her so closely that her hair brushed his chin. It smelt of tobacco smoke, but he caught a heady scent of flowers from her neck. 'What's your name, pet?'

'Iris,' she replied shortly without glancing round.

'That's a bonny name for a bonny lass,' Davie persisted, fighting his way behind her through the throng of drinkers. She did not reply, banging down the tray on one of the tables and off-loading her cargo. As she turned to go, she gave Davie an appraising glance, a half-smile and a 'Two pints was it?'

'Aye, bonny Iris,' Davie winked, and knew he was going to enjoy the rest of the Big Meeting far from the fiery speeches, the brass bands and the Cathedral service.

The voice of Ramsay MacDonald rang out over the crowds of pitmen and women, but Louie and Minnie walked away arm in arm, stopping to eye the passing bandsmen and gawp at the fair stalls by the riverside.

'So this is the first time you've come into the town?' Louie asked incredulously.

'Aye.' Minnie nodded her dark head. 'I'm that tired at the end of the day I haven't the strength to go window-shopping, even if I was allowed out. I'm up early, work all day - just look at me hands, Louie! Like raw carrot sticks. Washing for all the bairns at home was a holiday, I can tell you.'

'But what about the lads, Minnie? Must be grand to live in a house with all those posh lads.' She nudged her friend playfully.

'Lads,' Minnie snorted, 'I don't get to see any. Even if I did, I wouldn't be allowed to talk to them. One of the nannies got the sack this term for talking to boys.'

Louie looked at Minnie in horror; she was beginning to think life at home in Whitton Grange was not so bad after all.

'Let's go and watch the boxing, Louie,' Minnie was suddenly dragging her sideways. A short man in a striped waistcoat was beckoning in the passers-by, challenging the young men to fight his champion, the Black Bear from Germany.

'Eee, we can't go in there, Minnie!' Louie giggled nervously and looked behind her. They seemed to have lost Hilda who had insisted on tagging along behind. She must have stopped to gaze at the gaudy musical horses at the last roundabout ride. Her vague sister would never find her own way back to the Rechabites' tent where her mother was helping to serve tea to the thirsty bandsmen and their wives. 'I'll have to look for Hildy,' Louie said with exasperation.

'In a minute.' Minnie gave a cheeky smile that made her nose wrinkle and her green eyes narrow. 'Just for a laugh, Louie, I don't get many laughs these days. Haway, just for me.'

Louie could not resist her plea. With a last look around to make sure no one she knew was watching, she followed her friend behind the tent flap.

'Come on, ladies,' the fairman encouraged, 'you're about to see the fight of a lifetime. Come and cheer on your 'ero.'

Louie grabbed Minnie's hand in nervous anticipation. 'I can see fighting any week at the top of Hawthorn Street,' she whispered to her friend in mock disapproval.

'Well, the only wrestling I get is with the mangle, so come on.'

The tent was already crowded and the smell of bodies under the warm canvas was overpowering. Louie covered her mouth with her hand and wished she had not been so easily led. An enormous man, stripped to the waist, with thick growths of black hair sprouting from his chest and underarms, was parading around the raised ring. Louie blushed at the sight but could not take her eyes off him.

'Do we have our first challenger?' the man in the striped waistcoat boomed as he jumped up on the side of the ring. The Black Bear from Germany growled like an animal and the audience booed and whistled. There was a commotion on the far side as someone was pushed forward by his companions.

'Haway, man, and get up there!'

Louie started at the familiar voice, then she caught a glimpse of her brother John's excited mustachioed face across the canvas floor. What would her brother say if he saw her standing there? Louie shrank beneath her boater, eyes pinned to the ground.

A cry went up as a man pulled himself into the ring. Louie glanced up tentatively and saw a thickset young man, with cropped brown hair and a clean-shaven square face, rolling up his sleeves. His raised fists and forearms were hard and muscled, like the figure of the worker beside Keir Hardie on their lodge banner.

And that was Louie's first real impression of Sam Ritson.

Chapter Two

Iris was finishing the last refrain of 'Oh, Danny Boy' at the piano, and Davie was in heaven. The afternoon and evening had been spent in the stuffy warmth of the Market Inn, boozing with Tadger and flirting with Iris Ramshaw, the publican's daughter. Her interest in him appeared lukewarm, but with each beer, Davie fell deeper in love with her slim, petulant face and bright hazel eyes.

Finally Iris had been persuaded to sing to the accompaniment of the piano. Davie marvelled at the sudden vivaciousness that took hold of her the moment she began performing and the strong melodious voice that vibrated out of such a small body and mouth.

'You should be on the stage, bonny Iris,' Davie shouted in her ear amid the applause. 'You've the voice of an angel.'

Iris leaned away from the flushed face of her admirer, reeking as it did of stale alcohol. Admittedly it was a passably handsome face, with wicked blue eyes that promised fun, but it was boyishly young, the upper lip nurturing soft down that yearned to be a manly growth of hair. His smart appearance was marred by the stiff collar which had become disengaged and stuck out from his neck like small wings. Still, he liked her singing, and anyone who told her she should be a professional singer warranted some encouragement. She bestowed a smile on Davie Kirkup and her fate for the evening was sealed.

Abruptly, a fight broke out in the doorway of the pub and chairs began to fly. There was uproar and the splintering sound of bottles smashing as the dispute between two rival pitmen spread through the bar.

Davie ducked just in time to avoid a blow from an unknown fist, saw Iris in the doorway of the back room, turned her around and bustled her out of an open window into the marketplace.

'Get your hands off me!' she shouted with indignation, tumbling on to the cobbles. Among the sea of empty bottles in the square was a straggle of holidaymakers who had not yet retreated to the outlying villages.

Davie squinted in the sudden daylight that stabbed his eyes. 'You're best out of that battle, pet,' he said, pulling her up. 'I just want to protect you, Iris lass.'

Ramshaw's eldest daughter did not need much persuasion to abandon her post; she had been serving since morning and had seen none of the revelries in the town. She supported her rescuer as he weaved unsteadily across Elvet Bridge and down to the riverside. The noise of the town receded as they strolled along the riverbank, breathing in the warm evening air and listening to the birds' contented evening gossip.

'Sing for me, Iris,' Davie requested, pulling her down beside him under a tree. Walking was to him a fruitless pastime unless it got him somewhere.

'Why should I?' Iris pouted, straightening out her brown skirt.

'Because you've got the bonniest voice I've ever heard.' Davie put an arm around her shoulders. 'Just for me, Iris, please.'

She shook off his hold but could not prevent a smile at his persistence. 'Very well, then. What do you want to hear?'

'"Cushy Butterfield", for a publican's lass.' Davie grinned, and began to sing the chorus:

'She's a big lass an' a bonny one,
An' she likes her beer;
An' they call her Cushy Butterfield,
An' aw wish she was here!'

His laughed and gave him a swipe of her hand across his bristly fair hair. She began to sing 'Weel ay the Keel Row' and Davie joined in the chorus. After that she drew up her knees and clasped her hands round them as she sang a traditional love song in a strong, sweet voice.

'Aw've had mony sweethearts, in maw wooing life,
 And had mony offers to be a good wife;
But me heart beats for yen, aye an' faith it beats true,
He's a bonny keel laddie wi' bonnet se blue.'

Davie lay back, eyes closed, listening to the honeyed words drift over the sluggish water of the River Wear, the heavy scent of mature foliage all around. When she finished, they seemed spellbound by the silence the song left, until the sensuous summer sound of a wood pigeon hooting in the trees above released them.

'You're a canny singer.' Davie rolled towards her and sat up. They looked at each other as the light faded from the sky and the grass around them darkened.

Iris allowed him to kiss her on the lips. Singing always aroused a deep restlessness in her and Davie happened to be there, an audience to appreciate her talent. His kisses were enthusiastic, and in spite of his slim appearance, there was a pleasing strength in his shoulders and arms; but then he was a pitman.

At that thought, she pushed him away. No colliery lad was going to get her into trouble; a life of drudgery washing coal grime from his clothes, surrounded by a pack of squabbling bairns was no life at all.

'Just another kiss, Iris,' Davie urged, craving more of her moist mouth. His head swam from the effects of the drink and the closeness of her body.

'I'll be missed,' Iris replied, standing up and shaking out the creases in her skirt. She ignored the quickening thump in her chest that kissing him had started. 'And you'll have missed the last train.'

Davie heaved himself up, disappointed by the outcome of the day. She was right; he would have to walk the ten miles back to Whitton Grange and face the wrath of Jacob Kirkup for the next week.

'Can I see you again, Iris?' He fell in step with her, hoping with his usual optimism, to salvage the situation.

'You know where I live, Davie Kirkup,' she answered, then, seeing his dejection, added, 'If you ever get away from that pit, I'd be pleased to see you.'

He grinned and smacked her cheek with a kiss; all was not lost. There was something different about Iris Ramshaw that drew him like a moth to the oil lamp. He had notched up a few conquests in the village and thought he knew just how to please a lass, but not this one.

They parted in the marketplace and Davie began the long trudge home. Thoughts came, met and vanished in his head. What had happened to Tadger? Iris Ramshaw's eyes were the colour of honey. Would he be able to get into Durham to see her again before next Big Meeting? Louie would be furious with him for slipping away at the start of the day.

As Davie sobered up on the long march home, and the sky lightened his way into the valley that held Whitton Grange, he whistled the tune of 'Cushy Butterfield' and thought pleasant thoughts.

Mrs Eleanor Seward-Scott was holding a musical evening at The Grange, the modest Georgian country house that had grown up into a sprawling mansion with Victorian bell tower and turrets and Gothic windows and archways that proclaimed it the king of the countryside. She took pleasure in these musical gatherings that had been such a feature of her mother's entertainment when she had been alive; Lady Constance had played the grand piano beautifully and sung Scottish ballads in her soft, unaffected

Highland voice, before tuberculosis had robbed her of life.

Eleanor could not sing. Instead she thrived on the convivial companionship and conversation that such occasions brought; her close friend Isobel Joice, the local teacher, was there with her father Dr William Joice, and there were her own father's friends the Swainsons, who were shipping magnates. Eleanor's husband Reginald was a passably good singer in spite of his rather abrupt, military delivery; but the evening had really taken off when her younger sister Beatrice's friends from Cambridge had entertained them with a sketch from their college revue. Even stuffy Reginald had shouted 'Bravo!' and the Swainsons' rather silly daughter Harriet had gone into uncontrollable giggles.

'This has been a wonderful evening, Eleanor.' Isobel thanked her with a kiss on the cheek.

'Don't go yet,' Eleanor pleaded. 'Stay for a nightcap.'

Isobel smiled regretfully at her friend. 'Papa's really very tired. But you'll call and see us during the week, won't you? Now that term's finished I've got bags of time to chat. We'll discuss Winifred Holtby's new book.'

Eleanor's thin face lit up at the thought; she liked nothing better than to curl up on the Joices' sofa and discuss books and ideas with Isobel and her father.

'That's a promise,' Eleanor agreed. She turned and saw Mrs Swainson trying to extract her husband from the earphones of the new wireless set that her father was showing him. Eleanor smiled; her father had to have all the latest gadgets available and he had hardly been able to sit still through the entertainment in anticipation of showing his friend his latest toy. Thomas Seward-Scott was a man of action and progress who had kept a controlling hand on his estates and mines rather than trust all to his agent. His own father, Oswald Scott, had done the same before him. Eleanor's grandfather had secured the hand of the Seward heiress and injected her haphazardly run estates with his own ruthless energy. Thomas had all his father's energetic temperament and business sense, and had made a small fortune from his mines before the war with Germany, when prices had been high. But since Eleanor's elder brother Rupert had been killed in the Battle of the Somme, it was Reginald, himself a Scott and a second cousin of Eleanor's, who was to be successor to the Seward-Scott fortune. How very appropriate their marriage had seemed in 1914, Eleanor remembered ruefully. Reginald had even adopted the Seward into his name.

Eleanor glanced at her husband. He stood in his evening tails and starched shirt, propped against the grand piano, cigar in hand, chatting to Beatrice's latest boyfriend, Charlie Ventnor. Reginald was tall and good-looking, with a well-trimmed moustache and a strong chin; he was moderately intelligent, supremely confident and held strong opinions. Yet Eleanor could not now remember why she had married him.

'Fix me a whisky and soda, darling,' she said as she joined the young group that was staying at the house. Her sister Beatrice was often stupid and irresponsible, like so many of the young these days, but Eleanor loved it when her vibrant sister deigned to come home from her partying in London or Cambridge and filled the quiet house with guests.

Reginald gave his wife a censorious look as she flicked open her cigarette case and inserted a Turkish cigarette into the end of a long ivory holder. She ignored his disapproval.

'Turkish or Virginia?' She offered the case to Charlie.

'I'll have a gasper, thanks, Ellie.' Charlie reached for an ordinary cigarette.

'No one calls her Ellie, silly,' Beatrice slipped her hand playfully through Charlie's arm. 'Eleanor's far too highbrow for that.'

'Gosh, sorry.' Charlie blushed. 'Damn silly name anyway - Ellie, I mean, not Eleanor, of course.'

'Just shut up, Charlie,' Beatrice ordered, and took a puff of his cigarette. 'Let's all dance now those stuffed shirts have gone.'

'Beatrice!' Eleanor tried to sound disapproving.

'Oh, I know they're yours and Daddy's friends, sis, but they're not exactly ripping fun, are they? And as for that Harriet Swainson, she spent the whole evening simpering and making cow's eyes at Charlie.' Eleanor could not help laughing. 'Come on, Charlie, you wind up the gramophone and Sukie and I will show you how to dance the modern way. Harry's got some of those American jazz records from his cousin in New York, they're absolutely topping.'

'Not Negro music.' Reginald humphed in disgust.

'Oh, don't be so stuffy, Reggie,' Beatrice teased him, 'even Daddy listens to American jazz on the wireless, don't you, Daddy?'

'I shall retire to bed,' Thomas Seward-Scott grinned indulgently at his younger daughter, 'and leave you young things to dance the night away.' He kissed his daughters and withdrew.

Eleanor, watching Beatrice and her friends roll back the animal rugs and dance on the polished floor to a new Irving Berlin number, wished she had half their energy. A walk around the grounds with the aid of a stick still left her feeling breathless and exhausted. Neither could she join in their games of tennis, but preferred to lie in the shade of the trees and read. It annoyed Reginald that she did not join in any more, but then most things she did seemed to annoy her husband.

To avoid further disapproval from Reginald, she walked over to the decanter and poured her own drink. To her relief, he did not notice, being transfixed by Beatrice and Sukie's dancing. Beatrice looked so attractive, with her brown bobbed hair shaped with a new permanent wave and her green eyes underlined with black, giving her a vampish look. Her lips were shaped like Cupid's bows in a bright red which matched her nails, and she showed off slim legs as she hitched up her evening dress and kicked.

'Beatrice tells me you're a friend of Dr Marie Stopes.'

It was quiet, dark-haired Harry with the American cousin who spoke.

'I suppose I am.' Eleanor considered him and puffed on her cigarette holder. 'I took an interest in her birth control clinic in Holloway when she first started. I'd like to set up a similar thing here one day.'

'Bit risqué, isn't it, all this talk of sex and contraception for the masses?' He smiled.

'Maybe, but such education is necessary.' Eleanor was not embarrassed by the subject. 'If you saw the poverty and overcrowding in pit villages like Whitton Grange you'd agree.'

'So you're a bit of an expert on sex and marriage then?' Harry's look was disconcerting. Eleanor knew Reginald was suspicious of him because he wore outrageously wide Oxford bags, and shoes of brown and white.

'I may have read her books, but that doesn't make me an expert. As you can see, we have no children,' Eleanor answered sardonically; she would not let him see how she really felt about her infertility.

The record had finished and Reginald crossed the room to monitor his wife's conversation with the dubious Harry Stanton, who certainly did not seem like the youngest son of a baron to him. For a moment he viewed his wife objectively; she was too thin to be pretty in the conventional sense, although a lack of figure seemed to be all the rage these days. But she was elegant in the shimmer of black silk that swathed her svelte frame, her too-short cropped bob of black hair hidden in an exotic orange and black turban that complimented the prominent bones of her face and the large dark-brown eyes that dominated all. Her skin was so pale it was almost translucent, and in daylight she looked pasty and older than her thirty-one years; but in the electric lamp-light she looked energised and interesting, which was obviously what Harry Stanton thought.

'You have a modern wife,' the young undergraduate said in his easy drawl as Reginald joined them.

'Has she been boring you about the suffragettes again?' Reginald snorted. 'No, don't tell me; Eleanor has been recounting the speeches of those awful Bolshies who were haranguing my colliery workers in Durham today. Everyone else has the sense to avoid the city on Gala Day except my wife.' Reginald sounded more sarcastic than he had meant to be.

'Don't be ridiculous, darling, Durham was full of people today,' Eleanor countered.

'We were discussing Dr Stopes, actually,' Harry intervened quickly, sensing trouble in which he wanted no part.

'Really, Eleanor, this is hardly the time or place,' Reginald reproved.

'For what, Reggie?'

'For talk about - you know,' he blustered.

'Birth control?' Eleanor supplied the words.

'Exactly.' Her husband gave her a warning look. He was so tediously sensitive about the subject, Eleanor thought wearily, as if she was likely to go telling this boy details about their inability to produce a child. Reginald blamed her of course. He thought it was a result of her being force-fed in prison before she came to her senses and married him. But she had only been incarcerated for a week before her gaolers discovered she was someone of consequence and released her. No, their problems went deeper than that, but Reginald was the last person with whom she could discuss them. Their lovemaking was joyless and, more tragically, fruitless; but that was none of Harry Stanton's business.

'What would you like to talk about, Reggie, darling?' She smiled, knowing just how to annoy him. 'About your stocks and shares, or the price of coal? Harry, what do you know about mining?'

'Absolutely nothing, thank God.' Harry laughed. 'They say it's such a grubby little job.' He made his escape, finding Reginald Seward-Scott's conversation as boring as last year's fashions.

'Don't bite the hand that feeds you.' Reginald gave his wife a contemptuous glance. His spark of attraction towards her had dissipated; as a mark of his disapproval he would not visit her room later. 'Those grubby little jobs, as your admirer cares to call them, keep you in the house that you love. Always remember that.'

A few days later, Eleanor called on Isobel Joice and they sat on wicker chairs in the Joices' mature walled garden with its glimpse of the leafy dene beyond, facing away from the packed rows of colliery houses. Isobel's father was out on a call and they drank leisurely cups of tea, talking about everything from literature to Beatrice's latest escapades in Mayfair.

'I'm thinking of returning to London with her when she goes,' Eleanor said quietly, her gaze intent on a cascading clematis. Isobel shaded her eyes with a hand and squinted at her friend in surprise.

'For a shopping trip?' Isobel questioned.

'No, for longer. I had a letter from Marie Stopes yesterday; she's cock-a-hoop about the libel appeal going her way. She's asked me to plan a lecture tour for her around the north.'

'You could do that from here,' Isobel commented.

'Yes,' Eleanor admitted, 'but I also need to get away.' She looked directly at her friend. This fair-haired schoolmistress, her oldest friend, who should have been her sister-in-law had her brother Rupert survived the war, was the only person to whom she could really talk. 'Things aren't any better between Reggie and me; the only thing he wants from me is a son and heir and I can't give him one.' Eleanor reached for her cigarette case and holder on the portable Indian table. Isobel waited in silence as she lit up. 'If I can't be a mother, Isobel, I might as well be useful doing something else, like helping at Marie's clinic or something. Reggie's so wrapped up in selling coal to the Scandinavians or whoever he won't even notice I've gone.' She blew out smoke vigorously. 'I want to do something useful with my life like you have. You're a born teacher, you always have been.'

'I wouldn't have been one if Rupert had lived, remember,' Isobel replied reflectively.

'Oh, Isobel.' Eleanor reached over and squeezed her hand. 'I know. You would have been a darling of a sister-in-law too.'

They sat on in silence for a moment, each lost in private reminiscence. A light breeze brought the distant thrum of the pithead's ceaseless industry to them, but it was so much a part of the place that neither was disturbed by the noise.

'Remember the tennis fours we used to make up?' Eleanor smiled.

'Oh, yes.' Isobel joined in the game. 'Rupert and I always beat you and Reggie.'

'No you didn't! I was horribly athletic in those days, don't you remember?'

'Reggie was always shouting at you to leave the ball because it was going out, but you always had a go at hitting it.' Isobel laughed.

'Oh, dear Reggie, I was really quite fond of him before the war,' Eleanor mused.

'So was Rupert,' Isobel sighed.

'Yes, they were such good friends. Strange for cousins to be so close, don't you think? I mean, being forced on each other in childhood with Reggie's parents being abroad so much, you would think they would have loathed each other.'

The maid, Margaret Slattery, came and removed the tea tray. The breeze was becoming more chill, but both women were reluctant to move.

'You and Rupert should have married before the war, just as Reggie and I did,' Eleanor said after the maid was out of earshot.

'Would you have married Reggie after the war?' Isobel asked quietly. They both knew the answer.

'We seemed to be swept away with the urgency of it all.' Eleanor tried to excuse herself. 'Everyone was doing it. I was fond of him, but I also felt desperately sorry for him, Isobel. I really didn't think he was coming back. I suppose I looked on it as doing my own little bit for the war effort.'

'Oh, Eleanor, you are impossible!' Isobel couldn't help laughing 'You were in love with Reggie then, everyone could see it. Rupert was thrilled at the match, he took all the credit.'

'So I've got him to blame.' Eleanor rolled her large dark eyes and then realised what a crass remark she had made. Isobel glanced away. 'I've never told anyone this, Isobel,' Eleanor added quietly, 'but I used to pray that if one of them had to die and one was allowed to come home, Rupert would be the one to be spared. By the time Reggie came home, it was like being married to a man I'd never met.'

'Don't, Eleanor—' Isobel began to protest, but her words were cut short by the arrival of her father.

'What a delightful sight. Am I too late for tea, my dears?' Dr Joice greeted them.

'I'll get Margaret to bring some more out, Papa.' Isobel jumped up with relief. For a few minutes Eleanor chatted to the doctor about the garden; she knew it was his passion, but as local doctor and district medical officer he seldom had the chance to indulge it. Isobel returned.

'Is all well at the Kirkups', Papa?' she enquired, pouring out his tea herself. His long, chiselled face took on its world-weary look.

'Poor Fanny Kirkup is not at all well.' He shook his head. 'I'd like to get her into hospital, but the family want to nurse her at home - they're worried about the cost, of course.'

'The name sounds familiar.' Eleanor's brow puckered.

'You may know her.' Dr Joice sipped his tea. 'She used to work up at The Grange in Good Queen Victoria's Day.' It was a favourite expression of his which he applied to a past that had mellowed into nothing but happy memories; a time before his wife had succumbed to influenza. 'Fanny Beal she was called then.'

'Fanny Beal, yes!' Eleanor had a vague recollection of a plump and pretty housemaid who used to clean the nursery. 'I think I picked flowers for her when she left to get married. She was dark-haired and lively, could that be the one?'

'Probably.' Dr Joice slurped thirstily. 'She has a large brood in Hawthorn Street - not sure if all of them are hers. The place is stiflingly hot and full of dust from the men's clothes, quite the worst conditions for a woman suffering from a lung complaint like hers.'

'Mrs Kirkup collapsed on the day of the Miners' Gala,' Isobel explained. 'How will they manage with her so ill, Father?'

'Their elder daughter Louisa seems to have taken charge; she's a sensible girl,' Dr Joice assured his daughter. 'She'll have a job on her hands, mark you.'

'Oh dear.' Isobel looked worried. 'I hope it doesn't mean Hilda Kirkup won't return to school; she's such a bright girl.'

'You teach one of the family, then?' Eleanor asked.

'Isobel's taught at least three of them, haven't you, my dear?' Her father smiled.

'Yes, but Hilda's the most promising of them all. I've never known a pupil have such a thirst for reading at her age. She's only twelve and she's devoured all my Jane Austen and Charles Dickens and even Father's Matthew Arnold poems.'

'What a protégée, Isobel,' Eleanor teased.

'You'd find her interesting, Eleanor.' Isobel ignored the jibe. 'She's quite without inhibition with people like you and me.'

'Precocious, you mean.' Her friend gave an exaggerated roll of her eyes.

'Really, Eleanor.' Isobel sounded quite annoyed. 'For someone who professes to care about the working classes, you show a remarkable lack of interest in them as individuals.'

Eleanor felt rightly rebuked. 'If it makes you happy, Isobel, I'll lend her my banned copy of *Ulysses.'*

Dr Joice gave a theatrical tut and stood up. 'I shall leave you ladies to your seditious talk and go and tend my garden,' he announced, and strode away.

Shortly afterwards Eleanor took her leave and drove back to The Grange in her new Austin Seven. She always felt guilt at her relief at leaving behind the grime and squalor of Whitton Grange and the gaunt, menacing bulk of the Eleanor and Beatrice pits, clinging like black giants to the side of the escarpment. She never felt easy that a mine was named after her, that people died in her name. Thankfully this year, no one had; the Whitton Grange lodge banner held aloft at the Durham Gala had not been draped in the ominous black crepe that spoke silently of fatalities. But next year, or the following one, it might be different.

She shuddered, and then put such bleak thoughts from her mind. Tonight she had arranged a theatre party for Beatrice and her friends and would take them to Newcastle. Tomorrow she would brace herself to tell Reginald that she was going to London to visit friends. By next week, she thought with pleasure, for a while at least, she would have shaken the dust of Whitton Grange from her feet.

Chapter Three

The wind that lifted the billowing washing across the back lane was raw, but spring was on its way, Louie thought with relief. A clutch of yellow crocuses stood in solidarity at the stand pump, buffeted but defiant. In a minute, Louie knew, the coal cart would come, with its driver shouting his warning, and she would have to dash out and remove the half-dry clothes before they were blackened, but for a brief moment she could enjoy a welcome cup of tea and a chat with Mrs Parkin over the clippy mat.

'Your Louie makes a lovely scone, Fanny,' their neighbour was saying as Louie re-entered the kitchen. Her mother was propped up in the spare bed, which pulled out of the large mahogany press in the corner. She had had a bad week with her chest, but with the brighter weather a glimpse of her old liveliness was returning. Louie was thankful that this Monday was not a wet one and the washing could be hung outside. They seemed to have lived all winter with the dank smell of wet washing strewn about the cramped kitchen and her mother wheezing and coughing on her bed behind a screen of shirts and tea towels.

'She's a good cook, I taught her all I know.' Fanny Kirkup smiled jokingly at her elder daughter.

'More tea, Mam?' Louie reached for her cup. They had become close since last summer when her mother had been taken ill. Louie had been terrified of her dying, but Dr Joice had said she was of strong Durham stock and would survive worse than this; and she had.

She poured her mother another cup of the well-stewed dust tea they drank. After a couple of minutes the women settled to the task of adding a few shreds of cut-up cloth to the clippy mat stretched over the wooden frame before them. The pattern was largely grey and green, but they had managed a splash of red around the border made from an old petticoat of Hilda's. The mat was nearly completed and would take pride of place in front of the parlour fire.

'Your mam tells me young Sam Ritson's been calling at the house on Saturday evenings,' Mrs Parkin began. Louie felt her fair face blushing.

'John brings him sometimes,' Louie tried to sound disinterested, 'and we sing around the piano. I don't know why he bothers, though, 'cos he spends most of the time arguing politics with me Da, doesn't he, Mam?' She looked at her mother for support.

'He is a bit serious that way,' Fanny admitted, 'but he's a canny lad - Liza Ritson has brought him up with nice manners, he always compliments Louie on the spread.'

'That's good.' Mrs Parkin nodded with approval. 'And some men like to talk politics, Louie - after all, his father's been a union delegate before. Now my Wilfred isn't political; all he talks about is football, but then lads will be lads.'

'But Sam Ritson doesn't seem to have any interests apart from politics,' Louie complained. 'He blames the bosses for low wage packets, he blames them for bad conditions, I bet he'd blame them for the snow this last winter!'

'Well, perhaps he has a point.' Mrs Parkin's fleshy lined face grew serious. 'Wilfred says three of the pits at the top of the valley are closing soon. We need fighters like Sam Ritson to stop them closing the Beatrice 'n' Eleanor.'

'Aye,' Fanny wheezed. 'Our Eb's already on short time.'

Louie could not prevent a memory coming into her head of Sam Ritson, the fighter, standing bare-armed in the boxing ring, aggressive and uncompromising, about to fell the Black Bear from Germany with a thick fist. Perhaps underneath he had the same interests as other lads, but she had yet to be convinced. He never danced at the socials at the chapel hall, he did not appear to enjoy a sing-song like her family did, and he had not shown the slightest interest in her except to thank her politely for nice teas. Yet Sam was the only lad in a family of three lively sisters, so how had he turned out so boring? His sister Bel had been a cheerful classmate of Davie's, and Louie had been at school with Mary Ritson; she was normal enough, apart from an over-enthusiasm for religion. Well, what did it matter? Louie did not give a halfpenny for what Sam Ritson thought of her.

'Louie, there's the coal man on his way.' Her mother interrupted her thoughts, and she jumped up guiltily.

'I'll be off then.' Mrs Parkin heaved herself from the kitchen stool. 'My Wilfred's shift will be finishing shortly, so I'll have to get more hot water on. By, Monday's the devil's own day. Ta-ra, Fanny.'

'Ta-ra, Edie,' her mother answered.

For Louie the rest of the afternoon was a rush to finish the hectic round of chores that came with Monday: hauling in the mounds of washing to air by the fire, boiling up endless pans of water for the men's baths when they got home, frying up the Sunday leftovers for Sadie and Hilda's tea, dubbing Davie's pit boots before he went on night shift, and finally putting on a large pan of broth for the following day; with all the ironing and baking she had to do tomorrow there would be no time for extra cooking.

Only now had she begun to appreciate the weight of tasks her mother had borne for years, work that had finally left her on the point of exhaustion. No sooner was one man safely home from the pit, bathed and fed, than another one had to be roused and waved off with a bait tin full of jam sandwiches and a silent prayer. No matter what dark hour of the night they came and went, her mother had been up to see they left with a warm meal in their stomachs and clean boots on their feet. Louie had marvelled that she ever had time to sleep, her life a constant merry-go-round of meals and washing and boiling water and baking and blacking the hearth and cleaning and mending. Now Louie was learning the art of catnapping in a chair, or climbing into bed beside Sadie and Hilda without disturbing them, for a couple of hours of dreamless sleep.

Like her mother before her she felt as much a servant of the pit as her father or brothers. At times Louie resented the greedy, hungry monsters halfway up the hill, jaws whirring and clanking in anticipation, swallowing the men whole, day after day. The women fed the men who fed the pits. The pitmen toiled and clawed in the black dampness until they were spat out, exhausted and bent double, at the day's end. Louie rubbed the awful vision from her tired eyes; she was becoming as fanciful as Hilda from lack of sleep, she thought wearily.

'Where in the world has that sister of yours got to?' her mother fretted as she paused over a half-darned sock. 'Sadie came home an hour ago.'

Louie rubbed her nose with the back of her hand as she prepared to fry up egg and chips for the men. 'Goodness knows. Our Hilda gets more airy-fairy by the day. She's probably up at the allotment with Eb.'

'She should be here helping you.' Fanny Kirkup began to work herself into a fluster. 'The girl's getting above herself.' Louie knew the signs, there was always this subtle tension in the air that stretched more taut as the time for the changeover of shift drew near.

Louie hummed softly in time to the ticking of the clock on the wooden mantelpiece above the kitchen range, her actions mechanical and deliberate as she prepared for the men's homecoming. The sounds of the pits beyond the open door were soothing; the trundle of trucks on the line, the rhythmic chug of the winding engines. At last they heard the short blast of a hooter, followed by the blessed crunch of boots coming up the back lane and the click of the gate. Behind her, Louie heard her mother's breath hiss with relief like the large kettle ever ready on the hob.

'That's your father and John back.' Her mother's face lightened. 'Go and wake Davie, it's time he was up.'

Hilda had sent Sadie home with her friend Jane Pinkney, making excuses about having to see Miss Joice after school, which was true. But she omitted to tell them she was going to have tea at Miss Joice's house in the dene, and now here she was, trembling on the large doorstep of the solid redbrick house, wondering whether to press the bell. On the glass above the door, ornate gold letters announced with a flourish that this was 'Greenbrae'. This was the first time she had come to the house for books and suddenly Hilda was nervous. But Miss Joice must have been looking out for her because the green painted door swung open before she had time for second thoughts.

'Come in, Hilda.' She smiled encouragingly. 'I'm just back myself and saw you approaching.' Her teacher still wore her fair hair in an old-fashioned style, bound up at the back, but her flannel skirt was raised to calf-length from last year's ankle, and her Fair Isle jumper met with Hilda's approval.

'I've brought back *Tess of the d'Urbervilles* and *The Mill on the Floss*.' Hilda handed back the books.

'Did you enjoy them?' Miss Joice asked, taking the books and helping her off with her coat.

'Very much, thank you.' Hilda smiled. 'I love a sad ending.' Her teacher laughed and led the way into the drawing room. It was a beautiful room with large French windows looking on to a sheltered garden full of trees breaking into early bud; one cherry tree was already in blossom although the trees by the village green were still bare. Hilda gaped about her at the spacious room, the huge flowered chairs and sofas and the exotic red patterned rug beneath her feet. A cheery fire crackled in the wide brass grate although the room was filled with late afternoon sunlight. On either side of the stone fireplace two deep alcoves held a treasure trove of books stretching from the polished floor to the moulded plasterwork on the high ceiling.

'It's beautiful in here, miss.' Hilda's face shone with admiration, her bright-blue eyes wide in wonder.

'This is Mrs Seward-Scott, Hilda,' Miss Joice prompted her. 'She's been looking forward to meeting you. I hope you don't mind me asking her along.'

Hilda was momentarily startled; she had not realised there was anyone else in the room, and hearing the all-powerful name of the landowner brought a rush of blood to her pale cheeks.

'How do you do?' the slim lady asked from her seat in the corner of the room. She did not rise, so Hilda stood feeling foolish.

'Pleased to meet you, miss,' Hilda gulped, and then half crossed the room towards her. 'I mean, Mrs Seward-Scott.' The woman smiled graciously, her dark eyes fixed on Hilda. The girl's hand groped self-consciously at her hair where it had slipped from its ribbon and tried to hold it in place. She was at once struck by the elegance of the other visitor, dressed in a beige dress with a slim white collar and thin pleats. She wore a neat violet cloche hat which allowed a few wisps of dark hair to peep out and lie next to her prominent cheekbones. Otherwise her pale, slender neck was not fussed by hair, but showed off a necklace of pearls which wound around twice and then fell to her waist.

'Miss Joice tells me you are an avid reader.' Eleanor tried to put the girl at ease. 'Who is your favourite author?'

'Don't know, miss.' Hilda was mesmerised by the dark eyes and the pallid face and felt unusually shy.

'You enjoy Jane Austen, don't you, Hilda?' Her teacher came to her rescue. 'She's borrowed *Northanger Abbey* about five times now.'

'So Catherine is your kind of heroine, Hilda?' Eleanor asked, reaching for her cigarette holder.

'Well, yes,' Hilda agreed, feeling at once on familiar ground. 'I'd have been just like her if I'd gone to stay in a big old house. I'd have seen ghosts and things round every corner and made a fool of myself just like Catherine.'

The two women laughed.

'Take a seat by the fire, Hilda.' Miss Joice steered her from the middle of the room. 'We'll have tea in a minute.'

Soon they were in conversation about books and heroines from Jane Eyre to Joan of Arc. Eleanor was amazed by the girl's knowledge of literature and the way her mouth full of crooked teeth chattered away animatedly about the realms of fiction as if she really believed in the characters.

There was a pause while Margaret Slattery came in with the tea. Hilda pressed her lanky body into the back of her chair hoping Margaret would not notice her. She was the eldest of Mrs Slattery's family and Hilda only knew her by sight, though her younger sister Minnie was a friend of Louie's. But Margaret did not even glance at the visitors, leaving the tray on the octagonal table inlaid with mother-of-pearl and withdrawing with a nod from her mistress.

Hilda helped herself with youthful relish to the plateful of drop scones and cream cakes. She had not tasted such rich pickings for ages. Louie was very frugal with the household budget it seemed to her, though she was aware that less money was coming into the house since Eb's hours had been cut and her father and John were working in a difficult part of the pit.

She noticed that Mrs Seward-Scott did not touch a mouthful of the delicious food, but sipped occasionally at her sugarless black tea. Hilda listened with rapt attention to the conversation of the older women, who seemed uninhibited by her presence. They began by discussing some French book about homosexuals and then a writer called D. H. Lawrence of whom they both appeared to approve.

'And will Dr Stopes be coming to speak at the Cooperative Women's Guild soon, Eleanor?' Her teacher switched subjects again.

'I'm afraid not, Isobel.' Her friend stubbed out the cigarette in its long ivory holder. 'Marie has discovered she is pregnant at long last, so the lecture tour has been postponed for a while. Nevertheless I'm determined she will come sooner or later.'

Hilda was shocked but fascinated as the conversation about a birth control clinic developed. Her mother and her friends never talked about such things in front of their children, if at all. Sudden thoughts of her mother made her grow uneasy about the time. When they paused again she piped up, 'Thank you very much for the tea, Miss Joice. I think I should be gettin' home now.'

'Of course, Hilda, it's been nice having you.' Her hostess stood up.

Hilda turned to look at Mrs Seward-Scott who rose to her feet. Only then did the girl appreciate how incredibly thin she was, like a supple blade of grass that could blow away in the slightest breeze. But her voice was far from fragile.

'Perhaps you'd like to borrow some of my books, Hilda?' she asked.

The young girl was momentarily speechless.

'Well, Hilda?' Miss Joice smiled.

'I'd love - I mean - if you really think - well - yes please!' she stammered in reply.

Eleanor smiled at her enthusiasm. She could identify with the thrill of discovering

21

the rich world of books, but had not thought to find it in this gauche, lanky girl with the dull blonde hair who lived in one of the miserable cottages in the centre of Whitton Grange. It was an uncomfortable feeling to have her perspective on life altered so suddenly. Hilda had left the door ajar on another world just as much as she herself had done for this collier's daughter.

'Then I'll leave some here at Miss Joice's the next time I call,' she promised.

Hilda left with her small clutch of books and ran excitedly through the dene, skirting the woods above the village. She would have to be quick in hiding her store of knowledge in Eb's allotment shed because she was sure she had stayed too long and would receive a scolding for being so late home. Today though, she did not care. Her visit and meeting with Mrs Eleanor Seward-Scott had been wonderful.

'And she's so tall and elegant,' she panted at Eb in the seclusion of his vegetable garden, 'and she smokes cigarettes that smell like an oriental bazaar and she reads books which the government has banned.'

Eb smiled to himself, wondering how his sister, who had only travelled as far as Durham City, could possibly know how an eastern bazaar smelt. Still, it was obvious that the woman from the big house had impressed his sister; her eyes shone in adoration as she spoke of her.

'Eb, you mustn't tell, but Mrs Reginald is going to lend me her books. I bet they've got a few at the big house.'

'A few hundred, more than likely,' Eb grunted. He was surprised by the woman's gesture. No one could fail to be impressed by the scale and grandeur of The Grange and the glamorous family who came and went in shiny black Bentleys. But Eb Kirkup was less impressed than most. Perhaps they did hold riotous cocktail parties for Miss Beatrice and rub shoulders with the Prince of Wales in West End nightclubs, or so the rumours went, but he had met their type during the war and found them hollow to the core. Maybe the best of them had died, like Captain Seward-Scott, all too eagerly spilling their vital blood into the soggy soil of Flanders and on the bleak ridges of Gallipoli. But the hollow ones like Reginald Seward-Scott, who had frittered away much of the war at regimental parties, were in control of things now. A land fit for heroes was their promise, Eb thought sadly, but conditions here in Whitton Grange were probably worse than before that hellish war. At least he had his pocket of land here, away from the soot of the village and the furnace underground, up here on the hillside where the earth could breathe.

'Let's see what you're drawing, Eb.' Hilda had finally run out of things to say about Eleanor and was leaning over his shoulder curiously.

'Nothing really.' Eb tried to cover his pencil sketch of the two fat chaffinches which had been sitting on the battered fence.

'That's really good,' Hilda praised. 'They look like they're having a canny chat.'

Eb chuckled. 'They were.' It pleased him that he had caught the mood of the moment and not just the image. 'Anyway, what are you doing up here so late in the afternoon? Shouldn't you be helping our Louie?'

'Eee, what's the time?' Hilda's hand flew to her mouth. Eb checked his pocket watch in the growing gloom.

'Half past five,' he announced.

'I'll be skinned alive.' Hilda looked to be on the verge of tears, or the giggles, Eb could not tell which. 'Will you cover for us, Eb, please? Say I've been up here helping you. I'll carry some of the potatoes home, or the spring onions, or anything.'

Eb grinned and tousled her hair playfully. 'Long as you promise to read me some of your banned books,' he bargained.

'Aye, all of them.' Hilda laughed with relief. Together they gathered up a few early broad beans and some thick stems of rhubarb that Eb had gardened and set off down the slope to the village.

By the end of the week Louie and her mother had forgiven Hilda for neglecting her duties, but the younger sister realised she would have to forgo trips to tea at Greenbrae for a while. She made up for her transgressions on Saturday by spending the whole afternoon altering Louie's Sunday dress to the new length and embroidering some doilies to sell in their shop. At least Louie called the modest enterprise a shop; it was really a few odds and ends that they sold from the window of their outhouse in the back yard. Louie made ginger beer and lemonade to sell and sometimes when their mother felt strong enough she made peppermint creams that brought in a few pennies too.

This Saturday it was warm and sunny and they had done well selling pop to the children in Hawthorn Street and round the corner in Holly Street. They had sent Sadie round to tell everyone what was on offer and she had returned triumphant, like the pied piper, with a straggle of thirsty and inquisitive playmates behind her.

'She's coming out of her shell is Sadie,' Louie told her mother with satisfaction when she had shut up shop. 'Seems quite popular with the other bairns now. I gave her a toffee for helping out.'

'Mind you don't spoil her now, Louie,' her mother warned, glancing up from her mending. 'I know you can be soft inside like your father given half the chance.'

Louie smiled, pleased at the comparison and thankful that the heaviest of the week's work was over. She was going to sit with her feet up for half an hour with a cup of tea, and read a magazine that Mary Ritson had lent her. She did not like to admit that she had gone out of her way to be nice to Mary when she saw her working in Armstrong's the tobacconist's on the corner of Mill Terrace. Since then she always bought John's twist of tobacco for him at Armstrong's, though only if she saw Mary behind the counter. Well, she had always got on with Mary at school and there was no reason why they should not carry on being friends, Louie reasoned.

'Are you going to let me do it?' Hilda broke the peace of the moment.

'Maybe's.' Louie flicked over the pages. 'Do you think I should, Mam?' It was a question that had exercised the minds of the Kirkup women for the past fortnight; should or should not Louie have her hair bobbed?

'I think you'd suit your hair shorter,' her mother encouraged, 'and it would be more practical - you wouldn't have to boil up so much water to wash it.'

'It's all the fashion, Louie,' Hilda assured her with an air of authority, 'Mrs Reg—' She managed to bite back her words in time. 'Just look at the magazine you're reading, all the women in there have their hair short.'

'What do you think Da would say?' Louie's face wrinkled in doubt.

Fanny Kirkup looked at her elder daughter's tired face; it had slimmed down over the last year and her blue eyes had taken on the careworn look of a much older woman. She allowed herself to feel a pang of pity for Louie and the job she had taken upon herself; it would give her spirits a lift for her to have a new appearance.

'Go ahead and have it done,' her mother urged. 'He can't make you stick it back on, now can he?' They all laughed at the conspiracy and Louie submitted her long, flyaway fair hair to Hilda's dextrous scissors.

Eleanor leaned back into plump cushions on the comfortable sofa in the library. She had dined alone with Reginald; her father was staying overnight in Newcastle, having had some business to complete. Since her return from London just before Christmas her relationship with her husband had improved. Eleanor was almost sure he had missed her - not that he had said so exactly - and she had tried her best to bring a new enthusiasm to their marriage. They were sleeping together again. Eleanor did not delude herself that this was because Reginald suddenly found her desirable; there was a new unspoken agreement between them that they would once more try to conceive a baby.

'When does Beatrice arrive?' Reginald looked up over his copy of *The Times*.

Eleanor reached for another cigarette, but he did not admonish her. 'She's supposed to be here tonight. Bridget took a call to say she had reached York. Her new friend, Bill or someone, is driving her up here.'

'What happened to Charlie?' Reginald sounded disapproving. 'I thought he was a damn good chap. Played a good game of rugger too, a Cambridge Blue. Why couldn't your sister settle for him?'

Eleanor laughed. 'Really, Reggie, you know her as well as I do. Charlie may have been a good sport but he didn't have enough money. Beatrice will have to marry a maharajah or something to keep her in the clothes she buys and take her to all those nightclubs she seems to live in.'

'God forbid an Indian.' Reginald shuddered and folded his paper vigorously. 'It was bad enough her going about with that Jew from France last year.'

'I thought Marcel was quite charming,' Eleanor replied. Reginald could be so tediously narrow-minded at times.

'Shifty, I'd say,' Reginald said. 'I meet these people in business, old girl, they muscle in and take over wherever they get the chance.'

'And you don't, I suppose?' Eleanor mocked him from behind a haze of smoke.

'It's different for us British, we have a sense of fair play,' Reginald snapped back. Eleanor thought that some of the Whitton Grange miners might think there was nothing fair in the conditions they had to settle for, but decided to let the subject drop. It was impossible to argue with Reginald about such matters as race or class; his mind was like a book whose pages had been left uncut. Anyway, if she thought too much about the miners she became racked with guilt, and why should she be? She had struggled for women's suffrage and won, so they could fight their own battles for themselves.

She watched as Reginald uncrossed his legs and stood up. 'I think I'll go upstairs now. I've got a meeting with the mine manager early tomorrow. Don't wait up late for Beatrice and Bill what's-his-name, darling; if they can't turn up in time for dinner then Robertson can see to them. She'll rustle up something cold from the kitchens, no doubt.'

'Good night, Reggie,' Eleanor answered evenly. Secretly she hoped Beatrice would be late and she could carry on sitting here by the log fire, reading her Scott Fitzgerald novel and sipping her father's best malt whisky.

But twenty minutes later Beatrice burst in on the arm of her new man, an American called Will Hector Bryce Junior; and there was no more peace.

'Beatrice, when did you dye your hair blonde?' Eleanor chuckled when Will had gone to 'freshen up'.

'Last month,' her sister confessed. 'Not a word to Will, he thinks I'm a Teutonic goddess and he's madly in love with my flaxen image. He's also fabulously rich. For God's sake, tell Reggie not to put his big feet in it.'

'I like it,' Eleanor laughed. 'At last my little sister is a real vamp.'

Will returned. He said he was 'doing' Europe.

'I'm just reading about people like you,' Eleanor told him. 'I thought the British were decadent until I read Scott Fitzgerald.'

'Don't be boring, Eleanor.' Beatrice waved a decanter stopper at her then poured two enormous gins with Italian vermouth.

'No, but your sister's right, Bea honey.' Will accepted the large aperitif. 'We've perfected the art of doing nothing with as much expense and as little taste as possible. It's called Capitalism with a capital C, yessir. Let's drink to it!'

Eleanor watched in amazement as he chinked glasses with Beatrice, downed his drink in one, grimaced and smiled. She began to laugh. The next week with her sister and Will Hector Bryce Junior was going to be fun.

'What do you think?' Hilda stood behind Louie who was inspecting her new hairstyle in the mirror above the sideboard in the parlour.

'It's different,' Louie said uncertainly. 'Does it suit me?'

'You look all grown-up, Louie,' Hilda said excitedly.

'Yes,' she whispered back at her reflection. Hilda had cut it well. Released from the weight of long tresses, her hair even had a soft wave that wriggled over her ears. It made her narrow eyes somehow more noticeable. 'I think I like it, Hildy, ta for cutting it.'

Her father was horrified and warned her about the sin of vanity, but her brothers supported the change in their sister, especially Davie who told her she looked like a film star. Louie felt a new surge of energy as she changed into a clean blouse that evening and waited for her brothers to return from drinking at the club and her father from a game of billiards at the Institute.

Sadie played by the hearth with two wooden farm animals Eb had carved for her, while Fanny and Hilda picked at some embroidery. Louie found she could not settle to anything and kept jumping up to inspect the array of food she had laid out on the parlour table, glancing surreptitiously in the mirror on the way.

'Got ants in your pants, Louie?' Hilda smirked. Sadie giggled.

'That's enough, Hilda,' her mother reprimanded. 'You could warm the teapot now, Louie, they'll be here any minute.'

'Aye,' Louie smiled with relief. Just then the yard gate banged and they heard voices approaching. Louie flew to her task, pretending not to glance at the back door. Eb and John came in with Sam Ritson.

'Where's our Davie?' his mother asked suspiciously.

'Not with us,' John answered, unconcerned. He rubbed his hands and held them towards the blazing fire. 'It's clear tonight; there'll be a frost, Eb.'

'Aye,' his brother agreed and winked at Louie as she gave them a sly glance.

'Evening, Mrs Kirkup,' Sam greeted the older woman.

'Evening, Sam. Go on into the front room, lads,' Fanny ordered. 'Louie's just making the tea. Take a bucket of coal with you, Ebenezer, and add it to the fire.'

The men did as they were told. Louie scowled at their retreating backs.

'He hasn't even noticed!' Louie hissed to her mother. 'I might as well be part of the furniture.'

'Hush, Louie, and make the tea,' her mother answered calmly. Privately she felt like shaking Sam Ritson out of his political thoughts; he must be blind not to see how her daughter was trying to attract his attention.

Eb struck up on the piano and Jacob Kirkup returned, bringing the blacksmith Ernie Parkin with him. Fanny sent Hilda next door to fetch Edie and Wilfred. Louie was tight-lipped, pouring tea, when the neighbours arrived. Sam was still ignoring her.

'Eee, Louie! What in the wide world have you done to your hair?' Edie Parkin screeched on seeing the girl's shorn appearance. Louie blushed painfully at the silence this brought from the assembled company. Wilfred gawped at her in horror as if she had just declared she was a supporter of Sunderland FC, arch-rivals of his beloved Newcastle.

'Why d'you do it, Louie?' he asked.

'I cut it.' Hilda spoke up proudly. 'Would you like me to do yours an' all, Mrs Parkin?'

'Hilda,' her mother glared, 'don't be cheeky.'

At this point Sam Ritson stepped forward from the piano and took his hands out of his pockets. He picked up one of the freshly poured cups of tea from the table and said, 'Suits you, Louie.'

She looked at him in astonishment, but his brown eyes returned her look with genuine liking. She was filled with a flood of warmth which had little to do with the heat of the fire or the packed room, but much to do with the acknowledgement from this stocky man before her with the vital eyes and the fighter's arms.

'Thanks, Sam,' Louie smiled back.

Chapter Four

Iris sank back into the plush red velvet of her cinema chair and gave herself up to the images that flashed before her on the big screen. For once, Davie had impressed her; it had been his idea to treat her to an afternoon at the new Palladium picture house in Durham. She had gasped in delight at the glitter of gilt and chromium around them and the feel of new plush carpet underfoot. The Wurlitzer organ had played for them, filling this new palace with music, then leaving the stage like a glamorous star, glowing in a colourful shimmer of lights.

'That's him,' Iris squealed with pleasure, 'Ramon Novarro!'

Davie watched the dark and dashing film star jerking through his part in *The Prisoner of Zenda*. In the gloom he tugged at his own attempts at a moustache and cursed the Kirkup parentage that had made him fair. Still, Iris seemed happy, and when he slid his hand across to grasp hers, she did not resist.

He gazed at her profile, the small, neat features of her face framed by waves of short auburn hair. He had preferred her hair long but was growing used to the new style; it certainly made her look sophisticated - like Clara Bow. To Davie she was still the prettiest girl he had ever set eyes on, and then he told himself not to be so soft. A lass is a lass, after all, he thought ruefully, and this one was costing him a fortune.

Davie had bought her sheet music, cream cakes and now this expensive trip to the pictures. He had had to beg Louie to lend him some of the precious housekeeping money in order to come into Durham and take Iris out. If his mother found out there would be hell to pay. Louie had been annoyed with him for asking, but he had got round her objections in the end and he knew he could trust his sister not to tell of his debts.

'She must be Mary Pickford the way you go on about this lass,' Louie had said scornfully. 'When are we going to meet her?'

'Maybes the summer picnic,' Davie had rashly hinted.

'Where does she live?' Louie's curiosity was waxing.

'Now that would be telling.' Davie smiled infuriatingly. Even Louie could not be told that Iris was a publican's daughter; he could not risk his teetotal father finding out at this stage.

Iris's hand was warm in his and he squeezed it, then decided to slip his arm around her shoulders while she stared at the screen.

'Watch the film, Davie man,' Iris insisted without glancing away from the giant image of Novarro, but she did not push him away. Davie's pulse quickened; today might be his lucky day.

Louie was tidying away the men's clothes into the under-stair cupboard when Sam Ritson called. The back door was open and warm May sunshine spilled into the stuffy kitchen. Sadie ran in clutching a piece of washing line she used as a skipping rope.

'Sam's here, Louie,' she shouted breathlessly. Louie felt her stomach jolt but carried on with her methodical folding.

'Tell him John's gone to help Eb in the allotment.' She tried to keep her voice level.

'It wasn't John I came to see.' Sam was standing in the doorway, a few feet away from Louie. She turned round with a start. The sun shone in behind him and she could not make out his expression, but he stood there stiffly as if he were about to make a speech.

'Da's at the Institute and Mam's next door at Edie Parkin's,' Louie gabbled. Her voice sounded husky and nervous to her ears.

'I thought you might like to go for a walk,' Sam suggested, in a voice so stern it was almost an order.

'A walk?' Louie repeated.

'Aye.' Sam lifted his cap and scratched his head. 'A walk.'

'Where?'

He stood there nonplussed for a moment as if he had not expected to get as far as such practical details. 'There's a footy match against Waterhouses in the park. We could walk in the park.' Sam coughed and cleared his throat. Louie was just about to protest she hated watching football, but managed to stop herself.

'I'd like that, Sam.' She smiled. 'Just give me a minute to get ready. Can I get you a cup of tea?'

'No ta,' he grunted. 'I'll stop outside.'

He was gone, and Louie flew upstairs to change into her Sunday dress and comb her hair. Sam Ritson had come to the house to see her - it must be a dream. He had certainly shown her more attention over these last few weeks since she had cut her hair, but they had not exchanged more than a few words with each other. She wondered if Mrs Parkin had spotted the visitor from her kitchen window. One thing was for certain, by the time they reached the top of the street, all the neighbours would know about it.

Out in the bright sunshine she found him leaning up against the yard gate watching the children playing in the lane. A group of boys had chalked out goal posts against the midden wall and he was shouting words of advice and encouragement. Louie could see creases of coal dust in the leathery lines of his neck, where much scrubbing had been to no avail. He turned and smiled awkwardly, his strong, square face seeming boyish with doubt. He's as nervous as me, Louie thought with relief, and took charge of the situation.

'Let's walk down the dene, shall we? I'd like to see where they're building the new council houses.' She smiled.

'If that's what you'd like, Louie.' Sam looked relieved that a decision had been taken.

They walked up the back lane, Louie instructing the skipping Sadie not to wander further than Holly Street.

'What about the shop, Louie?' Sadie asked.

'It won't be opening this afternoon.' Sadie pulled a disappointed face. 'If you're good, I'll make you some toffee anyways,' Louie added quickly to avoid a protest.

They walked to the corner and turned into Holly Street and on up the hill till they passed the mine workshops and the gates to the pit yard. A clutch of old trucks rattled by on the makeshift tracks, taking away discarded stone from the screens. The gigantic caged-in wheel and gear of the Eleanor pithead loomed over them, panting and whirring in complaint. Beyond, a grey-black spoil heap sat like a suet pudding that had turned out wrong, misshapen and streaky. Louie was glad when they cleared the end of the fenced-in yard and left the pit and its coal heap behind.

'Mary says there's an evangelical mission coming to the Memorial Hall next week,' Louie began, desperate to break the silence between them. 'There's some of them visiting gospel singers going to be there. Mary says they've got smashin' voices. Will you be going, Sam?'

'Me?' He sounded shocked. 'You won't catch me at one of Mary's religious meetings.'

'Oh.' Louie realised she had said the wrong thing.

'Last year she joined the Salvation Army,' Sam continued, unaware of Louie's embarrassment. 'Now she's going evangelical.'

'You're not religious then?' Louie ventured, remembering the rumours that Sam was a Communist.

'Religion is the opium of the people,' he announced. 'The establishment use it to keep working men in their place, Louie. They promise a glorious afterlife instead of making things better for the working man in this one.' Louie looked at him doubtfully. Her father would not approve of Sam if he talked like that about the Methodists.

'But you do believe in an afterlife, don't you, Sam?' Louie asked anxiously. 'It says so in the Scriptures; you must believe what the Bible tells you, surely?' He stopped and gave her a quizzical look from his brown eyes, then tugged at his clean-shaven upper lip. 'I believe in an afterlife, any roads.' Louie held his look defiantly. 'And I'll not hear a word said against the Methodists, so there's an end of it.'

Unexpectedly Sam laughed. He raised his cap, scratched his head and wedged his cap back on more firmly.

'Not a word against the Methodists,' Sam agreed, still chuckling. Louie did not see that there was anything funny about such matters but it was better than the serious Sam of moments before. They continued their circular walk through the back streets of Whitton Grange, the terraces gradually thinning until finally giving way to an unkempt copse of trees and the dene itself.

The bushes and trees had broken into the vibrant emerald green of early summer and in sheltered spots a carpet of violet bluebells was unfolding underfoot. They walked a rigid foot apart from each other, until the path narrowed and Louie went ahead. By the time they emerged on to the railway line and the path that led round to the village green and the new council houses, they had exhausted all conversation about their families, their neighbours and the price of tea.

Louie was about to tell Sam of Davie's trip into Durham to see the 3.45 performance of *The Prisoner of Zenda*, but thought that he would probably disapprove. He appeared to disapprove of Davie altogether. Sam's idea of entertainment seemed to be a night at a political meeting or delivering speeches over a pint to his comrades, Louie thought glumly.

'Aren't they big,' Louie gasped as she saw the new houses. There were only six, standing two by two, with a large area of ground cleared between them and the railway line for several more.

The building's stopped now, though,' Sam sighed. 'The council say they can't afford to build any more just yet. Here we have the first Labour Government in our history and we still don't have the right to a roof over our heads. Our Bel got married last year but she and Johnny Pearson are having to share a two-roomed cottage with Johnny's parents, his two sisters and brother. It's not decent.'

Louie remembered Bel from school with admiration. She was two years older than Louie and had the same brown eyes as Sam. But Bel was always laughing; Hilda had once described her as all bubbly like lemonade.

'And Bel's expecting in August,' Sam added. Louie felt uncomfortable with talk of marriage and babies.

'Can't they rent one of these houses from the council?' she asked.

'There's a waiting list as long as my arm,' Sam grunted. 'I wouldn't be surprised if she came back home once the baby's born, not that we'll have room to spare.'

Louie sighed and turned to look at the large redbrick houses across the railway line, sitting in grand isolation with the sweep of hillside beyond and the thick woods of Highfell Common behind. These were the homes of the well-to-do of Whitton

Grange; the colliery manager, the agent, the doctor and the vicar, Reverend Hodgson. Louie had never been inside any of these houses, though Margaret Slattery, sister to her friend Minnie, was housemaid at Dr Joice's. According to Margaret they rattled around in the eight-bedroomed house and although they used only a third of the rooms, all of them had to be kept clean in case they had visitors. Imagine a widower and his spinster daughter taking up all that space when there were people like Bel who would have been grateful for a single room in such a place! Sam was right to be angry. But that was the way things were, Louie thought with resignation, and complaining about it would get them nowhere.

'Isn't that your Hilda?' Sam startled Louie out of her thoughts.

'Where?' He pointed across at the big houses.

'Coming out of the doctor's house,' Sam persisted. 'I'm sure it was your Hilda.'

Louie caught a flash of straw-coloured hair and blue skirt dashing away from the large dark-green front door of Dr Joice's house, and then she was gone. Sam was right, but it would not do to say so; he would want to know why her sister had been hobnobbing with the middle classes.

'Can't be our Hilda,' Louie replied lightly. 'She's up at the allotment helping Eb and John. Been there all afternoon.' She slid Sam a look. She knew he did not believe her; he was certain of what he had seen. For a moment she was tempted to confide in him about Hilda's passion for books and how she hid them at the allotment. Her sister was obviously growing bolder and calling on Miss Joice at home for her reading matter. But she was not sure of Sam yet. He was a radical when it came to pitmen and the working-class struggle, but what did he think about girls like Hilda getting an education in literature and the like?

'Let's go and see the end of the footy match.' Louie gave him a sly smile and touched his arm briefly. Sam grinned in agreement, though he did not return the gesture. Walking a foot apart they made their way across the village green to the park gates.

Hilda was dismayed to find John helping Eb in the allotment. He was tying strips of newspaper to the canes supporting the runner beans, to warn off the greedy birds. She quickly dumped her bag of books in the shed, resisting the urge to flip through the titles of her new haul.

'Can I help?' she asked before John questioned her parcel.

'No, we're nearly done,' Eb answered with a wink. He ran the back of his hand across his balding head. 'By, it's warm in this sun.'

'I'll get you some water from the burn,' Hilda volunteered.

'There's still some cold tea in the flask, Hildy, fetch that instead,' Eb replied.

'I thought you were going to help us all afternoon.' John's blond head shot up and his bright-blue eyes looked accusing. She hoped he was not going to lose his temper over her truancy.

'Sorry.' She looked contrite. 'I had an errand to run.'

'Who for?' John straightened up and put his hands on his hips.

'Louie, of course,' Hilda lied, crossing her fingers behind her back. 'I'll get you some tea.'

To her relief John did not stay long. 'See you at the club later?' he asked Eb as he went.

'No, I've got band practice tonight.' They both knew that on Eb's reduced wages he could not afford to drink on a Saturday night, but it was John's way of saying he would stand him a pint if he wanted one.

'So what have you got for me today, Hildy?' Eb demanded when their brother was

30

out of earshot.

'Mrs Reginald's books!' Hilda could not suppress her excitement any longer. She pulled a parcel out of her string bag. The books were neatly wrapped in brown paper and tied with string. Hilda fumbled with the knots.

'Let me,' Eb grinned at her impatience. 'You're all fingers and thumbs.'

He undid the ties and folded back the paper to reveal four volumes. Two were novels, one by Somerset Maugham, the other by Arnold Bennett. There was a play by George Bernard Shaw and a collection of poems by Wilfred Owen. Hilda picked up this last one and began to read out the introduction by someone called Siegfried Sassoon. It was at once obvious that they were poems about the recent war.

'I don't want to hear any more,' Eb said abruptly. He turned his back and began clearing away his tools.

'But you were there, Eb.' Hilda was surprised by his sharp tone.

'Yes, Hilda, I was there and I don't need some dead poet to remind me what it was like. Put your books away,' he ordered. 'I don't know what that Seward woman is thinking of lending you books like that.'

'Sorry, Eb.' Hilda's enthusiasm for her new books was dashed. She wrapped the brown paper around them once more and hid them behind the seedling boxes with Eb's sketches.

Eleanor had thoroughly enjoyed the past month with Beatrice and Will. On the spur of the moment they had persuaded her to join them on their visit to her mother's relations in the north-west of Scotland. With Reginald's grudging permission she had packed two modest suitcases and they had all crammed into Will's Model T Ford and headed north, Beatrice sending a trunkload of clothes ahead by train. The MacKenzies had given them splendid hospitality in their rambling country house with its breathtaking views over the Kyle to Skye. They had hiked across the moors in the spring sunshine and been drenched in squalls that whipped off the sea; they had spent cosy evenings by a roaring log fire playing cards and charades with their cousins after gargantuan meals in the draughty dining hall by candlelight. Will had been garrulous with praise and wonder at the Highland hospitality, though he found the temperature in his bedroom 'icier than the rocks in a White Lady', as he put it.

Now they were returning home and Eleanor was feeling gloomy at the thought of Beatrice and Will leaving The Grange. They sat in silence, Beatrice dozing in the front, Will yawning at the wheel.

'Reggie will be pleased to see you after all this time,' Will said softly. 'I sure would be.'

'I doubt it,' Eleanor answered wearily and then regretted the disloyalty. Will threw her a look over his shoulder, but said nothing. They had grown close during the holiday; Eleanor found him attractive and she knew he liked her, but she would never hurt Beatrice by flirting with one of her boyfriends just because she was bored with Reginald. In her opinion, men were an unnecessary complication in life. Nevertheless, the holiday had left her feeling discontented and restless.

They were reaching the outskirts of Durham and the silhouette of the Norman cathedral shimmered before them in the twilight, like a ship launched into the sunset.

'Are we nearly home?' Beatrice asked sleepily.

'This is Durham, Bea honey,' Will announced. 'Shall we stop for something to eat?'

'No, let's just get home.' Beatrice sounded petulant and Eleanor wondered if she had been awake all the time. She directed Will through the narrow streets and up the hill that took them south and west back to Whitton Grange. Eleanor's heart sank with each mile they sped nearer to Reginald.

'You're a canny lass, Iris,' Davie sighed, and stretched in the long grass. Below them on the riverbank an animal scavenged in the undergrowth. She lay quite still next to him, her breathing still fast, but said nothing. 'Are you happy?' He leaned over her on one elbow, a look of quick concern on his fair face.

'S'pose I am,' Iris whispered, listening to the sounds of evening. The cathedral clock was chiming languidly, and a rowing boat slipped quickly past with a man racing it along the towpath, shouting instructions through a loud-hailer. She was content. Ramon Novarro had been wonderful, the whole afternoon in that palace of make-believe and dreams had been wonderful. Even the bag of chips and Davie's compliments had seemed romantic after such a day, so she had given herself up to his kisses and caresses. Now Davie was her man and she had enjoyed it all more than she had expected.

'Will you come on our village picnic then, Iris?' Davie sat up, his unbuttoned shirt revealing a hairless chest. She wanted to run her hand over its smoothness again, so she did.

'Maybes.' She smiled. 'Will we be able to kiss and cuddle like this, Davie Kirkup?'

He stopped her hand because it tickled and pushed her back playfully. 'No, so we better do it now,' he laughed. Iris closed her eyes and opened her lips, imagining it was Novarro leaning over and pressing himself to her body.

Later they parted, drunk with kissing, and Davie promised to come into Durham before the June picnic. At the station he bumped into Tadger Brown and two other mates who persuaded him to go for a drink. Davie was full of his conquest and drank long and deeply. They caught the last train home but in a burst of alcoholic high spirits Davie was bundled off at the stop before Whitton Station, and found himself having to walk the extra miles. It was almost dark and he whistled as he went, breathing in the rich smell of new-mown grass and weaving unsteadily between the hedgerows. His thoughts were full of Iris Ramshaw, the girl of his heart.

The car dipped and rose along the narrow lanes; Eleanor and Beatrice stared ahead, mesmerised by the dim light that the headlamps cast on the road ahead. Will accelerated, yearning to be out of the car and stretching his long legs.

Eleanor saw the figure first, a shadow that grew out of the dark.

'Look out!' she screamed. Will slammed on the brakes and swerved automatically to the right. The figure half turned and froze like a terrified rabbit caught in the glare of the lights. He was young. The car clipped him and bounced him into the ditch.

'Jesus!' Will cried, horrified, and leaped out of the car. Eleanor was close behind. At first they could not see him, then a voice groaned.

'He's over here, Will,' Eleanor shouted, peering into the ditch. 'Are you all right?' The man groaned again.

'I'll lift him. Out the way, Eleanor!' Will ordered.

'Is he dead?' Beatrice called from the safety of the car.

'Don't be so dramatic,' Eleanor snapped back, her heart still thumping at the thought of how close that outcome might have been.

'Stupid bugger,' Davie cursed, wincing as Will heaved at his throbbing leg. 'Didn't they teach you to drive?'

Eleanor rushed to the car for the flask of whisky Will kept in the glove compartment and put it to Davie's lips.

'Been drinking already by the smell of him,' Will said, his fear giving way to annoyance.

'Then it was his own silly fault.' Beatrice, feeling brave, had stepped out of the car.

'You were going too fast, Will,' Eleanor said quietly.

'Damn it, Eleanor, the boy's drunk,' Will defended himself. 'He was all over the road.' Davie rolled on to his side, moaning about the pain in his leg and the stupidity of car drivers.

'Can you walk?' Eleanor asked him.

'I cannot bloody well stand,' Davie shouted angrily.

Eleanor took command. 'Help me get him into the car, Will.'

'We can't take him with us.' Beatrice looked horrified. 'Not in the car.'

'Do you suggest we just leave him in the ditch?' Eleanor asked tersely.

'Why not?' she pouted back. 'He's just a drunken lout from the village by the looks of him. He'll get himself home once he's sobered up, I'll bet.'

'Oh, do shut up, Beatrice.' Eleanor lost all patience with her sister. 'Come on, Will.' Together they heaved a protesting and disorientated Davie into the back of the car.

'We'll drive him to Dr Joice's house and he can fix him up,' Eleanor decreed. She sat in the back with the young miner while Beatrice sat in frosty silence beside Will. She had to admit that the smell of beer and stale sweat was unpleasant in the confined space, but tried not to let her distaste show.

'What's your name?' she asked.

'Davie Kirkup,' came the sullen reply. The name sounded familiar. Yes, of course, Eleanor realised, he must be a relation of Hilda, the gangly girl who read books. She had left a few volumes for her at Isobel's before setting out for Scotland. This fair-haired youth with the mousy moustache could easily be her brother. What else had Isobel said about the family? She recalled her mentioning that the mother, Fanny, who had worked at The Grange, was an invalid and there was a lay preacher father who would no doubt disapprove strongly of his son's drinking. Eleanor felt somehow responsible for the unfortunate boy. 'I'm Mrs Seward-Scott. I've heard of your family, Davie.' She tried to sound friendly. 'Is your mother any better?'

Davie stared at her in surprise. He had been wondering who these grand people were, the women in fur coats and the man in plus fours. So this was the famous Miss Eleanor from the Big House; he'd seen her in the distance, skinny as a scarecrow, walking on the hill. But he had never been this close to posh folk before.

'She's better these days,' Davie answered cautiously. 'Thank you for askin'.'

Dr Joice was out on a call when they arrived but Isobel took them in and Davie was laid on an old sofa in the large kitchen. Margaret was off duty so Isobel made him some tea herself. Eleanor took Will and Beatrice into the drawing room and poured them stiff drinks. They downed them without much conversation; Will was on edge and Beatrice grumpy about the end of the holiday being spoilt.

'Papa's here at last.' Isobel popped her head round the door. 'He's with David Kirkup now.' Eleanor slipped out to join them.

'His left leg is badly bruised but he doesn't appear to have broken anything,' Dr Joice told her. 'I've strapped him up, as you can see, but it would be best if someone could give him a lift home.' He turned to Davie. 'You've been a very lucky young man. If Mr Bryce hadn't taken avoiding action you'd have been off work for a good while.'

'Lucky?' Davie muttered. 'The bugger had me in the ditch, he was driving too fast. Mrs Seward-Scott said so an' all.' He cast Eleanor a challenging look.

'You shouldn't have been in the road,' Eleanor answered uncomfortably. 'But we won't take it any further. We'll see that he gets home, Dr Joice.' Looking at Davie's forlorn, accusing face, handsome in a foxy sort of way, she felt she had somehow betrayed him for Beatrice's American friend. But there was no harm done, she assured herself; the boy would be walking again soon and there was no point bringing in the police to complicate matters.

Will drove them to Hawthorn Street and Eleanor saw a flurry of curtains throw chinks of light on to the uneven road as the car stopped outside the Kirkups' house. Will left the engine running and Beatrice, sitting inside, sank into her fur collar as he helped Davie out of the car.

'I'll go in with him,' Eleanor offered, and Will looked relieved. Davie did not like to tell her that they never used the front door; visitors always came and went the back way. There was the sound of piano music and singing coming from the front room, but it stopped as Eleanor knocked.

'Go in, it's open,' Davie said, feeling important yet embarrassed by the woman who guided his elbow. A tall girl with short, wavy fair hair came to the door; she looked like a prettier version of Hilda.

'Davie!' she cried. 'Where have you been?' She looked taken aback to see the well-dressed woman at his side.

'He had an accident,' Eleanor explained quickly, 'but Dr Joice says he'll be fine.'

'What happened?' Louie looked at the other woman with a mixture of suspicion and awe.

'I stepped in front of a car, Louie,' Davie spoke up. 'Mrs Seward-Scott saw me right, though,' he added gallantly. Eleanor felt a pang of gratitude towards the youth.

'Mrs Seward-Scott,' Louie gasped, colouring pink. 'Well, it's an honour! Will you come in?'

Eleanor hesitated, then said, 'Just for a moment.'

Louie led her in as if she were royalty visiting, and the reception in the tiny parlour was equally deferential. Louie's parents sat her in the best chair and pressed her to a cup of tea and a ham sandwich. She refused the latter. The tall girl stood possessively close to a dark-haired, thickset young man who seemed embarrassed by her presence and did not speak. There were two other brothers besides Davie; one red-faced but handsome, the other with very blond receding hair and a look of detachment. And there was Hilda. She gave Eleanor a beseeching look and Eleanor had the wit not to register recognition. The books were apparently their secret and the secret would be safe with her.

'Please don't stop the entertainment on my account,' Eleanor insisted. 'I love a musical get-together.'

'We were just about to turn in,' Jacob Kirkup growled with pride and bashfulness, 'it being the Sabbath shortly. But Eb will play something for you, ma'am. Go on, Eb,' his father instructed, 'play for the lady.' Eb, reluctant, gave his father a sardonic look. Jacob had never uttered a good word about Eleanor Seward-Scott until she'd come breezing in as if she owned the place. Then Eb half smiled as he realised that was exactly what she did do - own the place. He turned to the piano and began to play 'Sweet Lass of Richmond Hill', while Louie and Hilda sang.

Eleanor sipped at her strong, milky tea, pretending to enjoy it and at the same time fighting off the faintness she felt from the heat in the room, smelling as it did of candle grease and paraffin. Davie sat in the corner, relieved that the attention was focused away from him for the moment. No doubt there would be recriminations later.

Eb finished and glanced round as Eleanor politely applauded.

'Thank you, but I really must go.' She rose. 'The others are waiting for me.' As if to stress the point, the Model T Ford tooted impatiently outside. 'I hope you'll be better soon, Davie,' she smiled at him. 'Please let me know if there's anything more I can do.'

He nodded wearily, wondering why he was suddenly being made to feel beholden to the people who had nearly run him over.

There were stilted goodbyes and Louie saw their guest to the front door. As Eleanor passed Eb she said, 'You play very well. Where did you learn?'

'In the army,' he answered, fixing her with blue eyes that did not slide away nervously as the others had done. It was not necessary for him to specify the Durham Light Infantry; everyone who had volunteered from Whitton Grange had joined the DLI.

'Which brigade?' she asked.

'The Fifteenth,' he answered.

'Then you knew my brother, Rupert?' Her voice was hopeful.

Eb had known him. He remembered the thin young officer lying in a ditch with half his head blown away. His hand had still been moving.

'I knew him,' Eb answered quietly. Without knowing why, he added, 'He was a good officer - more popular than most.'

Eleanor gave him a considering look and then her gaunt face broke into a wistful smile. 'I'm glad,' she replied, 'and good night.'

Back in the car Will closed her door for her and drove off in silence. Labouring up the hill to The Grange, Beatrice yawned. 'Really, Eleanor, I feel quite unclean being made to wait in that sordid little street. It was perfectly lousy of you. Wasn't it, Will darling?'

Eleanor ignored her and Will thought better about replying. All at once, Eleanor could not wait for them both to go.

Chapter Five

'And she wore a silver fox coat, Minnie, and you could see her knees when she sat down an' all.' Louie recounted the visit of Mrs Reginald Seward-Scott for the third time that morning.

'Fancy,' Minnie replied, catching her breath, 'showing off her knees at her age.'

They walked arm in arm up the street while Hilda and Sadie struggled behind with the food that Louie had prepared. The motor coaches were waiting at the chapel hall to transport them all to Finchale, site of a monastic ruin by the tree-lined River Wear where the annual village picnic was to be held. Minnie was on a rare holiday home from her job in Durham and found her friend bursting with the news of their illustrious visitor. The neighbours had long since grown weary of the Kirkups' bragging, once the initial interest had waned.

'She's a real lady, Mrs Reginald.' Louie's tone was reverential. 'She had nothing but concern for our Davie. Even my da had to admit what a lady she was, though he doesn't hold with her ideas about women gettin' the vote.'

'What about her hair?' Minnie was impatient for more details.

'Short like a lad's,' Louie was able to report. 'I thought it was too short, mind you.'

'Yours looks canny,' Minnie said, scrutinising her friend's wavy fair hair.

'Our Hilda cut it,' Louie answered, pleased. 'She'll do yours while you're here if you want, won't you, Hildy?' Louie glanced behind but Hilda was not listening. 'Well, she will anyway.'

'So is Davie all right now?' Minnie questioned as they turned into North Street and saw the gathering crowds ahead.

'Aye,' Louie pulled a face, 'but he was off work for a week with his bad leg. Da went light with him for losing work-time and wages. He still won't let him go into Durham, he has to spend his free time doing jobs.'

'So what about the lass he was seeing?' Minnie asked with interest. She had always had a hankering after Davie Kirkup.

'Iris? Hasn't seen her, as far as I know.' Louie shrugged. 'Don't suppose he was serious about her, not our Davie. He'll be the last of us to settle down.'

'Aye, I hear you're courting.' Minnie dropped her voice and gave Louie's arm a squeeze. Her friend's fair face coloured quickly and her fleshy lips pouted.

'If you mean Sam Ritson, there's nothing going on there, Minnie,' Louie said severely. 'He's hardly said two words to me since that bother with Davie and Mrs Seward-Scott. I can do better than Sam Ritson, any road.'

Minnie giggled. 'No wonder he's not speaking to you, Louisa Kirkup, with your nose above your face. You've got above yourself with this visitor from the big house, anyone can see that.'

Louie turned to her friend in shock at the outspoken criticism. But she could not think of a rebuff, so just pushed her away and walked on in high dudgeon. Minnie laughed out loud at this and caught up with her, grabbing her arm again.

'Please, your ladyship, be kind to an old washerwoman.' Minnie mimicked an old woman's voice. Louie's mouth was still set in an offended thin line, but she did not try to shake off Minnie's hold. Her friend was never one to mince her words or care about people's sensibilities, but they were still friends after all.

'Get us a seat,' Louie ordered. 'I'll help the bairns with the picnic bag.'

Squashed on to a bench in the open charabanc, Louie had time to look around for Sam Ritson. He was not on their coach. Surely he would be coming on the village picnic? She was certain his sister Mary had said so when she had been in the tobacconist's last week. Even Sam must take some time off from championing the rights of the working man. Louie hated to admit that Minnie might be right about Sam's reason for not speaking to her. Perhaps she and her mother had gone on a bit about Miss Eleanor; Sam had not appeared the least interested in tales of the landowner's daughter as a girl, when her mother had been a maid at The Grange. Well, he was wrong to think that everyone who lived in the big house was wicked and against them, Louie thought with annoyance. All the same, as the bus chugged off down the hill, she craned in vain to catch a glimpse of him in any of the other vehicles.

By the time they reached Finchale, the early morning clouds had broken up and the sun was warm on their faces as the residents of Whitton Grange disembarked for a day of fun away from their routine drudgery. With the colliery band playing them down the hill, the miners and their families jostled together in festive mood. Children ran screaming with delight to the river's edge while their parents found sheltered positions against the old stones of the ruined priory in which to lay out their picnics.

Louie and Minnie eventually found the rest of the large Slattery family and shared what food and drink they had. When the band finished playing, Eb joined them with John. To Louie's concern there was no sign of Davie and she hoped he had not jumped off the bus as it passed Durham. Neither of her parents had come today; her father had decided to stay as her mother did not feel well enough to travel. He would spend the day reading in the Institute library while her mother darned at home. That's all she seemed to do these days, Louie thought sadly, sit by the smoky fire coughing and darning.

'Can I have a donkey ride?' Sadie rushed up expectantly to Louie. 'There're gypsies over-by giving donkey rides.'

'Oh, I don't know ...' Louie looked dubiously at the scruffy boys who were in charge of the mules. Sadie squirmed with impatience, hopping from one foot to the other.

'I'll take her,' Hilda volunteered, so Louie handed over two pennies.

'Be careful now, the pair of you,' she cautioned as Sadie went off happily clutching Hilda's hand.

'Haway, Eb, let's join in the footy.' John hauled himself up and nudged his dozing brother in the back.

'Later,' Eb mumbled from under his cap, and did not stir.

'We'll come and watch you.' Louie leapt to her feet and brushed down her best lilac dress that she had purchased on credit from the co-operative store. 'Won't we, Minnie?'

'You don't like football,' Minnie answered suspiciously.

'I do now.' Louie glared at her to keep silent.

'Away you go, girls.' Mrs Slattery waved her hands, 'I'll keep an eye on the bairns. You enjoy yourselves.' Louie smiled at her gratefully, amazed at how happy-go-lucky her friend's mother was. She had eight of her own to look after but Mrs Slattery would take in the bogeyman's offspring as well if he asked her, Louie was certain.

The men were shouting and tearing after a worn leather ball, about twenty to each team as far as Louie could make out. The noise was deafening. Small children who wandered on to the makeshift pitch did so at their peril. Ernie Parkin the blacksmith was attempting to keep order as referee, his large red face panting and bawling as he ran after the players. A gap opened up in front of Louie and she spotted Sam for the first time that day. He half turned, caught her watching and kicked the ball too far. It whistled into touch, hitting Minnie who was standing next to her. A short, athletic man with red hair and a large mouth who was castigating Sam, chased after it. He seized the ball from Minnie, winked and gave a breathless, 'Ta, bonny lass.'

As he disappeared back into the game Minnie giggled and nudged Louie. 'Who was that then?'

'Bomber Bell,' Louie told her. 'He's the captain of Whitton Grange now. Works with Sam Ritson - one of his marras.'

'I think he looks canny.' Minnie grinned as she followed his progress. 'You'll just have to make up with Sam Ritson, Louie, so you can introduce us.'

'There's nothing to make up,' Louie protested, feeling her mouth going dry. Sam had looked at her but had not smiled; he was not interested in her after all, she thought bleakly. She was wearing her new dress with the thin pleats and the cut-away neck, but she might as well have been dressed in a coal sack for all he had noticed. 'I'm going for a walk. Are you coming, Minnie?'

'I'll catch you up,' Minnie replied, her attention fixed on the game. Louie wandered off towards the river, keeping to the sun-baked path. The woods rang with the laughter and calls of children as they swung from branches and made dens in the bushes. Courting couples walked arm in arm, smiling in companionship, and Louie wished with a pang she was one of them. She felt caught in a strange limbo; no longer the child who used to run after Davie, scraping her knees and joining in his pranks. Yet neither was she the adult that she yearned to be, with a house of her own and a man to look after and a pink-faced baby to nestle in her arms.

This past year she had held the family home together and taken on the cares of a woman much older than her sixteen years. Perhaps no man would want to marry her and she would have to live out her life keeping her parents and her brothers until she was old. A picture of the four spinster Dobson sisters ageing like summer blooms in Railway Terrace came into her mind. A gurgle of panic rose in Louie's throat and left a bitter taste on her tongue.

'Louie!' A voice called to her from the opposite bank and she jumped at the sudden intrusion. 'Comin' for a dip?' She squinted across the water and saw Davie swinging half-naked from the long branch that stretched out over the river. The water beneath him did not look deep; it moved in a sluggish swirling motion. There was a group of lads drinking and laughing on the bank beside him. Trust Davie to be in the middle of it. Louie sighed; he would never change.

'Careful, our Davie,' she shouted back with a wave. Tadger Brown took a leap from the bank fully clothed and plunged into the river with a yell. He splashed back to the bank and heaved himself out. Davie whooped his approval and started shaking the branch vigorously. The next few seconds unfolded like a film before Louie's eyes. Suddenly the branch snapped and dropped with Davie clinging to it like a skinny squirrel, amazement on his face. He hit the water with a smack and went under the dull blue surface, then bobbed up, hitting his head on the moving branch as it fought its way free of the reeds and trailing foliage.

'Davie!' Louie screamed, but his mates just laughed and swigged their beers. Her brother splashed out in panic for the bank but the more he struggled the further away he seemed to float. 'He cannot swim,' Louie cried. 'Tadger, he cannot swim!' But they were making such a noise on the far side that no one heard her.

She looked on in horror as her beloved brother spluttered and choked in the water, the treacherous hidden current pulling him away and under. They think it's just daft carry-on, Louie realised, her movements paralysed by fear. An ear-piercing scream ripped out of her and then from behind someone shouted at her to get out of the way.

She turned to see Sam Ritson pulling off his boots, his jacket discarded on the ground; a moment later he had hurled himself into the river with an almighty splash. Sam swam after Davie's disappearing body with short, strong strokes, speeding up when he reached the middle of the snaking river where the current flowed fastest. He grabbed for the branch and hung on and as Davie came whipping past him he seized his hair and pulled his head above water.

Louie ran along the bank, following their bobbing bodies. Tadger and his drinking friends hurried down the opposite bank, now aware of their appalling mistake. Sam, realising he could not keep hold of Davie and the branch in such a current, pushed the branch away and grabbed Davie from behind, forcing his chin up. They went with the swirl of the river, Louie running desperately along the bank to keep up with them.

Quarter of a mile downstream the pull on them lessened and Sam swam for the bank with what remained of his strength. Louie helped him drag Davie's body on to a small sandbank and turned him on to his side while he vomited foul water into the sand.

'Davie man, are you all right?' She held his head in her lap. Davie spluttered back incoherently.

'He'll live,' Sam gasped, his chest heaving as he drew breath. Louie looked at him, his short parted hair glistening, his shirt torn and clinging to his body.

'Sam, thank you,' she whispered, tears springing suddenly to her eyes at the thought of what might have happened to her brother. Then she realised she was crying because Sam might have drowned too trying to save him. 'I can't ever thank you enough,' she sobbed.

He leaned over and patted her shoulder awkwardly, 'There's no need to cry, bonny lass. There's no harm done.'

Louie crumpled under his gruff kindness. He had called her a bonny lass too. Somehow she found herself leaning into his shoulder and crying in relief. Sam gently folded his arms about her shaking frame and felt the softness of her fine hair pleasant against his wet face.

Davie turned, coughing, and, through eyes bloodshot from the half-drowning, saw them clinging together. He cleared his throat and spat. 'Give him a kiss, man Louie,' he spluttered. 'He deserves it, doesn't he?'

Later, when Tadger arrived with Davie's shirt and jacket, the young lads left Sam and Louie alone on the sandbank. Louie did not protest when Sam removed his wet shirt and hung it on a bush to dry. He leaned back in the sun and closed his eyes, and Louie slid sideways looks while pretending to pick flowers. His chest was broad and muscled, ingrained with coal dirt in the hairline creases; there was a blue scar across his shoulder where coal dust had got into a wound before it healed. His upper body and arms were testament to his other life underground that Louie would never know about, each muscle telling a tale of coal hewn from the rock, of twisting and crawling through seams less than three feet high, of digging and pulling, shovelling and dragging.

'What are you staring at, Louie Kirkup?' Sam suddenly opened his eyes.

'Not staring.' Louie blushed red-hot and buried her face into her posy of flowers.

He sat up, hooking his arms over his knees. 'Come here then,' he beckoned.

As Louie crept forward nervously, her eyes met his and she saw he was amused at her shyness. He no longer seemed unsure of himself in her company, as if his diffidence had been shed with the soaking shirt. She knelt beside him. 'What about that kiss then, that your Davie suggested? It's the first sensible thing I've heard him say.' Sam's look was teasing. 'Or is the friend of that Seward woman too grand for the likes of me?'

Louie laughed coyly and leaning across pecked him lightly on the cheek.

'I'm not your da,' Sam complained and sliding an arm about Louie's waist, pulled her to him and kissed her roundly on the lips. Louie gasped in surprise, her insides leapfrogging at the contact. She was about to protest when he kissed her again, this time more lingeringly. She liked it. When he stopped she did not pull away but nestled under his arm.

'You won't tell me mam or da about Davie will you?' Louie looked into his brown eyes. 'Not about him drinking and fallin' in the river, please, Sam.'

'It's our secret,' Sam promised.

'It's the first time he's had a bit of fun since the accident,' Louie went on. 'You can't blame him carrying on now and again, can you? It's in his nature.'

'You'd stick up for Davie if he brought the devil home for tea, wouldn't you, Louie?' Sam laughed.

'He's my brother,' Louie answered defensively.

Suddenly Sam hugged her. 'I like that in you, Louie - loyalty. You're loyal to your own kind, and that's a good thing.' Louie glowed at this praise, though she had never thought about it before. Sticking up for her own kin just seemed the natural thing to do.

'Will you stick by me too, Louie?' Sam asked, searching her bright-blue eyes for the answer. For a moment she was taken aback by his directness.

'What d'you mean, Sam?' she asked, her voice husky.

'I want a lass that'll stand by me and what I fight for,' Sam said firmly.

Louie gulped at the gravity of what he was asking. Was she strong enough to take on Sam Ritson, not just the fighting man in the boxing ring, but the fighter against the bosses? That meant no more chitchat with the lady from the big house, or dreams of working in a milliner's in Durham City. It would mean putting Sam before anyone else, even Davie. He would provide for her and in return she must sacrifice everything to give him the home comforts he would expect as his right. She would probably have to attend a lot of political meetings, she thought ruefully.

A dream of their future together floated before her eyes; a new council house with its own outside toilet, Sam on good pay and well respected as an official of the Durham Miners' Association, her lovingly embroidered table linen spread out for all to see, a baby rocking in a cot Sam had made for it. She would escape the responsibility of nursing her invalid mother and ageing father until she was past a marriageable age. She pushed that last thought guiltily from her mind.

'Aye, I'll stand by you, Sam.' She lifted her small chin and held his direct look.

Sam nodded, as if he had been certain of the answer, then shivered as a gust of wind rippled up the river. He drew away from Louie, and she watched him button up his damp torn shin and fix his tie methodically as if they had merely been discussing the weather. She felt a prick of annoyance that he should have been so sure of her reply, as if she had had no say in the matter.

'How come you were on the bank when Davie fell in?' she asked him, getting to her feet and shaking the sand from her dress. Sam turned and saw her regarding him, clutching her arms in front of her protectively.

'I was looking for you,' he replied, pulling on his jacket. 'Saw you leave on your own.' So he noticed more than she gave him credit for, Louie thought with surprise.

'And why did you want to get me on me own?' Louie's mouth twisted into a half-smile.

'To ask you if you were courting any lad.' He turned down his collar as he spoke.

'Well, I'm not.' Louie waited for him.

'You are now, bonny lass.' Sam grinned and crooked his arm for her to hang on to. Sam wanted her and she liked a man who knew his own mind. Louie happily slipped her arm through his, a warm glow of triumph spreading through her as they took to the path together.

'Is your marra, Bomber Bell, going with anyone, Sam?' she asked.

'Bomber? No, he's too busy with football,' Sam answered as if that were explanation enough. 'Why d'you ask?'

'No reason,' Louie said lightly, thinking of how pleased Minnie would be at the information. All in all, the village picnic had turned out far better than she could ever have hoped. Life was just as good as it could be, Louie smiled in triumph.

Iris came out of the Palladium red-eyed from crying. Rudolph Valentino had distracted her from her own affairs of the heart for a brief time, but in the glare of the outside world they returned. She felt washed out from the self-indulgent tears she had cried over a make-believe romance which had turned out well in the end. There was no such luck for her, she thought bitterly; her lover had got what he wanted and never returned. All at once she was furious at Davie Kirkup for discarding her. How dare he win her with sweet words and a trip to the pictures and then not turn up for over a month? Why had she ever allowed herself to be taken in by his good looks and boundless energy? She should have stuck to her screen lovers.

Walking listlessly back through Durham's crowded and cobbled streets, Iris decided she would not allow herself to be abandoned; instead of wallowing in self-pity she would act. If Davie refused to come to her, she would seek him out in his dirty little pit village. But what if he had a girlfriend or wife at home? Such an explanation had not occurred to her before. Well, she thought vengefully, she would delight in causing him no end of trouble. Without going home first she crossed the river and headed up the North Road to the station. She bought a ticket for Whitton Station and waited for the train.

On the way back to Whitton Grange the buses stopped in Durham for fish and chips. The Methodist minister, Mr Stephen Pinkney, had raised funds from the chapel to treat the trippers to the final feast. Louie and Minnie ate theirs hungrily, while John and Sam and Bomber Bell argued about the outcome of the football match.

'You let in three goals,' Bomber criticised John.

'Two!' John protested. 'And where was my defence? Halfway across the pitch like a bunch of old pit ponies,' he scoffed.

'You would think you'd lost, the way you're arguing, Bomber.' Minnie threw her eyes heavenwards.

'What do you know about football, eh? Nothing.' Bomber dismissed her impatiently.

'Our Michael was captain of Whitton Grange for longer than you've been, Bomber Bell,' she retaliated, 'and I've watched him plenty. Don't tell me I don't know nothing about football.'

Bomber's large mouth froze in mid-sentence and he gawped at her for a moment. He was not used to lasses arguing back. Who was this lass with the curly black hair who kept interrupting him? She was pretty enough, with her shiny green eyes.

'Michael who?' he asked, his tone condescending.

'Michael Slattery,' Minnie answered proudly. 'They said he was good enough to go professional if he hadn't been injured in that fall of rock down the Beatrice.'

Bomber turned with a look of interest. 'Michael Slattery, did you say?'

'Aye, and sometimes I used to play in goal when my brothers played in the lane,'

Minnie crowed. 'Didn't I, Louie?' Her friend nodded, thinking of the sight of the Slatterys and their relations taking over the back lane of Durham Road near the Catholic church to play their rowdy games of football. Minnie had been a real tomboy in those days.

'Didn't know you were a Slattery,' Bomber mumbled, torn between his contempt for her as a Catholic and his admiration for her footballing brother Michael. 'He was a canny striker, Michael Slattery, I'll give you that.' Over the last of their chips they began a heated conversation about past Whitton Grange teams.

Davie slipped away without anyone noticing. He headed for the town centre, wondering whether he was mad or doing the right thing. He had not been in contact with Iris for weeks and the separation had been hard at first. Several times he had wanted to disobey his father's decree that he should not go to Durham, and if he had had the money to do so he would have done. But he could not risk getting Louie into trouble by asking for precious housekeeping again, and he had no pocket money of his own.

Since the accident and his week off work, he had given Louie all he earned and he was lucky to still be working, judging by the increasing number of lads hanging around the street corners on short time.

But he had missed Iris Ramshaw and, loath as he was to admit that a lass could put him off his food, this one had. If he turned up now after weeks of absence she would probably throw him back out the door and give him a piece of her wisdom. But an angry Iris was better than no Iris at all and he would take his chances.

The door to the Market Inn was open and he saw Mr Ramshaw, fat and perspiring behind his bar. Market days were always busy ones and Iris would probably not be allowed off duty. Still, he could speak to her.

'Where's my Iris, then?' Ramshaw demanded on catching sight of Davie.

'Isn't she here?' Davie asked, disappointed.

'Said she was going to the pictures,' Ramshaw grumbled. 'I assumed it was with you.' Davie felt dashed. Far from missing him, Iris had obviously found someone else to take her to the Palladium. Why had he expected anything different? She was a beautiful lass, he had had his chance and thrown it away. Still, his pride made him angry with her all the same.

'Do you want to leave a message for her?' Ramshaw asked more kindly, seeing he had hurt the boy's feelings.

'No.' Davie gave a false smile. 'I was just passin' by.'

'Probably just as well.' Ramshaw poured Davie a half of beer. 'She's got her heads in the clouds, my Iris. Should be here helping me.' Davie was about to refuse the drink because he could not pay for it, but Ramshaw said, 'Have one on the house. She's been quite contrary these past weeks. Aye, but that's Iris for you.'

Davie bolted down his beer, thanked the publican and raced back for the bus. He saw the last one pulling away up the North Road and out of sight.

Louie's face was glowing from the midsummer sun and the events of the day when she led the girls in at the back door. The men had gone straight to the club for a final drink. At first, her mind taken up by other things, she did not notice her mother's agitation.

'Sam and Louie are courting, Mam,' Hilda announced gleefully. 'I've seen them holding hands.' Louie flushed with embarrassment and pleasure and looked to her mother for approval. The older woman's face was pale and drawn, her dark eyes darting from the girls to the parlour door.

'What's wrong, Mam?' Louie asked in concern.

'Hildy and Sadie straight up to bed now,' Fanny Kirkup insisted. Still excited from their day out, the girls began to protest.

'Do as Mam says,' Louie ordered firmly. 'Hildy, take Sadie upstairs.'

When they had gone her mother whispered, 'She's in the front room. She came about two hours ago. Your father was here. By, what a shock he had. He's gone to the chapel to prepare for his service tomorrow, not a word said.'

'Mam, who's in the front room?' Louie sat down on the arm of her chair. 'You're not making any sense.'

'She says she's called Iris Ramshaw.' Her mother took a deep breath and tried to speak calmly. 'She turns up here bold as brass demanding to see our Davie.' Louie's heart sank as the story unfolded. 'Said she'd found out where he lives from the store grocer and she won't go until she sees him. Well, your father wanted to know exactly who she was.'

'Well?' Louie held her breath, the suspense of having Davie's secret girlfriend sitting just feet away behind the closed door proving unbearable. 'Tell me what she's like, Mam.'

'Her father runs a public house in Durham.' Fanny shuddered as she spoke. 'You can imagine what your father thought of that. He stormed out the door and he hasn't been back since. I mean, Louie, that's not the place to get yourself a wife.'

'Has she had anything to eat?' Louie was immediately practical. If there was going to be a domestic crisis they might as well all face it on a full stomach. Her mother looked blank for a moment.

'I gave her a cup of tea an hour ago, but she hardly touched it.'

Louie, able to wait no longer, marched into the parlour. Iris was sitting in the half-gloom, back erect on the horsehair sofa. The room smelt cold and unused with no fire in the grate.

'I'm Davie's sister, Louie,' she said to the shadowy figure. 'Can I get you something to eat?' There was no reply. 'I'll make you a sandwich anyway and a cup of tea. How do you like yours?'

'I'll do without, thank you,' Iris replied quietly.

'Don't be daft,' Louie cajoled. 'You've been here hours and not had enough to keep a mouse going.' Iris leaned forward and in the light from the window Louie saw her smile. She had a lovely oval face with wavy hair that shone auburn at the edges.

'You're like Davie,' she said. 'I like my tea without sugar, thanks.'

By the time Davie finally trudged down Hawthorn Street, his bad leg was aching with the fatigue of the walk from Durham. He braced himself for his father's wrath, knowing he would think the worst of him and not believe his story about missing the bus. Davie hardly cared; he just wanted to lie down and rest his throbbing leg.

To his astonishment, most of the family were still gathered in the kitchen when he hobbled in the back door. There was a pot of tea on the table and the heel of a loaf of bread reminding him how hungry he was.

'By, I'd love a cup o' tea,' he said breezily, thinking it best to go on the attack first. 'Any pie left, Louie?' He glanced at his sister for support. She gave him a frosty look and he wondered in dread whether she had told them about his escapade in the river. Looking round he saw both brothers turn away awkwardly, his father's face thunderous.

His mother broke the silence. 'You've got a visitor, Davie.'

'Stand up, young woman,' his father added in his loud preaching voice, 'and tell him why you're here.'

In a dark corner of the room, Iris stood up. Davie's stomach lurched to see her, his mouth dropping open in disbelief.

'Iris,' he gulped, 'what are you doing here?'

'So you admit you know her?' his father barked.

'Aye, of course I know her,' Davie became defiant at his father's implied disapproval. 'She's the lass I've been seeing in Durham.'

'So it's true.' Jacob Kirkup rapped the table with his knuckles.

'Oh, Davie,' his mother sighed.

'And why shouldn't it be true? Iris is a grand lass and just as good as any of you.' Davie turned to Iris. 'I tried to see you in Durham today - that's where I've been. I missed the bus home.' Iris gave him a nervous smile; she looked so pale, Davie thought.

'Don't you compare your mother and sister to this woman,' his father barked.

'Just tell the lad.' Eb spoke up, glaring at his father. 'Keep the sermon for later.' His father looked at him with indignation.

'Davie,' Iris interrupted, finding her voice at last, 'I came to tell you.'

'Tell me what?' Davie's eyes were full of concern.

'I'm expecting.'

'Expecting?' Davie repeated, quite astounded.

'She's going to have your bastard.' His father's voice was more disappointed than angry. There was a tense silence while they waited for his reaction.

Davie swallowed down his shock.

There won't be any bastard,' he said resolutely. 'Iris and I are going to be married.'

Chapter Six

Eleanor, alone in the dining room, toyed with her kedgeree. Reginald had breakfasted early and gone to meet Hopkinson, the mines agent, and her father was spending the weekend with his shipping friends the Swainsons, at their Northumberland country house. Beatrice was in Scotland, or was it London? Eleanor could not recall. She pushed away her plate, rose and told Bridget her maid that she was going out for a walk.

Taking her ebony walking stick from the elephant's-foot holder in the hallway, Eleanor headed aimlessly past the glasshouses and the walled garden and found herself taking refuge in the water garden with its languid green pools and dribbling stone fountains hidden among the thick overhanging trees and rhododendron bushes. As children, she and Rupert had played endless games of hide and seek in these woods, along with their friends Isobel and Reginald.

'Reginald,' Eleanor sighed aloud. Reginald thought she was pregnant and she was carrying on the pretence because she did not have the strength to tell him the truth. When she did not eat and went straight up to bed after dinner he gave her a possessive kiss on her head, as if she were a child, and told her to rest. It was true her monthly periods had stopped, but Eleanor knew she was not carrying Reginald's longed-for son. Her belly was shrivelled and barren, like the rest of her, she thought with self-loathing. There was nothing in her life that seemed able to lift her from her mental and physical fatigue, not even the concerned friendship of the Joices. She had no appetite for anything any more.

Summer was drifting on and soon she would have to tell Reginald that there might never be any hope of a child. They had tried and failed; she had failed. God did not mean them to have children. Eleanor no longer knew what was the purpose of her life.

Perhaps Reginald would be relieved that he would not have to visit her stark room at night. She knew he found her bedroom a depressing place, but its black furniture and white walls expressed better than words how she felt about her colourless life.

Crossing the stile above the waterfall she stepped into open fields and kept on walking. Breathless now, she halted every few yards to shield her eyes and squint over the ripe, rustling corn fields spread below, and to listen to the sounds of sheep munching the turf around her on the moor. Gaining the top of Highfell Common she could look into the valley that held Whitton Grange. It was hazy with smoke from scores of coal fires burning away on this hot August day, obscuring the lines of brick houses and the dark sentinels that were the Beatrice and Eleanor pitheads.

An image of Hilda Kirkup, the miner's daughter with a head bursting with ideas and a zest for life, came into her own mind. How could this squalid village have given birth to such a vivid imagination, while she, with all the advantages of privilege and a good education, was bereft of a single original thought? Reginald still believed their class was born to rule because nature had bestowed on them a higher intelligence. But the ruling class had led all those young men into war with Germany, and what could have been more stupid than that?

Eleanor stopped and fingered the small volume of poems she carried in her pocket. She would go now and hand it to Isobel for Hilda to read and enjoy. Greenbrae lay like a doll's house on the edge of the dene far below; it would take half an hour at her slow pace. Eleanor set off for the woods that confined Whitton Grange to the valley floor.

Hilda and Eb sat in companionable silence against the rough wooden fence that marked their allotment. Not for the first time Eb had slipped the book of war poems by Wilfred Owen out of its brown paper wrapper and edged haltingly across the bleak and angry words. As Hilda immersed herself in her novel he read again 'Anthem for Doomed Youth'.

'What's a pall, Hildy?' he asked diffidently.

'What's a what?' she asked, her finger keeping her place in the book as she looked up.

Eb read the line.' "The pallor of girls' brows shall be their pall", it says here.'

'It's the cloth they put over a coffin,' Hilda explained. 'It means the soldiers that died and didn't have a proper funeral will still be remembered by the lasses that miss them.'

Eb nodded and bent his head to read on. 'Their flowers the tenderness of patient minds, And each slow dusk a drawing-down of blinds.' That last line haunted him. The other poems, with their graphic descriptions of the horror of the trenches that conjured up the very smell of death, were too much for him to bear. He could not read them. But this poem was simple and sad; it opened up a crack of light on his memory of the war and through it he was able to remember the friends who had not come back.

He started and dropped the book at the scream that rang through the woods just to the left of them. Hilda jumped, her eyes wide. Eb scrambled to his feet and vaulted over the fence. As he ran along the path into the woods a pheasant came flapping out of the trees and skirted the top of the corn in the neighbouring field. Emerging after it was a fragile figure in a cream dress and a short-brimmed black hat, walking with the aid of a stick. As she came out of the shade he recognised her pale thin face and dark-ringed eyes.

'Are you all right, Mrs Seward-Scott?' he asked, seeing how her breath was wheezing and laboured. She stared at him oddly as if he had no right to speak, and then her face changed as she smiled.

'I'm sorry, I didn't mean to cause alarm,' she apologised. 'It was that bird. It just flew up in front of me and I screamed. Quite ridiculous.' She laughed falsely, embarrassed to have been heard.

'That's all right then.' Eb felt at a loss as to what else to say. When the lady from the big house had visited them in their own home he had not been the least bit in awe of her. But here out in the open on her estate, he was acutely aware of the gulf that divided them, and to his annoyance found himself blushing like a schoolboy.

'Do I know you from somewhere?' Eleanor asked, unsure.

'Eb Kirkup, ma'am,' he answered, lifting his cap and scratching his head self-consciously.

'Ah, yes.' Eleanor smiled at him again. 'Hilda's brother. How is your sister?' Before Eb could answer, Hilda ran up, having come round through the allotment gate.

'It's you, Mrs Reginald.' Hilda beamed in delight.

'Yes, Hilda, it's me.' Eleanor smiled with pleasure at the girl's open enthusiasm. 'I have something for you, as a matter of fact. I was on my way to Miss Joice's house—' Abruptly she stopped, glancing warily at Eb, wondering if she should mention the books in front of him.

'Oh, Eb's canny,' Hilda assured her. 'He knows about my books and reading.'

'Good,' Eleanor said with relief and pulled the volume of verse from the pocket of her thin lace jacket. 'It's Yeats, he's an Irish poet.'

'Thank you, miss.' Hilda took the book reverently. 'I've nearly finished *Wuthering Heights*. Is it going to have a sad ending? Eb and me were reading in the allotment. We've got some of Louie's shortbread with us, would you like some?'

Eb looked at his sister in astonished annoyance; he did not want anyone to spoil the quiet of their morning, especially this Seward woman. His heart sank when Eleanor replied, 'That's most kind of you, Hilda.'

Hilda led the way back excitedly to the allotment. Eb glanced around to make sure no neighbour was watching. There was only old Mr Stephenson nearby, pottering about behind a veil of sweet peas. Eb heard the pitman's habitual cough and spit as he carried on unaware of the nugget of gossip that lay within his grasp.

Eleanor picked up the book Eb had been reading before he had time to hide it.

'What do you think of Wilfred Owen?' she asked him directly. Eb tugged uncomfortably at his blond moustache and shrugged.

'My brother doesn't like to talk about the war, miss,' Hilda answered protectively.

'No, I'm sorry.' Eleanor found herself apologising again to the tall miner with the impassive fair face. He was ill at ease with her, his sharp blue eyes dodging away from hers every time she met them. As Hilda disappeared inside the corrugated hut she tried to explain.

'You probably think I shouldn't have lent such harrowing poems to Hilda. But then how can the young learn how terrible war is if they don't read such things?'

'A poem can't ever tell how terrible it was,' Eb replied, anger igniting . What did this woman know of war, cocooned as she had been in a beautiful house far from the mud and stench and agony of the Front?

'No, you are right,' Eleanor admitted humbly. 'I can never understand what men like you went through. But when I read the accounts of soldiers like Owen I believe war is a horrible evil that must never be allowed to happen again.' She fixed her dark eyes on his face. 'So many friends lost - so pointless. I lost a brother who meant the world to me,' she added softly.

Eb was taken aback by her quiet passion; the things she said echoed his own hidden, unexpressed feelings. Suddenly his anger evaporated. In her face he saw a glimpse of her brother Rupert, though her look was reflective and world-weary while his had been full of boyish zeal. She had old eyes, he thought, under the thick, dark brows.

'So you're a pacifist,' Eb said, pulling out for her a low stool that he had used below ground.

'Isn't everyone now?' Eleanor countered. 'Even the old warmongers don't have the stomach for fighting any more. Everyone's happy to drink cocktails and make money these days as if none of it ever happened.' Eb was surprised by the bitterness in her voice.

'Not all of us are making money,' Eb grunted, glancing at her silk dress with the lacy collar and beaded front, 'or drinking cocktails.'

'No, how stupid.' Eleanor's pallid cheeks flushed pink at the edges. 'There I go again, saying the wrong thing.'

For all she knew, this sturdy man in his grubby striped shirt and ragged necktie was not working at all. Perhaps that was why his face and forearms were weathered from the sun instead of showing the grey pallor of most colliers. There was an awkward pause, then Hilda appeared from the hut with shortbread and a bottle of homemade lemonade. Eb was embarrassed by the frugal offering, although the shortbread had been made as a treat. But their guest accepted the proffered biscuit gracefully as if she was always served shortbread off old newspaper.

'And are you looking forward to the start of term, Hilda?' Eleanor asked the girl.

'Yes, miss.' Hilda squatted at Eleanor's feet and watched her eat. 'Our Louie'll be glad to have me out from under her feet too,' she laughed. 'I'm not very handy at cooking and cleaning and the like.'

'Hildy would have her nose stuck in a book all day long if she could,' Eb said gruffly.

'Don't you approve of girls reading?' Eleanor eyed him.

'Oh, Eb likes books too, miss,' Hilda answered for him. 'He gets me to read to him while he digs the garden.'

'Helps pass the time,' Eb mumbled, 'and keeps Hildy out of my way.'

'Of course.' Eleanor bit on the shortbread, amused by Eb's bashfulness.

'Mind you,' he added, 'it's a shame Hildy has to leave school at Christmas, seeing as she likes learning so much. It was different for the rest of us - couldn't wait to leave school and start work. But our Hildy's got more brains than the rest of us put together.'

The young girl smiled at her brother's description.

'Why should you leave school, Hilda?' Eleanor asked, concerned. 'Miss Joice says you are her best pupil and I can well believe it.'

'I'll be fourteen, miss,' Hilda answered.

'But surely you can stay on longer? You could be a teacher or anything you wanted if you persevered at school,' Eleanor urged.

Hilda looked at her in surprise at the fanciful suggestion. 'Mam says I'll have to find work - maybes domestic work in Durham if I'm lucky.'

Eb saw Eleanor's slim face crease in perplexity.

'We can't afford to send Hildy to the grammar school in Durham - what with the train fares and the uniform - even though she won a scholarship at eleven. Anyways, my father doesn't hold much with girls having an education. Hildy will be needed at home or to bring in a wage if she can.'

Hilda sighed. 'It's worse now, what with our Davie and his new wife Iris living with us and a bairn on the way—'

'Davie's married?' Eleanor asked in surprise.

'Yes,' Hilda nodded, 'last month. Iris is canny, but she doesn't lend much of a hand. And the baby will be with us after the New Year and you know what a handful they can be—'

'That's enough, Hildy,' Eb warned. He slid Eleanor a look and saw spots of pink grow along her prominent cheekbones. Hilda was unaware of the embarrassment she had caused. All at once her face lit up with an idea.

'Miss, d'you think you might find me a place up at the big house?'

'Hilda, mind your manners!' Eb protested.

'The domestic arrangements are not my concern, Hilda,' Eleanor answered, flustered. 'I leave such things up to the housekeeper, Mrs Robertson. Perhaps you would care to write to her - I would put in a good word,' she added hastily, seeing the girl's downcast expression.

'Thank you, miss.' Hilda brightened. 'Mam would be so pleased if I went to work at the big house like she did.'

Eleanor steered the conversation away from the subject of domesticity and soon was in deep discussion with Hilda about *Wuthering Heights*. Eb rose and began to busy himself in the allotment, leaving them to chat. It was only later, when he came back to the hut for the wheelbarrow, that he discovered Hilda showing Eleanor his bird sketches.

'They're good.' The older woman gave him a considering look. 'They're so expressive.'

'Hilda shouldn't have shown them to you,' Eb said crossly. 'I don't show them to anybody.'

'Well, you should,' Eleanor told him. 'They're almost like cartoons. These three finches are positively taunting that fat cat,' she laughed.

'I just do them to amuse m'self.' Eb blushed, trying to hide his pleasure in her praise.

'Well, they amuse me, and Hilda too, don't they?' She smiled at the girl.

'Yes, and Miss Joice says Miss Eleanor knows quite a few artists, Eb, so she should know a good picture when she sees one.' The other two laughed at her earnest face.

'Well, at least I can understand these drawings.' Eleanor held them up again. 'Modern expressionist artists leave me feeling I've missed the point completely. But then I'm shamelessly old-fashioned about art.'

'I just draw what I see,' Eb answered self-consciously.

'No, it's more than that, Eb.' Eleanor shook her head. 'You're saying something about nature - and people.'

'People's natures reflected in birds?' Hilda suggested.

'That's exactly it.' Eleanor sounded triumphant. 'Hilda hits the nail on the head as usual.'

Eb looked at the two of them, baffled. He had never given his drawings much thought before and he certainly did not think he was trying to say anything through them. Still, if it pleased them both so much, he was not going to spoil their fun.

'Eb'll let you keep that one, I'm sure,' Hilda said enthusiastically. 'You can show it to your friends.'

'Can I, Eb?' Eleanor asked tentatively. 'I won't show it around if you'd rather not.'

'Take it,' Eb replied, and turned from her as if he did not care. 'It'll only go on the bonfire if you don't.'

Eleanor rolled it up and put it in her jacket pocket. She could see that Eb was embarrassed and wanted to get on with his work. Rising, she said goodbye, thanking them for the hospitality. As she turned at the gate, Eb's sunburnt face was already bent over his spade, blond curls sprouting from under his cap on to his leathery neck. Hilda waved. Eleanor waved and smiled back, feeling a sudden lifting of spirits that sent her on the path towards Greenbrae with a lightness of step that hardly needed the aid of her pearl-handled stick.

Louie turned from the open oven door with a tin of hot bread. Her face was radish red and running with perspiration. Plonking the bread on the scrubbed kitchen table top she let out an angry puff. From the parlour she could hear Iris and her mother laughing with Edie Parkin and Clara Dobson over their embroidery. They gathered here every Saturday afternoon now to make clothes for the forthcoming baby; for although Fanny's racking cough had mellowed with the summer sun, she rarely left the house. Beautiful day gowns and night gowns were being created and refashioned out of old cotton shifts; vests, bodices and cot blankets assembled. Her mother was adding yellow braid to a tiny coat and Mrs Parkin was knitting endless pairs of booties.

'You would think Iris Ramshaw was her own eldest daughter,' Louie had complained to Sam in a fit of frustration.

'She's Iris Kirkup now, Louie,' Sam had reminded her. 'Any road, she's a canny enough lass and your mam is looking forward to her first grandbairn. You can't begrudge her that, Louie.'

Louie had bitten her tongue in annoyance; even Sam did not support her. Everyone seemed to think Iris was a 'canny lass', in spite of the fact that she never lifted a finger to help around the house or ease Louie's burden. It was like having two invalids at home. 'She's company for your poor mam,' her mother would say when Iris was out, strolling to the shops, dressed in her fancy green velvet hat with the cameo brooch pinned to the front. Or from Edie Parkin: 'She's expecting, Louie, you mustn't upset her with your twisty face. Iris is a delicate lass, she doesn't have half your strength, pet.'

Even more galling was her father's attitude; he, who had so disapproved of his prospective daughter-in-law. 'Your time will come, Louie, be patient and don't be envious of others. To covet is a mortal sin.'

When Iris sang at the piano on a Saturday night in that earthy, melodious voice like black treacle oozing off a spoon, the family thought she could do no wrong. But what hurt Louie the most was the way this publican's daughter had usurped her place in Davie's affections. He hardly appeared to notice her these days, so moonstruck was he over his pretty pregnant wife. A sister was good only for making his meals and clearing up after Iris. And she was not the only one to notice the change. One day in Armstrong's the tobacconists, she had overheard Tadger Brown complaining that Davie had gone soft, staying at home on a Friday night instead of going out drinking with the lads.

Sadie ran in asking for a glass of lemonade.

'You can have water or go thirsty,' Louie snapped, pushing back the damp wayward curls that stuck to her temples.

'Please, Louie,' Sadie began to protest.

'I can't afford to make any more pop for you bairns - not with all the housekeeping going on fancy ribbon for the baby's clothes.' Somehow Louie couldn't help her words. 'Now do you want a drink of water? If not, then scarper!'

Sadie pulled a face and skipped out of the back door to rejoin her friends. Her cousin Louie was always bad-tempered these days; she could not understand it. She thought people who were courting should be smiling all the time, like Iris and Davie. She would lie in wait for Iris when she went out to the shops and hang on to her yellow dress until she bought her some sweets. Iris never said no to her like Louie did.

When Hilda and Eb arrived home, Louie had the tea ready; bacon, bread and jam, semolina pudding and tinned peaches, and strong, hot tea in the pot. Hilda was bursting to tell Louie about their visit from Miss Eleanor, but she thought better of it when she saw her sister's fraught tired face. Sam would be calling for her any moment to take her to one of his meetings, but she was not changed. She had not even had time to wash the sooty film from her face or comb her hair.

'I'll clear the dishes,' Hilda volunteered as Louie rose to do so, 'and Sadie will help me wash up, won't you, Sadie?' The dark-haired girl grimaced but did as she was told. Louie looked at her sister in surprise, but did not argue. She would go and lie down upstairs for five minutes before Sam came. At this rate she would fall asleep during whatever meeting they were attending. She would far rather be going to see the lantern-slide lecture on the Egyptian king with the unpronounceable name that was showing in the Memorial Hall. Davie and Iris were going; strange how her sister-in-law seemed to have the energy for entertainment but not for housework.

The next thing she knew was Hilda shaking her awake. 'Sam's waiting for you, Louie.' Louie groaned and turned over, her body weighted as lead.

'Tell him I'm too tired,' she muttered. 'He'll have to go without me.'

'Louie!' Hilda remonstrated. 'You cannot say no to Sam. He'll go off you, Louie, and you'll end up a spinster.'

Louie shot up in bed and glared at Hilda. Her younger sister was grinning, pleased with the effect of her words.

'Help me get ready, Hildy,' Louie pleaded. 'Will you style my hair for us?'

Hilda did so, persuading Louie to add a string of glass beads to her dress. She did not look as sophisticated as Iris, who wore beads around her head, but it made her feel better.

'Thanks, Hildy.' Louie gave her a sudden kiss on her cheek. Hilda grinned back, pleased at her sister's rare gesture of affection. 'What was it you wanted to tell me before? I could tell you had some secret up your sleeve,' Louie coaxed.

Hilda bit her top lip. How could she possibly tell Louie about her meeting with Eleanor Seward-Scott and her hopes about going to work at The Grange? She had a daydream that after a bit of dusting and polishing around the vast mansion she would escape out of doors with a pile of books and read all afternoon. But life was not like that. It was only too obvious to Hilda that Louie needed her here at home, and she did not want to spoil her sister's night out with talk of her madcap scheme. Perhaps she could make a little bit of money doing dressmaking or sewing to help out too.

'Eb thinks he's going to win a prize with this year's leeks,' Hilda answered quickly.

Louie stared at her. 'Is that all?'

'Aye.' Hilda nodded.

'Don't believe you.' Louie sounded suspicious.

Hilda changed the subject and flew to the door. 'Hurry up, man Louie, Sam's waiting.'

Sam looked smart in his brown suit, and Louie felt proud walking down the back lane on his arm. In her best buckled shoes they were the same height and she thought they made quite a handsome pair, he dark and well-built, she fair and her figure filling out into a young woman's.

'Who's speaking tonight?' Louie asked, stifling a yawn, as they walked down Mill Terrace towards the centre of the village.

'MacAlister. He's from Glasgow - Independent Labour Party.' Sam was enthusiastic.

'Oh.' Louie tried to sound interested. 'How long is he speaking for?'

'Bout an hour,' Sam guessed, 'then there'll be a discussion, of course.'

'Of course.' Louie's heart plummeted. The things a lass had to do to please her man, she thought ruefully. Sam began to tell her about MacAlister and the sorry state the new Labour Government was getting itself into and how their leaders were selling out the working man for a taste of power with the bosses. Louie only half listened. At least it got her out of the house for a brief time. She hardly ever got beyond the yard wall these days.

Sam said they would take a diversion up South Street and as they approached the Memorial Hall, Louie gave a wistful glance at the crowd streaming in to see the lantern lecture.

'What's going on here then?' Sam asked.

'Some talk about Egyptians and treasure,' Louie answered, pretending not to be bothered.

'You mean Tutankhamen's Tomb?' Sam questioned.

'That's right.' Louie slid him a look.

'You're not interested in foreign kings are you, Louie?'

'No.' Louie sighed and dropped her head. As she walked on, she realised Sam was not at her side. Glancing round she saw him standing still, grinning at her. 'What's so funny?' Louie asked tersely.

'Are you coming in or not?' Sam said by way of an answer.

'To the lecture?'

'Aye. Gan' on, pet, it starts in five minutes.' Sam turned towards the steps of the hall.

'Sam Ritson,' Louie shouted, 'you've been leading me on all the time!'

'Easy to do.' Sam laughed and took her by the arm. 'Hildy told me you were going on about these Egyptians and I thought you deserved a treat.'

'Sam!' Louie squeezed his arm in return and gave him a wide smile.

'Not my choice of entertainment, mind, all these kings,' he added gruffly.

Thanks.' She leaned over and pecked his cheek.

'Not now, Louie.' Sam turned his face away in embarrassment. Louie could not take the smile off her face. Not now, she thought, but later, Sam Ritson, I'll get my kisses.

Reginald had been playing in a cricket match that afternoon over at the Fishers', the new landowners at Waterloo Bridge; they had bought the bankrupt estate from old General Peters. Bernard Fisher was a bicycle and car dealer. Reginald came back satisfied and with a burnt nose, talking animatedly about the wickets he had taken to win the match for the home team. Normally he would have insisted on Eleanor going along to support him but, as he'd mentioned with a proud smile to Rose Fisher, a woman in Eleanor's condition needed rest.

At the first gong Eleanor went upstairs and changed into a brown and cream backless dress, shimmering with long fringes. She had not worn it for months and it accentuated the flatness of her chest and stomach and the leanness of her upper arms.

She smoked three cigarettes while Reginald, dressed in his new double-breasted dinner jacket, helped himself to brandy cocktails and talked *ad nauseam* about Bernard Fisher's fleet of fast cars and his white Rolls-Royce.

'Some people find him rather vulgar, but he's a shrewd man of business - nothing wrong with that.' Reginald jutted out his chin and swigged at his drink. 'Poor old chap's only got daughters to inherit his wealth. They're jolly enough girls though, especially Libby - she's the golfer. Quite a sport, ol' Libby,' he laughed. 'She insisted on playing cricket with us this afternoon. Dash it, she hit Major Marshall for four!'

Eleanor listened to him pontificate about the poor calibre of the opposition and Bernard Fisher's collection of rare birds' eggs filched from remote nests in the Scottish Highlands. They dined alone. Eleanor sipped at the consommé and pecked at the fish course, skipped the entrée of pheasant and barely touched the beef Wellington. Her irritation at Reginald's boisterous talk grew with every mouthful.

'And how did you spend your day, Eleanor?' he asked at last, wiping his mouth after the cheese. She wanted to scream that she had spent it with two pit villagers in a rude allotment, that she had sat on a splintered stool and eaten shortbread blackened with newsprint and talked about art and pacifism. She yearned to tell him that she had spent the most enjoyable day for months with these ordinary, unaffected, kind people. She wanted to tell him that she was attracted to a man with calloused, earth-ingrained hands and a thick sunburnt neck and creased blue eyes. Eleanor could visualise Eb now, raising his cap to reveal a tanned bald head which he scratched to hide his awkwardness at having to talk to her.

Instead she said, 'I'm not pregnant, Reggie.' The words came from nowhere; she had not planned them, and they hung in the air like an independent puff of smoke.

He gawped at her for a moment, then waved Laws the butler back out of the room as he was entering with a tray laden with the silver coffee service. Eleanor reached for her cigarette case and lit up. She knew the habit of smoking at table disgusted him, but she had to do something with her shaking hands.

'What do you mean?' he asked, his tone hardening.

'I'm not having your baby, Reginald, that's what I mean.'

'Have you been to see Dr Joice?' He pushed back his chair and walked round to her side of the table. Eleanor could not look up at him.

'I don't need to. I know,' she insisted quietly.

'But I don't understand. You led me to believe - I thought we'd agreed to this child!' Reginald sounded almost petulant. 'You've been using birth control, haven't you? You and your precious Dr Stopes and her modern ideas. You've deliberately made me a laughing stock!'

'No, Reggie. It's hardly my fault if you've been bragging to the Fishers. You shouldn't have jumped to such a conclusion.'

Eleanor stood up and walked away from him to stare out of the window. The soft light of the evening sun was throwing beams like stage lights on to the terrace steps.

More gently she added, 'I want a baby too, really I do. But I'm infertile. I'm sorry, I don't think we'll ever be able to have a baby, Reggie. And I don't see the point in trying any more. Can't we just accept things as they are?'

She turned and looked at him, feeling a pang at the shattered expression on his handsome face, the disbelieving furrow carved between his light-brown eyes. She could not tell him that in truth she had never wanted his child; just a hypothetical child with rosy cheeks who would be hers and hers alone.

His look turned to contempt; she had let him down. She was his gaoler, imprisoning him in a loveless, childless, meaningless marriage. At least I have given him The Grange and its estates, Eleanor thought bleakly; he cannot resent me for that.

'I'm going over to Waterloo Bridge,' Reginald announced abruptly. 'Fisher has a card table tonight. Don't wait up for me, Eleanor. Tell Sandford to bring the Bentley round to the front door.'

It was a rude and humiliating gesture to abandon her after dinner for the company of people with whom he was only just acquainted. But she sent a message to the chauffeur anyway. It would be a relief to have Reginald and his raw hurt pride out of the place. She heard Laws ringing ahead on the telephone to alert the Fishers of his master's unexpected arrival.

Eleanor wandered out on to the terrace and breathed in the air, rich with the perfume of roses. She thought inconsequentially how her mother had planted the yellow Jacobite rose that crept up the side of the French windows, tangible proof of Lady Constance's existence. She, Eleanor, was proof of that too. She shivered and felt achingly alone.

Perhaps the idea had been crouching in the back of her mind all evening; a few minutes after her husband had left, Eleanor pulled on a warm cashmere shawl and collected her walking stick. She told Laws not to lock up before eleven. It took her half an hour to walk down the far side of Highfell Common and through the woods of Whitton Grange. Dusk was edging all about her as she reached the patchwork of allotments, beginning to burgeon with their late summer crops. There was no sign of anyone about and Eleanor was overcome with a wave of disappointment. Eb Kirkup would be socialising with his friends, or perhaps he was engaged to some dependable pitman's daughter who was providing him with the companionship and love that he needed. Strange though, because she had sensed in him a self-sufficiency, an ability to cope without others. He did not strike her as someone who needed company.

Eleanor leaned on the rickety fence and listened to the contented cooing of the pigeons. In a moment, when she had regained her breath, she would turn for home.

'By, you startled me!' a voice accused from over the fence as a man loomed out of the twilight. It was Eb.

'You gave me a fright too,' Eleanor gasped, her heart thudding. 'I didn't think anyone was here.'

'I like sitting here at this time,' Eb replied. '"Each slow dusk a drawing-down of blinds",' he quoted softly. Grateful that he didn't question her presence there, Eleanor followed his gaze over the field of corn, smouldering orange in the sunset. The trees behind them were already swathed in darkness like widows' robes.

'I hoped you'd be here,' she whispered, not knowing from where she got the courage to say so. He turned and studied her face, lit by the red light, the dark eyes unsure. Strange how he had been thinking of her when he had strolled up from the dene, whistling back at the sleepy chatter of the birds. He turned from her and pointed to the lip of the hillside.

'If you walk out-by, you can see the sun setting in Weardale. It's a bonny sight.'

'Yes,' Eleanor agreed, letting go the breath she had held in check, 'I'd like that.' As they walked together, an intimate silence fell about them that neither felt the need to disturb.

Chapter Seven

Eleanor continued her country walks to Whitton Woods throughout the late summer and on into the autumn. In October, Eb Kirkup was laid off at the Eleanor pit and spent the shortening days working the allotment. She would go on the pretext of leaving books for Hilda, but she only appeared if the other gardens were empty, knowing Eb would be there in all weathers. Sometimes she would look for him sketching up on the hill and they would talk together, as the trees around them turned rusty gold and the garden fires of damp leaves sent up pungent smoke signals to the cobalt-blue sky. Eb was diffident towards her and she sensed a reserve between them, but in a strange way his link with her brother was a bond and she felt more at peace in his company than with any other man she knew. She became physically stronger and could walk for several miles without the aid of her stick. With the return of an appetite for life, she allowed herself to eat again without the self-disgust she had been experiencing. If Reginald had not spent so much time hunting and dining with the Fishers over at Waterloo Bridge, he might have noticed the subtle changes in her. As it was, he no longer seemed to care. When he was at home, he spent the time closeted with her father and the mines' agent in his study, worrying over shrinking profits.

Eleanor turned a deaf ear to her estates' business problems; she had never been encouraged to get involved and so she did not. She much preferred to spend her mornings wandering the countryside and her afternoons drinking tea by a roaring fire with her friend Isobel.

Then December came and with it the argument with Eb that choked the sprouting of their tentative friendship. It was just before Christmas and the schools were breaking up for the holidays. Hilda was about to leave the classroom for the last time.

'I would like to pay for Hilda to stay on at school,' she announced, watching Eb's pencil strokes shaping into a boastful robin. Momentarily he stopped, shooting her a surprised look, and then resumed his careful caricature. 'I've been thinking about it a lot,' she continued, encouraged by his listening, 'and I've talked it through with Isobel Joice. She would be more than happy to teach Hilda up to certificate level. Do you think your parents would agree, Eb?'

'No,' he answered firmly without looking up.

'Why?' Eleanor felt deflated.

'Hilda will have to find a job, that's why.' Eb put down his pencil. 'I'm out of work, Davie and my father are on short time. Only John is bringing in anything like a wage to our house, and he's on the minimum. Iris is about to have a baby and my mam needs medicines for her chest. Do you need any other reasons, Mrs Seward-Scott?'

Eleanor hated it when he addressed her formally with that edge of mockery in his voice. At times he could be irritatingly stubborn.

'But it's so short-sighted.' She dismissed his excuses. 'Hilda could get far superior employment once she has some qualifications. Your father should be proud of her talents, not embarrassed by them. If she was a boy he'd let her stay on at school, wouldn't he?'

'If she was a boy she'd be out looking for work like the rest of the school leavers.' Eb stood up angrily. 'The pits are not taking them on, so they're scavenging for farm work or selling bags of coal or anything for a few pence. Aye, they're not above stealing mistletoe from under the nose of your gamekeeper just so they can buy a few treats for Christmas. It's not a matter of superior employment as you call it - it's a choice of odd jobs or no job at all.'

'Well, I'd still like to hear your father's opinion,' Eleanor replied, feeling the argument slipping away from her. 'I intend to call on him tomorrow evening.' Suddenly Eb whipped round and caught her by the elbow.

'Don't you go interfering, Mrs Reginald.' He spoke with quiet menace. 'We don't want charity from any of you Sewards. We've lived without it so far and we'll get by on our own wits.' She gawped at him in astonishment. Self-consciously, he dropped his hold on her. 'Aye, and it might be better if you don't come visiting here again.'

Eleanor felt herself redden at his blunt rebuff. 'I know what this is all about,' she retorted. 'Your stupid pitman pride. You think I'm playing Lady Bountiful and you won't have any of it. Well, it's Hilda who will be the loser, not me or you, Eb Kirkup. Just remember that when she's scrubbing someone else's doorstep for the rest of her life!'

Eleanor pulled her fur-trimmed coat about her in the frosty air and left, tossing a bag of small Christmas gifts on to the wheelbarrow as she went. But she did not go to confront Jacob Kirkup about his daughter's education, and she did not go back to visit the allotment.

Beatrice came home, bringing with her a young fair-haired Scots officer, Captain Sandy Mackintosh, whom she had met at the Highland Balls the previous September. He stayed over Christmas and then took her younger sister north for the New Year celebrations. Eleanor had thrown herself into the festive arrangements, holding a party on Christmas Eve for thirty neighbours and friends. To please Reginald she even invited the Fishers who turned up in their white Rolls-Royce and talked several decibels louder than the rest of the guests. But by New Year, she was glad to have a nightcap in the library with just her father for company, while Reginald went out to the Fishers' fancy-dress party got up as a sheikh. They quietly toasted the portrait of her mother Constance who looked down on them from above the mantelpiece with a quizzical smile. Then with 1925 acknowledged, Eleanor went to bed.

In January, Isobel's maid Margaret Slattery left to marry Joseph Gallon, a young pitman, and at Eleanor's suggestion, her friend employed Hilda. She was not the most efficient of domestics but she was lively company to have about the house, and Isobel allowed her to dip into her collection of books when off duty. Eleanor felt a flush of triumph that Hilda's education was still continuing, albeit in a diluted form. Eleanor had one other suggestion to make to her old friend as the first early snowdrops appeared from the soggy black earth.

'You need a gardener, Isobel,' she said decisively. 'Your father is far too busy to keep a controlling hand on all this.' She waved her hand expansively over the view from the French windows.

'I suppose you have someone in mind,' Isobel replied knowingly.

'As a matter of fact I do. Eb Kirkup seems to have green fingers, from what I can gather,' Eleanor replied lightly, not daring to meet her friend's curious look. 'And Hilda says he is still without proper work.'

'I'll see what Papa has to say.' Isobel made no promises. 'He may well be glad of the assistance. It really is a full-time job, I suppose.' Isobel guessed from Eleanor's casual comments that she had formed some kind of relationship with Hilda's older brother and was wary of encouraging it. Still, she trusted Eleanor not to do anything foolish, and they really could do with a gardener. Eb came to work for Dr Joice in the middle of February.

Louie lifted the hot coal out of the fire with the pincers and dropped it into the iron. About her on the brass fire rail hung pressed shirts and sheets; in the warming oven the men's trousers were airing. With the incessant rain of the past week, the kitchen had been strewn with wet washing for two days, and only now was she able to tackle the ironing. She hit the final tea towels with a monotonous thud, the noise dulled by the old blanket on the wooden table that did for an ironing board.

Iris sat with her feet propped up on the cracket, Sadie's stool that normally stood by the fireside. She was listening through headphones to the crackling wireless that she had brought from Durham, and singing along to tunes Louie could not hear. Fanny, whose chest had given her a wheezing cough all winter, sat unravelling old stockings to knit up again. Even she had begun to lose patience with Iris's baby, who showed no signs of wanting to come into the world. It was the beginning of March and they had been holding their breath for a month.

'Who'd want to be born when the weather's like this?' Iris laughed and carried on singing. 'My bairn will be born when the sun's shining.'

Louie humphed and clattered the iron on to its stand. She refrained from saying that the baby appeared to be as lazy as its mother and would probably have to be coaxed out with chocolate or a trip to the picture house. She glanced enviously at Iris's huge pregnant bump and her contented pink face. Her auburn hair was luxurious, although Iris complained it was growing too long. Louie admired the dramatic way her sister-in-law stood, hands supporting her back, and moved, like a stately overweight queen, making sure everyone knew what an effort walking was for her these days. They had made sure Iris had not gone without nourishing food for the eight months she had been with them.

'That baby's overfed and doesn't want to come out,' Louie had said to Sam recently. 'I've given it a better start in life than if it had been my own.' He had studied her for a moment and seen the longing in her eyes. He was content with Louie as his girl, but there were far more pressing concerns on his mind before he could commit himself to marriage. The pitmen of Whitton Grange would be fighting for their very survival if things got much worse. So he ignored Louie's unspoken pleas.

'Are you going to that talk at the store hall, Mam?' Iris asked Fanny Kirkup, slipping off her headphones. Louie still felt a pang of jealousy when Davie's wife used this endearment when talking to Fanny, instead of referring to her as Mrs Kirkup.

The union meeting?' Fanny answered, clearing her throat.

'Not that one.' Iris yawned. 'The one about child rearing.'

'It's that Dr Stopes, Mam,' Louie explained, 'the one who wrote them books on - you know. Mrs Seward-Scott has arranged the lecture. Clara Dobson said she's wanting to start up a clinic in Whitton Grange.'

'Doesn't sound natural to me.' Her mother looked dubious. 'And I don't want you going, Louie, you're not even engaged. Young lasses shouldn't be listening to such things.'

Louie was annoyed. She was a young woman now taking on all the responsibility of running the house, and if she had her way she would be married this year. It was only sensible that girls like her should get some education on marriage; she could not bring herself to use the word 'sex' even in her own mind. Her mother had never spoken of such things, so how was she going to know what to expect?

'I'm going to listen to Sam tonight anyways,' Louie said shortly. 'He's speaking after the man from the Miners' Federation.' She gave a smile of satisfaction at his importance.

'I'd like to hear the lady doctor,' Iris raised a slim hand to cover a theatrical yawn, 'but I'm too tired to do anything these days.' Her other hand rested protectively on her swollen belly. It was too late for her to learn about birth control, Louie wanted to say; she was proof of the need for a local clinic. But she bit back the words.

Hilda came home after tea and said she would have to return to Greenbrae later in the evening as the Joices were entertaining Dr Stopes. Their father and Davie came home from the pit and with tired resignation said they were being laid off for the rest of the week. This set off a bout of coughing from Fanny, whose face crumpled into worry. When Eb also returned from Greenbrae and Sadie came in from playing under the gas lamp in the street, the house felt as if it would crack at the corners from the crush of people. The foul odour of pit clothes and damp bodies hung in the fusty air like ghostly washing.

A squabble broke out between Davie and John when Louie prepared John's tea first, as he wanted to get some rest before the night shift started. The brothers hardly spoke to each other these days unless it was to quarrel, Louie thought wearily. Several days of the whole family around the house with nothing to do was going to be purgatory. So it was with relief that she escaped out into the drizzle of the cold, damp March evening to go to Sam's meeting. It was being organised by local members of the Labour Party and the union lodge, and they had hired the main store hall, expecting a large turnout for their guest speaker from the Miners' Federation of Great Britain. In the room above, wives of the pitmen were drawn out of curiosity to the meeting of the Women's Co-operative Guild where the celebrated Dr Stopes was about to lecture. Louie glanced wistfully at the married women who chattered expectantly as they took the stairs, then made her way into the hall.

Sam barely had time to speak to Louie, so she settled into a seat near the front, next to his sister Mary, who had also come to support him. By eight o'clock the hall was full and latecomers had to stand at the back. Sam Ritson was beginning to attract attention as a forceful speaker, and his reputation was spreading outside the pit gates. He was becoming more than just a spokesman for the disputes of his group of face workers, and many had come to hear what he, rather than the official from the national organisation, had to say.

Louie fidgeted while the guest speaker urged them to stick together with miners from the other areas, so that together they could negotiate from a position of strength. Her mind wandered to and fro like a fretful, broody hen. She thought of Iris's baby and whether it would look like Davie; wondered if the store would extend their credit; itched to know what was being discussed by the women in the room upstairs. Even her friend Minnie Slattery had been allowed to go, because much to everyone's surprise, she had got herself engaged to Bomber Bell. They appeared to enjoy arguing with each other so much they were going to formalise the rules of engagement. She would make Minnie tell her everything.

Eleanor was pleased with the turnout for the lecture. Marie Stopes had shown a film entitled *Maisie's Marriage*, which the women had watched attentively. Now they were having a break for a cup of tea before Dr Stopes answered their questions. Eleanor decided to slip out and see what was going on in the hall downstairs. She had heard Reginald complaining to her father that some rabble-rousers in the village were organising discontent by inviting a spokesman from the Miners' Federation who was openly critical of the owners. He had wanted the local superintendent of police to send an observer to the meeting to note down any seditious speechmaking. Thomas Seward-Scott had told him he was getting things out of proportion and left to attend a musical in Newcastle with the Swainsons.

The door to the downstairs hall was open because the press of people had spilled out into the corridor, so packed was the body of the room. Various officials dressed in their best suits sat on the stage on upright wooden chairs, a table in front of them. Standing up, left thumb crooked into his waistcoat pocket, and right forefinger prodding the air, was a man she recognised but could not place. He was dark, short and stocky, his head bare and his brown suit ill fitting. None of this mattered to the audience, who were listening avidly. Eleanor pressed forward to try and catch what he was saying. From the far end of the hall his flat voice carried without any effort.

'. . . But they've shown us they cannot be trusted. They promised to build us more houses, but not one brick has been laid since before the War. Why should we have to live herded together like animals? Why shouldn't our young 'uns have a decent home to bring up their bairns? Why should our widows and orphans be evicted when their men die in the pits the bosses won't make safe?' With each question he stabbed the air with his finger and his face grew more passionate. 'The reason, comrades, is that the owners don't care about the conditions we put up with, they don't care about our safety, they don't care that we can't afford to keep our bairns healthy. They only care that there's coal coming out of the ground!'

Eleanor felt an uncomfortable prickle at the back of her neck and she glanced at her neighbours to see if they were aware of her identity. Everyone was concentrating on the speaker's words.

'And things are going to get worse not better,' he predicted. 'The bosses are blaming us for falling productivity. But we all know that the seams we're working now are hard seams, they're wet seams. The good coal in the Eleanor has been worked out. We're crawling in gassy tunnels two foot high, in six niches of water. If the bosses spent a bit of their profits on better conditions and better transport below ground, they'd get better productivity. 'Cos the pitmen are grafting just as hard as ever!'

There was a cheer and clapping at this. Eleanor felt herself squirm at the accusations. She wanted to run from the man haranguing her but she could not stop listening. Could things really be as bad as he maintained or was he just out to make trouble as Reginald believed? She knew that Reginald was capable of being ruthless, but surely her father would not allow his men to work in such conditions.

'I tell you this, comrades,' his voice dropped level again, 'we've seen none of the profits that we've made these past years. Instead we've seen thirty-eight pits close in County Durham alone since May of last year. But we're not going to let them close down our pits. I'm telling you now, they'll try and cut our wages and bring back district bargaining. They want to undermine our solidarity with our comrades in other areas. But we're not going to let them get away with it! Ah¹ we're asking is a fair day's pay for a fair day's work.' His voice rose to a shout with his final battle cry. 'It's time we stood up to the Seward-Scotts of this world and showed them we can still fight, comrades!'

The audience jumped to its feet, the applause and shouts of agreement deafening. The young man had spoken without a note or sign of hesitation. As Eleanor watched him step back, it came to her that she had seen him before, at the Kirkups' house; he was Louie's young man. Eb had told her Louie was being courted by a political hothead called Sam Ritson. Feeling suddenly exposed, as if his brown eyes had focused their scorn on her all along, she withdrew and headed thankfully upstairs. She was sure he had not seen her, but her heart pounded fearfully even so.

He was filled with a conviction of the justness of his cause that Eleanor recognised; it emanated from his thick hands and his strong voice. Years ago, as a very young woman, she had felt just such a calling, one that had led to her involvement with the suffrage movement. She sat down, her hands still shaking and thought of her father and Reginald moving towards confrontation with this pitman. God help them, she thought, the image of Ritson's uncompromising face imprinted in her mind.

Louie clapped enthusiastically with the others, a surge of pride bubbling through her at the thought of how well her Sam had been received. At that moment she felt she would follow him anywhere, do anything he asked of her. He was going to be a great leader of then-people, perhaps an important official in the Durham Miners' Association or even a Labour MP in time. And she, Louisa Frances Kirkup, would be beside him, championing his cause. She experienced a twinge of shame that her head had been so turned by a visit from Mrs Seward-Scott. Sam was right. The people in the big house were all the same; they did not care about the pitmen who worked for them, or the poverty their families had to endure. Stirred by Sam's speech Louie vowed never to betray her own folk.

For a while she and Mary hung about below the stage, but Louie could see Sam was too engrossed talking with the officials. No doubt they would adjourn to the club for further discussion and she would not see him again that evening. She turned to leave the hall and saw Hilda pushing her way towards her against the flow of the crowd. Her younger sister's face was puckered with breathless anxiety.

'What is it, Hildy?' she asked alarmed.

'Louie, you've got to come,' Hilda gasped. 'Quickly, Louie!'

'What's happened? Is it Mam?' Louie took hold of her sister's skinny arm and shook her.

Hilda gulped for air and then panted out her message. 'It's Iris, she's started. Mam sent me for Clara Dobson, but I can't find her. You'll have to help, Louie.' Louie stood dumbstruck for a few seconds. Iris's baby was coming at last.

'But- ' Louie stuttered.

'Come on, Louie, she's screaming the house down!' Hilda pulled her sister after her, ignoring Mary's gasps of surprise.

Outside it was raining hard again and by the time they reached Hawthorn Street both sisters were soaked through to their underclothes. They clattered through the back door and found their mother attending to Iris on the spare bed, that had been pulled out of its press. Iris was half propped up, with towels about and beneath her. Her face was contorted in a spasm of pain. She cried out as she caught sight of the girls and Louie's stomach lurched in fear.

'Come here, Louie, and bathe her face.' Fanny spoke calmly and beckoned her daughter with a frail hand. Louie pulled herself together, and, sitting on the chair next to the bed, dipped a flannel in cold water and wiped the sweat from her sister-in-law's brow. Her face was red, the auburn hair damp and stuck to her temples.

'I can't bear it!' Iris shouted, and writhed as a new contraction took hold of her body. Louie made quiet, comforting noises as she wiped Iris's face. She looked questioningly at her mother.

'She started just after you left,' Fanny explained. 'The contractions are getting stronger now, but it could be hours yet.' Louie gulped in horror. She had never attended a birth before, she had always been considered too young and shooed away with the other curious children. Clara Dobson, the local midwife, had delivered all of Fanny Kirkup's children and borne four daughters of her own, and Louie prayed that the bustling, no-nonsense Mrs Dobson would arrive soon. The thought of herself and her mother having to deliver Iris's baby alone filled her with dread.

Hilda left swiftly to go and serve a late supper at Greenbrae, relieved to escape from the hot kitchen and the sounds of Iris in labour. John was despatched without ceremony to his night shift and Sadie was told to stay in bed upstairs. A while later, Davie, Eb and their father returned from the meeting, but were sharply banished to wait next door at the Parkins'. Davie protested that he could wait in the parlour, but his mother would have none of it.

'I've told Edie to get the pot warmed, she's expecting you.' Fanny was adamant. 'We'll send word when there's anything to tell.' Louie looked admiringly at her mother; she was so sallow and old about the eyes, but her voice had taken on its former air of quiet authority. She felt encouraged by her presence.

The hours stretched on interminably, but Iris's waters did not break. At one point she dozed off in a faint of fatigue, and Louie found a strange wave of pity sweep over her at the sight of Iris's flushed, vulnerable face. She sat holding her clammy hand while Fanny moved slowly about the room, preparing for the baby's arrival.

Finally word was brought by Susan Dobson that her mother had gone to visit a sister in Durham and would be away for the night. Louie's heart jumped in panic.

'Shall we send for Dr Joice, Mam?' she almost pleaded. Her mother was silent for a moment, then shook her head.

'We'll manage,' she answered. 'Dr Joice is entertaining. There's no need to bother him if we don't have to. We women can manage on our own, unless there's any complications.' Louie could not bring herself to ask what complications there might be, her mind filling with ghastly imaginings.

Shortly after four in the morning, there was a gush of fluid from Iris's womb and the labour proper began. They were all worn down with tiredness and nervous anticipation, but gently Fanny encouraged Iris through the severe contractions that left her racked and weeping. Louie lost her fear as her whole being concentrated on the job of helping to bring the baby safely through the traumatic pangs of birth.

This time, when you feel the spasm come, push hard!' Fanny urged. Iris clenched Louie's arm and shrieked like a madwoman. 'Again,' Fanny coaxed, 'push, push!'

'No!' Iris screamed, and lay back panting.

Louie felt a calm determination settle on her as she helped support her sister-in-law in a half-crouched position. Engulfed by a warm protectiveness towards them, she would do everything she could to bring Iris and her baby through this agony to safety.

The baby's on its way, Iris.' She talked gently. 'Don't fight it. Try again, we'll help you.'

Iris focused frightened, dilated eyes on Louie and clutched her free hand. 'Oh God, I'm scared, Louie,' she whispered.

As the labour seized Iris's body again, Louie and her mother together encouraged the terrified girl through the pain.

The head's appearing,' Fanny announced with an edge of relief in her voice, as Iris sank back once more. Louie leaned over and looked between Iris's shaking legs. Strangely, she no longer felt disgust at the mess or the young woman's nakedness, only an excited wonder at the sight of a new being thrusting itself out into the world.

'It's got hair,' Louie cried in amazement. 'Haway, Iris, and push again!'

The clock on the mantelpiece chimed five, and a few minutes later, in a cacophony of shouts from Louie and her mother and yells from Iris, the baby emerged.

'It's a boy, Iris,' Louie told her, her eyes shining with emotion. Iris sank back with a grunt and closed her eyes.

Under instruction from her mother, Louie lifted the slippery, bloodied scrap of human life on to a clean sheet and wrapped him up loosely. As she placed him gently in Iris's arms, the baby gave out a small bleat.

'I think he's hungry.' Fanny smiled.

'What are you going to call him, Iris?' Louie asked, finding it hard to hold back the tears of relief and joy.

'Raymond,' Iris answered simply, looking curiously at the tiny bundle. 'After Ramon Novarro.'

Louie looked at her in disbelief. 'You can't call a bairn after a film star! What does Davie think - ?'

'Leave her be.' Her mother put a hand on Louie's shoulder and squeezed it affectionately. 'I'll bathe him and then you should try and feed him, Iris pet. After that you must get some rest.'

'I just want to sleep,' Iris protested.

'I'll go and tell our Davie.' Louie's face glowed with pride at what they had achieved.

'Yes, pet.' Fanny gave her a warm, tired smile that told her she had done well.

Louie arched her back to release its stiffness and reached for her coat which had been drying by the fire. As she opened the back door to leave, Iris called, 'Thanks, Louie. You're a canny sister to me.'

'Don't be daft,' Louie replied, embarrassed, and turned away quickly.

But as she ran next door to break the good news to Davie and the men, the emotion that was choking her throat rose up and overwhelmed her. Tears streaming down her cheeks, she sobbed out loud in the dark of the cold March morning.

Chapter Eight

The following morning, Eleanor drove Marie Stopes to the station in Durham and put her on the early train south. Marie did not want to spend any more time than was necessary away from her work, her clinic and her new baby. The meeting at Whitton Grange had been a moderate success, with the younger women showing interest in new ideas in child health and family planning. Dr Stopes had given Eleanor much to think about in developing her project for a local clinic. As she swung her green Austin Seven down the steep hill away from the city and back towards Whitton Grange, Eleanor resolved to speak to Dr Joice about it at the earliest opportunity.

Talk of babies made her feel uncomfortable, and she preferred to think of birth control in the clinical context of general family health and helping to eradicate the overcrowding and poverty of the pit villages. But last night, as if to spite her, Hilda had come breathless to Greenbrae with the news that Iris's baby was on its way. Eleanor wondered if it was a girl or a boy. She would send a present for it; she still felt guilty about Davie's accident the previous summer.

As she pulled up in the drive outside The Grange, a splash of white and purple crocuses waved their welcome. Suffragist colours, Eleanor thought with pleasure, and her spirits lifted at this natural sign of rebirth and the promise of spring. The hardy bright flowers gave her the courage to confront Reginald about something that had been gnawing at her conscience since the previous evening. She found him in his study, alone.

'Has your visitor gone?' Reginald asked, glancing up from the papers strewn across his desk in the bay window. It irked Eleanor that he did not refer to Marie by name.

'Yes,' she answered, advancing into the room. 'Marie was sorry to miss you at breakfast - and at tea yesterday. You could have made the effort to be around for just one meal, Reggie.'

'You know I'm busy, Eleanor.' He gave her a dismissive look. 'And I'm expecting Hopkinson any moment.' She knew this. She had seen the agent's car pulling up at the front of the house just after she had arrived home. She had asked the butler, Laws, to make him wait in the drawing room for ten minutes. Reginald valued his mines' agent for his blunt speech and frugal economics in managing the pits, but Eleanor disliked his abrupt manner and the coldness of his shrewd grey eyes. It gave her a perverse pleasure to think of him impatiently pacing the Persian carpet in the downstairs room while his time ticked on like a meter.

'I heard some of the union meeting in the co-operative hall last night,' she plunged in, knowing how to gain his attention. Her husband's head of wavy brown hair jerked up in surprise. 'I popped in during the interval in Marie's talk.' She waited.

'And what did you hear?' Reginald asked cautiously, his light-brown eyes searching her face for clues.

'Words that shocked,' she answered carefully, going to the mantelpiece and reaching for a brass Indian ashtray. She deliberately took her time lighting up a cigarette. Tipping back her cropped head of hair she blew smoke at the new electric light fitting.

'That doesn't surprise me.' Reginald followed her movements with irritation. 'I told your father it was a meeting of damn Communists, but he wouldn't listen. He takes less and less interest hi the affairs going on under his nose. It's just as well I'm de facto manager around here, or goodness knows what state we'd be in.'

'So it's you and not my father who's responsible for the squalid conditions in the village?' Eleanor rounded on him. 'They're living like animals in those slums you call houses. I was shocked by what I heard. I thought the speaker was exaggerating, so I asked Isobel's father. There was no exaggeration.' She challenged him with her dark eyes. 'They have to cross a muddy lane just to answer the call of nature, and even then it's just to an open earthen sewer. Disease spreads among them like wildfire, half the children are malnourished. And apparently the men aren't even taking home a living wage to keep hunger from the door.'

Reginald looked at her unmoved. 'I haven't time for one of your hysterical speeches now, my dear. Things are better now than they were under your grandfather or your Seward ancestors before them, did Dr Joice tell you that? No, he wouldn't - he's got Socialist tendencies himself, for all his talk about "Good Queen Victoria's Day". But I'm surprised, Eleanor, that you've been taken in by the rantings of some grubby Bolshevik. Who was he, by the way?'

Eleanor laughed harshly. 'I really have no idea.' She was not going to let slip Sam Ritson's name, just so Hopkinson could persecute him.

'No matter.' Reginald bent over his papers again, as if her information was inconsequential. 'I'll find out soon enough.'

Eleanor could see she would get nowhere by moralising at him. After all, she was just as guilty for allowing such conditions to exist; they were plain to see if she had but opened her eyes.

'Are you going to close the Eleanor or Beatrice, Reggie?' she asked him directly. 'I have a right to know. Dr Joice tells me five of the Seward pits have already closed in the past year.'

He stood up suddenly, glared at her and then turned to stare out of the window. His hands were locked tightly behind his back as he spoke.

'Those other pits were worked out,' he answered tightly. 'Hopkinson and I are doing our damnedest to keep the Whitton Grange pits open. Costs are rising all the time and productivity is not. We've lost valuable markets abroad to France and Germany and even the Americans. The price of coal we were getting overseas has consequently fallen. Durham coal has a valuable market in Scandinavia, but now the Poles are undercutting us.' He turned and confronted her, his face hard. 'What your precious miners can't understand is that we have to compete to survive, and to survive we must make economies.'

'By cutting their wages instead of our profits?' Eleanor accused body. His jaw tensed as he struggled to control his anger.

'Most of them can see the sense in what we are proposing, but there are a few reds - agitators - who want to see us fail, because all they are interested in is bloody revolution. Make no mistake, such men want to see the end of our British way of life - of people like you and me, Eleanor. They won't thank you for championing their cause. What happened in Russia can happen here.' He waited for her to interrupt him, but when she said nothing, he smiled briefly and untensed his hands.

'I'm not an ogre, Eleanor, and neither was your father or grandfather before me. We provide these people with free housing and gifts of coal. We pay for their funerals if there's an accident at the pit. We pay them wages we can realistically afford. Our hands are tied by what the market dictates, my dear. And we are providing valuable jobs for these men. Think of the poverty there would be if there were no mines on our estate. Trust me to look after your interests best, Eleanor,' he swept his hand over the papers before him, 'and the interests of the miners.'

She looked at him bleakly. How could she begin to argue with him about things whose importance she was only beginning to grasp? She had a gut reaction that in his explanation moral values had been turned on their heads. But she could not put what she felt into words; she did not have the arguments at her fingertips as he did. As usual, her husband had got the better of her. He had spun a plausible story and bound her up in his words.

Reginald was already seated at his desk again, once more immersed in his papers. She stubbed out her cigarette in frustration and marched from the room. If she had glanced back for an instant, she would have been surprised by the look of uncertainty on Reginald's face as he watched her brittle body turn from him in defiance.

Louie was thrilled that she had been asked by Davie and Iris to be baby Raymond's godmother. He was less than a month old now, but Louie found it hard to remember a time when he had not been around, so familiar was his tremulous cry when he was hungry, his serious frown of concentration when he sucked from his bottle in her arms. Iris would not feed him herself; she was only concerned with regaining the shapely curves of her former figure, and Fanny helped her wrap a sheet tightly about her stomach each day to force her sagging belly back into shape.

'Oh, if only I could go out,' Iris sighed in frustration, gazing longingly through the net curtains of the parlour. She and Davie had moved into this room with the baby until they found their own home, while Fanny and Jacob now slept upstairs. Hilda had removed to the spare bed, which Louie shared with her for a few hours a night.

'You know you mustn't go out until you've been churched and the baby christened,' Louie answered firmly, rocking Raymond gently in his crib. 'And don't let in the light, Iris, it'll hurt the baby's eyes.'

Iris let the curtain fall back and stood up impatiently.

'I'll go mad if I have to spend one more day in this house!' she cried. The baby started at her raised voice and gave a yell of fright. Louie reached to pick him up at once.

'There, there, bonny lad, Mammy didn't mean to shout,' she crooned. Iris looked at them both in desperation. She felt no stirrings of maternal love for this strange, pink, crinkled bundle of humanity with its demanding appetite and cry that set her teeth on edge. She would make a hopeless mother; she would never cope without Louie's help. What would she ever do if they moved to a place of their own? She would be tied to this stranger for ever. Her dreams of being a famous actress or singer were gone for good, ruined by Davie and his son. She hardly thought of Raymond as her own.

'I wish he were your bairn," Iris suddenly shouted at Louie, and burst into tears, flinging herself on the stout iron-framed bed.

Louie gaped at her in shock. She was quite bewildered by Iris's lack of affection for her son. She thought he was the most perfect and beautiful baby she had ever seen. Already he had his father's spiky hair and neat nose. His eyes were dark blue still, but they would lighten into Davie's sky blue in time.

She let her sister-in-law cry for a minute and then said, 'Hold him, Iris.' Louie offered him gently, folding a lacy knitted shawl about his head. Iris's sobbing stopped as she raised her tear-streaked face. Louie thought she was prettiest when her green eyes were sad and her sum face moody.

'He looks better in your arms, Louie,' Iris replied quietly, without malice. 'You hold him and I'll make the tea.' She dragged herself wearily off the bed and unconsciously smoothed her hands over her shrinking stomach. As she went into the kitchen, Louie bent and kissed Raymond on his button nose.

'Auntie Louie will take care of you, pet,' she whispered sadly.

The day of the christening was a bright, blustery Sunday in early April. Louie and Hilda and their mother had been busy for days baking for the christening party, and Iris's family had been invited from Durham for the occasion. Her father brought them on the train, a gaggle of unruly children and a thin wife, with Iris's auburn hair, who scolded Iris for not breastfeeding her baby and pressed a silver sixpence into Raymond's podgy hand for good luck.

To Louie's relief, Iris seemed to have shaken off her gloom and revelled in putting on her best dress with a new beige felt hat she had bought on credit from Lake's the haberdashers. Davie, besotted with both wife and child, hardly seemed to notice Iris's disinterest in Raymond, and looked at her in admiration. Though he had not touched a drop of alcohol since the night of the birth, he felt in a permanent state of intoxication.

The two grandfathers regarded each other warily, neither really approving of the other. Louie thought her father looked the more distinguished, tall and erect, his white beard and red and white hair neat above the starched collar and best black suit. He bore the authority of an Old Testament prophet, Louie thought with pride, while Iris's father was overweight, with a pallid face and a weeping brow he kept having to mop with his handkerchief.

'Well, Louisa,' her father spoke so everyone could hear, 'are you ready?'

'Yes, Da.' Louie smiled, taking Raymond from Iris's mother, careful not to crease the long white robe that fell luxuriously to her knees. It was the only family heirloom that her mother had, a delicately embroidered christening gown, already three generations old. One day, she thought with pleasure, her own babies would be baptised hi this dress.

'Do you have the christening parcel, Louie?' Hilda asked excitedly.

'Aye, it's in my coat,' Louie answered, feeling the lump of wrapped cake and silver sixpence heavy in her pocket.

Stepping out into the street ahead of the parents and family, Louie felt as grand as Queen Mary, carrying her precious godchild to the chapel. The stiff breeze buffeted the proud party as they made their way up Hawthorn Street and into Holly Street, smiling neighbours watching from their doorsteps or falling in behind to follow the procession to the Wesleyan chapel in North Street.

The first young girl that Louie met after leaving the house was May Little, a schoolfriend of Sadie's who had been waiting on the Parkins' doorstep so that she would be the recipient of Louie's parcel.

'Reach into my pocket.' Louie smiled at the anxious girl. She fumbled for a few seconds and then triumphantly drew out the package of treats.

'I've got it, Sadie!' she cried to her friend, waving her treasure in glee. Then she remembered the baby who had caused her this good fortune. She peered at the puckered face all but hidden in the warm shawl. 'He's tiny.'

'Isn't he bonny?' Louie demanded.

'Aye,' May agreed quickly and dived away with her good-luck prize.

At the chapel they filed into their regular pews and the Reverend Stephen Pinkney led the service from the pulpit, with rousing hymns and exhortations that stirred the congregation and filled the high-ceilinged chapel with noise. Jacob Kirkup gave one of the readings in his powerful bass voice, and when Louie and the parents went forward to have Raymond baptised she thought she would weep with happiness.

As the minister took the baby from her and sprinkled his head with water, Raymond gave a shriek of protest. Louie knew this would please her mother and the older women who thought it bad luck if the baby did not cry.

Afterwards, members of the congregation crowded about Iris and Davie to see the baby. The schoolteacher Miss Joice and her father the doctor were there, and Louie's parents invited them back to 'wet the baby's head', as they had been so kind in taking Hilda into their employment. The Parkins and the Dobsons came back to the house too, and Aunt Eva, a sister of Fanny's who had travelled from up the valley where her husband worked on a farm on the Waterloo Bridge estate.

'He's going to be a footballer,' Wilfred Parkin was telling Davie over a glass of ginger wine. 'I can tell by the square head. He'll play for Newcastle, will your lad.'

'He'll play for England, this one.' Davie laughed proudly and reached for another ham sandwich.

Louie busied herself making tea for the visitors who called all afternoon, and she and Hilda brought out reserves of currant bread and homemade biscuits for late arrivals. While Davie and Iris walked to the station with her family and put them on the train, Eb thankfully changed out of his suit and went off to the allotment to be alone, and John and Jacob went upstairs for a rest.

'Can we take Raymond for a walk?' Sadie asked Louie.

'Not today,' Louie answered, 'but we'll take him out in the pram tomorrow.' Sadie wasted no more time trying to win her cousin round and instead disappeared to join in the skipping game outside.

'Where's this bairn?' a voice asked at the door. Louie looked up, startled, to see Sam standing awkwardly with one foot in the kitchen.

'He's through in the front room with Mam and Edie Parkin,' Louie told him and turned to cut him a piece of cake. 'I didn't expect to see you today,' she added without glancing round.

'Came to pay my respects,' Sam said stiffly.

'That's what you do at funerals.' Louie could not keep the amusement from her voice.

'Well, I'm not very good with bairns - or christenings,' he said defensively. 'You know I'm not the religious type.'

Louie turned to look at him and saw the flush of uncertainty colouring his square jaw. Not for the first time she marvelled at how he could be so assured when speaking in front of scores of strangers and yet so tongue-tied with her.

'But you won't say no to a piece of christening cake, even if it has been blessed with a grace?' Louie smiled as she held it out to him.

'Ta.' Sam took the fruit cake in his rough hands. He still appeared uncomfortable. 'Louie—' he began. Edie Parkin interrupted him, bustling in and demanding that the baby's bottle be warned.

'He's hungry for his tea now, bless him,' she said, giving Sam a suspicious look. Louie stood the bottle in a pan of warm water and listened to Edie chatter about Iris's family.

'You can pick your friends, but you can't pick your relations,' she announced with a shake of her grey head. 'Still, Iris is one of us now.' Louie had her doubts about this, but kept quiet. Eventually Edie disappeared into the parlour with the milk and they were alone again.

'Louie,' Sam tried once more, his voice rising in desperation, 'before anyone else comes in, I've got something to say to you.'

'What, Sam?' She shot him an anxious look. His nervousness was infectious. He was going to finish with her; why else was his face so severe? 'Say what you have to say.'

'We've been courting for a year now, Louie.' He addressed the kitchen range.

'Eleven months,' she corrected him.

'It hasn't been much of a courtship for you,' he ignored her interruption, 'what with me at meetings all the time, and things at the pit uncertain. I haven't given you much fun, but.' He shook his head. 'And things will only get worse, Louie; we've got a fight on our hands with Hopkinson and Seward-Scott.'

He was going to spoil this special day, Louie thought, her stomach churning. He was going to end their courting.

'What've they got to do with us, Sam?' she asked miserably. 'If you're sick of me why don't you just say so?'

He jerked his head round, his brow perplexed. 'Why should I be sick of you, Louie? I just want you to know that if you marry me, things aren't going to be easy for us, not for a long time - maybes never. So will you marry me on those conditions, Louie?' Sam demanded sternly, grasping his cake in a closed fist.

'Marry you?' Louie repeated in astonishment.

'Aye.' Sam glanced anxiously at the back door as if preparing for rejection and escape. 'I need a strong lass like you beside me, Louie, and it's time I did something about it. We've been courting long enough to know we're suited - and I can see you won't be happy till you have a family of your own.' Sam blushed.

'Sam Ritson,' Louie laughed with relief, 'you're a right one! On those conditions indeed - you make it sound like union bargaining.'

'I'll only ask the once.' His eyes were defiant.

'Of course I'll marry you.' Louie rushed towards him and threw her arms about his neck. 'I've looked at no other man since I saw you, Sam Ritson.' She pecked him on the cheek and felt an answering squeeze of his arms about her waist. What a perfect, perfect day, Louie thought, shutting her eyes tight as she clung to him. 'We're going to be so happy, Sam,' she assured him, 'you just wait and see.'

They pulled away from each other and Louie noticed Sam's crushed cake at their feet. For once she did not care about the mess.

'It might be best to wait until after the summer with things at the pit so bad,' he cautioned.

'Oh, let's not wait, Sam,' Louie pleaded, thinking how much she yearned to have a home of her own, away from the cramped strictures of Hawthorn Street. She would miss Raymond the most, but wherever they went they would be close by to see him every day. And maybe by next year she would have a bairn of her own.

'There are no pit houses available at the moment, Louie,' Sam reminded her. 'We'd best wait until one becomes vacant. There's no room at home now Bel and Johnny have moved in with their bairn.'

'What about Gladstone Terrace? We could take a room like Minnie and Bomber have done,' Louie suggested eagerly.

'Those cottages aren't fit for rats to live in.' Sam sounded offended.

'We don't need much,' Louie smiled persuasively, 'and it would just be to start with.'

Sam laughed at her persistence, wondering briefly if marriage had been Louie's idea all along and not his suggestion.

'We'll see,' he promised.

'See what?' Davie asked, coming in at the back door. Louie and Sam sprang apart guiltily. Her brother chuckled at the furtive looks passing between them. 'I've broken up a union meetin' I can see,' he teased. 'What are you plotting with my sister, Red Sam?'

Louie saw Sam's shoulders stiffen.

'Sam and I are going to be married,' she announced proudly, lifting her small chin, 'this summer, aren't we, Sam?'

'Well . . .' Sam hesitated, taken aback by her decisiveness.

'Married, you bugger!' Davie clapped him on the back. 'You're a lucky man, Sam Ritson, to be marrying our Louie. She's one of the best.' Davie grabbed his sister and swung her around in a playful hug.

'I'm pleased for you, pet.' He kissed her fair hair and turned to Iris, still with an arm about Louie. 'That's grand news, isn't it, bonny Iris?'

Iris stood in the doorway, her face pale and drawn as she stared back at them. All at once, her mouth sagged and her brow crumpled as she burst into tears. She hid her face behind slim hands and shook with racking sobs. Sam looked at her dumbfounded. Louie and Davie stood helplessly, wondering if they would ever understand this contrary girl from Durham.

While Louie revelled in the preparation of her 'bottom drawer', with Hilda helping her sew when she had time away from Greenbrae, Sam found himself increasingly at loggerheads with the pit management and even the officials of the Durham Miners' Association. He despised their conciliatory attitude towards the owners and their desire to avoid head-to-head confrontation. Their representatives at the Miners' Hall had gone soft with their own importance. But he would fight to the last drop of his blood to defend his marras' jobs and wages.

Much as he hated the work they were forced to do, the pit was a part of him and he was proud of the men he worked beside, the stoical courage they showed risking their lives each time they went below ground. His father Samuel was a loyal member of the Whitton Grange lodge, as his father had been before him. His grandmother, Mary Graham, had been born down a pit in East Lothian in the 1830s. To hew coal was Sam's reason for being; to work was his pride. The pit was his lifeblood. As a frightened young boy, sitting in the pitch-dark, opening and shutting the trap doors and listening out for the hiss of gas or the call of voices, he had developed his pit sense. He won himself a name as a hard worker, a lad who was picked on at the bully's own peril, a marra who would stand up to the deputy and the overman for the rest of his team. He soon became a spokesman for the men, bargaining for and sharing out their wages, drawing the cavels each quarter of the year to see who worked in which part of the pit.

So in June, when the owners decreed there would be a cut in wages and a lengthening of the working day, Sam Ritson led his men out on strike. The local lodge was behind him even if the Association in Durham was horrified by the unofficial action. By 1st July, exactly a month before the date Sam and Louie had set for their wedding day, Reginald Seward-Scott declared that wages would be cut by half or the pits would remain closed.

Sam caught Louie alone in the back yard as she came in with a jug of milk from the dairy cart, and, tight-lipped, she listened to him tell her that the management had officially locked them out of the pit.

'How can we afford to get married now, with you and my Da out of work?' she asked when he'd finished, close to tears.

'We can still do it, Louie,' Sam cajoled. 'We could just have a quiet trip to the registry office, no need for a big fuss, is there?'

'No!' Louie shouted at him as she stormed into the house. 'If we don't get married in the chapel, we don't get married at all.'

For a moment Sadie and May stopped their game of leapfrog to stare at the slamming door and an embarrassed Sam, until he strode stormy-faced back down the lane.

It was late evening but only just darkening into night when Eleanor wandered out of Whitton Woods on to Highfell Common. She'd rather walk all night, she thought, communing with ghosts, than go home to an empty house. Her father was in Scotland making up a house party with Beatrice at Sandy Mackintosh's estate in the central Highlands. Beatrice seemed very taken with her Scots officer, but then she had waxed enthusiastic about men before, only to wane when someone more desirable came on the horizon. Reginald had left that morning to go fishing with Bernard Fisher and she knew he would stay over at Waterloo Bridge. He had seemed in high spirits for someone who had just slammed lock-out notices on the gates of the Whitton Grange pits. But then Reginald gloried in fighting, as long as it was not his blood which got spilt.

Eleanor shuddered. What ironic thoughts for this particular day, the anniversary of her brother Rupert's death. Nine years it was since the first day of the Battle of the Somme, the day that had sealed his fate along with that of tens of thousands of other soldiers - and their families, she thought bitterly.

Something close by stirred in the thick bracken and a dark shape emerged right in front of her. She stifled a cry as the becapped man got to his feet.

'Didn't mean to scare you,' he said, hastily removing his cap and scratching his head.

'It's Eb, isn't it?' Eleanor felt a surge of relief.

'Yes, Mrs Seward-Scott,' he mumbled. 'I'll be off then.'

'Don't go.' She stopped him quickly with her hand outstretched, 'Not yet.'

Eb thrust his hands into his jacket pockets, feeling ill at ease so close to this woman who troubled his peace. She was a link with the War and all that he tried and failed to forget. On this of all days, did she think of the brother she had lost, just as he remembered his long-dead friends?

'Let's walk on to the brow and look at the sunset over Weardale,' she suggested.

He felt better once they started to move. They had not been alone together since their argument over Hilda's future last Christmas. It bothered him that he had missed her visits; her staying away had only served to highlight his own solitude in the world. He belonged to a big family and yet lived apart from them, cut off by experiences and feelings they could never fathom. This woman from the big house knew him better than his own kin, though she had made little attempt to speak to him again, even when he had gone to work at Greenbrae.

'I went to St Cuthbert's today and put some roses on Rupert's memorial stone.' Eleanor broke into Eb's thoughts. He was unnerved by the way she seemed to read his mind. 'Yellow roses from a creeper my mother planted. Rupert used to write about it in his poems.'

'I didn't know your brother wrote poetry.' Eb stopped by a stone wall and leaned on its coldness.

'Most young men did in those days, didn't they?' Eleanor mused. Eb did not reply. He had never confessed to anyone about the stilted verses he had scribbled on the back of cigarette packets as the rain dribbled down the back of his greatcoat in a soggy Flanders trench. None of them had survived.

'Rupert wrote of childhood and home in all of his poems - the ones he sent to us at least,' Eleanor continued. 'He used to describe some idyllic past of hot summers and walks on Highfell, tennis at The Grange, punting on the river at Durham - that sort of thing. Not once did he write about the War or death or sadness, though they must have been overwhelming. Don't you think that strange?'

'No.' Eb turned his face into the remnants of the sunset. 'It was his way of coping with his friends dying around him.'

'I would have been so angry.' Eleanor clenched her hands and knocked them against the stone wall. 'Rupert was the one going through hell but I was the one consumed with bitterness at the futility of it all. And I still am!' she cried, feeling her throat choke with sadness. 'Every day I wish the War hadn't happened, every morning I wish Rupert were still alive and running this estate.'

Eb was at a loss as to how to answer her despair. 'We can't bring any of them back,' he said gently. 'We can only hope that we'll meet them again in another life.' Eleanor swung round and scrutinised his face; its fairness was hidden in shadow.

'Do you really believe in that, Eb, in this life-after-death business?' she asked, as if proof was demanded.

'I have to believe in it.' He faced her as he spoke. 'I've lost too much in this one.'

'Your father's a lay preacher, isn't he? Is that why you're religious?'

'Maybes,' Eb shrugged, 'maybes not. 'Eleanor waited for him to explain. 'During the action at Loos there was a young subaltern wounded in a crater. We couldn't get to him with water or medical supplies, 'cos the shelling was that heavy. He lay out there for two days.' Eb paused as he struggled with his memories. 'Finally, me and this marra Dickie, we went out under fire to take him some water. We expected to find him dead but he wasn't. Between the two of us we managed to bring him back in alive. Well, Dickie wanted to know what had kept him going, and do you know what he said? He told us he'd been reading his Bible - a small one he kept in his pocket.' Eb smiled wistfully at Eleanor. 'Me marra Dickie couldn't believe it, but the proof of it was the officer was still alive, and he insisted it was God had kept his spirits up in that crater till we arrived.'

'And you believed him?' Eleanor searched his face, wanting to feel conviction too.

'I believed he had faith,' Eb answered, 'and that his faith had kept him alive. And it's because of that subaltern that I have hope - perhaps beyond reason - that we'll all meet up some day. I can't explain it any other way.'

Eleanor sighed. 'I wish I could hope, Eb. You know, you're like Rupert in so many ways; I've felt that before. It's your sensitivity, your love of nature, your quietness. Rupert believed in God too. I wish I still did.'

Without knowing why, Eb stretched out his hand and covered one of Eleanor's. She let it rest there, warming her cold, fragile bones, letting the life flow from him in to her numbed being. She raised her dark eyes to meet his blue ones and saw the need in him too, a raw, physical need for human comfort. Eleanor felt herself shaking under his touch like a nervous girl. Could she, dare she, allow herself to step over the invisible boundary that kept them in their separate worlds? She had drawn close to it before and peered into Eb's life like a voyeur, but had shrunk from touching it; a world too insecure and impoverished, yet too vibrant and giving. But her desire for him at that moment made her sick with wanting, swamping her fear of an embarrassed rebuff from this gentle pitman.

'Will you kiss me, Eb?' she whispered. 'Please.' He hesitated, shocked, held back by his sense of their differences, the social void between them, the decades of distrust and hatred that they carried. But her simple request touched him and he could not deny the excitement within at the thought of kissing this alluring woman with the dark, appealing eyes. So he leaned towards her and placed his lips tentatively on hers. He could not remember the last time he had kissed a woman like this and something inside him broke free at the contact, like one of his pigeons released at last from its coop.

Eleanor stepped close to Eb and kissed him again, the warmth from his body washing away the pain of her loneliness. How odd to find the answer to her empty life here all the time in Whitton Grange, in the person of Eb Kirkup, ex-private soldier, ex-miner. For the first time in years Eleanor felt no fear of the present. The future would have to take care of itself.

Chapter Nine

Louie and Sam patched up their quarrel, and despite the growing hardships at home with only Hilda's wages from Greenbrae to see them through July, Louie doggedly prepared for her wedding day. Her mother, filled with sympathy for her elder daughter who was to have such a frugal start to married life, did what she could to help. She got up early to make the most of the daylight to sew pillowcases out of old sheets, as they could not afford to burn paraffin in the lamps at night.

They had enough to eat, as Eb worked hard in the allotment and brought home vegetables and fruit to feed both their household and the Dobsons who had no garden. Their friends contributed scraps to feed the chickens which Eb was fattening up for the wedding meal. Davie and John got casual work on Stand High Farm where their Uncle Jack and Aunt Eva lived. For the week Davie was away picking vegetables, Iris fretted and lost her temper with them all. Raymond, however, was turning into a sunny-natured baby. 'Just like his father,' Fanny would say proudly, and tickle his chin to release a gurgle of delight from her grandson.

Towards the end of July, Sam appeared at their back door with some good news.

'The TUC are backing us, Mr Kirkup.' He came in triumphantly, his shirtsleeves rolled up to reveal strong hairy arms, the sight of which made Louie's stomach vault.

'About time.' Jacob Kirkup looked up from his book and peered at his future son-in-law over his recently acquired wire-rimmed spectacles.

Sam took the chair Louie pulled out for him and continued eagerly. 'The Triple Alliance is going to show the bosses that they can't ignore the pitmen this time. The other unions have agreed not to move the coal - not by road, nor rail, nor nothing. The seamen won't touch it either!'

Louie looked expectantly to her father for his approval. This might at last break the deadlock and they could all get back to work.

'We'll just have to see,' Jacob replied cautiously. 'We'll have to pray Prime Minister Baldwin sees sense at last.'

Amen, Louie thought fervently. 'Would you like a glass of water, Sam?' she asked her fiancé. She was saving their stock of tea for the wedding feast.

'No, ta, pet,' he answered briefly, getting to his feet again. 'I've got a meeting to attend.' As an afterthought, he turned in the doorway and smiled at her. 'You be looking out your wedding dress, Louie Kirkup, 'cos we'll be celebrating a victory on that day, you just see.'

As he left, Louie sighed and looked at her mother. They both started to laugh.

'You're marrying the whole union when you take on Sam Ritson,' Fanny chuckled quietly, 'but he's a good lad all the same.'

To the relief of all Whitton Grange, save the landowners at The Grange itself, the coal embargo worked. A flustered Baldwin intervened in the dispute and agreed to continue the coal subsidy to the industry for another nine months. In the meantime a commission of enquiry would be set up to investigate the problems. Friday, 31st July 1925, was christened Red Friday by the gleeful miners. Sam knew they had won an important victory over the owners in their fight for a decent wage, but he knew too it was just a temporary halting of the forces amassed against them and that they would gather to fight another day.

Eleanor found Reginald in a foul mood at luncheon. Her father was quiet, but thankful that the government had come to their aid.

'We've been made to look idiots by men like Ritson,' Reginald fulminated, stabbing his fork into the cold chicken and pushing it away without appetite.

'They've forced a climb-down, and now we've given hi on their wage demand. It's just fuel to their revolutionary fire, it's damnable!'

'Calm down, Reggie,' Eleanor said evenly. She was secretly relieved things had turned out well for the miners. For the last month she had lived through the Kirkups' uncertainty and anxiety, hearing first-hand from Eb of Louie's hopes for an August wedding. She had offered him gifts of food from The Grange or a loan of money, both of which he had adamantly refused. She knew now not to ride roughshod over his proud independence. There had been no impropriety since their embrace on the anniversary of the Battle of the Somme, but the bond between them still remained. Eleanor would have to take care that Reginald did not learn of her visits to Whitton Woods.

'Don't tell me how to behave.' Her husband spat the words at her. 'You've been less than loyal during this dispute.' Eleanor's head jerked up guiltily. Surely he knew nothing about her friendship with Eb and with Hilda? 'You spend your time aimlessly wandering about Whitton Grange like a lost pup, instead of entertaining people who would be useful to us.'

'I suppose by that you mean the tedious Fishers and their moneyed friends?' Eleanor asked him sarcastically.

'They're a damn sight more jolly company than you are, my dear.' Reginald was spiteful in return.

'That's quite enough, Reginald.' Thomas Seward-Scott got to his feet. 'If I'd wanted to witness a dog fight, I'd have lunched in the kennels.' He turned to his daughter. 'Do you wish to ride this afternoon, Eleanor?'

'Thank you, Papa, but I'm going into town to collect an item.' She smiled at him gratefully. Whatever she did in her life, her father had always supported her, even if he had not always given his approval. The invitation was his way of backing her against his son-in-law, who appeared to run The Grange these days without any consultation. Her father was an amazingly tolerant man for his generation, she thought.

Once Thomas had gone, Reginald rose and went to glare out of the wide bay window framed by its heavy burgundy velvet curtains.

'They haven't won yet,' he muttered, directing his wrath at the terrace, its rockery burgeoning with yellow tagetes and bright orange nasturtiums.

'Who haven't?' Eleanor asked him with irritation.

'Red Sam Ritson and his bunch of Communists.' Reginald clamped his hands behind his back. Eleanor wanted to point out that Sam Ritson was nothing of the sort - he merely put the interests of his own kind first, just as Reginald did - but she bit back the retort.

He swung round abruptly and fixed on Eleanor like a hound who smells a fox nearby. 'I swear to you, Eleanor, that Sam Ritson will rue the day he ever tried to cross me.' She felt a sudden shiver run through her at the threat of vengeance in his face. 'When I'm finished with him, there'll not be a colliery in County Durham that will have anything to do with him.'

Later that day, as Eleanor drove herself down to Greenbrae, she experienced a thrill at her rebelliousness against Reginald. She was going to deliver a wedding present from The Grange to Louie and her victorious Sam. She had gone into Durham straight after lunch and collected the silver tea service she had chosen from a jewellers on Elvet Bridge. It was wrapped now and resting on the back seat. She knew it might cause embarrassment if she went openly to the Kirkups' house, so she would hand it over to Hilda.

But Louie's sister had already left. Isobel had let her off duty early so she could go and help prepare for the wedding the following day.

'Eb is still in the garden, though,' her friend told her as she brought her into the drawing room. Eleanor needed no further encouragement and went to seek him out. Apprehensively, Isobel watched her go, sensing the growing friendship between her schoolfriend and the gardener; it was a long time since she had seen Eleanor as animated as she was in his presence. Others might have been shocked, but she knew of her friend's deep underlying unhappiness and was glad that Eb Kirkup could give her something to brighten her life. Isobel was sure that, as yet, they did not know the depth of their regard for each other, but from her objective standpoint she could tell when two people were falling in love.

Eleanor found Eb picking strawberries. He looked round and gave his slow, shy smile, his moustache showing pale gold across his sunburnt face.

'Miss Joice said I could have a basketful for Louie's wedding. There'll be a canny few mouths to feed tomorrow.'

'That's nice of her.' Eleanor smiled in return. 'As a matter of fact, I was wondering if you would deliver a present from me. It's a tea set, I've left it in the house.' Eb stood up and took off his cap. Eleanor was suddenly filled with doubt. 'Do you think she'll accept it?'

'Louie will be touched,' he assured her. His ruddy face broke into a grin. 'Sam Ritson probably won't drink from it, but Louie will invite the whole of Whitton Grange to view it.'

Eleanor laughed with him. "That's all right then.'

Eb finished off his fruit gathering in silence, then Eleanor spoke. 'The pits will be opening again on Monday. Will you go back to work at the Eleanor?'

Eb looked up at her. 'Not if the Joices will keep me on here.'

'Good,' she said with relief. 'I'd never get to see you otherwise.'

'No, suppose not.' His eyes did not slide away from hers as they used to. 'I can't say I miss the pit one bit.' Then he did turn from her as he added, 'I'm happy here. It's a grand life to work out of doors. And I'm happy when you're here, Eleanor.' The last words were spoken so quietly she hardly caught them. But they thrilled her. He was talking to her as a friend, an equal, no longer as a labourer to the squire's daughter. Eb trusted her. Her heart leapt inside her like a skittish kitten.

In reply she leaned down and ran a hand over the ruddy-brown of his tanned scalp. She had always wanted to touch his head; it was smooth and warm. The blond hair that framed his ears felt coarse in comparison. He did not seem to mind her touching him, so Eleanor let her hand rest there.

'Your friendship means so much to me, Eb,' she said in a low voice. 'Since knowing you, I've come alive again.'

Saturday morning began with a blustery shower, then the grey sky cracked to reveal splinters of blue. By nine o'clock the clouds were rolling into puffy balls of white and racing across the terraced roofs.

'It's a grand day for it,' Davie said amiably, watching Hilda giving Raymond his milk, 'and you're looking in the pink, our Louie.'

Louie's insides wobbled like jelly, and she rushed about the kitchen trying to hide her nervousness. 'I hope you're going to polish your shoes before the service,' she scolded her brother.

'Iris'll do that,' he answered confidently, 'won't you, pet?' He pecked his wife on the head as she sat reading a magazine.

'She can do mine an' all,' John said, chewing over a stale crust of bread. Iris scowled at her brother-in-law.

'Do your own,' Davie told him, foreseeing an argument.

'What's the use of having an extra lass around the house if she won't work?'

John replied grumpily.

'She's not your lass.'

'And she doesn't do what you tell her neither,' John ridiculed. Davie flew at him with a fist. John caught it and jabbed him in the stomach. Louie turned and ran upstairs in tears, her nerves too frayed to bear their bickering.

'That's enough,' their mother shouted, coming in from the parlour to see what the noise was about. 'Can't you stop your fighting for just one day - your sister's wedding day?' she cried at them in exasperation. The brothers pushed each other away, suddenly guilty that they had upset Louie.

'Hilda, go upstairs and see that your sister is all right.' Fanny took command.

'I'll go,' Iris volunteered unexpectedly, and went for the stairs.

'Well, Hildy, find Sadie and tell her to come in and wash,' her mother ordered. 'You lads get yourselves tidied up before your father comes back.'

Iris found Louie staring out of the window of the small bedroom.

'They don't mean any harm.' Iris put a hand on her shoulder. 'Some brothers just like a scrap. They're sorry now.'

Louie took a deep breath, intending to show her usual practical, no-nonsense exterior. Then she saw Iris's kind smile, and burst into tears. They hugged each other for a minute and then Louie pulled away and wiped her eyes on her sleeve.

'I'm frightened, Iris,' she whispered. 'I've longed for this day, and now it's come, I don't want to get married. I can just imagine Sam standing there waiting for me - and - and it's like going to meet a stranger.' She looked at the older girl miserably. 'I shouldn't feel like that, should I? There's something wrong with me, isn't there?'

Iris put an arm around her shoulder and laughed sympathetically.

'There's nothing strange about getting cold feet on your wedding day,' she assured her. 'I was a bundle of nerves myself.'

'Not you?' Louie was amazed. 'You looked champion to me - all calm and glamorous like a film star.'

'Not inside I wasn't.' Iris shook her head with a smile, pleased with the compliment. 'But once we were married everything was better. I knew Davie was the man for me. Just like Sam is right for you, Louie.'

Louie dropped her head so Iris could not see the rising flush in her cheeks. 'Aye, but it was different for you and Davie,' she mumbled. 'You'd like - well, knew each other already.'

Iris felt a sudden pang of sympathy for her young sister-in-law, worldly-wise in so many ways and yet a complete innocent about men. She knew that if she laughed now, Louie would never forgive her.

'That'll just come natural too,' she told her gently. 'You mustn't be afraid. Has your mam never told you about marriage, Louie?'

Louie shook her head bashfully. 'Only about housekeeping and that.'

Iris sighed. 'Listen, we'll start getting you dressed,' she said firmly, 'and old Iris will tell you the facts of life while we're about it.'

Looking back, Louie remembered floating through the service, the lusty hymn-singing and the scent of flowers washing over her. Then she was outside with Sam in the bright sunshine, clutching the bouquet that Eb had made up for her and smiling happily at the crowd of well-wishers in the street. She glanced surreptitiously at Sam and thought how handsome he looked with his parted hair newly cut, and his collar stiff and white below his cleanly shaven square chin. His diffident smile changed his whole face and softened the intensity of his brown eyes.

Then to the delight of them both, they heard the colliery band strike up and appear from behind the chapel to play them back to Hawthorn Street.

'It was Eb's idea,' Hilda told Louie with a broad smile of crooked teeth. 'He knows how you like to hear the band.' Louie squeezed Sam's arm as she proudly slipped her own through his. It's a mark of how important they think Sam is too, she thought with a thrill.

Back at the house, the parlour and kitchen were packed to bursting with relations and friends tucking into the spread of food that the Kirkups had managed to lay on for their guests.

Liza Ritson, a handsome woman in a large-brimmed old-fashioned hat covered in mock flowers, complimented Louie and her mother on the quality of the chicken sandwiches and the homemade cakes and biscuits. However, her husband Samuel, a small wiry man with deep-set dark eyes, was not so happy about the lack of alcohol to celebrate the proceedings. Jacob Kirkup had been adamant that tea and ginger wine or lemonade were all they needed to refresh their thirsts. Davie saved the situation by taking Mr Ritson into the wash-house where he had hidden a few bottles of beer that he had persuaded Iris's father to donate. Soon Sam and John and Sam's brother-in-law Johnny Pearson had all found it necessary to call in at the wash-house on their way back from 'going across the road' to relieve themselves of vast amounts of tea.

By the time Jacob became aware of the illicit drinking party in the outhouse, the crime was committed and the bottles were empty. Iris calmed the rising tempers by starting off the singing. Soon Eb was striking away at the piano and Iris was joined by Sam's sister Bel who loved a singsong. Together they sang 'It Ain't Gonna Rain No Mo" and other musical favourites, then they all joined in traditional songs, such as The Lambton Worm' and 'Do Y'Ken John Peel?'

Davie started off 'Cushy Butterfield' and sang it raucously with Iris, slipping a possessive arm around her waist and thinking of the time they had first sung it, when they had met two years ago at the Big Meeting.

Louie looked at them enviously, wishing she and Sam were so easy in each other's company. She turned to find Sam eyeing her. His brow was furrowed, as if something was causing him doubt, and her palms began to feel clammy in the hot parlour. Was he regretting their marriage already, she wondered anxiously? Soon they would have to leave. Sam had managed to procure a room from the colliery management, a tiny dwelling in Gladstone Terrace, a row of temporary cottages thrown together when the first pit had opened. The previous week, Louie, with Hilda's help, had scrubbed it clean, and her brothers had carried in a large bedstead and a solid kitchen table and chairs. One room was hardly a glorious start to their married life together, but it would be their own and was already crammed with the presents and second-hand furniture they had been given. Louie had not yet dared tell Sam about the magnificent tea set gifted to them by the lady of The Grange. It was still in its luxurious box, under her brothers' bed upstairs.

All at once she was nervous about leaving the crowded conviviality of her parents' home, its cosy familiarity. Now the memories seemed so precious to her; the touch of the well-polished mahogany furniture, the noisy chatter of Sadie and Hilda around the hearth, the sight of her mother quietly knitting while her father read by the light of the paraffin lamp. She would miss Davie's friendly banter, Eb's silent presence as he wandered in after a day out of doors, even John's flashes of temper. They were all a part of the home's character like a well-worn clippy mat that she could not bear to throw out; they represented her girlhood here. And she would miss Iris and her bonny baby Raymond. Her moody, infuriating, generous, lazy, beautiful, funny sister-in-law, whom she had determined to hate, had ended up as her friend. Louie knew the grudging affection was mutual. Tomorrow morning it would no longer be her job to give her nephew his early bottle by the warmth of the kitchen range. With a pang she watched him gurgling and clutching Davie's finger as her brother showed him off to the Ritsons. Louie missed Raymond already.

Suddenly Sam was at her side, clearing his throat. 'It's time we were off, Louie.' The singing had stopped, and attention was focused on the departing couple. Sam took his leave of his family.

'Louie.' Her mother kissed her cheek, her eyes filling up with tears. Louie knew she would not cry, she had never seen her cry, but it touched her all the same to know her mother would miss her too. She hugged her father and he kissed the top of her head affectionately.

'You'll be just up the road,' he smiled encouragingly; 'we'll see you in chapel tomorrow.' Louie nodded, knowing her father would be preaching.

She hugged her brothers, cuddled Sadie who had burst into tears at her going, and promised her cousin she could come and stay one night soon.

'Bye, Hildy.' She hugged her younger sister. 'Take care of Mam, won't you?'

' 'Course I will,' Hilda reassured her. 'I'm not as daft as you think.'

'I've never thought you were daft, our Hilda.' Louie flushed to think of how bossy she had been at times.

She ignored the nagging guilt she felt at leaving Hilda to cope with the household as well as her job at Greenbrae. They would all just have to manage without her; she was entitled to a life of her own with Sam. She took Raymond in her arms and kissed his soft cheeks. Reluctantly she allowed her mother to remove him firmly from her hold.

'Give us a hug then.' Iris grinned, her slim face rosy from singing. Her eyes sparkled knowingly as she whispered in Louie's ear, 'Remember what I told you and there'll be nowt to be frightened of.'

Louie laughed nervously.

'What's the joke?' Sam took Louie by the hand.

'Women's talk,' Iris replied cheekily, and winked.

Minutes later they were out in the street, waving goodbye to their friends and neighbours, Sam clutching a canvas kit bag borrowed from Eb, full of Louie's clothing. Louie stepped out of number 28 Hawthorn Street as Mrs Sam Ritson, leaving behind the ghost of Louie Kirkup the spinster on the scrubbed and sandstoned doorstep.

At the end of the street they turned into Holly Street and then on up to the top of the village. Neither of them broke the awkward silence until they reached 16 Gladstone Terrace. I'll clean the window again come Monday morning, Louie vowed, seeing how the small downstairs window of their one-roomed cottage was once more thick with grimy dust from the pits which now loomed over their home. 'You know the inside's clean when the outside's good,' her mother always said. But in Hawthorn Street it had been possible to turn away and look down towards the dene and pretend that the pits and their clouds of filth were not there. Here, the squat, blackened group of houses seemed to huddle together for protection from the vast brick buildings, and the two pitheads with their unblinking wheel-eyes that watched fortress-like over them.

'It's a start,' Sam said defensively, seeing the dismay on his young wife's face. 'It's more than a lot have got to start with an'all.'

'Aye,' Louie sighed, and followed him inside.

She found comfort in busying herself about the cramped dwelling, rearranging her few possessions and spreading her best tablecloth over the rough square table that Wilfred Parkin and his father had made for them. The yellow and blue embroidered flowers with which Hilda had helped decorate the cloth brought a splash of colour into the dingy room.

'I'll get the kettle on,' Louie said with false brightness, then realised the fire was not lit and the stove was cold.

'I've had enough tea to float the Fleet,' Sam grunted, loosening his tie and stiff collar. He gave a groan of satisfaction as it relieved the constriction around his neck.

'I'll go and get the coal in for the fire anyway.' Louie felt the panic rising in her throat.

'In your wedding dress?' Sam laughed in surprise. Louie looked away, feeling tears pricking behind her eyes. She was at a loss as to how she should act. The wretchedness of the room with its smell of damp pressed around her like prison walls. She was trapped in here with this strange man, and his proximity was frightening. To her shame she allowed herself to succumb to the overwhelming need to weep.

'Louie?' Sam's voice was puzzled as he stopped his undressing to stare at her. 'What you crying for?' Louie could not answer except with louder sobs. He'll never forgive me for this, she thought miserably, he'll send me back home and I'll be a disgrace to all the family.

A moment later she felt his arms around her shoulders. 'Come here, Louie pet,' Sam said gently. 'You would think you'd been locked in with one of the bosses the way you're carrying on. I'll treat you right.'

Louie half laughed and half cried at his kind humour, burying her face into his broad shoulder.

'I'm sorry, Sam,' she apologised, her voice muffled in his shirt. 'It's been such a grand day; I don't know why I'm crying like a silly bairn.'

'It has been a grand day, Louie,' Sam patted her head, 'but you mustn't get too emotional, it doesn't do you any good.'

'No.' Louie drew away from him and blew her nose hard on her handkerchief. She felt her self-control returning rapidly.

They changed out of their wedding clothes and went for a long walk, over Highfell Common and back through the dene. As they stood on the Common and looked over at the woods that surrounded the secluded mansion, Louie told Sam about the present from the big house. To her relief, Sam found it amusing that his enemy Reginald Seward-Scott should have spent, probably unknowingly, a fraction of his profits on a wedding gift for a man he despised and feared.

Arm in arm they strolled back to the village.

'She seems canny, Mrs Reginald,' Louie ventured, testing Sam's good humour. 'Our Hildy sees quite a bit of her over at Greenbrae. She says she's not like other posh people, she treats her like a friend. Hildy says she's always speaking to our Eb, too.'

Sam frowned with disapproval. 'They shouldn't let her get too friendly,' Sam warned. 'Her type aren't like us, Louie, even Eleanor Seward-Scott - no matter how canny she may seem, she cannot change who she is. When it comes to a fight, she'll stick with her own, and her friendship with Hildy or Eb won't be worth tuppence-halfpenny.'

'Why does everything have to be a fight with you, Sam?' Louie asked impatiently.

'Because that's the only way our class ever gets anything,' he answered emphatically. 'Nothing gets handed to us on a plate, Louie, remember that.'

When they got home the fire that Sam had lit before going out had taken, and Louie boiled up a bowl of potato soup for them both. They ate hungrily and in virtual silence. Afterwards, she made up the bed that stood in the corner taking up a third of the room.

While the evening light still shone in through the thin curtains, Sam and Louie consummated their marriage; at first awkwardly and with fumbling bashfulness, later, as it darkened, with more assurance and growing intimacy.

Louie lay peaceful at last, nestled under Sam's arm, listening to the calls of men passing along the street on their way home from the pub.

'Will you come to chapel tomorrow?' she asked him softly. Sam shifted his arm.

'I've got a meeting,' he answered shortly. 'Meetings come first, Louie.' Yawning, he turned over and settled himself to sleep.

Louie lay awake for a long time, envying Sam his even, untroubled breathing as he slept. She tried to work out if she was happier now than she had been yesterday, and thought that she probably was. Anyway, it did not matter now; she had chosen a life with Sam Ritson and she was going to make the best of it. The clock on the mantelpiece struck twice, and then Louie remembered nothing more.

Chapter Ten

Married life for Louie was working out fine as far as she could tell. She had made their tiny home as comfortable as possible, with new nets at the window and her mother's best second-hand clippy mats by the hearth and bed. At the weekend, out would come the polished silver teapot from Mrs Seward-Scott, with its dainty sugar bowl and cream jug to match. With it sitting on a lacquered tray given by the Dobson family, and placed on her best embroidered linen tablecloth, Louie imagined she had the finest tea table in the county.

Through the week she would scrimp and save the meagre housekeeping that was left after their bills had been paid, so she could put on a special spread for the Saturday tea. Sometimes Sam would invite in Bomber and Minnie from down the street, as Minnie was now hugely pregnant and her mother, Mrs Slattery, had more than enough mouths to feed without helping them out. Bomber's parents had refused to speak to their son since he had married a Catholic.

The week before Christmas they sat around Sam and Louie's kitchen table, having had their fill of teacakes and jam, cheese and scones, wholemeal loaf and - Sam's favourite - Louie's homemade custard tart.

'Have some more jelly and pears,' Louie pressed Bomber.

'No ta.' Sam's redheaded workmate leaned back in his chair and patted a full stomach. 'That was grand. I only get to eat as good as this when I'm here.'

Minnie was immediately riled. 'Don't expect me to go baking all week, Bomber,' she retorted. 'I've hardly the strength to walk up the street, with carrying your baby.'

'Looks like you're carrying a football team in there,' Sam teased, not wanting a row to spark after Louie's hard work in laying on the large tea.

'Feels like it an' all.' Minnie gave out a loud sigh, her face flushed beneath her thick, curly dark hair.

Louie got up quickly to clear the plates. Minnie had asked her to be there at the birth; she was now considered a trainee midwife after delivering Iris's baby, and Mrs Dobson had taken her to help out at several births since. She slipped a look at Sam, but he was not watching her. They had been married nearly five months and yet nothing had happened. It was the only blight on her happiness that she was still not pregnant. She avoided her mother's look of enquiry each time they went to Hawthorn Street for the traditional family Saturday evening around the piano. It was even worse with Sam's mother when they called for Sunday lunch and she would be making a fuss of Bel's baby daughter, Betty. 'This'll all come to you soon, Louie,' she would smile as she bounced Betty playfully on her knee. 'It'd be nice to have a grandson next, wouldn't it, Samuel?' And she would nod her greying head of hair at her husband absorbed in the newspapers.

Louie could only escape to help Sam's sisters, Bel and Mary, with the washing-up. 'Don't mind Mam.' Bel squeezed her arm after one embarrassing mealtime of unsubtle hints from Louie's mother-in-law. 'She's just daft about bairns. She misses our sister Lizzy and her two boys, that's all.' Louie hardly knew Sam's eldest sister; she had moved away to Yorkshire with her mining husband at the end of the war.

Mary had snorted. 'Can't think what all the fuss is about - they're either crying or dirty or wanting feedin' - or all three. I'm never going to have bairns.'

'Mary's going to be a nun.' Bel raised her eyes to the ceiling.

'I'm going to be a missionary,' Mary corrected. 'A Presbyterian missionary like Miss Kennedy who spoke to the Guild last week.' This surprised Louie, who thought she was still with the Evangelicals.

'You mean like in foreign countries, preaching to the heathens?' Louie asked with interest.

'Yes.' Mary nodded decisively. 'I'm going to convert the heathens to God like Miss Kennedy and help all the poor people.'

'God help the heathen bairns,' Bel said under her breath as she went to claim Betty from her doting grandmother.

Still, Louie felt the pressure from her family and Sam's, whether spoken or not, the continual watching for signs that their marriage had been blessed. 'Babies only happen to the good ones,' she had heard Mrs Dobson say repeatedly to the mothers of the babes she had just delivered. Louie thought that was so unfair; she was no worse than either Iris or Minnie. But she was learning to be less impatient with life, and told herself that if it was meant to be, it would happen all in good time.

By the time Louie had stacked up the plates in the small pantry that was curtained off from the room, the conversation had thankfully switched from babies.

'It's bad,' Sam was saying. 'There'll be men idle by the end of the week who won't see work again for months.'

'Not just before Christmas?' Minnie cried in dismay. 'They won't be laying you off will they, Bomber?'

'Why no!' Bomber was falsely cheerful. 'You know how Sam likes to paint the picture black - they don't call him Lenin at the pit for nothing.'

'It won't be us just now,' Sam ignored his friend's joking. 'We've got a good cavel and they need us where we are. But they'll try and cut our wages and make us work more hours for less - that's the Christmas present the Seward-Scotts have for us this coming year.'

'Us pitmen will never agree to longer hours,' Bomber said hotly.

'We can't manage on less than we have now,' Minnie responded horrified, 'not with the bairn on the way. We can hardly manage as it is.' Her neck was a flushed red and Louie noticed tiny beads of sweat bubbling next to her hair line.

'Don't upset her, Sam,' she reproved quickly. 'No one's going to starve around here. Let's talk of something more cheerful. Our Sadie said she'd come over to help make some decorations.'

Louie sat Minnie by the fire and they began to cut shapes out of old newspaper to make into streamers. But the men sat on arguing about the worsening situation at the pit. Louie shut her ears to Sam's gloomy predictions. She could not believe the Seward-Scotts would have so little pity on them; things were bound to work out all right in the end. Anyway, their first Christmas in their own home was not going to be spoilt by anxious thoughts of the year ahead.

Sadie came rushing in at the back door, stamping her boots on the mat.

'It's started to snow,' she announced excitedly. 'Hildy's sent some coloured paper she got from Miss Joice, she said you can use it all for your streamers, 'cos she's made ours, and Davie's sent some mistletoe - he won't say where he got it from.' Sadie stopped her chatter to pull her store of treasure from the newspaper parcel tucked inside her over-large coat. Louie remembered wearing the frayed blue garment before handing it down to Hilda.

'Good for Davie,' Louie laughed.

'Look, Sam.' Minnie grabbed the mistletoe branch and waved it aloft. 'Plenty of kissing for you and Louie this Christmas, eh?'

'Minnie!' Louie tried not to look amused. 'Watch yoursel' while our Sadie's present.'

'Well, I know all about kissin' and that,' Sadie answered boastfully.

'And how do you know?' Louie asked sceptically.

'Iris tells me things.' Sadie looked triumphantly at her cousin.

'Does she now?' Louie's voice was full of disapproval.

'And I've seen May Little kissin' Frank Robson after school. Frank Robson's got a piece of mistletoe and he makes all the girls kiss him before he lets them out the school gate. Me and Jane Pinkney climbed over the wall so we didn't have to kiss him.'

Minnie and Louie burst out laughing. 'It was never that much fun when we were at school, was it, Louie?' Minnie grinned, her green eyes shining in the soft firelight.

'I'm surprised Miss Joice allows any carry-on,' Louie said, putting on her prim expression again.

'Well you might as well enjoy it, Sadie,' Minnie encouraged,' 'cos there's precious little carry-on once you grow up.' She flicked a look at Bomber, but he ignored the jibe.

'Fancy a beer at the club?' he asked Sam.

'Aye.' Sam stood up.

'Remember we're going to Mam's later.' Louie tried to hide her disappointment that he was not going to stay and help them put up the streamers. She had got a bag of chestnuts to roast on the fire too.

'I'll meet you there,' Sam told her. 'You just go on ahead. I need to speak to a couple of the committee before the meeting tomorrow.' Louie groaned inwardly. It had been the same every Saturday since Sam had been elected on to the lodge committee in the autumn, along with several of the younger, more radical pitmen. Louie was used to the lodge coming first in Sam's priorities, but it still rankled at times like this.

When the men had gone, Louie brought out some homemade ginger beer she had been keeping for Sadie, and they spent a happy hour making the decorations and catching up on the news from Hawthorn Street. Although Louie visited every week to help her mother with the large wash and Hildy with the ironing, she liked to hear Sadie's account of the household. As her mother was still plagued by a bad chest and coughing fits that left her exhausted, Louie's young cousin frequently stayed over at Gladstone Terrace at the weekends, to give Fanny a bit of peace, and because tempers in the crowded home often flared and Sadie got upset at cross words.

'And has Raymond taken any more steps since Tuesday?' Louie asked, thinking fondly of her nephew. He still had Davie's face and eyes, but his short fluffy hair was turning auburn like Iris's.

'He took four steps yesterday,' Sadie reported, 'but Iris isn't speaking to Davie since he forgot they were supposed to go to Durham last weekend to see her family.'

'She can be so moody at times.' Louie spoke up immediately in Davie's defence. 'He can't always be at her beck and call.'

'She doesn't know how lucky she is, with a lad like Davie for a husband,' Minnie added with feeling. 'You said he never goes out drinking now and he dotes on that bairn of his; I've seen them out in the park together.'

Louie nodded in agreement.

'He was out last night with Tadger Brown,' Sadie contradicted them. 'He woke me up when he came in and fell over me and Hildy in bed. When he went into the front room Raymond woke up and there was a terrible row, we could hear Iris shouting at him.' Sadie's dark eyes widened in fright as she remembered the uproar.

Minnie shot Louie a look of concern.

'She wouldn't mean anything by it,' Louie assured her hurriedly. 'Everyone has a tiff now and again. Now tell me about our John. Has he been courting Marjory

Hewitson again?'

'Aye,' Sadie stopped stabbing the paper with the scissors and looked up, 'and he's bringing her home tonight for supper.'

'Who's she then?' Minnie asked with interest.

'You know Marjory Hewitson, don't you? Works in drapery at the store. Her father's a joiner at the pit. You'll know her - plump lass with curly brown hair and pretty eyes.'

'Does she have a brother who plays for Whitton Grange? There's a lad called George Hewitson plays with Bomber.'

'Think he's some sort of cousin,' Louie replied. 'She's got a younger sister but no brothers. Marjory's very homely, just right for our John, specially now he's on the committee. She knows what's expected of a pitman's wife, not like our Iris, fond of her as I am,' she added, glancing at Sadie. Louie did not want to be too critical of Iris in front of the girl.

'I like Marjory,' Sadie said, pulling out a string of dancing figures from the red paper Hilda had provided. 'She brings me sweets and she made me a rag doll out of scraps from the store. She promised Iris she'd make something for Raymond too.'

'She must be serious about John then,' Minnie winked at Louie, 'making toys for the bairns.'

'Well, he's a lot less bad-tempered since he's started courting,' Louie smiled, 'so it can't be a bad thing.'

Minnie cracked open another chestnut as Louie hung up the first streamer, above the kitchen range.

'And what about Ebenezer?' Minnie asked, juggling a piece of hot nut in her mouth.

Sadie shrugged. 'He's never at home.'

Louie chipped in from her perch on the kitchen stool. 'Mam thinks he's courting, but he's that secretive no one knows who it is. I think our Hildy has her ideas but she won't say. I mean, he can't be out gardening in the dark every evening, now can he?'

'Didn't think your Eb was interested in girls,' Minnie answered, intrigued by the mystery. 'He's always been a one for his own company.'

'Don't ask me what he gets up to all day on his own,' Louie sighed. 'Hildy's the only one who seems to understand him. They're both a bit airy-fairy in the head, those two.'

Louie climbed off the stool and stood back to admire the bright-red decoration adorning the mantelpiece. Tomorrow she would pick some holly from the dene after chapel and place it around the tapestry picture of a horse and cart which Edie Parkin had made for her and which hung above the fireplace. She glanced at the darkened window and saw through the nets flecks of snow on the glass panes. Louie felt a childish thrill of anticipation ripple through her at the thought of the Christmas festivities that were about to begin.

Davie came home that Monday and told Iris he had been laid off at the pit. When he then announced he was going out to meet Tadger, she picked up his wet boots from the hearth and threw them after him. One caught him on the shoulder as he ducked, the second smashed against the kitchen door as he slammed it behind him. Fanny Kirkup came rushing and wheezing down the stairs to see what had caused the commotion.

'What in God's name was that about?' she asked sharply. 'Jacob and John are trying to get some sleep upstairs before their shift. Have you no consideration, girl?'

Iris turned towards her mother-in-law, her hazel eyes blazing with indignation. 'You can blame the noise on your precious son Davie, it's him who's got no consideration!' she screamed, pushing straggly strands of hair off her face. 'We've no money to do anything these days - not a bloody penny.' Fanny gasped in shock at her daughter-in-law's language. 'Now he tells me he's lost his job, and what does he do? He goes off drinking with scum like Tadger Brown. That's how much he thinks of his wife and bairn. So don't go telling me I've got no consideration, just don't go telling me!'

Iris's face was flame-coloured, her cheeks hardly distinguishable from the red lipstick she still insisted on wearing. For a moment Fanny was frightened by her wrath, unsure how to respond to this young woman who showed her feelings so easily. It had never been her way to betray her hurt or anger so publicly, and she and Jacob had never fought openly in front of the children. She went to pick up Raymond who had stopped his crawling exploration of the hearth and the specks of coal which he was methodically placing in his mouth. He seemed too shocked to cry at his mother's angry words.

'There, there, pet,' she crooned, 'Mammy isn't shouting at you.' He clung to his grandmother for a moment and then stretched out his arms for his mother and began to cry. Iris responded, though her whole body was shaking with fury. She clutched Raymond to her defensively.

'I should have known your Davie wasn't the type to change,' Iris continued accusingly. 'He'll always be a bad'n. I thought my head was in the clouds, but not compared to Davie. He'll always run from his responsibilities, that one.'

Fanny could not bear to hear her third son attacked so disloyally by his wife.

'He stood by you when you needed him,' she replied sharply, her face tense. 'Don't you ever forget that, Iris. And he's given Raymond a better start in life than if he'd been running loose in a public house.' She could not keep the indignation out of her voice. 'You're just a publican's daughter and you always will be, so don't you go looking down your nose at us pit folk. Davie may be a wild'n at times, but he's got a heart of gold. My son's worth twice as much as your kind.'

The effect of Fanny's words was more forceful than a slap to the face. Iris visibly reeled from the attack. Never before had her mother-in-law been critical or unkind in such a way. She had expected the older woman to understand her frustration and anger over Davie's behaviour, to stick up for her as another woman. Instead it was clear Fanny resented her in the family, blamed her for not fitting in, rather than Davie for turning back to drink and his mates when life began to get tough.

Without another word, Iris tossed her head back and marched with Raymond into the parlour, kicking the door shut behind her. Only then did Fanny notice Sadie crouched behind Jacob's large armchair, where she had been listening to Iris's wireless with the headphones on. The girl sat hugging her knees into her chest, her eyes tightly closed, black hair falling like a curtain across her face. Fanny did not know if she had heard their terrible argument, or whether she was oblivious to all, absorbed in her world of music. She cursed herself for allowing her temper to get the better of her. Then something that Iris had shouted returned to give her a second jolt; Davie had been laid off at the pit.

Iris sat down on her bed and let the tears come. Raymond had calmed down and was trying to yank the glass beads from around her neck.

'They don't want us here,' she whispered to him and sniffed. 'They think we're common as muck. Well, if that's the way they feel, we won't stay to be insulted, will we, Raymond?' She unclasped his fingers from her necklace and rolled him playfully on the patchwork eiderdown. The baby smiled widely, two teeth glinting in his gummy mouth. Iris tickled him and he giggled.

'They won't miss us,' she continued, enjoying her self-pity. Except she knew they would miss Raymond; Davie, Fanny, Jacob, Louie, they would all miss him terribly. Right now, Iris really wanted to hurt them for rejecting her, so hurt them she would.

'I'll get a job entertaining folk,' she told Raymond, 'singing or dancing. I could track down that man in Whitley Bay.' Iris thought back to the summer trip they had taken to the seaside at the end of August. She had dragged Davie along to the entertainment on the beach where a touring troupe was performing. She had been captivated by the bizarre costumes and actions of the characters; Pierrot, Columbine and Harlequin. Afterwards there had been a talent competition and Iris had got up and sung and won a twist of barley sugar. The leader of the troupe, an odd-looking showman called Barny, had approached her and only half jokingly invited her to go on the road with them. At the time Iris had laughed at Davie's rude reply to the manager, glad of his possessiveness towards her. Now she was almost tempted to try and find the troupe. But they would be far away from the north-east, scattered around the country and impossible to trace.

So instead, Iris waited until the following afternoon, when Davie and John were out playing football in the park, the rest of the men were sleeping and Fanny and Sadie had gone with Louie to help decorate the chapel with holly for the Christmas services. She packed her scant possessions into a carpet bag of her mother's, along with Raymond's things, and left 28 Hawthorn Street with Raymond clutching the soft stuffed ball that Marjory Hewitson had given him at the weekend. At quarter to three that afternoon, just as the wintry silver light was draining out of the sky, she boarded the train for Durham City.

She sat straight-backed, her slim face resolute, concentrating on how she was going to explain her actions to her parents. Her mother would scold her for being a bad wife and her father would give her a hug and ask her to help out in the bar. Neither would force her to go back against her will. Stepping on to the platform at Durham, her neat shoes ringing on the cold stone and echoing into the metal rafters, she brightened at the thought of seeing her family again.

Eleanor sat in the back of the Bentley, rubbing the window so she could catch her first glimpse of Beatrice coming off the London train. The chauffeur, Sandford, kept the engine running, but she still felt the cold under the kaross spread over her legs. She saw a pretty young woman muffled in a green coat and battered velvet hat leave the station clutching a baby. Only after she had disappeared down the hill towards the town did Eleanor recognise her as Iris Kirkup, Davie's wife. She had not seen her since calling with a book of nursery rhymes during the summer. It had been a useless present for such a tiny baby, but she had not known what else to give. Eleanor assumed she was visiting her family before Christmas and thought no more about it.

Five minutes later the London train arrived and Beatrice finally appeared leading a posse of porters laden with her suitcases. Sandford jumped out to help heave them into the boot of the car.

'Beatrice,' Eleanor kissed the proffered cheek, 'you must be coming home for a month.'

Her sister waved a careless hand at her luggage. 'This is nothing. I've sent another trunk north with Sandy. He'll be arriving on Christmas Eve. He's got three weeks leave; it's going to be marvellous.'

Sandford held the door open for them and the women climbed into the car. He tipped the porters and slid a hat box on to the seat beside him.

'So what's the news you said you had for me?' Eleanor smiled and leaned back on the leather upholstery. Beatrice grinned and snuggled the animal skin rug around her knees.

'It's about Sandy.' She almost purred as she said his name, 'He's asked me to marry him. Isn't that wonderful?'

Eleanor had suspected this would be the cause of Beatrice's excitement. She had stuck with Sandy Mackintosh for over a year now and at twenty-three had obviously decided it was time to stop playing with the bright young people and settle to the task of finding a suitable husband. Then Eleanor chided herself for being critical of her younger sister's calculating practicality. If she herself had only stopped to think through her reasons for marrying Reginald, she could have saved them both a lot of trouble and pain.

'That's marvellous news.' She leaned across and squeezed Beatrice's fur-gloved hand. 'You said yes, I take it?'

'I let him stew for two days,' Beatrice smiled, 'then agreed. Don't tell Daddy yet, though. Sandy is insisting on going through the rigmarole of asking his permission. He's terribly old-fashioned that way. Still we can go ahead and organise a party.'

'When do you want it?' Eleanor asked. It was ages since they had held one at The Grange and she found herself quite looking forward to the idea. 'I've invited the usual friends for Christmas Eve.'

'Then that's when we'll announce our engagement. It must be a huge party though.' Beatrice began to enthuse. 'We won't tell Daddy it's for anything special until after Sandy has spoken to him.'

As the car slipped through the twilight of a crisp December afternoon, they talked over the arrangements that would need to be made.

Eleanor frowned. 'It doesn't leave much time to send out extra invitations. We'll have to do it by telephone.'

'I suppose Reginald's awful friends the Fishers will have to be invited?' Beatrice pulled a face, and Eleanor flushed.

'Not if you don't want them there,' she answered.

'Oh, I don't care.' Beatrice changed her mind. 'It'll be quite a laugh for Sandy to meet such vulgar people. He'll be very diplomatic, of course, he's a complete gentleman. How is Reggie, by the way?'

Eleanor smoothed the rug with her hands as she answered. 'Totally caught up in some secret committee. Something to do with organising supplies in an emergency - though emergency for what, I can't think.' Beatrice looked uninterested, and Eleanor had to confess to herself that she paid little attention to his activities unless they had a direct bearing on Whitton Grange. She tried to stay alert to any news that might affect Eb or his family, but apart from that she stayed out of her husband's way.

'So life at The Grange is as exciting as ever?' Beatrice mocked.

'Life here is just fine,' Eleanor replied, her mouth twitching at the corners.

'Oh?' Beatrice tried to scrutinise her sister's face in the gloom, alerted by something in her voice. 'I thought you found life here tedious beyond words. That's the impression I got when I was last home, anyway.'

'You haven't been home for months,' Eleanor accused.

'Come on, then.' Beatrice's curiosity was momentarily aroused. 'Tell me what's happened to change things. Have you got yourself a rich lover?'

'Beatrice!' Eleanor was scandalised by her sister's bluntness in front of the chauffeur.

'Oh, Sandford can't hear us.' She dismissed Eleanor's warning gesture. 'He's as deaf as an old post. So tell me who he is and has he got pots of money? Gosh, I bet Reggie would revolve in his stuffy shirt if he suspected. Does he suspect?'

'There's nothing to suspect.' Eleanor looked away out of the window, unnerved by her sister's accuracy. She and Eb could hardly be called lovers. Since their first shattering kiss on Highfell last summer they had only snatched moments together, but their meetings were always laced with a delicious sense of clandestine rebellion.

'I don't believe you,' Beatrice crowed at so easily getting at the truth. 'I could tell there was something the minute I saw you. You look younger - your face looks plumper. I can tell a woman in love; you're giving off a scent of lust like an expensive perfume.'

'Don't be ridiculous,' Eleanor snorted with embarrassment. She could never tell Beatrice about Eb; her sister was a snob and would never understand. It saddened her to think she could not share her joy in Eb's company with anyone close, except Isobel; only her friend knew how she felt.

'Well, I think it's about time,' Beatrice commented. 'Reggie was turning you into a bad-tempered old maid.'

The following two days were filled with frantic preparations for Beatrice's party. Mrs Robertson the housekeeper oversaw a rigorous polishing of the furniture, silver and brasses until the lofty rooms of The Grange sparkled in the crisp winter sunlight. Meanwhile Mrs Dennison, the cook, set her staff to the task of preparing a large buffet of soups, pies, winter salads, soufflés, game, cheeses and puddings. Laws, the butler, directed the preparation of enormous tureens of hot punch to be served on the guests' arrival.

Sandy Mackintosh arrived at midday on Christmas Eve and Beatrice clung to him possessively with girlish smiles, hanging her blonde head coyly as they went to confront her father in the library after lunch. Eleanor watched them go with amusement, feeling a stab of pity for the young fair-haired officer who seemed much too gentle and diffident to be a match for her self-willed sister.

However, they all emerged smiling twenty minutes later. Eleanor thought her father's enthusiastic reaction was an indication of real approval of his future son-in-law, verging on relief. He would have hated Beatrice to have married any number of her past boyfriends; he had been seriously worried when the American, Will Hector Bryce Junior, had shown himself keen to win Beatrice's hand. Unlike many of the aristocracy who were looking to America for an injection of wealth and vitality into their fortunes, Thomas Seward-Scott was aggressively chauvinist.

He patted Sandy on the back. 'My dear Constance was Scottish,' he declared. 'Don't mind the Scotch - you're good fighters. And you'll need to be strong to keep my Beatrice in check,' he laughed.

'Oh, Daddy, don't be such a bore. It won't be like that with Sandy and me - we're madly in love, aren't we, darling?' She smiled up at her fresh-faced fiancé.

'Beatrice has made me very happy, agreeing to be my wife,' Sandy answered gallantly, enchanted by her forthrightness.

'Good show.' Thomas Seward-Scott clapped him on the back again then turned to go and search for Laws. 'We'll bring up some of the best champagne tonight to celebrate.'

Davie sat by Louie's fireside. He ran bony fingers through his stubbly hair and sighed. 'Tell me what to do, Louie. I'm that mixed up inside, I can't think.'

Louie was finishing off icing some cupcakes she had prepared for the weekend. The trick was to prevent the icing running off, as she had rationed the sugar and watered down the icing to make it go further.

'You know what I think.' Louie straightened from her task. 'You can't think right 'cos your head's fuzzy with drinking all week. Why else has Da put you out the house until you sober up? You've only yourself to blame that Iris upped and left for home.'

'Is that where you think she's gone?' Davie asked in a small voice.

'Of course she has, where else would she go?'

'I half worry—' Davie stopped his conjectures. What if Iris had run off with some music-hall act or travelling players? He had always feared she might get sick of Whitton Grange one day and go off to be a singer somewhere. Louie was right. What had he done to try and make life bearable for her as a pitman's wife? Nothing. The little money he had had, he had wasted on beer or chucked away on pitch and toss on the street corner after dark. Iris had been on at him to buy Raymond a coat or take her to the pictures, but he had not done either and now they were both gone. He might never see either of them again and the thought made the pain in his head start to throb again.

Suddenly he felt Louie give him a sharp kick on his shin.

'Ayaa, Louie man!' he cried. 'What was that for?'

'Stop feeling sorry for yoursel', Davie Kirkup.' She stood back, hands on her hips. 'You love that lass and that bairn. You may deserve Iris, but you don't deserve that happy little lad. Well, if you want them, go after them and fetch them back,' Louie ordered. 'Let them know you care about them - more than you do a bottle of beer and a game of footy with Tadger Brown.'

All at once Davie's astonished face broke into a grin. He had never before been told off so roundly by Louie, and it made him feel quite ashamed.

'By, you can tell you're married to Sam Ritson,' he laughed. 'You'll make a better leader than he will, Louie. You frightened the hell out of me for a second.'

She flicked a tea towel at him and grinned back. 'Well, while I'm in the bossing mood, you can help me fill the tub with water for Sam's bath. He'll be home for his breakfast shortly. And don't tell him you slept off your hangover here last night; I don't want him worrying about your problems. I want this to be a happy Christmas for us all.'

While Louie fetched the zinc bath from its nail in the back yard and poured boiling water into it from the pot on the range, Davie went down to the stand pump and filled two pails of water. Dawn was breaking slowly at the bottom of the valley, a cold pearly light rising from the trees as if someone carrying a bright lamp was heading their way. He could smell the cheerful whiff of coal fires from the houses around, although in the half-dark, the blanket of smoke was indistinguishable from the grey sky.

Davie splashed icy water from the tap over his face and grunted aloud as it stung his eyes. He would never touch a drop of alcohol again, he promised himself. From now on, it was goodbye to Tadger and the lads.

When he got back, Sam had returned from the pit and was discarding his wet clothes by the hearth. His body was black with dust and knotted with fatigue. Louie was bustling about him with tea and jam sandwiches. Davie realised he was ravenously hungry.

'That looks good, Louie,' he said brightly, picking a sandwich off as she went by. 'Morning, Sam. That you done for the holiday?'

'Aye,' Sam groaned in relief. 'What you doing here?' He was suddenly suspicious.

'I'll explain later,' Louie said quickly. 'Davie's just leaving, aren't you, Davie?' She shot him a warning look. 'He's got an important errand this morning that won't wait.'

'Aye, well, I'll be off then,' Davie said, making for the door. 'Louie,' he hesitated outside and dropped his voice, 'you couldn't lend us the train fare back? I cannot make Iris and Raymond walk all the way like a couple of tinkers, can I?'

Louie sighed and slipped back into the house. Sam had his back to her as he sat in the tub and was singing vigorously, so he did not hear her reach behind the tea caddy on the mantelpiece for a couple of coins.

'This is the last time I bail you out,' she said severely as she handed over the money.

'Ta, Louie.' Davie gave her a sloppy kiss on her cheek and deposited the coins in his trouser pocket. Fixing his cap on the back of his head he strode off down Gladstone

Terrace whistling happily, turning once to wave, knowing his sister would still be watching out for him.

Louie went inside to make Sam's breakfast. He was drying himself in front of the fire and she glanced bashfully at his nakedness, proud to think he was her husband.

'You're too soft with that lad,' Sam commented gruffly.

'Maybes.' Louie shook her head at the thought of her wayward brother.

'How much did you give him?' Sam asked, reaching for a clean shirt. Louie gawped at him. 'I don't need eyes in the back of my head to know what you're up to.' He smiled at her guilty expression.

'I'm sorry,' Louie mumbled, 'I won't do it again, it's just he needed the train fare —'

'You don't have to explain,' Sam cut in, seeing her blush in confusion. 'Hey, Mrs Ritson, why haven't you hung up that mistletoe yet?' he teased, pulling her towards him. 'It's Christmas Eve and we haven't had a kiss under it.'

Louie giggled. 'You're in a good mood this morning. Have we time for kissing before the next committee meeting?'

'Today there's time for both, you cheeky lass,' he laughed, and began the kissing.

Durham was in a festive mood, with gaudily decorated Christmas trees in people's windows and the town bustling with last-minute shoppers beckoned in by cheerful traders. The Salvation Army band stood playing carols in the marketplace and Davie felt his waning courage return with the rousing music.

He found Mr Ramshaw in the bar.

'I've come for Iris,' Davie waded in aggressively.

'And a happy Christmas to you too,' Ramshaw replied, his brow trickling with perspiration in the fug of the room. 'Not that you deserve it from what I hear.'

Davie nearly lost his nerve and turned to run, but the ten-mile walk had made his leg stiffen up painfully and he wanted to sit down. 'You'll find her upstairs,' his father-in-law said more encouragingly, 'arguing with her brothers and sisters. I thought you were never coming.' He gave a lopsided smile. Davie grinned back and disappeared through the back door.

'So, Davie Kirkup,' Iris pouted at him disdainfully, 'sobered up at last, have you?' Davie was nearly swamped by the din from the younger children. Percy, one of Iris's brothers, dived through his legs and punched Tom, the younger one.

'Haway, Iris,' he said, ignoring her sarcasm, 'you don't belong here any more.' He stepped forward and picked Raymond up from the floor. 'Hello, bonny lad, I've missed you.' Raymond responded by sticking dirty fingers into his father's mouth.

Iris sat defiant, her green-brown eyes full of accusation. 'And what do we have to go back to?' she demanded. 'You're out of work, there's no chance of getting our own home now. You spend every spare minute away from the two of us, boozing and carrying on like the other bad lads you knock around with. You must be joking if you think we're coming back with you.' She reached out and pulled Raymond from Davie's arms.

They stood for a minute glaring at one another, each wanting the other to swallow their pride first. Iris had spent the last three days watching out for any sign of her husband coming to fetch her, but now he was here she could not help the hurtful words. She wanted to hear him say he was sorry and that he loved her, the way he used to tell her so easily.

'I can't change the person I am,' Davie answered crossly. He had expected her to rush into his arms like all the romantic heroines in the films. Then it would have been easy to apologise while comforting her and telling her he could not live without her or Raymond. 'So are you coming or not?'

Iris's brothers stopped their tussle, aware that a more serious battle was taking place over their heads. There was silence in the room for a moment, and nobody moved. Outside the band was playing 'O Come All Ye Faithful'. But Iris just stood rooted to the floor, clutching Raymond, who was beginning to fret.

'No, Davie,' she answered him helplessly, 'we're not.'

Chapter Eleven

Eleanor knew that, having been given their Christmas boxes, Eb and Hilda were to be allowed the afternoon of Christmas Eve off from Greenbrae. Isobel had shown her the beige stockings that she had chosen for Hilda, knowing the girl's love of fashion. For Eb, on Eleanor's recommendation, she had bought a box of watercolour paints. For the family, instructed by her father, Isobel had ordered a large basket of fruit and two tins of ham. Doctor Joice had been worried the younger members were not getting enough vitamins in their diet at this time of the year. Baby Raymond's face had been covered with sores and streaming with cold the last time he had visited the household at Hawthorn Street. Vitamins, Isobel had told her friend wryly, were all the rage among doctors these days.

Cutting through the frost-spangled trees of Whitton Woods, Eleanor arrived at the allotment to find it deserted. Disappointment enveloped her. She only had an hour away from the house, as there was still much to do before their party that evening. Beatrice's friend Sukie had unexpectedly invited herself for Christmas as her parents were holidaying abroad. More surprisingly, she was bringing her new boyfriend, who happened to be Beatrice's former escort, the American Will Bryce. Beatrice assured her sister that it made no difference to her, as they were both still her friends, and Sandy was not the jealous type.

Eleanor so wanted to wish Eb a happy Christmas before tomorrow. But the short afternoon was growing dark and she reluctantly admitted she should return to The Grange and all its frenetic preparations.

Instead of retracing her steps back through the woods and over the Common, Eleanor took the path that skirted the village and crossed the main road that led eventually to Durham. It would take her twenty minutes longer to walk home by road, but there was just a possibility she would bump into Eb along the way.

For once she found the tightly packed terraces of Whitton Grange inviting in the gathering twilight. Lights shone out of kitchen windows and red and silver baubles glinted in their cheery glow. Funnels of smoke drifted up from every chimney into an indigo sky, where the evening star hung like a fairy light to guide her home. As Eleanor circled the village, the sound of children playing under the gas lamps was as clear as the evening chorus of birds. There was a frisson of expectation in their calls that was only heard at this time of year. She marvelled at how children could enjoy themselves whatever their circumstances.

Leaving Whitton Grange behind with a strange feeling of being left out of a party, Eleanor quickened her pace for home. But before she reached the lane that wound up the hillside to The Grange, a figure loomed menacingly out of the dark towards her.

His cap was askew and he reeked of alcohol as he lurched at her, cursing. Eleanor's heart thudded in fright.

'Out of my way,' he slurred, and knocked into her shoulder. His cap fell to the ground and in the dim light Eleanor recognised the thin, wolfish face.

'Davie!' she cried, catching his arm as he staggered and lost his footing.

'Leave me be,' he answered crossly, trying to shake her off.

'It's your friend, Davie,' Eleanor persisted gently, no longer afraid of him, 'Mrs Seward-Scott.' The name seemed to halt his aggression and he tried to focus on her, his expression puzzled.

'Mrs S'ward-Scott?' he repeated with difficulty.

'Yes,' Eleanor encouraged, 'come and sit over here for a minute.' She guided him to the side of the road and sat him on a stone that had come loose from the field wall. 'What's happened, Davie?' she probed. 'Should you not be home with your family?'

Davie belched unhappily. 'She won't come home,' he told her. 'She's got my bairn and she won't come home.'

'Iris?' Eleanor guessed. Davie nodded. 'She's gone back to Durham then?' Davie nodded again.

'She thinks I'm a bad husband,' he mumbled, 'but what sort of wife gans off with your only bairn without a word?'

'And do you want her back?' Eleanor asked quietly. Davie's head sagged and he hid his face in his hands.

'I love 'em both,' he whispered. 'Iris and Raymond mean everything to me.' Then, his emotions loosened by drink, the young miner began to cry. Eleanor let him sob for a minute and then placed a hand on his shoulder.

'I think we should get you home now,' she said briskly. 'You don't want to spoil Christmas for the rest of your family, do you? No doubt they'll be wondering where you are. How long have you been wandering about here?' She helped him to his feet and he wiped his eyes on the sleeve of his jacket, suddenly embarrassed.

'Can't remember, miss,' he grunted.

'Cheer up,' Eleanor cajoled. 'If I was Iris, I'd be hoping to see you again. And when you do, you can tell her what you've just told me.' She smiled at him and handed him back his cap.

'I'll not go begging,' Davie replied stubbornly, his head beginning to clear. 'It's her who'll have to come to me.'

Eleanor huffed in disbelief. These pitmen could be so intractable at times, she thought impatiently. It was little wonder Iris had got fed up with him.

She accompanied Davie back along the Durham Road to the first few houses which ran parallel to the railway line and wound down to the village green. As the gas lighting revealed the steep banks of terraced housing beyond, Eleanor stopped, reluctant to be seen walking with this half-inebriated youth; she felt vulnerable, realising she had never walked through this part of the village before, but had only visited it by car. Before she had time to extract herself, two figures hurried out of a side street and spotted them.

'There he is!' a girl's voice cried, and the slighter of the two hurried towards them. 'Where the devil have you been, Davie? We've been searching all over. And where's Iris?' She peered suspiciously from under her over-large hat at the woman beside him. With a gasp she stuttered, 'Mrs R-Reginald, eeh, beggin' your pardon!'

Eleanor recognised the young woman at once. 'Louisa, I'm glad it's you. I found Davie on the road. I think he's a little the worse for drink,' she explained as politely as possible. Louie's tall companion caught up with her and Eleanor's hopes were confirmed.

'Mrs Seward-Scott.' Eb touched his cap diffidently.

'Eb.' Eleanor smiled at him distantly, keeping up the charade of slight acquaintance. But Louie was too busy fussing over Davie to detect any warmth in the looks they exchanged.

'You'll come home with me first and get washed and sober up before I let you home,' she scolded. 'What would Da say if he caught you like this? Give you a hiding into next week, that's what.' She turned to the lady in her fur-trimmed coat and hat. 'I'm that grateful, Mrs Reginald, you've saved our Davie again. Thank you, ma'am.'

'There's no need to thank me,' Eleanor assured her. 'I hope you all have a very merry Christmas, Louisa. Please remember me to your husband and family.'

'Yes, ma'am,' Louie beamed in reply. She pushed a morose Davie - who was trying to overcome a bout of hiccups - before her.

'I'll see Mrs Seward-Scott along the road,' Eb spoke up, 'it's almost dark now.'

Louie agreed that was a sensible suggestion and Eleanor watched her go with a remorseful Davie in tow.

Together, Eleanor and Eb retreated into the dark, not speaking a word until they had left Whitton Grange behind. The sky was scattered with bright stars above them and the chill air nipped at their faces as they walked. Only after they had turned up the hill to The Grange and were surrounded by dark, bare trees, did Eleanor slip her cold hand into his warm one.

'I hoped I'd find you at the allotment this afternoon,' she told him.

'I would have been there,' Eb sighed, 'but Hildy came to fetch me. Louie was in a right state about Davie not coming home. She feared the worst and as usual Louie's instincts were right. Davie can't help himself.'

'He doesn't seem to be much help to Iris and Raymond either.' Eleanor could not resist the criticism.

Eb did not jump immediately to his brother's defence as Louie would have done. 'She took him on knowing the kind of lad he was,' he replied.

'She didn't have much choice, did she?' Eleanor countered.

'They were too young,' Eb sighed, all at once feeling older than his twenty-eight years. 'Iris has ambitions beyond this pit village. I can only see unhappiness for them both.'

'But Davie says he loves her.' Eleanor did not want their conversation to become depressing.

'That's as may be.' Eb stopped and considered her pale face shrouded in soft fur. 'But people can love each other and still not be able to overcome the differences between them.'

'Don't say that,' Eleanor whispered fiercely, pulling him close to her. Impulsively, she kissed him to try and dissolve his doubts, and they clung hungrily to each other in the cold dark. She spoke low. 'You know I love you, Eb.'

'Aye,' Eb answered, feeling his stomach knot. He wanted to say the same to her, but he could not admit it. There could be no long-term future for them together, so why pretend there was? Theirs was an impossible love that should never have been allowed to grow. They could hardly ever meet, and when they did they had to stifle their feelings in front of others in case anyone guessed.

'I'll walk you to the gates.' He disengaged himself and broke the intimacy between them. As they went on, the sound of singing grew louder through the trees.

'Carol singers,' Eleanor said excitedly. 'Reverend Hodgson will have brought the Sunday School to sing at the house, they come every Christmas Eve.'

From the end of the drive they could see a throng of children and a few adult singers huddled under the stone portico of the house's main entrance. A blaze of electric light flooded out of the open doorway before them, where her father and the housekeeper stood. Eleanor linked her arm through Eb's to keep him there and they stood and listened from a distance, entranced by the young voices ringing out across the lawns.

When they had finished, the singers were handed glasses of lemonade and a mince pie each by Mrs Robertson. Eleanor smiled as she saw them receive money from her father; it was a ritual her mother had so enjoyed. The choir left chattering, a glow of miner's lamps swinging about them as they approached the silent watchers by the wrought-iron gates.

Eleanor pulled Eb behind a rhododendron bush and minutes later the children filed past noisily, the vicar herding them out of the grounds. Two girls straggled behind.

'Watch for us, May,' one of them said and turned directly towards the pair in hiding. Eb saw with astonishment that it was his cousin Sadie. She was not a member of St Cuthbert's Sunday School, but her friend May Little was and she had obviously come on the jaunt for an extra mince pie or two.

'Don't sit on the bogeyman,' May giggled as her friend pushed into the bushes and squatted down. Eleanor and Eb froze in disbelief as the young girl relieved herself just feet away from where they stood.

'Hurry up, Sadie.' May's voice was edged with fear. 'The others are halfway down the hill.' Sadie needed no encouragement and sprang quickly from the bushes, running after her friend.

But moments later, the dark-haired girl realised she had dropped her new hand-embroidered handkerchief, a present that Louie had allowed her to open early because she could not wait for Christmas Day.

'Wait for us while I go back,' Sadie pleaded, her fear of her cousin's scolding overcoming her nervousness of the dark. 'Louie'll kill us if I lose my hanky before Christmas.'

She reached the gates just as Eb and Eleanor, laughing with relief, stepped on to the drive. Sadie screamed to see the dark figures emerge from the trees. Eb reached her quickly.

'It's me, Eb,' he reassured her, and pulled her to him in a protective hug.

'Eb,' Sadie began to cry, 'you frightened me.'

'I'm sorry, pet.' He kissed her head under the woollen hat. Sadie looked nervously at Eleanor, recognising the lady who had occasionally visited their home. 'I was walking Mrs Seward-Scott home. She found Davie out on the road - it's a long story. Best if we keep it as our secret, eh?' Eb suggested in his easy voice. Sadie nodded but said nothing. He let her go. 'Now get on quickly and catch up with the others.' Without a glance back, Sadie raced for the safety of the retreating band of carol singers, quite forgetting that she had not retrieved her handkerchief.

'I heard you scream,' May said, frightened, as her panting friend reached her. 'What did you see?'

'The bogeyman,' Sadie answered, deciding to make the most of her adventure, 'and the bogeywoman!'

Eleanor watched the two girls scurrying off into the distance. 'Will she say anything?'

Eb shrugged. 'What's there to say?' He turned to her. 'I've got something for you.' He fumbled in his inner jacket pocket and pulled out a rolled-up piece of paper. 'You can't really see it in the dark.'

By the light of the frosty moon, Eleanor could just make out the outline of a woman bending over a book against a background of foliage. Eb lit a match as she held it, so she could see it better. In the flare of yellow light she saw herself in vivid colours against a pale backdrop of leaves and flowers.

'It's too flattering!' she protested, overjoyed that he should think to paint her.

'Miss Joice gave me the paints and I wanted to use them straight away. That's how I see you,' Eb answered bashfully, 'full of life.'

'Thank you.' She kissed him and carefully rolled up the painting. 'And this is for you.' She handed him the long, thin package from her coat that held four differently sized paintbrushes. She laughed at his genuine pleasure.

'That's grand,' Eb grinned, 'and I suppose that means I have to keep painting for my patron?'

'Of course.' Eleanor hugged him. 'Happy Christmas, Eb.'

This time it was Eb who pulled her close to him and kissed her warmly on the lips. Only with reluctance did she let him go at the gates. She turned once to wave, but he had been swallowed up by the dark. Eleanor hugged herself, still revelling in the warmness of their embrace.

Somehow, she knew, they would keep their love alive. But now she would have to put her energies into making Beatrice's engagement party a success.

Just as she arrived at the house, a car swung on to the gravel behind her, hooting noisily. Eleanor glimpsed Sukie's face at the passenger window. The car squealed to a halt and the doors swung open. Will Bryce jumped from the running board and came round to greet her.

'Will!' Eleanor greeted him warmly. She was fond of this affable, carefree friend of Beatrice's.

'You're not angry at me for inviting myself with Sukie?' he asked, kissing her flushed cheek.

'Not at all,' Eleanor assured him. 'The more the merrier.'

They both turned to the woman descending from the car in swathes of heavy fur.

'Eleanor, darling,' Sukie lisped, 'it's wonderful to see you - you're looking marvellous.' She brushed Eleanor's cheek with her own. 'How's Bea? Is it true she's announcing her engagement to Sandy tonight?'

Eleanor glanced at Will, but he continued to smile. 'You'll have to ask Beatrice, won't you?' she answered noncommittally.

'It's sure good to see you again.' Will took Eleanor's arm and led the two women inside.

'And you,' Eleanor smiled and thought she was going to enjoy this Christmas more than she had expected.

After the morning service in the Methodist Chapel, the Kirkups went, as tradition dictated, to the Dobsons in Railway Terrace for a glass of non-alcoholic ginger wine and a mince pie. Louie had managed to persuade Sam to join them and he tagged along reluctantly in his starched white shirt and dark brown suit, looking ill at ease with a dainty crystal glass in his hand.

The white-haired Clara Dobson pressed another mince pie on him. 'Your Louie's a grand help to me. Practically delivered Margaret Slattery's baby all by herself. She'll make a wonderful mother one of these days.' She smiled, her mouth spreading into soft crinkled cheeks and chin. 'I've raised four daughters of my own, but not one of them's as maternal as Louie.' She passed on with her plate laden with pies.

Sam manoeuvred himself across the parlour, squeezing past the heavy dark furniture and his numerous relations-in-law. He found John.

'Fancy a quick pint at the club?'

'Aye,' John answered swiftly and they disengaged themselves from the party.

'Coming, Davie?' Sam asked as they passed him. He shot them a bloodshot scowl and shook his head.

'Leave him,' John muttered unconcerned. 'He's bad company and he's off the drink.'

Louie pretended not to notice their going. Sam had already compromised by agreeing to be with her family for Christmas dinner and visit his own parents for tea. She contented herself with the memory that they had woken alone in their own home with no Sadie or Minnie or Bomber to interrupt their morning together. She had made breakfast for Sam, though she had had no appetite for the smoking bacon and fried bread. However, her lethargy had disappeared when they had opened their presents to each other. Sam had given her a beautiful necklace of fake pearls, and joked that she would no longer have to borrow jewellery from Iris, before realising what he had said. Louie had dismissed the subject - 'Let's not think about that Iris' - and given Sam his present. He unwrapped a pipe.

'But, Louie, I don't smoke,' Sam had said baffled.

'No, but I thought it would suit you.' Louie defended her choice. 'Since you're becoming an important leader, I thought it would make you look distinguished like.'

Sam had burst out laughing and Louie had been hurt. 'It's just what I wanted,' he teased and gave her a tickle.

'You don't like it,' she pouted trying not to laugh.

'I do,' he insisted, 'I just don't like smoking.' He grabbed her round the waist and Louie had laughed as they began kissing.

So she forgave him for slipping away for a drink with John, and Eb soon diverted attention by opening up the Dobsons' piano and starting to play. Susan and Eva Dobson, the two youngest sisters, who had courted friends of Eb's who did not return from the war, joined him in a singsong. Eva, the most emotional of the four, always sang with tears streaming down her face, no matter how happy the song. This Christmas Day was no exception.

Louie turned to see Davie quietly letting himself out of the house. She followed him, telling Mrs Dobson that she had to go and check on the dinner. She caught up with her brother as he turned into Hawthorn Street.

'Reminds you of her, I suppose - the singing?' Louie asked not unkindly. Davie tramped on as if he had not heard. 'Are you going to be a twisty-face all holiday?' she demanded more brusquely. 'Well, you've brought this on yourself for not facing up to your responsibilities.'

'I never asked your opinion,' Davie sulked. 'Just leave us alone.'

Louie sighed. 'Listen, Davie,' she linked her arm in his to slow him down, 'would you like me to go and speak to Iris?' Davie stopped and looked at his sister.

'You'd really do that for me, wouldn't you, Louie?' he said.

'For you, aye, I would,' she replied.

He hugged her suddenly. 'When will you go?'

'Tomorrow if you like.' She smiled resignedly. 'I can do without your Iris complaining around the place for a bit longer, but I miss that bairn Raymond too much.'

'Aye,' Davie agreed. 'You fetch them back and everything'll be canny again, won't it, Louie?'

'That depends,' Louie answered, not half so confident as her brother that Iris would settle down once and for all.

For the rest of the day she pushed from her mind the thought of the ordeal of winning Iris round, and busied herself with helping Hildy and her mother with the Christmas dinner. They carried the kitchen table into the parlour and covered it with a linen cloth, so all nine of them could sit round together. Fanny Kirkup carved the turkey, while Hildy, Louie and Sadie served up roast potatoes, mashed potatoes, roast parsnips, carrots and sprouts, along with bread sauce, sausagemeat and herb and onion stuffing. Not for the first time that week, Louie had to fight back the feeling of nausea that rose with the smell of the cooking. She disappeared outside for fresh air, blaming herself for being ill at such a special time of year. Her mother came to find her and put her hand to her forehead.

'I'm all right, Mam.' Louie pushed her away and returned inside, her mother following her with a concerned look on her face. They let Sadie find the silver three-penny bit and then ate the plum pudding with bowlfuls of custard. Louie hardly touched hers and avoided her mother's questioning look.

The meal complete, the men snoozed in front of the fire, under the sparkling tinsel festooned across the room, while the women cleared and washed up and prepared the tea. Sadie and Eb played Snakes and Ladders on the floor, while Hilda sat at the table and read last year's Girl's Own Annual that she had given to her young cousin for Christmas.

'That's typical of our Hildy.' Louie rolled her eyes at her mother. 'She buys everyone books that only she will read.'

Shortly afterwards Louie and Sam took their leave and went to visit the Ritsons. They hardly did justice to the massive tea that Mrs Ritson and her daughters had prepared, but Sam waded in to the cake and sandwiches as best he could. Later they played party games with Sam's young nephews who were visiting with his sister Lizzy from Yorkshire, while Bel's baby, Betty, toddled among the discarded presents and the wrapping paper.

They walked home happily in the crisp dark, taking a detour through the dene and across the park to ease their unusually full stomachs. Sam was talking about some meeting he had to attend the next day, when Louie's throat watered and she began to retch violently into the grass.

'Louie, are you all right?' Sam put a concerned hand on her back. 'It's all that rich food, you're not used to it these days.'

Louie straightened, the wave of nausea subsiding. She dabbed her mouth with her handkerchief and shook her head.

'I don't think so, Sam.' She smiled at him though her face was ghostly.

'Then what's wrong?' Sam felt a stab of worry for his young wife. Louie had always been a strong and healthy lass; Sam could not bear the thought of illness striking at their happiness.

'Nothing's wrong,' Louie assured him. 'I can't be certain, Sam, but my instincts tell me there's a reason I'm being sick.'

'What are you talking about, Louie? What instincts?' Sam was cautious.

'I think I'm going to have a baby.' Louie took his hand shyly.

'A baby?' Sam repeated, nonplussed.

'Well, it shouldn't be a complete surprise, Sam Ritson,' Louie laughed, thinking of the vigorous loving nights in their old bed.

'No,' Sam laughed tentatively. 'By heck, a bairn of our own, eh?' He grabbed her in a joyful hug. 'I love you, Louie Ritson, so I do.'

At The Grange they finished Christmas evening with charades. Isobel and her father had been invited for dinner, which had been a relatively light meal of soup and poached salmon, duck and desserts, following the gargantuan feast at midday. It was a relaxed, intimate evening after the impressive engagement party of the night before, when half the county had braved the icy roads to drink Beatrice and Sandy's health in champagne and eat the vast buffet prepared by the cook, Mrs Dennison, and her staff.

'Show us how to Charleston, Bea.' Will was egging her on as the charades came to an end.

'Oh yes, come on, Bea,' Sukie squealed with delight.

'Well, I don't know.' Beatrice put on a prim face and slid Sandy a look. He was standing on guard, close to his new fiancée, as if to protect her from the bad influence of her bright young friends.

'I hear it's pretty shocking,' Reginald huffed in disapproval. 'Negro influence and all that.'

'Don't be stuffy, Reggie,' Eleanor chided. 'I'd like to see it.'

Reginald flushed and gave his wife a resentful look. Her appearance tonight was stunning, dressed as she was in a shimmering silver dress, tasselled from the waist downwards and beaded with pearls across the front. Her short hair was completely hidden in a black satin cap, intricately embroidered in silver thread and pearl drops. In contrast to Beatrice and Sukie, she wore no make-up, yet her dark-brown eyes dominated her pale face. They watched him with disinterest from behind a spiral of smoke from her ivory cigarette holder. He felt goaded by her quiet contempt for him, in contrast with her lively conversation with the other guests. It infuriated him that she could still attract his interest, even though he knew he was no longer welcome in her bedroom.

'Oh, very well.' Beatrice needed no other encouragement than to shock her brother-in-law.

Reginald threw back his brandy in one swig. Sukie and Will were already rolling back the animal-skin rugs and Beatrice was instructing Sandy to wind up the gramophone. Eleanor had made him look foolish in his opposition to this vulgar dance.

'Well, I'll not stay to watch,' Reginald muttered. 'I shall retire to bed. Good night.' He nodded briefly at the Joices. Eleanor shot him a furious look for his deliberate breach of hospitality.

'We must be going anyhow.' Isobel touched her friend's arm, not wanting to make an issue of Reginald's rudeness. 'It's been a wonderful evening, as always.' Eleanor and her father accompanied their friends to the door.

'If you're interested in coming up in my aeroplane, you'll let me know,' Thomas Seward-Scott urged the doctor.

'If I ever find the time, I'd be delighted,' Dr Joice laughed.

'You'll just have to,' Eleanor pleaded. 'It's all Daddy will talk about these days. The thought of flying makes me feel quite ill, but it's become his passion, hasn't it, Daddy?'

'It's the transport of the future,' her father declared enthusiastically, 'we'll all be flying about in aeroplanes soon.'

'Not me. I'll stick to my bicycle, thank you very much.' Isobel smiled. 'Good night, and thank you for a lovely evening.'

The Seward-Scotts waved their guests off into the frosty night. Behind them in the house the up-tempo music of the Charleston mingled with shrieks of delight from the remaining revellers.

'I think I'll go for a short stroll,' Eleanor announced, beckoned by the starry night and the cool air outside.

'You won't go too far, will you, my dear?' her father insisted.

'Just on to the terrace,' Eleanor assured him, and they kissed good night. Her father turned back to face her as she wrapped herself in a large red cashmere shawl.

'I know things aren't too good between you and Reginald,' Thomas Seward-Scott said forthrightly, 'and I'm sorry that should be so. I'll say no more on it.' He raised a hand to block Eleanor's protest. 'I just ask that you don't do anything rash.' Eleanor felt her face flush red.

'What do you mean?' Her mind raced to think of the kisses she had exchanged with Eb within sight of The Grange.

'Reginald will need your support in the coming months,' her father answered mysteriously. 'It's not going to be an easy year for us coalowners, Eleanor, so we'll all have to put up a united front. Close ranks. Do you understand what I'm saying?' For a moment Eleanor saw the shrewdness in her father's eyes, the hard-headed businessman beneath the amiable, eccentric country-gentleman exterior he liked to cultivate.

'I'm not sure I do understand,' she replied warily. Her father came towards her and dropped his voice.

'There's conflict ahead, my dear, and you must make up your mind whose side you are on. For my sake and The Grange's, if not for your husband's, I hope you will see your duty lies in supporting us.'

Eleanor was shocked by his bluntness. Then almost as if nothing had been said, her father smiled and kissed her forehead. 'Enjoy your walk. It's been a most agreeable day and you've been the perfect hostess as usual. Good night, dear Eleanor.' He turned and headed purposefully up the central staircase, leaving his elder daughter quite unnerved.

She wandered round to the terrace and lit a cigarette, calming her thoughts as she looked in the direction of Whitton Grange. It was all so peaceful, belying her uneasy feeling that her father and Reginald were equipping themselves for some great battle ahead. And where did her loyalties lie? she wondered. Eleanor tried to picture what Eb was doing at that moment. She could not see the village, for the bank of thick woodland and the curve of the hillside hid it from view. It was as if The Grange rested in an idyllic rural Never-Never Land, divorced from the grim realities of the pit villages which dotted the valley below. Under the arch of inky black sky speckled with stars, it was impossible to think it would ever change.

'Sure is cold out here.' Will's voice startled her from behind. 'Did you think the dancing was that bad?'

Eleanor laughed in response. 'No, Beatrice and Sukie are wonderful dancers. I just needed some fresh air,' she replied.

'It doesn't come much fresher than this.' Will gave a theatrical shiver. 'Don't suppose you'd like to warm me up?' He put a casual arm around her waist. Eleanor gently removed his hold.

'Why did you really come here for Christmas, Will?' she asked him quizzically. 'Was it to try and stop Beatrice becoming engaged? I can tell there's nothing between you and Sukie. It was just an arrangement, wasn't it?'

Will laughed disarmingly. 'You have ten times the intelligence of the rest of your family.'

'Nonsense,' Eleanor rebuked him, 'and I'm not easily flattered.' She scrutinised his face. 'So why are you here?'

'I came to seduce you,' he answered without a qualm.

'You're quite impossible!' Eleanor laughed, embarrassed by his directness. 'You'll say anything to shock.'

'It's God's honest truth,' Will replied and, cupping the back of her head in his hands he kissed her roundly on the mouth. Eleanor pushed him away.

'Don't.' She was firm.

Will sighed. 'Then it's true.'

'What is?'

'Beatrice said you already have a lover. I'm just sorry I'm too late,' Will answered, not the least abashed by her rejection.

'Beatrice shouldn't say such things,' Eleanor said crossly. 'It's just not true.'

'Then you'll still consider me?' Will's voice was hopeful.

'No.' Eleanor grew impatient. 'I'm not looking for an affair.'

Will brushed her cheek gently with a finger. 'I think you've already found one,' he said reflectively, 'and I envy him, whoever he is.'

Eleanor turned abruptly and left the terrace. It worried her that she was failing to hide her feelings for Eb. Perhaps even her father suspected that something was going on. She would have to be more careful.

From the edge of the woods, staring up towards the terrace lit by the gaudy electric chandeliers, Eb watched the American stub out a cigarette and follow Eleanor inside. It had been a stupid, romantic notion to climb the hill and see if he could glimpse Eleanor at home, dining in the splendour of The Grange. He had wanted to capture a memory of her to paint and surprise her with later.

Eb did not recognise the man who had sat so close to her on the edge of the stone balustrade, and he did not want to know. He was overwhelmed by a feeling of being totally cut off from the fairy-tale scene before him; it was a world he did not know and could never enter, like the officers' mess in his army days.

A lump formed in his throat as he scrambled back over the high wall and jumped on to the rough ground that bordered the estate. He knew then that his love for Eleanor was futile.

Chapter Twelve

'Your place is with Davie,' Louie told Iris firmly, above the noise of the children in the Ramshaws' crowded upstairs sitting room. Raymond was trying to stand up and was steadying himself against Louie's knees. His aunt put out her hands to help him take a couple of wobbly steps. Raymond beamed with the achievement and sank on to his bottom.

'Why hasn't he come himself?' Iris asked moodily. 'Too drunk from Christmas to find his way out of Whitton Grange?'

'He hasn't touched a drop all holiday,' came Louie's retort. 'He asked me to come,' she added less hotly, 'and he wanted me to come straightaway after Christmas, but it's been that busy at home I haven't been able to come into Durham until now.' It was New Year's Eve and Louie thought it as good a time as any for new resolutions and reconciliation. 'Minnie had her baby on Boxing Day - a boy, they've called him Jack.' Louie omitted to tell her sister-in-law that she herself had been so sick the past week that she had hardly moved from the house.

Iris stood up restlessly and went to peer out of the window at the busy market square below.

'I'm frightened, Louie,' she whispered. 'I'm frightened to go back.'

'What in the wide world for?' the younger woman asked in astonishment. 'Davie's not the type to give you a beating for taking off with Raymond.'

'And I wouldn't let him lay a finger on me like that!' Iris spun round, giving a flash of her normal spirit.

'Then what do you mean?' Louie was baffled.

'I'm scared of being poor,' Iris admitted, her green eyes looking to Louie for understanding. 'Oh, I know my family aren't rich or anything, but we've always had the pub - a steady business - we've never gone without. But Davie's out of work now and we've got no savings, nothing to fall back on. We haven't even got our own home - the room we sleep in belongs to everyone else during the day. I'm not used to living like that, Louie. I have this bad dream that Davie won't get taken back on at the pit, that Raymond will never have any new clothes again, that I'll never be able to afford to go to the pictures.'

Louie laughed derisively at this last fear. Iris pursed her lips together in annoyance. 'Don't laugh at me. I'm serious.'

'Aye.' Louie felt a twinge of pity for her sister-in-law; at least she was being honest. 'But you mustn't worry about Davie not working - they'll be taking lads on in the New Year - Sam and the others will see to that. And you'll never starve in our village,' Louie insisted. 'We all help each other in bad times; pit folk are the most neighbourly folk you'll ever come across. You're one of the family now, Iris, and we all want you back.'

Iris smiled gratefully at her tall, fair-haired sister-in-law, though she was sure Louie was exaggerating the degree to which she was missed. She watched her rumbustious brothers Tom and Percy fighting over some lead soldiers that one of them had got for Christmas and both wanted to play with that minute. Her sisters Nora and Jean were using the furniture as imaginary ships at sea, so there was no room for anyone else to sit down. The noise was deafening. To stay here was impossible. Louie was right; she had thrown in her lot with Davie and the Kirkups, and she had no choice but to return to their drab pit village. Her fanciful ideas of being a famous singer were mere childish dreams; her fears of sinking into poverty childish too.

'I'll come home then,' Iris sighed without enthusiasm.

'Grand,' Louie answered brightly, swinging Raymond into her arms. 'Come on, little lad, Auntie Louie will get you dressed.' She kissed his red cheeks and wiped his runny nose. 'Won't your daddy be pleased to see you, eh?'

Eleanor served tea in the drawing room. The Fishers had joined their house party for New Year at Reginald's insistence. The morning had been spent hunting across Highfell Common, the red of their hunting uniforms a ribbon of garish colour fluttering over the dead browns of the moor. Rose Fisher had stayed at the house with Sukie and Will and Harriet Swainson, who had no appetite for the chase but preferred to while away the short day over a large jigsaw that was spread out on a carved table in the bay window.

Eleanor had been distant with Will since his approach to her in the garden, but he seemed quite happy to allow Mrs Fisher to flirt with him. Even now, with the others present, Rose Fisher's dyed blonde waves of hair were bent towards Will over the table, her hands, heavily ringed and bangled, brushing against his as she attempted to force the wrong piece of jigsaw into the puzzle.

'Do you take milk in your tea, Mrs Fisher?' Eleanor interrupted. In spite of the woman's insistence that she should call her Rose, Eleanor felt a perverse pleasure in addressing her formally.

'Please, darling,' she turned her heavily made-up face towards her hostess, 'and two lumps of sugar.'

Her eldest daughter, Libby, strode across the room still in riding breeches and exuding an air of rude good health. 'Let me help you, Eleanor,' she insisted, grabbing the cup Eleanor was pouring and spilling tea into the saucer. 'You missed a jolly good day's riding,' she continued, unabashed by her clumsiness. 'Superb stable Reggie's got.'

Eleanor considered the young woman for a moment as she handed her a plate of drop scones to distribute. She was fresh-faced, with sandy eyebrows and short, straight red hair which she kept flicking away from her brown eyes. Except they were not quite brown, but flecked with a pale green that made one want to keep looking at them.

'My father's always been proud of his horses,' Eleanor replied, reminding the girl that it was he and not Reginald who still owned The Grange. Libby held her look coolly for a second and then smiled.

'Daddy is much more comfortable in a car seat than the saddle,' Libby joked, and gave a nervously loud laugh.

'Hurry up with those scones, Libby.' Reginald beckoned her across the room. She turned and gave him a broad smile that Eleanor did not miss. Neither did she fail to intercept the admiring look that her husband bestowed on the buxom Libby.

'You don't ride then?' Sandy Mackintosh asked quietly, appearing at her elbow and holding a cup for her to refill.

Eleanor smiled at him. 'When I was younger, my brother Rupert and I used to ride all over the county. I've lost the enthusiasm for it now - I'd really rather walk.'

'Yes, I've seen you out on the hill in all weathers,' Sandy replied, amusement in his blue eyes. 'It must be your Scottish ancestry, this desire to be out in the rain.' Eleanor laughed. She was growing fond of Beatrice's shy, diffident fiancé with his flashes of humour.

'Well, you should feel at home in this weather, Sandy,' she responded, nodding her head towards the window as a fresh squall hit the panes. Eleanor loved this time of the day, just before the curtains were drawn and the world became swallowed up by night. It was so cosy in their brightly lit drawing room, with a log fire blazing in the wide marble recess and the conversation muted among the chink of china tea cups. Only one thought spoilt her enjoyment, and that was her failure to see Eb at the allotment that afternoon. She had found it sadly empty, a solitary robin waiting on the fence to have his picture painted.

'Come on, Bernard!' Reginald's hearty cry jarred on her nerves. 'Let's leave the ladies to prepare for dinner and have a game of billiards.' He steered the stout and jovial Mr Fisher towards the door, winking at Libby as he went. Eleanor turned her back and went to talk to Beatrice.

'It's going to be a long evening,' her sister muttered, rolling her eyes.

'Will seems to be enjoying himself,' Eleanor commented.

'Yes, well, Will is an opportunist, in case you hadn't noticed,' Beatrice said with an edge of disapproval in her voice. It amused Eleanor to see her young sister becoming more respectable by the day, as she settled into her role as prospective wife of an army captain.

'I'm going to lie down for an hour,' Eleanor announced.

'Well, don't suddenly develop a headache,' Beatrice warned her. 'I'm not coping with the Fishers on my own.'

Louie had half hoped Davie would have been at Whitton Station to meet them, but they had to trudge the half-mile up the hill to Hawthorn Street alone, with the baby and Iris's possessions piled high in the pram the Ramshaws had bought. Neither of the girls spoke, and Raymond had fallen asleep.

Sadie was the first to spot the weary troupe. She waved and then dashed into the house.

'Louie's coming,' she shouted excitedly, 'and she's bringing Iris and Raymond!'

Fanny Kirkup let out a sigh of relief. 'Go and tell Davie,' she ordered. 'He's moping upstairs.' Sadie clattered up the steps to the bedroom and found her cousin asleep on the bed.

'She's here, Davie.' Sadie shook him awake. 'Iris is here.'

Louie flopped thankfully into a chair by the fire, too tired to even remove her coat. Iris looked bashfully at her mother-in-law, and at Eb who was whittling a piece of wood in the corner of the kitchen. He smiled and said hello. Fanny immediately took Raymond from his pram and searched for him among the folds of scarf and blankets and knitted hat. She did not know what to say to her daughter-in-law; she still felt guilty at having lost her temper and spoken such hurtful words to the young girl. In part she felt responsible for the rift that had come about between the Durham lass and the family.

'There's tea in the pot.' She nodded towards the table. 'Pour a cup for yourself and Louie.'

'I'll just have a glass of water,' Louie replied; she had mysteriously lost her taste for tea. 'Then I must get off home. Sam will be wondering where I've got to.'

Just then, a sleepy-eyed Davie appeared at the door, with Sadie leading the way like an ambassador. His hair stuck out at angles and his soft chin was shadowed in tawny bristle.

'Iris.' He said her name tentatively and stood feeling foolish.

'Davie.' She slid him a semi-defiant look.

With only a moment's hesitation he stepped forward and plucked Raymond from Fanny's arms. 'Hello, little man,' he said, then kissed him and tossed him in the air. Raymond's eyes opened wide in fright at the sudden movement and he started to cry. Davie laughed and threw him higher, until Raymond howled in protest.

'Take Iris's things into the parlour.' Fanny took command of the situation quickly, disengaging her grandson from Davie's arms. 'I'll give the bairn something to eat. You two go and make things up.'

Iris closed the parlour door behind them, feeling awkward in her husband's presence. For once she was at a loss as to what to say. She took her bag from Davie and began to unpack her clothes. He watched her in silence.

'I've—'

'You've—' They both began at the same time, and then stopped.

'You say first,' Davie insisted.

'It's nothing.' Iris shrugged. 'I was just going to say, you've got a very loyal sister in Louie. It must have taken a bit of nerve to come and fetch me back.'

'Aye,' Davie admitted candidly, 'more nerve than I've got.' Iris continued to fold away her possessions into the boxes under the bed. 'She's been that desperate to see Raymond again, I think she would have gone to Newcastle for him.'

'She might not be so interested in him soon,' Iris answered.

'What do you mean?' Davie asked, puzzled.

'Well, it's obvious to me she's pregnant.'

'Our Louie?' Davie gasped in amazement.

'And why not?' Iris laughed for the first time. 'She's been married long enough.'

'She hasn't said anything,' Davie said with an edge of reproach in his voice.

'I'll bet you a shilling she is,' Iris challenged.

'Don't have a shilling,' Davie answered, then with a grin reached over and grabbed his wife around the waist. 'I'll bet you a kiss an' cuddle though.' Iris giggled and twisted to face him, happier than she had expected to feel his arms about her again.

'A kiss and a cuddle then,' she agreed.

'I've missed you, Iris,' Davie whispered as their lips met.

'Good,' Iris replied and said no more.

In the kitchen Sadie stood on one leg, trying to listen at the parlour door.

'Come away from there,' Fanny ordered.

'I want to listen to Iris's wireless. Why are they taking so long?' she asked impatiently.

'Never you mind,' her aunt replied shortly. 'Here, you can take these biscuits round to Louie's, I've done extra.' Sadie's dark eyes lit up with interest at the sight of food. 'And don't you go eating them all before you get there.'

'Can I stay over at Louie's tonight, Aunt Fanny?' Sadie was suddenly taken by the idea.

'You'll have to ask Louie,' Fanny replied. The young girl buttoned on her blue coat and pulled her woollen hat down over her ears, then took the parcel of warm biscuits in her hands. Forgetting about Iris and the wireless she rushed out of the back door.

'Peace at last,' Fanny sighed, spooning some rice pudding into Raymond's compliant mouth. Eb carried on his methodical carving as if she had not spoken. 'You haven't been up to the allotment this week,' she said. 'I thought you would have been there while the Joices don't need you - it's not like you to sit around the house.'

'Nothing to do up there just now,' Eb replied without taking his eyes off his task.

Fanny did not press him, although she sensed her eldest son's glumness. Questioning Ebenezer never did any good; he was as secretive as a badger. Like her, he carried his burdens alone. Together they sat in companionable silence, enjoying the brief quiet before the revelries of bringing in the New Year.

Cocktails and dinner at The Grange had been followed by games of mah-jong and bridge in the library. Now they were gathering in the ballroom, the large glass-roofed room they had used for Beatrice's engagement party. Laws was distributing glasses of champagne and the atmosphere was jovial as they awaited midnight. Thomas Seward-Scott was tuning in the wireless to get a clear signal. He called for hush as the chimes of midnight crackled across the airwaves.

'Nineteen twenty-six!' cried Beatrice. 'Happy New Year, darling.' She kissed Sandy, setting the tone for the rest of the evening. The guests circled each other, kissing and wishing each other good luck in the coming year. Then the band they had hired for the evening struck up a waltz and the dancing began.

Later on Eleanor saw Reginald take Libby on to the floor for a foxtrot. She was bedecked in old-fashioned flounces, low-cut across her young bosom, and Reginald seemed entranced. Eleanor mocked herself for feeling a niggle of jealousy as they moved energetically around the dance floor. She wondered what they were saying to each other under cover of the music.

By three in the morning Sandy was leading them all in riotous Scottish reels, shouting instructions with cool authority as if they were his soldiers. After that the dancing seemed anti-climactic and the party began to break up. Eleanor was exhausted, but beyond sleep, and she stayed up reading in the library long after the house guests had retired to bed. What would 1926 hold for them all? she pondered over a cigarette. A time of change, perhaps. Beatrice planned to marry and follow Sandy in whatever posting he was given. Her father and Reginald seemed bent on confrontation with the miners' leaders; there might be real hardship ahead for the pitmen and their families if the owners got their way. Reginald would not stand idly by and watch his profits evaporate like morning mist. Eleanor shivered as she watched the embers in the fire turn white and dusty and lose their heat. What would happen to her and Eb this year if the community was rent by dispute?

She mounted the stairs in silk-stockinged feet, carrying her satin shoes rather than suffer further discomfort. The lights in the hallway had been turned off and only one dim lamp lit the stairway, halfway up. About to take the last flight of steps to the first landing where her bedroom lay, Eleanor became aware of someone else there in the dark. It was not that she had seen or heard anyone, just felt their presence.

Straining in the half-dark through the banisters she saw a pair of bare feet, and heard a silk dressing gown rustle past her at eye level. Some romantic corridor-creeping, Eleanor thought to herself with amusement. How anyone still had the energy for that after such an evening of dancing she could not imagine. She waited for the woman to pass so as not to embarrass her and then quietly climbed the remaining steps.

The figure had reached the end of the corridor and stopped at the corner. Eleanor thought it odd, as only Reginald's rooms lay beyond. The woman tapped softly on his dressing-room door. The door next to it opened and Eleanor caught her breath in surprise as Reginald peered out in obvious anticipation of his visitor. In the gleam of lamplight thrown momentarily into the passageway, she saw the redheaded Libby illuminated as she passed into the bedroom.

The door closed. Below in the dark the grandfather clock chimed five times. It was at least an hour before any of the servants would be stirring and setting about their early-morning duties. Eleanor's hand slipped from her mouth where it had flown to stifle her astonishment. Reginald was having, or at the very least embarking on, an affair. Libby Fisher's brazenness under her hostess's roof was staggering, Eleanor thought with incredulity.

But undressing in her own room, shock gave way to a wave of relief. She felt liberated by Reginald's infidelity; it assuaged her feeling of guilt at meeting Eb in secret. Until now, their affair had amounted to a few snatched embraces, yet she felt Eb's quiet passion. In future she would strive for ways for them to be alone together so that she could let him know the strength of her love for him. Eleanor fell asleep feeling almost grateful to the bumptious Libby Fisher for releasing the bonds which still held her to Reginald. She thought of him now with no shred of affection.

At five to midnight Sam was sent out of the Ritsons' house to wait for the New Year. He huddled from the rain under his mother's wash-house wall, cursing the tradition that dictated that the first visitor over the threshold after twelve o'clock must be dark. He heard the cries from inside the house as the clock on the mantelpiece struck midnight, picked a piece of coal from the heap in the shed and knocked at his parents' door.

'Come in, lad,' his father shouted, and pulled him in from the rain. He submitted to being kissed by his sisters while his brother-in-law Johnny Pearson poured him a whisky from a half-full bottle which had not been touched since last Hogmanay. Sam swigged it back and grimaced as the fiery liquid burnt its way down his throat. He did not know how people could drink spirits; he would rather have a pint of beer any day.

'Happy New Year, Sam.' Louie hugged him. 'It's going to be a good one for us.' She gave him a secretive, knowing look.

'Aye,' Sam answered, putting an arm around his wife's shoulders. Yet he could not shake off his mood of depression that had grown during the day at the thought of the year ahead. He was filled with foreboding about the future.

'Let's have a singsong,' Bel suggested. 'Come on, Mary, you know lots of songs.' The two sisters sang together and then Samuel Ritson brought out his old fiddle and gave his family a few tunes. By the end he had their feet tapping and the girls dancing in the tiny parlour.

Later they were first-footed by Louie's brother John and his girlfriend Marjory Hewitson, who was also a friend of Bel's.

'They've all gone to bed at home,' John said with derision. 'Eb didn't want to play the piano and Hildy did nothing but yawn after she got in from work. As for Davie and Iris — well it's like the reunion of two lovebirds,' he announced with disgust.

'John,' Marjory nudged him in the arm and simpered, 'you shouldn't tell tales.'

'It's nice to hear they've settled their differences,' Liza Ritson interjected kindly. 'They make a bonny pair - and Fanny's proud to bits with that wee grandson Raymond.' She winked at Louie.

Louie itched to tell her mother-in-law her news, but she swallowed the words with difficulty. Better to have her pregnancy confirmed before she told the world.

Sam saw the tired shadows around his wife's eyes and knew she had made a special effort to appear to enjoy the evening, while feeling nauseous at the sight of food.

'Come on, pet. It's time we were off,' he declared to the room.

Louie thanked her mother-in-law. 'It's been a lovely evening, Mrs Ritson, grand company.'

'Nice to have you here for once,' Liza Ritson smiled, tipping her grey-haired head to one side. 'You seem to be that busy looking after the waifs and strays of Gladstone Terrace these days.'

Louie smiled but said nothing; she knew the older woman was referring to their befriending of Minnie and Bomber. Any free time she had had since Minnie's baby Jack had been born on Boxing Day had been spent helping out at her neighbours'.

She knew Mrs Ritson disapproved of Minnie and her chaotic family because they were Catholics, and thought Sam's workmate Bomber had married beneath him. But Minnie had always been a good friend and Louie was not going to abandon her now just to please her mother-in-law. Besides, Bomber was Sam's marra, they grafted together at the same coal face and there was no greater bond of loyalty than that between marras.

They said their goodbyes and hurried up the muddy back lane towards the top of the hill. Lamps still burned in several homes and occasional first-footers could be seen darting through the dark, undaunted by the rain. Passing Minnie and Bomber's they could hear a roomful of loud voices and the quavering wail of a very new baby. Sam and Louie looked at each other in tolerant amusement.

'Well, baby Jack is getting a taste of his first Slattery Hogmanay by the sounds of it,' Sam laughed.

'It's nice to be going back to an empty house, isn't it?' Louie replied, pressing close to Sam's arm as they walked the final yards home.

'Aye,' he grinned.

They entered their tiny home and Sam lit a candle on the mantelpiece with a taper from the fire. The room was warm and cosy in the soft yellow light. Louie had already started to undress when she saw the small figure curled up in their bed.

'Goodness, it's Sadie,' she whispered loudly, sucking in her breath. 'She must have been here for hours.'

Sam puffed in annoyance. 'So much for an empty house,' he complained.

'We can't shift her now, Sam.' Louie's voice was pleading. 'She's sound asleep.'

'I'll kip in the chair,' Sam volunteered resignedly. He was beginning to realise that taking on Louie Kirkup meant taking on all the relations and feckless friends who needed her too. But he could not blame her; Louie's generosity was part of what he loved in her. Yet in the pit of his stomach he felt a tension, a dread that he would not be the only one leaning on Louie for support in the months to come.

Chapter Thirteen

In early March, A. J. Cook, the firebrand leader of the Miners' Federation of Great Britain, visited Whitton Grange. It was organised that he would stay with Samuel and Liza Ritson the night that he spoke, as Samuel was a respected union man and former official. Louie's Sam was responsible for collecting him from the Durham train and getting him to the Memorial Hall in time for the open meeting. Louie went round to her mother-in-law's to help prepare the meal for their important guest.

'And how are you keeping, pet?' Liza Ritson asked her young daughter-in-law. Everyone now knew that Louie was three months pregnant.

'Canny,' Louie smiled, though her face was pasty. 'The sickness is wearing off at last.'

'That's good.' Mrs Ritson nodded. 'Now you just take a seat. Mary will be in from the shop in a minute and she can peel the vegetables.'

'I can peel spuds sitting down,' Louie laughed, enjoying the fuss Liza was making of her. She took the large basin on her knee and began to clean the potatoes.

'I hope our Sam is looking after you,' Bel said as she gave Betty her tea at the table.

'Sam's been that caught up with organising this meeting I've hardly seen him lately,' Louie sighed. 'He's so excited about Mr Cook's visit. Sam's heard him before - over at Lanchester in January - says he's a wonderful speaker.'

'Yes, so I believe.' Mrs Ritson grunted as she leant down and reached into the oven to pull out a large pot of stew. She lifted off the lid and gave the thick gravy a stir. 'Mind you, there are those who don't trust him - him being Welsh and all.'

'Mam!' Bel remonstrated.

'No, it's true.' Mrs Ritson was adamant. 'They think he's going to lead us into trouble instead of talking to the bosses.'

Louie jumped to Cook's defence. 'Well, Sam says the bosses don't want to talk. We need men who'll stand up for us.'

Bel backed her. 'That's right. Johnny says we should be preparing for the worst now.'

'Oh, you don't mean another lock-out?' Liza looked across anxiously at her daughter.

Bel shrugged resignedly and glanced at her baby daughter. 'Let's hope it won't come to that.'

Instead of attending the meeting, Louie stayed at the Ritsons' to help. She sang Betty to sleep in the cot upstairs and talked with Bel and Liza about babies and childrearing. With the easing of her nausea, Louie was beginning to revel in the anticipation of her baby. Mrs Parkin and Fanny had started knitting already, and Mrs Ritson was constantly telling her she must eat for two.

Mary, unimpressed by the maternal chatter, bolted down her tea and rushed off to a Bible class meeting she was leading at the Presbyterian church. It was late by the time the men returned, and Louie was dozing by the kitchen fire.

All at once the room was buzzing with conversation as the discussion from the public meeting was resumed in the Ritsons' home. Louie gazed in awe at the visiting Welsh miner with his intense look and his powerful singsong voice.

'You must prepare for the emergencies of war, Samuel,' he urged his host as they tucked into the food the women served them. 'We're flying into one of the biggest industrial crises we've ever known. And the miners are going to be in the cockpit, Samuel. The struggle will succeed or fail by how we lead.'

'He's right, Father.' Sam nodded his head vigorously. Louie could see he was as inspired by this man as Mary was by her seasoned missionary, Miss Kennedy. 'We must take the lead in this battle; no one else can do our fighting for us.'

'Well spoken, Sam,' Arthur Cook said with approval.

'But you make it sound like a political battle,' Samuel Ritson pointed out uneasily. 'To us, this is about wages and hours. Like you said at the meeting; not a minute on the day, not a penny off the pay.'

'That's where you're wrong, Samuel.' Cook raised a finger to make his point. 'You see, it's not just a matter of your local bosses trying to cut your wages. It's the conspiracy by the whole establishment to deny us freedom. The government commission into the coal industry has as good as said wages must be cut to save costs. They're in this together - the coal owners and the Government. And they'll use all the power of the capitalist state to keep themselves in power - the police, the law, the army if necessary.'

Louie looked with concern at Sam. 'Surely it won't come to real war, will it?' she spoke up, her fear overcoming her shyness. The miners' leader turned his gaze to include her.

'We are already on the road to battle, Mrs Ritson,' he told her, 'and there must be no retreat - no compromise on our conditions of work. I tell you this, the whole labour movement will be up in arms if they try to cut our wages or suspend the seven-hour day. You've put up with too much hardship already. I'll not see my people starved to death by the capitalists.'

Louie was mesmerised by his words, delivered in that lilting Welsh voice. She felt strengthened by them, just as she was when Sam spoke of protecting the pit folk. She smiled back at him, encouraged.

'Well, let's hope it's all settled swiftly.' Samuel Ritson drew the conversation to a close and stood up. 'Come and sit by the fire and Liza will fetch you another cup of tea.'

Arthur Cook followed his host and sat in the deep armchair that was normally reserved for the head of the household. Only then did Louie notice the dilapidated state of his boots. They were through at the toes and scuffed and unpolished. She felt a nervous twist in her stomach at the sight. A great leader like Cook should not be going about in such scruffy footwear; it was like discovering a flaw in his character. She quickly dismissed the thought that his boots were a bad omen and hurried into the kitchen to help wash up the dishes.

Eleanor was still puzzled by Eb's avoidance of her. Since New Year the weather had been miserable and she had often had to forgo walks across the Common, but even at Greenbrae he had resisted her attempts to talk to him alone. She was hurt by his coolness and baffled by the change in their relationship since Christmas, when he had kissed her so warmly. She blamed herself for being preoccupied with entertaining over the holiday period and not making an effort to see him when the weather had been bad. Now that March was well under way there would be more opportunity to find him painting up on the hill or working at the allotment. Sooner or later she would discover what it was that bothered him.

She was picking daffodils from the sheltered gardens behind the stables when Reginald appeared. Since discovering his affair with Libby Fisher, Eleanor had not tried to hide her contempt for her husband. She had not confronted him with her discovery, but was sure that Reginald suspected she knew. She did not care what he did these days and was happiest when he stayed away at Waterloo Bridge on the pretext of a shooting weekend or riding to hounds.

'I've been looking for you, my dear.' Reginald bounded up purposefully in his bracken-coloured plus twos and brown brogues. Obviously he was about to go out, dressed as he was in casual clothing. Eleanor carried on amassing her wicker basket of yellow trumpet heads. 'I wondered if you'd like to go riding this afternoon?'

The request took Eleanor by surprise and she looked at him sharply. His brown eyes watched her, as if calculating her response.

'What do you want, Reggie?' she asked, knowing his offer was not motivated by a desire to spend time with her.

Reginald considered for a moment and then answered directly. 'I want you to use your influence with the Kirkup family to help me - to help us,' he added quickly.

Eleanor put down her basket abruptly. Now he really had surprised her. 'What makes you think I have any influence with them?' she asked cautiously.

'From what I gather, you have become some sort of benefactress to the family.' Reginald could not keep the edge of mockery from his voice. 'Showering them with gifts and securing them jobs. You've caused quite a stir in the village with your generosity, from what Hopkinson tells me.'

'Hopkinson!' Eleanor repeated with disdain. 'Your little mole.'

Reginald ignored the slight to his agent. 'Eleanor, I know you don't always trust my motives, but I'm trying to avoid a calamity for both us and the miners. You may be the only one who can bring the two sides together before a disaster occurs.' His handsome face was openly expectant, his tone quietly pleading.

Eleanor was taken aback by the supplication; gone was the confident arrogance of moments before.

'How do you think I can help?' she asked tentatively.

Reginald squatted down on his haunches beside her and fixed her with his light-brown eyes.

'I want you to approach the daughter, Louisa,' he began earnestly. 'Ask her to arrange a private meeting for me with Sam Ritson. He can choose when and where. From what I hear, she holds you in high regard; I'm sure she'll do as you ask.'

Eleanor was doubtful. It was true Louie Ritson was grateful for the way she had brought Davie home on Christmas Eve, and she knew the girl had been pleased with the wedding present from The Grange, but they were only acquaintances. Should she be getting involved in Reginald's business dealings at all? 'Why do you wish to see Sam Ritson so desperately? I thought you loathed him,' Eleanor countered.

Reginald's brow flushed pink below his short wavy hair and he clasped his hands together, cracking a knuckle tensely. 'I'm no admirer of Ritson,' Reginald admitted, 'but he's a man of great influence among the young radical pitmen. If I can persuade him to avoid a confrontation with us - come to some mutual agreement - then we can save Whitton Grange from a damaging and drawn-out dispute. It's to the benefit of us all, Eleanor,' he urged. 'You'd be helping your friends in the village as well as saving The Grange from a ruinous dispute. It may be our only chance of avoiding a stoppage.'

Eleanor was reluctantly swayed by her husband's words. For once he really did seem to be considering the lives of the villagers as well as his own business interests. The idea of a bitter and protracted feud between the miners and The Grange filled her with dread; it might finally kill her relationship with Eb as well as with the rest of his family. At this moment, the young ex-miner was the only person in her life who made living at The Grange bearable. If she were to be cut off from him because of her association with the owners, her existence here would be bleak indeed.

'I'll try,' she promised at last. Reginald smiled gratefully at her, brushing his well-trimmed moustache with relief.

'I'm grateful for your help, my dear,' he said quietly. Eleanor felt a faint leap of fondness for him which she quickly quelled.

'It may come to nothing.' She turned away and gathered the remaining picked flowers into her basket. When she looked round again, Reginald was standing up and straightening down his jacket with his usual brusqueness.

'I'll be out riding for the rest of the day,' he told her. 'I'll see you at dinner.' He did not stay to tell Eleanor with whom he would be riding, and as she watched him stride away with the eagerness of a young lover, she knew she did not need to ask.

It was towards the end of March before Eleanor plucked up the courage to visit Louie in her squalid one-roomed house dwarfed by the giant pitheads and spoil heaps at the end of the row. She marvelled at how the small window somehow managed to stay clean and the doorstep scrubbed and whitened, while all about them lay the black soot that permeated the very pores of the skin. Eleanor had discovered from Hilda that Louie was pregnant, and she had sent word via Louie's younger sister that she would like to call with a contribution towards the baby's wardrobe.

Now they were sitting by Louie's kitchen range sipping cups of tea. The room was spartan, but tidy and spotlessly clean. Bright-blue checked curtains hung at the window, matching the bedspread over the iron frame, and a gold-fringed covering adorned the mantelpiece, adding a splash of colour to the dark room. The range was crowded with heavy black pots, a kettle and an old-fashioned iron. Clean laundry hung from a pulley above their heads and the walls were dotted with pictures of animals and religious texts exhorting the occupants to be good and sober. The chairs they sat in were hard and the brown linoleum that covered the floor was worn down to the canvas. Eleanor had thought Louie's parents' house cramped, but she had never imagined that a married couple could live in such restricted conditions as this one room, which served as bedroom, kitchen and parlour. Where on earth did they wash? she wondered briefly.

Despite her first claustrophobic impression, Eleanor found herself relaxing in the room's welcoming cosiness. Louie was delighted with the small white coat and matching bonnet that Eleanor had brought, along with a thick woollen cot blanket.

'You shouldn't have, Mrs Reginald,' Louie said with unconcealed pleasure. 'It's going to be the best-dressed baby in Whitton Grange.'

'I consulted one of our housemaids, Jenny Bell, about what to get,' Eleanor confessed. 'She's got a baby nephew who was born on Boxing Day, I believe.'

'Oh, that's Bomber's sister,' Louie exclaimed. 'Jenny's brother is a good friend of Sam's - he and Minnie live down the street. Their baby Jack's a bonny bairn - lots of red hair like his dad.'

Eleanor smiled politely and used the pause in the conversation to turn the subject round to the real purpose of her visit.

'I was wondering if you could do something for me, Louie,' she began. The young miner's wife looked at her guest expectantly.

'Me, Mrs Reginald? I'd be glad to do anything, but what use can I be to you, miss?'

Eleanor took a deep breath. 'My husband, Mr Seward-Scott, wishes to speak to Sam privately. He says it is of the utmost importance to Whitton Grange that he do so soon. He wishes to avoid trouble for the village and feels Sam has it in his power to help. Would you persuade your husband at least to agree to listen to what Mr Seward-Scott has to say?'

Louie's deep-set blue eyes were narrowed in thought, her generous mouth pursed into a tight rosebud.

'The meeting would be completely confidential,' Eleanor continued, 'at a time and place to suit your husband.'

Louie nodded and then her solemn face broke into a cheerful smile. 'I'll ask him, Mrs Reginald. If Sam can help prevent hardship for the pitmen then he'll do so.'

'Thank you, Louie.' Eleanor returned the smile gratefully. 'And thank you for the tea, it was most refreshing.'

'Pleased you came, miss,' Louie answered warmly. 'You're a good friend to my family and I'm grateful for all you've done for us.'

Eleanor rose, embarrassed by the young woman's gratitude for so little. She could not resist asking, 'Is your brother Ebenezer well? I've not seen him at Greenbrae for several weeks.'

Louie glanced at her in surprise. 'Eb's grand as far as I know,' she replied, 'but he keeps himself to himself. I'll tell him you were asking after him.'

'Yes, do.' Eleanor turned quickly from the girl's enquiring look, cursing herself for raising the subject. She left with a promise to call again soon. From the window, Louie, wondering, watched her go. There had been something in the woman's voice when she had asked about Eb that betrayed more than a passing politeness. Sadie had once let slip that she had seen Eb with Mrs Seward-Scott in the grounds of The Grange, the time she had confessed to losing the embroidered handkerchief Louie had made her for Christmas. Louie shook her head in disbelief; the woman from The Grange could not possibly be the secret person they suspected existed in Eb's life. But perhaps Eb admired this lady in the same way that she and Hildy did? Poor Eb, he would never find happiness in yearning after such an exalted person. Still, she would keep her suspicions to herself for the moment.

It was with reluctance and a great deal of suspicion that Sam agreed to a meeting with Reginald Seward-Scott. Louie cajoled and persuaded until he could no longer refuse without appearing churlish. It was just possible the haughty coalowner had had a change of heart since the publication of the findings of the Samuel Commission, which advised against the lengthening of miners' hours. Maybe he wanted to reach a face-saving agreement, Sam thought, allowing a glint of optimism to colour his natural caution. Through Hilda, a message was relayed that Sam would agree to see Mr Seward-Scott at The Grange one Thursday afternoon before going on night shift.

As Sam strode up the long drive to The Grange, he barely noticed the awakening of the trees to spring, their young green buds opening like sleepy eyes after the buffeting of winter gales. Louie would have been alert to every detail of the grand house sprawled among the terraced gardens. But Sam paid no attention to the bowls of scented pink and white hyacinths standing in the bay windows, or the gleam of the old rosewood table in the hallway. He was only aware of a general air of extravagance and wealth beyond the dreams of the people with whom he lived, and he was offended by the disapproving aloofness of the greying butler who, with obvious reluctance, showed him into his master's study.

Sam gripped his cap defensively, resisting the urge to wipe his boots on the back of his trousers before stepping on to the highly patterned carpet. He had deliberately come dressed in his work clothes, ready to go straight to the pit, rather than show any deference by dressing in his Sunday best as Louie had wished.

'Do sit down, Mr Ritson.' Reginald beckoned him in courteously and indicated a comfortable leather chair by the fireplace. Sam nodded and perched awkwardly on its edge, his legs placed apart, as if he would spring from it like a whippet the moment the carved door was opened to let him free. 'Can I order some tea for you?'

'No thank you,' Sam replied, unnerved by the civilities. 'I'd rather just hear what you have to say, if you don't mind, Mr Seward-Scott.'

'Of course.' Reginald turned and walked to the window before continuing. He locked his hands behind his back and licked dry lips as he gazed out of the tall window.

'We both know the outcome of the independent report into the coal industry.' Reginald spoke to the early April shower splattering the flowerbeds below the window. 'The government will no longer subsidise us and there has to be drastic cost-cutting if we are to maintain our markets abroad. The Durham coalfield is more vulnerable than most to overseas competition.'

'I don't need a lecture on the state of the industry,' Sam replied impatiently. Reginald held his annoyance in check and turned slowly to meet the stoical face of his adversary.

'You have made a name for yourself as a man who represents his men well, a man who will argue but also negotiate with the pit management on behalf of others. I feel I can do business with forward-looking young men like you.' He smiled tightly. 'You understand the problems we face locally better than rabble-rousers who come into the area and try to stir up trouble in our coalfield.'

'If you mean Arthur Cook, he's a legitimately elected leader,' Sam answered gruffly.

'Quite so.' Reginald cleared his throat and looked directly at the miner. 'The Government is urging us to accept the Samuel Commission report. I can tell you confidentially that there are many coalowners who do not want to settle on those terms - they wish to extend the working day as well as cut wages.'

'The union will never agree to that,' Sam said emphatically.

'Hear me out," Reginald interrupted swiftly. 'I do not wish to alter the traditional working hours that you enjoy at Whitton Grange. I'm aware that an eight-hour day would make the hewers even worse off than their counterparts in other areas.'

'Then what are you offering?' Sam asked bluntly, tired of this man's pandering approach.

'I want someone I can trust to help negotiate with the local lodges, help steer through a realistic wage agreement. In return there will be no change in hours.'

'You mean you want a tame lapdog to make sure we'll agree to a reduction in wages,' Sam mocked. 'Well, you've asked the wrong man. I'll fight to maintain every penny that we earn - our families can't live on any less than they get now. It's the owners who must bear a cut in their huge profits, not the pitmen, who see none of them anyway.'

'If this comes to a head-on collision the miners don't stand a cat in hell's chance of winning,' Reginald snapped, giving way to his frustration at getting nowhere with this proud pitman with the hostile eyes.

'The people will see that we are in the right - that justice is done to the working man.' Sam spoke with quiet conviction. 'And then we'll see who'll be the winners.'

Reginald felt fear clutch his belly at the uncompromising words. For a moment he was filled with awe at the sacrifice this man was prepared to make for his cause, the hardship he was prepared to inflict on his family in order to stick to his principles. He knew then, instinctively, that a strike could not be avoided. Yet he must try one last tack to steer them all away from the impending storm.

'You have a charming young wife and a baby on the way, my wife tells me.' He forced himself to smile at the miner. Sam shot him a look of surprise and then nodded with bashful pride. 'I also know they deserve a better house than the unsatisfactory dwelling in Gladstone Terrace. Those cottages were never meant to accommodate families.'

'That's all the colliery offered us when we married,' Sam replied accusingly.

'A deputy at the pit would do better,' Reginald countered softly. 'Hopkinson tells me he is looking for a new deputy, and the one he has in mind would be able to move into a splendid two-bedroomed house on the green. I'd like to see you do well at Whitton Grange, Sam; a man like you could progress to overman or even under-manager in time.'

Sam looked at him speechless for a few seconds while the implication of what he was saying sunk in. The man was blatantly trying to bribe him into collusion with the management. Fleetingly he let his mind consider the possibilities. Louie would have the home she hankered after, the baby would be brought up with the village green to romp across and a bedroom to call its own. They would have money to spend on treats and trips into Durham. He would be given the blue cap and the yardstick of the deputy, with all the importance that went with such badges of office. No longer would he have to sweat and graft with his pick to earn his meagre daily crust or risk his life with the cutting machine they nicknamed 'the widow-maker'. This powerful man in front of him had the means at his fingertips to turn this dream into a reality. All Sam had to do in return was persuade the lodge not to resort to striking over their pay. Suddenly he was filled with self-disgust for even contemplating such thoughts, and his anger flared at the coalowner's apparent contempt for his principles.

'You can keep your bag of silver.' Sam almost spat the words out. 'I'll not betray my comrades to the likes of you. If you think a pitman can be bought off with such bribery then you don't know the men you're dealing with. You can take away all we've got, but we'll still have more self-respect than a dozen of you lot. There's one thing you'll never break, Mr Seward-Scott,' he trembled as he spoke, 'and that's our spirit!'

'Then you're a fool,' Reginald answered coldly. 'You'll not win against your superiors, Ritson. All you'll achieve will be misery for yourselves and your families. I'll not make such an offer to you again.'

'And I wouldn't listen a second time.' Sam stood, picked up his cap from the ornate table by his chair, and jammed it firmly on his head. Reginald glared at him in fury. For the first time he was struck by how short Sam Ritson was; he carried about him the air of a much larger man. 'I'll see myself out,' Sam added stoutly and strode across the room.

As soon as he was gone, the double doors that connected an adjoining sitting room opened and Hopkinson entered.

'I suppose you heard all that,' Reginald said in a clipped manner, barely controlling his anger.

'Yes,' the mines' agent answered, satisfaction glinting in his grey eyes. He hated the disdainful miner who caused his management continual bother at the pit. 'He's a very silly man.'

Reginald went quickly to the window, ignoring the comment.

'I want notices drawn up terminating all contracts at the pits on the thirtieth of April - when the government subsidy is withdrawn.' Hopkinson raised his eyebrows in surprise. 'We'll announce the conditions available to the miners who wish to reapply for employment on the first of May. Such things as free housing, rent allowances and free coal will be calculated as part of their wages in future.'

'That means a reduction in wages in real terms,' Hopkinson commented dubiously. 'They're used to those things as extras. Some may find it hard to manage.'

'And the working day will be extended to eight hours,' Reginald continued, as if the other man had not spoken. 'I want a draft by the end of today. And now I'm going out riding.' He spun round abruptly and marched towards the door before Hopkinson had time to query the command. Turning at the last moment, Reginald added, 'Red Sam Ritson has declared war on the Seward-Scotts, and that's exactly what he's going to get.'

As spring stirred in Whitton Grange and the first yellow primroses sprang into life in the dene, Eb retreated to the allotment once more to escape the increasing tension in the village. April was nearly at an end and there was little sign of any agreement being reached on wages for the pitmen or how the industry was to be run. Prime Minister Baldwin was making half-hearted attempts to press the two sides to settle the dispute, but the owners were in no mood to compromise and the miners refused to accept an eight-hour day. Already the Seward-Scotts had shown their vindictiveness in declaring the men would be finished on the 30th April. Those who were lucky enough to be re-employed would have to agree to a reduction of over two shillings a shift. How could the majority of them cope? Eb wondered bleakly. His family was luckier than most, with both himself and Hilda employed outside the pit. But Davie was still out of work and if his father and John were laid off too, life would be very tough. And what of Louie and Sam, with their first child on the way? He shuddered to think how they would manage. Eb looked around his small shed, cobbled together with bits of old fencing and advertising hoardings. The walls were covered with his pictures, for he no longer denied his passion for painting. He even drew at home, sketches of his family sitting around the kitchen. John and Davie thought his craving to draw odd, but he sensed that both his parents were quietly proud of his skill. Hilda was his greatest admirer and Sadie had begun a lucrative trade with her friends in swapping his drawings for sweets. She got Eb commissions from her schoolfriends May Little and Jane Pinkney, for which Sadie received a comic and a postcard of some dreamy-eyed actress.

He looked at a picture he had done of Eleanor, head bent, reading a book as she sat in the allotment, framed by creeping sweet peas. Often he had wanted to tear it from its hook on the wall, but he could not bring himself to do it. Every day he thought of her, longed to see her, in spite of the way her arrogant husband and hard-nosed father were intent on bringing the pitmen to their knees.

Galvanised by a sudden restlessness, he picked up his box of paints and left the allotment, striding purposefully through the woods up to the Common. Eb walked for half an hour but found only sheep occupying the high ground. He turned reluctantly for home, calling in at the allotment to tidy away his tools. A figure in the gloom of the shed startled him.

'I'm sorry,' Eleanor said quickly. 'I was looking for you. I couldn't help seeing the paintings on the wall. You've done a lot this winter. They're very fine.' She was aware of how she was gabbling, trying to fill the awkwardness between them with words.

'I was out on the hill,' Eb answered diffidently.

'Why have you been avoiding me?' Eleanor plunged in. Eb turned away and began a deliberate sorting of his garden implements. 'What's happened, Eb?' She could not bear his coolness. 'Am I an embarrassment to you? Perhaps you have an intended? Tell me what it is, please. I will never stand in the way of your happiness; I just need to know what troubles you.'

He faced her, his expression resentful under his grimy cap. 'I saw you with another man on Christmas Day,' he said in a dull voice. 'I climbed up to The Grange to catch a glimpse of you. Soft as muck, aren't I? You were with someone else - not your husband.'

Eleanor blushed as she remembered Will's approach to her on the terrace. No wonder Eb had avoided her since. He must think her heartless in the extreme.

'I'm sorry you saw that.' She dropped her head. 'He was a friend of Beatrice's and in too high spirits. There is absolutely nothing between us. Please believe me.'

Eb sighed. He did not know if he did believe her. Perhaps people of her class played games with each other like figures in chess? Well, he would not be a pawn to divert her when she was bored with her aristocratic friends.

'What do you want from me?' he asked in a tight voice.

'Your friendship,' she answered softly. 'As much as you can give me.'

'What's the point in being friends?' he questioned, his blue eyes sad as he spoke. 'We live in different worlds, Eleanor. Things are only going to get worse between your people and mine. Besides, you have a husband,' he added with a note of finality.

'A husband who is unfaithful to me,' Eleanor said bitterly. Eb shot her a look of surprise and she cursed inwardly for allowing her self-pity to make her indiscreet. It was not Eb's sympathy that she sought, but his love.

'Am I your way of getting back at him?' Eb accused her.

'No,' she answered vehemently. 'How can you even think that of me?' She gazed at him unhappily, feeling tears of frustration sting her eyes.

'I'm sorry,' he replied more gently and stepped towards her. Eleanor put out her hands and grasped his.

'I care for you deeply, Eb,' she whispered. 'I can't bear the thought of not being able to see you.'

'Then you must decide whose side you are on,' he insisted quietly, gripping her hands in his.

'Why must there always be division?' she asked forlornly, thinking of the way her father had demanded her loyalty too.

'It's the way of men,' Eb replied. 'Where there's self-interest, there will always be division and hatred.'

'But not between us, surely?' Eleanor pleaded. 'Don't let the dispute force us apart.' In reply, Eb put his arms about her and held her tight for a moment.

'I hope not,' he said in a low voice, though his spirit felt heavy with dread. They kissed briefly, as if they could keep the outside world from touching them while they clung to each other. Then Eb brushed away the tears that were slipping down Eleanor's pale high-boned cheeks.

'That husband of yours must be mad, going looking elsewhere,' he comforted her gruffly.

Eleanor laughed with relief. 'Thank you, Eb,' she whispered, and kissed him again.

For a further week, life continued as normal in the village, with the men tramping off up the lanes to the pits at the top of the hill as if nothing concerned them. The women and families at home carried on the pretence that this was an ordinary spring, going about their daily chores and ignoring the ominous headlines in the newspapers. But the uncertainty and fear gathered around them like black storm clouds intent on blocking out any last rays of hope for a peaceful settlement in the coalfields.

Louie stood at her doorway late on a Friday afternoon, watching Sadie skipping with May Little, the two of them jumping as one as the rope descended and bound them together. Minnie was chatting to her on the doorstep while baby Jack kicked contentedly in his battered old pram.

Arms crossed, Louie glanced occasionally up the street, watching for signs of the changeover of shift. The whistle blasted and she relaxed to think of Sam coming to the surface again. Then, unusually, it blasted a second time, the signal that work was finished for the week, although it was only Friday.

'How are things with your Davie?' Minnie asked, shaking dark curls out of her green eyes. Louie was momentarily distracted.

'Canny,' she smiled. 'Iris seems to have settled down at last. And Raymond's a treasure - walks like Charlie Chaplin - all bow-legged.'

As Minnie busied herself fussing over Jack and making him gurgle, Louie lingered, enjoying the contented street scene of women leaning on their half-doors, chatting in the bright spring sun and listening to the call of their children at play. Unconsciously she unfolded her arms and slipped a hand down to cover her stomach where the small bump swelled the flowers on her apron. She felt a flutter from the baby in her womb, right under her hand. It sent an excited thrill through her whole body to feel it moving inside her.

'I felt it move again, Minnie,' Louie told her friend breathlessly.

'Going to be a footballer, this one,' Minnie smiled back, teasing. 'Don't tell Bomber, else he'll have him signed up for Whitton the minute he's born.'

Louie laughed and then turned at the sound of men clattering out of the pit gates, their boots thudding like troops on the march. Gradually she realised that something was different. The men who were supposed to be beginning the evening shift were returning too, as well as those finishing the day stint.

Murmuring spread down the street as the tide of pitmen surged back from the gates, grim-faced. Louie spotted Sam in the midst of a group of men, Bomber and her brother John among them.

'What's happened?' Minnie shouted.

'They've locked us out,' Bomber called back over the heads of the others, confirming what they had all feared. Behind them the gates were being swung closed by a group of officials. They were arguing hotly with some retreating pitmen.

'Mary, Mother of God, protect us,' a frightened Minnie whispered, automatically crossing herself.

Sam reached his front door and nodded at his wife.

'They've done it,' he told her grimly, his tired face blackened with dirt and streaked with sweat. 'The battle's begun.'

Chapter Fourteen

On May Day, the weekend newspapers and Iris's crackly wireless carried the doom-laden Royal Proclamation. The Government was declaring a state of emergency in anticipation of a General Strike. The country had never been threatened with such industrial unrest, never before had there been a full-scale withdrawal of labour.

Yet strangely, life in the village appeared normal during that first weekend in May. Louie went to chapel as usual, had lunch at her mother's, helped with the Sunday School in the afternoon and went to her mother-in-law's for tea. There was an uneasy quietness about the place, a subdued atmosphere of waiting for the unknown. The children's play in the lanes sounded over-boisterous and discordant by comparison.

Sam was constantly absent at lodge meetings, but that was not out of the ordinary. Louie went through the motions of preparing his bait tin and bottle for the pit on Monday, even though she knew he had no work to go to. She could not quite believe the men would be idle come Monday.

That night as they lay in bed together, he told her what to expect. 'The TUC has called for certain trades to strike at midnight tomorrow, if the lock-out continues. We've set up a Council of Action to help co-ordinate the strike effort. We'll show them how working men can unite against tyranny, Louie. There won't be a bus or train running come Tuesday, unless Baldwin and the bosses back down.'

Louie felt cold and snuggled closer to Sam for warmth, even though their tiny room was airless and stuffy.

'Is there any chance an all-out strike will be avoided?' she asked anxiously, holding her breath for the reply.

'I don't think so, pet.' Sam slipped an arm around her shoulders. Louie had the impression that he was relishing the fight ahead, as if he had a score to settle more personal than the struggle for a decent wage. He had refused to discuss what had passed between him and the coal owner at The Grange and she had not pressed him for details. All she knew was that Sam had been livid when the subject was raised, and the name of Seward-Scott had been forbidden in his company.

Monday was warm and sunny. Sadie appeared at Louie's kitchen door with her friends, May and Jane.

'Can we go and see the Gallowa's in the field, Louie?' Sadie asked excitedly. 'Uncle Jacob says they brought them up from the pit over the weekend.'

'Why not,' Louie agreed with unusual lenience. After all, there was no urgency to prepare dinner for Sam, as he would be out at meetings all day. She even reached for the sugar bowl and dropped a few white lumps into the pocket of her apron for the girls to feed to the pit ponies.

Sadie skipped joyfully ahead, chattering with her friends. When they got to the fields below the Common, they discovered other families had had the same idea. Parents lazed around on the grass eating sandwiches, while the children fed titbits to the stout bewildered ponies, blinded by the unexpected light of the world above ground.

Davie and Iris joined them, with Raymond staggering along and flopping into the lengthening grass.

'Which is your pony, Davie?' Sadie demanded, clutching the precious lumps of sugar. May had given hers away all at once in a wild generous gesture, but Sadie wanted to make the moment last for as long as possible.

'Frisky.' Davie pointed over to a squat tan-coloured beast with a light streak down its nose.

'He's tiny.' Sadie marvelled at the pony. 'I bet I'm taller than him.' She ran towards the animal and leaned over the fence. 'Here, Frisky, here's some lovely sugar!'

Davie held up Raymond to get a better look at the ponies. 'Never thought I'd miss the bugger so much.' Davie looked affectionately at his work horse who had helped him pull countless heavy tubs of coal below ground. Frisky recognised his voice and came towards the source of the sound with a soft neighing. Davie put down his son and stroked the pony's mane.

'Haven't seen you for a few weeks, marra.' He patted the short flanks.

'Few months, more like,' Iris pulled a face. Davie ignored his wife's jibe. 'And at least the Gallowa's get fed by the management, strike or no strike,' she continued.

'Give over,' Davie said with an impatient look. 'Can't you stop your complaining for just once?'

Louie glanced up from encouraging Raymond in his walking and saw Iris bite back a rejoinder. Her slim face looked tense and petulant, as if nagging was growing into a habit. Louie wondered if a winter of being closeted together with Davie out of work was taking its toll on Iris's brittle patience. At least summer was on its way, and if they were all to be idle, they could do it out of doors in the fresh air.

'Let's go up to Eb's allotment and get some vegetables,' Louie suggested, to put an end to their bickering.

'Iris'll go with you,' Davie announced. 'I've got a game of footy in the park in twenty minutes.' He ruffled Raymond's hair and sauntered off before anyone challenged his right to do so.

'Come on then,' Iris sighed, and lifted the little boy into her arms, flinging a reproachful look after her husband.

Sadie and her friends ran ahead, playing hide and seek through the trees. When Louie and Iris arrived, they found Eb in his shed. He seemed unnerved to see them, and Louie was conscious of her eldest brother constantly glancing towards the door.

'I'm off down to Greenbrae in a minute,' he told them. 'You can take some rhubarb with you though.'

'Let me sit down for a minute, man,' Louie said breathlessly. 'That walk up the hill has done me in.' She plonked herself on an upturned bucket and put her hands to her growing stomach.

'Sorry, I forgot about your condition,' Eb apologised, handing her his water bottle. 'I'll just be outside, then,' he continued. 'Make sure the lasses aren't pulling up the beans.' He disappeared quickly.

'What's wrong with us this morning?' Iris pouted. 'None of the Kirkup men want to know us.'

'Eb likes the allotment all to himself,' Louie laughed. 'Like his own home this shed. Look how he covers the walls with pictures.' She scanned the curling drawings with amusement, then caught her breath at the picture of the woman reading. The allotment background was unmistakable and so was the gaunt face of Eleanor Seward-Scott. So she came to Eb's garden; Louie was shocked by the discovery. There was substance to her suspicions about them, after all. She was filled with foreboding at the thought of her brother being involved with a Seward-Scott. He had never had any sense of his place since his time in the army. Could he not see that the people from the big house were not their kind, that he could never be theirs, for all his love of painting and music? Besides, Mrs Reginald was a married woman. What could Eb be thinking of, allowing her to befriend him?

Suddenly, Louie was afraid that if they stayed any longer the lady from the big house would appear. If Eb was expecting a visit from her, that would account for his being on edge with them. Louie knew that Iris would be quick to put two and two together and she did not trust her forthright sister-in-law to keep the liaison secret.

'Let's be off.' She stood up, trying to control her breathlessness.

'But we've only just come,' Iris protested, swigging water from the bottle.

'Sam'll be back and I've things to do,' Louie answered briskly, and made for the door. Iris followed, reluctant to return so soon to a full house.

Louie saw Eb standing by the fence, giving quick glances at the path that snaked out of the woods.

'Thanks for the rhubarb,' Louie said, and saw the relief on her brother's face that they were leaving. 'Better be getting off to Greenbrae,' she could not resist adding. 'We'll walk down with you if you like.'

'No, you get off, Louie,' he mumbled. 'I've got to finish off the planting first.' Their eyes met for a moment, before Eb turned away. His look was silently pleading.

'Come on, Sadie.' Louie called for her cousin, who was already munching a stick of the sour fruit, dipped in a crumbled sugar lump she had kept back for a treat. Louie led her party away down the hill to the dene.

Eb let out a long sigh of relief. Eleanor was due at the allotment at any moment. He was unsure whether his sharp sister had read anything into his guilty behaviour. With the men laid off work, the allotment would become a busier place and no longer safe for them to meet. He would have to tell Eleanor not to visit him here again until the dispute was settled. Perhaps not even Highfell Common was safe, Eb thought with desperation. Was it not just a matter of time before their relationship was discovered? He plunged his spade angrily into the soil and worked out his frustration on the black earth.

When Eleanor returned from her assignation with Eb, she found Reginald in a bullish mood. He was fulminating about the gathering unrest over tea and madeira cake on the terrace with her father. Beatrice had arrived home from London the day before and was already yawning with boredom.

'They've done it now,' Reginald said gleefully. 'Those Bolshie print workers have refused to print the Daily Mail because it's too patriotic. It's tantamount to revolution. Baldwin can't possibly negotiate with the TUC now.'

'It's very worrying.' Her father's face was stern. 'We're on the verge of a general strike; the trade unionists will reduce the country to chaos.'

'Not a damn chance,' Reginald contradicted him, 'we're ready for them - we've been preparing all winter for such an eventuality. We'll call for volunteers to man the transport, that sort of thing.'

'You mean we'll all have to drive buses?' Beatrice laughed incredulously.

'And why not?' Reginald challenged her. 'We can't let the Communists hold this country to ransom. People like you and me, Bea, must stand up and be counted. You'd be doing it for your King and Country, saving them from revolution.'

'How thrilling!' Beatrice clapped her hands together.

'You make it sound like the Great War all over again, Reggie,' Eleanor butted in, sickened by his enthusiasm for confrontation.

'That's just what it is like,' Reginald replied roundly. 'Same threat - different enemy.'

Eleanor's anger boiled over. She was already resentful that the dispute engulfing them all was making it increasingly difficult for her to see Eb. 'Your so-called enemies are the very men who sacrificed their lives on the fields of Flanders; they're the war heroes who returned expecting a better lot for themselves and their families.' Eleanor glared at her husband. 'They're the men who slave away in your pits and dig out the wealth that allows us to live comfortably here at The Grange. How can you sit there so glibly talking about these people as your enemies?'

Reginald sprang up and faced her with narrowed eyes full of contempt. 'Well, it's perfectly obvious whose side you are on, my dear. I'm disappointed in you - a husband expects more loyalty than that.'

Eleanor could not bear the criticism. 'Don't you lecture me about loyalty! That was forsaken by you a long time ago it seems.' Reginald flushed furiously and Eleanor knew she had hit home about his affair with Libby Fisher.

'That's enough!' Thomas Seward-Scott decreed. 'This is a trying time for us all, but please conduct yourselves with a shred of dignity.'

Eleanor sat down, chastened by her father's reproof, and Reginald did the same, glowering at his wife.

Beatrice broke the hostile silence. 'Well, I think it's going to be absolutely topping; something exciting to do around here at last.'

With Tuesday came an eerie stillness over the valley that held Whitton Grange. Crowds of onlookers walked down the Durham Road to see how the world had changed since the strike call the night before. The road was deserted. The railway station was empty. In the woods above, a cuckoo called out and the sound of a dog barking a mile off carried clearly through the breathless air.

Groups of young men hung aimlessly around on street corners, talking, watchful, waiting for something to happen. Older miners sat in the park sharing a cigarette, coughing up phlegm in the clear air. The women, troubled by the brooding silence of the pits at the top of the hill, could not settle to their tasks. The ironing lay in piles on kitchen tables while they drifted to their doorways and leaned over yard gates to catch a whiff of gossip from their neighbours. None came. There were no daily newspapers to buy and circulate. The village was set adrift from the outside world, like a ship becalmed on a tranquil, uncharted sea.

In the back room of the Durham Ox, Sam and his Council of Action were holding their first meeting since the General Strike had been declared.

'The lads need something to do,' Johnny Pearson urged his brother-in-law.

'We'll keep them occupied,' Sam promised. 'Bomber, your father works in the rent office, doesn't he?' Bomber nodded. 'Can he get the use of a duplicator?'

'I can ask,' Bomber agreed. 'What are you thinking of?'

'What we need is to put about information - let everyone know the success of the strike and how they can help our cause.'

'You mean put out a bulletin?' John Kirkup queried.

'Aye.' Sam nodded, then leaned forward and dropped his voice lower. 'But we'll have to keep the operation secret. The bosses mustn't get a sniff of where the bulletin's being produced, else they'll smash it up, and Bomber's dad will likely lose his job. But we need to tell our side of the story, 'cos the capitalist press is going to try and make us out as criminals, just wait and see.'

'We could move the duplicator to a different place each night,' Johnny suggested.

'What about distributin' the broadsheets?' Bomber asked.

'Anyone who can lay their hands on a bicycle or who can run like you, Bomber, can take them around the villages.' The others nodded. 'Now,' Sam continued, 'we need to organise picketing of the main road. Nothing is going to get in or out of this valley, unless it's essentials like milk or food.'

Superintendent MacGuire stood attentively in the library at The Grange, his heavy black boots sinking into the hearthrug. The windows were open and the sweet scents of early evening wafted in with the birdsong. He grasped a dainty sherry glass awkwardly in his hand, his ruddy face creased in concentration as he listened to the tall coalowner.

'I want your men to be vigilant,' Reginald instructed the policeman. 'It would be useful to know the names of troublemakers, those leading the picketing. In return I can supply you with names of likely subversives, men who will delight in trying to flaunt the law.'

Robert MacGuire shifted uneasily and cleared his throat. 'We don't want relations in the village to become heated, sir. The police must be seen to be impartial.'

Reginald eyed the bulky man studiously. 'I understand that, Superintendent. However, it is also your duty to protect the persons and property of this estate. We cannot turn a blind eye to law-breakers and hoodlums. I want you to deal severely with anyone found breaking into the pit yard to steal coal, or any man who violently attempts to stop any of my vehicles. I shall expect police protection on the highways.'

'It's all quite peaceful at the moment, Mr Seward-Scott,' MacGuire assured him. 'There have been no incidences of unruly behaviour among the pitmen. No one has broken the law.'

'These are early days - it may not remain so peaceful,' Reginald said brusquely. He marched over to a large oak table and picked up a sheet of paper. 'These are the names of suspected Bolsheviks.' He flourished the list at the policeman. MacGuire took it gingerly. A quick glance showed him the names of Sam Ritson and Bomber Bell, two hotheads among the younger pitmen. He knew their families well; his wife was a cousin of Liza Ritson's and he had helped coach Bomber at football when he was a boy. His heart sank at the thought of what might lie ahead.

Quickly swallowing the sickly sherry, Robert MacGuire took his leave, eager to be released from his briefing. It irked him that he should have to take orders from the prickly coalowner; he would rather have dealt with the older Thomas Seward-Scott; he at least had his roots in Whitton Grange.

'Don't forget to keep me informed,' Reginald reminded him once again as he held the door open for his visitor. Constable Turnbull was hovering outside the double library doors.

'Sir.' MacGuire nodded stiffly and strode away down the corridor with the young constable attempting to keep up with his tight-lipped superior.

Sam's strike committee produced its first bulletin on Friday, 7th May. John Kirkup, in charge of distribution, persuaded Eb to borrow Miss Joice's bicycle, and the two of them took it in turns to cycle to neighbouring villages with copies of the cyclostyled news-sheets. Bomber and Davie organised a relay of runners from the football team to go around the houses and deliver copies too. Even Sadie and her friends were co-opted to help.

People seized on the news avidly, starved as they were of information on how the strike was going, except for the odd copy of a national newspaper which condemned the action with hostility. Sam had come home on Wednesday brandishing the British Gazette, the Government's strike bulletin, edited by someone called Winston Churchill. Louie had listened to Sam almost choking with anger as he haltingly read out snippets from the paper.

'They say we're holding the nation to ransom. By heck, listen to this,' he shouted.' "It is a conflict between Trade Union leaders and Parliament. ... must only end in the decisive and unmistakable victory of Parliament." Well, if that's not biased then I don't know what is,' Sam cried. 'You wouldn't think the Government was supposed to represent the whole nation would you? They're just interested in serving a small bunch of profiteers and exploiters, Louie, so they are!'

Louie had tutted and let him rant on, her mind half distracted with worry over the credit they were already amassing at the store. The grocery manager was being lenient with her because of the good name of Kirkup, but for how much longer? Their meagre savings would see them to the end of the month if they were careful, but no further.

On Friday Sadie ran in with a copy of Sam's news-sheet.

'Read this, Louie.' The dark-haired girl waved the chemical-smelling paper in her face.

'You read it to me, pet,' Louie encouraged, knowing how her cousin now enjoyed showing off her ability to read long words. Sadie settled herself on to a kitchen chair and creased her brow in concentration.

'"Workers of County Durham be of good courage!"' she began. '"The General Strike is a success." Success is in capital letters, Louie,' Sadie explained for her cousin's benefit. Louie hid her smile at the girl's serious expression and nodded as if impressed. '"Don't be taken in by the lies you read in the Cap-it-alist press. The workers cannot fail. Across the country, Ind-us-try has answered the call from the General Council of the Trades Union Congress. They are resisting the unprovoked attack by the owners who locked us out. The Power Stations are closed down. No coal is being shipped from Sunderland or Seaham Harbour. The response of our fellow workers has exceeded all ex-pec-tations."' Sadie pronounced the word carefully.

'That's good news,' Louie commented, encouraged by the words. At least they were not alone in their time of trouble. Perhaps the nation would listen to their plea at last.

'It goes on,' Sadie followed her finger as it drew across the page, '"Fellow trade unionists will not allow the miners to be starved into sub-miss-ion. The wages and welfare of all our families are at stake. If we fight together, we will win. Victory is ours!" That's in big letters too.' Sadie looked up triumphantly.

Louie smiled and put her arms impulsively around her young cousin. Sadie slipped her arms around the older girl's waist and hugged her, enjoying the sudden show of affection.

'Eeh, Louie,' she looked up in wonder, 'I can feel your baby kicking.'

A week after the lock-out began, Reginald was growing nervous about the sweeping success of the strike in paralysing local commerce and industry. He was virtually marooned at The Grange as a picket on the Durham Road had prevented him from motoring over to Waterloo Bridge to see Libby. Instead he had taken to riding across the moor, but the experience had left him stiff and saddle-sore from hours on horseback.

Furthermore, picketing had been orderly and well organised, and his operations at the Eleanor and Beatrice had ground to a standstill. The strike was solid. He could not even move the coal from its tubs in the pit yard. All that the union would allow through the gates were officials detailed to do essential maintenance work below ground. The Government had commandeered his coal stocks lying unshipped at Seaham and the electricity supply at the house had packed up and they had had to resort to using smelly oil lamps and candles. Mrs Robertson, the housekeeper, was beginning to complain about household stocks running low.

Out of sheer frustration at his impotence, Reginald decided he must act. He called a meeting with Hopkinson, the only ally he felt he could trust completely with the plan he was formulating. When the agent left to put the plan in action, Reginald went to look for his high-spirited sister-in-law Beatrice. To his relief she was on her own in the conservatory, listening to the gramophone and sipping an iced gin.

'I've got something to relieve your boredom, Bea.' Reginald smiled. 'A little errand I'd like you to run.'

Early on Monday morning Sam received disturbing intelligence that a convoy of lorries, packed with non union labour, was likely to be travelling through the valley. Rumour had it that they were miners from out of the area, being brought in as blacklegs to work the Seward pits. Some said they were Cornish, others maintained they were Italians or Poles. Their origin did not matter; what mattered was that a large enough picket was mustered to blockade the pits at Whitton Grange.

By nine o'clock in the morning members of the Council of Action had been alerted and word was put round that as many men as possible should rally at the pit gates and on the road into the village. Louie watched them streaming past her window, dozens of pitmen, cheerful and resolute as they gathered at the top of Gladstone Terrace.

'Aren't you going to join them?' Minnie appeared at her kitchen door, her pretty face flushed with excitement, Jack balanced on her hip.

'At the picketing?' Louie asked in surprise.

'Aye, why not?' Minnie replied. 'Our Margaret's made a banner and she needs someone to help carry it. Why shouldn't the lasses join in and have some fun? I'm going to leave Jack at Mam's for the morning.'

Louie hesitated a moment. Sam had already left with Bomber to go down the Durham Road and block the way into Whitton Grange. The picketing had been good-humoured when the women had gone with refreshments for the men, and the police had avoided any clashes with the miners during the past week. MacGuire kept his men under tight control. It might be fun, she thought, untying her apron.

'Wait while I pop across the lane,' Louie answered with a grin at her friend.

Eleanor stopped Beatrice in the hallway, surprised to see her donning her riding hat. She was dressed in an old pair of riding breeches and an army jacket that had belonged to Rupert.

'Why are you dressed in such an extraordinary fashion, Beatrice?' Eleanor enquired.

'I've got a job to do,' her sister answered, strapping on her hat over her short dyed blonde hair.

'What job?' Eleanor looked at her in amusement.

'I'm driving a van for Reggie,' Beatrice announced proudly. 'Got an important delivery to make in the village. He wants someone who can drive fast, like me,' she added with delight.

'What are you delivering?' Eleanor's tone hardened. 'You realise there'll be pickets on the road to stop you.'

'They don't frighten me one bit,' Beatrice answered disdainfully, glancing at herself quickly in the gilt-framed mirror above the rosewood table. 'Anyway, it's medical supplies or food, or something like that - so I've every right to be let through. Reggie will be there to protect me,' she said mockingly.

Eleanor felt a twinge of concern. It did not make sense. Why would Reginald be responsible for delivering medicines? Unless it came within his responsibilities as a member of the local OMS, the emergency committee set up by the Government. 'I don't approve,' she said doubtfully, 'but take care, won't you? It may be more dangerous than you think.'

'Don't nag, Eleanor.' Beatrice dismissed her warning. 'You're just jealous because I'm going to have a bit of fun out of this tedious strike.'

Eleanor sighed resignedly and retreated to her upstairs drawing room to read.

By late morning, the numbers on the Durham Road had swelled to several hundred. But the road was empty of traffic and the picketers were beginning to get restless. Sam felt a growing unease at the situation. They had certainly had a good response to their call for help, but there were faces present that he had never seen before, men who claimed they had travelled from Durham and as far away as Gateshead to stop the convoy. Sam wondered how they had heard and responded so quickly. Still, he had no time to question their enthusiasm, as rumour spread that extra police were being drafted in from Durham to cope with the numbers on the road to the pit.

At midday, four vanloads of police motored in from Durham and nosed their way through the phalanx of vocal miners. There were jeers and jostling around the vehicles but the men fell back to let them through, with little more than a shake of their fists.

Shortly afterwards, Johnny Pearson pushed his way through to Sam at the head of the picket and took hold of his arm urgently.

'Two wagons have been spotted coming in the back road,' he shouted over the noise of the crowd. Sam was stunned; it had not occurred to him that they might attempt to slip into the village down the steep and narrow back road from the neighbouring valley, past St Cuthbert's and the old churchyard. He had assumed a large convoy would travel along the main route from Durham. Inwardly he cursed himself for being so easily fooled.

'You stay here with a couple of dozen men,' Sam ordered John Kirkup. 'I'll take the rest back to the pit and reinforce the picket on the gates. We may be too late to stop them reaching the village.'

Shouting commands as he went, Sam led his men back into Whitton Grange like a swarm of ants on the march, spilling into the tightly packed lanes that led uphill to the pit.

Louie, Minnie and Margaret stood clutching their banner, pressed close to the pit yard wall. At first they had enjoyed the banter with fellow picketers, basking in the pleasant sunshine and throwing ribald comments at the policemen on duty at the gates.

'That Alfred Turnbull's a nice-looking lad.' Minnie nudged her friend playfully.

'You shouldn't be thinking of lads now you're a married woman,' Louie reproved, but could not help a smile.

'Just looking,' Minnie pouted, then shouted across to the young constable.

'You're making him blush, the poor lad,' her sister Margaret laughed.

'Don't encourage her,' Louie said, seeing Minnie's glee at provoking a response.

Then, inexplicably, the atmosphere around them changed and the press of bodies became uncomfortable. The shouts of the pickets grew hostile and the mood menacing.

'They're drafting in more police,' someone beside them said angrily. 'Strangers from outside.'

The crowds pushed back to let the police vans through to the pits, and the reinforcements set up a cordon of truncheon-bearing men to keep the picketers at bay. People began to sway around them, as the mass of bodies took on a momentum of its own.

'I don't like this,' Margaret said anxiously to her sister. Louie caught her infectious rising panic.

'I feel a bit faint,' she muttered to Minnie and grasped her arm. Her friend looked at her in concern.

'We'll get you back home,' she reassured Louie. 'Here, Margaret, you take the banner and I'll see to Louie.' She slipped a supporting arm around Louie's back and coaxed her forward. But they soon found their way blocked by a surge of people running up Gladstone Terrace and the parallel streets.

The sound of boots on the rough cobbles thudded in Louie's ears like bass drums and the throng of men before her lurched unsteadily like crazy puppets. Minnie pushed with all her might to force a way for them through the crowd, but they were fighting against a determined tide of picketers. Just when Louie felt she could stand the heat and the pressure of jostling bodies no more, Minnie gained a foothold in a neighbour's doorway, felt for the handle, which thankfully gave way, and bustled Louie inside. Her friend flopped in a faint and crumpled to the floor.

Sam and Bomber heaved their way through the crowd to the front of the picket, the air thick with the noise of abuse from both sides. It was their intention to try and simmer down the most vocal pickets and restore a sense of orderly resistance but before the leaders could gain control of the situation, the impatient hooting of the first lorry was heard down the street. Someone was challenging the driver to produce their permit to prove they were carrying essential supplies. Sam thought he saw a woman's face behind the wheel, but knew he must be mistaken. The driver did not stop to talk; instead the vehicle leapt forward with a long, strident blast of its horn, and the questioners jumped out of the way.

The arrogant hooting of the lorry's horn was like a spark to tinder. There was a roar from the crowd and a surge towards the offending vehicle. Sam shouted vainly for people to keep back until they could discover if the cargo carried was indeed blackleg labour. Incredibly the van kept on coming, revving its engine and tooting loudly at those who tried to block its progress towards the pit gates.

Suddenly, a man next to Sam, whom he did not recognise, pulled out a broken brick from under his jacket and shouted, 'Let's get the scabbing bastards!' He hurled his weapon at the lorry's windscreen. It was a good shot and the glass on the passenger's side shattered. Pandemonium followed.

The police at the gates took the offensive, charging into the crowd with batons raised, to be replaced by a second wave of constables. A shower of stones buffeted the uniformed men as the two sides met in an angry clash. The waste ground in front of the pit yard was in uproar. Defenceless pickets around Sam were beaten to the ground by the armed police. Disbelieving, he saw the brick-throwing pitman point out Bomber to the police. A moment later, Bomber, capless and fists flying, was felled by two policemen who continued to kick him as he lay doubled up in the dust.

Sam waded in to help his friend. He swung a fist into the jaw of the nearest policeman and heard a muffled crack as it made contact. The man reeled backwards and Bomber rolled out of the way. Seconds later, Sam was knocked sideways by a truncheon blow to his head and a brutal jab in his kidneys. He slumped with the pain, a wave of nausea flooding through him. Someone tripped over him and he passed out.

Eb and Davie, who had merely joined the crowd out of curiosity, saw Sam being trampled underfoot. They pushed their way through the battling pitmen, Eb taking a crack on his shoulder as he ducked out of the way.

'Grab his legs,' Eb shouted to his brother, and heaved at Sam's limp body. They managed to move him from the middle of the riot and Eb put his ear to Sam's chest, ripping his necktie loose.

'He's breathing,' Eb said with relief.

'Good job you were a stretcher-bearer in the war,' Davie grinned.

'That's them there!' someone shouted close by, and in an instant the Kirkup brothers were surrounded by police. One seized Davie by his jacket and two others began to drag Sam away from the wall against which he was propped.

'Leave him be,' Eb shouted angrily. 'He needs medical attention.' They ignored him and continued to haul the two men away, Davie raging obscenities at them in protest. Eb jumped to defend Sam. 'I said leave him!' He glared at the constable nearest him, and grabbed him by the arm.

'Arrest him too,' a burly policeman with a bushy moustache ordered.

'Come on, you Commie bastard!' the constable jeered at Eb as he wrenched him into an arm-lock. Eb allowed himself to be bustled into a waiting van, determined to keep Sam in sight.

It was an hour before Minnie judged it safe to poke her head out from her neighbour's door. She had refused to let Louie stir, shaken by her sweaty pallor and laboured breathing. The lane was deserted, strewn with caps and the debris of bricks and broken glass. The street was ghostly quiet, as if a rampaging storm had blown through and swept all humanity from its path. She stepped out tentatively to search for news of the pickets, urged on by Louie's fretful questioning about Sam and Bomber. Torn and muddied, Margaret's banner lay on the ground like discarded washing, its message of resistance trampled into the dust.

Minnie found her own house empty. At the top of North Street she saw a group of pit folk gathered outside the Methodist chapel. From the first woman, Minnie gathered that the hall was being used to administer first aid to the injured. Pushing her way inside, she spotted Mary Ritson bandaging the hand of a young pitman.

'Have you seen Sam or Bomber?' she asked her old schoolfriend urgently. Mary looked up, her dark-eyed face pale with shock. But her voice when she spoke was steady.

'Give us a hand will you, Minnie?' she asked.

The other girl cried out with impatience. 'Tell me, Mary man, where are they? Louie needs Sam - she fainted in the crush. Now she's sick with worry for him.'

Mary glanced up in concern, but said nothing while she finished methodically tying the ends of the bandage. Then she stood up and put a hand on Minnie's arm.

'They've both been arrested,' she answered quietly. 'Sam and Bomber. Eb and Davie Kirkup with them. Dozens of others, so they say.' Minnie looked at her, stunned, unable to take in what she was saying. 'I didn't see them,' Mary continued in a low voice, 'but when we got there, it was like a battleground. I've never seen the like of it before, Minnie, and I hope I never will again.'

Minnie looked at Mary properly for the first time, as the dreadful words registered through her shock. Tears were streaming down Mary's small sallow face. It was the first time she could recall seeing Mary Ritson cry.

'Oh, Mary, Mother of God!' Minnie whispered fearfully. 'What am I going to tell Louie?'

Chapter Fifteen

'She's quite all right.' Dr Joice assured Eleanor as he closed the library doors behind him. Inside, Beatrice was lying on the deep sofa, propped up with cushions, a large whisky by her elbow. 'She's had a bad shock, but mercifully escaped without injury. It's just as well Reginald was with her and got the van into the pit yard before they were lynched. What on earth possessed her to attempt such a damn-fool escapade?'

Eleanor shook her head at the craggy-faced doctor. 'You know how wilful my sister can be. I blame myself for not stopping her when I saw her leave this morning. I had no idea there was so much trouble brewing in the village,' she sighed, walking Dr Joice back down the corridor.

'It was out of all proportion,' he muttered, his tired face creased with concern. 'They'd rallied pickets from out of the area - and there was a huge police presence too - all for a couple of vanloads of spare parts for the pit. It doesn't make sense.'

Eleanor turned to him in surprise. 'Beatrice told me she was delivering food or medical supplies. Reginald asked her to do it.'

Dr Joice tutted angrily. 'If she had been carrying food into the village, she would have been issued with a permit to pass the picket line and none of this would have happened.'

'You mean Reginald lied to my sister and put her life in danger?' Eleanor demanded furiously.

'That's something you had better ask him yourself,' the doctor replied shortly, as they reached the hallway.

'I shall,' she said with a determined jut of her chin. Dr Joice took his hat and stick from the footman waiting by the entrance. As he made to leave, Eleanor detained him with a question. 'You said there were arrests and injuries - have you heard who was involved?'

Dr Joice's stern face softened a moment at Eleanor's troubled frown. He knew from Isobel that her friend had a fondness for their gardener Ebenezer, and though he did not strongly disapprove, he saw only unhappiness in such an attraction.

He lowered his voice. 'I believe Sam Ritson has been arrested, though as for the others I couldn't say.'

'Poor Louie,' Eleanor whispered in distress.

'Quite. Now, my dear, I must hurry to see to my other patients - most of them should have managed to limp home by now,' the doctor continued more briskly. 'We used the chapel as a temporary first aid post. If I hear anything more I'll let you know.'

'Thank you.' She smiled with gratitude, touching his arm briefly. Watching him go down the steps of The Grange, Eleanor marvelled at how his stooping shoulders never failed to carry the increasing burdens of Whitton Grange upon them. The greater the plight of his patients, the more driven he was to help them, she thought with admiration. Then the stupidity of Reginald's actions came into her mind. She turned back with her indignation rising like sap.

Reginald was with Beatrice in the library when Eleanor re-entered. His left hand and wrist were bandaged; they had been cut by glass from the broken windscreen. Apart from that he appeared unscathed.

'How do you feel?' Eleanor asked her sister coolly, ignoring Reginald's quiet look of triumph.

'Terrible,' Beatrice answered petulantly. 'I'll never get over today. All those awful people - their dirty, shouting faces.' She shuddered. 'I never want to go into

Whitton Grange again. I don't know how you can bear to visit those savages, Eleanor - I've seen how they behave. They don't deserve the consideration that Reggie gives them.'

Eleanor felt her patience snap. 'You shouldn't have been there in the first place,' she was quick to retort. 'Reggie shouldn't have put you at such risk. All for the sake of a few bits of machinery which are useless while the strike continues.' She flashed an angry look at her husband and then added tartly to her sister, 'And you don't know the first thing about the people you denigrate with your sweeping generalisations.'

'Beatrice was doing her bit to get this country back on its feet,' Reginald goaded his wife. 'It was a brave mission which Bea succeeded in accomplishing.'

'Don't talk such rot,' Eleanor replied sharply. 'Beatrice thought she was carrying essential foods; you tricked her into driving the van, hoping the pickets wouldn't give her trouble because she was a woman. Isn't that the truth?'

'What does it matter what I was carrying?' Beatrice interrupted irritably. 'They behaved like a pack of dogs out there anyway. They deserve to starve after what they did to us.'

'Beatrice!' Eleanor was shocked at her callousness.

'Your sister has a point.' Reginald seized the opportunity to isolate Eleanor. 'Perhaps Bea is being a bit over-dramatic after the scare she got, but today just demonstrated that we're up against a bunch of Communist agitators - lawless criminals leading the majority of my colliers astray. But decency and order won the day.' He stuck his chest out proudly. 'The troublemakers have been rounded up. It's happening all over the country. This strike won't last another week.'

'Good,' Beatrice answered. 'It's all been ghastly. I just want to get back to London and civilisation until Sandy gets some leave.'

Eleanor could not bear to stay in the room a second longer. 'You're both contemptible,' she declared, and flinging a last indignant look at her husband she marched out of the library. She was shaking with anger at their complete lack of concern for the havoc they had wreaked that morning. Their provocation of the miners would only feed the hatred and bitterness that was growing like weeds, threatening to choke them all.

Later, she would discuss Reginald's tactics with her father, who was still out riding and knew nothing of the morning's events. He at least might see the folly of what had been attempted. She went swiftly to her room and dressed for walking in flat shoes, a primrose-yellow coat and matching hat with a short brim to shade her face. Despite Eb's warnings that they should not meet at the allotment, she had to find out if he and his family were unharmed. If Sam Ritson was involved, the Kirkups might well have been sucked into the fighting too, Eleanor thought with dread. Ten minutes later, she set out for Whitton Woods.

At 28 Hawthorn Street they waited for news of their men. Louie lay resting on the pull-out bed in the kitchen. She felt a lot better now; the tightness in her stomach had eased and her pulse beat at a normal pace. Fanny Kirkup had shown only a moment's alarm when Minnie had brought her in, almost hysterical with the news that Sam and Bomber and her brothers had been taken by the police. She had put Louie straight to bed with a hot cup of tea from their precious stocks, and had forbidden her to move.

Minnie confessed it had been her idea for them to join the picket line, and when the Ritsons called to wait with the Kirkups, Liza gave the girl a severe telling-off.

'What were you thinking of?' stout Mrs Ritson demanded. 'Dragging her out in that crowd, with her five months gone. Did you want her losing that grandbairn of ours?'

'I said I'm sorry,' Minnie wailed. 'It was all right until the extra coppers arrived.'

'Aye,' Jacob Kirkup agreed. 'It got out of hand on both sides. I'm ashamed our Eb and Davie got mixed up with the troublemakers.'

'They just went to watch.' Hilda jumped to their defence. 'They saw the crowds and were curious. Eb wouldn't start any fighting.'

'Davie might,' Iris grimaced, trying to quieten a fractious Raymond with a bottle of sweetened water.

'Anyways,' Liza Ritson was not prepared to see her wrath deflected from Minnie, 'you should be home looking after that bairn of yours, so get yourself off.'

'She can stay if she wants,' Louie piped up from the bed, not afraid to defend her friend against her mother-in-law, 'until we have news of Bomber at least.'

'Thanks, Louie.' Minnie smiled and shuffled on to the edge of the bed, throwing a look of satisfaction at Mrs Ritson. Her mother had always said Liza Ritson was a snob, thinking herself above the likes of the Slatterys because her husband had been secretary of the lodge and her cousin was married to a superintendent of police. Well, being more posh than the rest of them did not help at a time like this, Minnie felt like saying as Mrs Ritson pursed her lips together; they were all in the same leaky boat now.

It was into evening and the kitchen was shadowed from the lack of sunlight by the time news of the arrested picketers came. Fanny had stretched their meal of vegetable soup and rhubarb and custard to feed the Ritsons and Minnie too. Jacob and Samuel were playing a listless game of dominoes in the parlour and Raymond and Sadie had been put to bed when John came running in at the back. The women, sitting in the gloom of the unlit kitchen, looked at him expectantly.

'They've released them,' he panted. 'MacGuire brought them back a short time ago.'

'Thank the Lord!' Fanny Kirkup gasped, and Louie thought her mother would cry in front of them all. She felt a sudden pressure on her own throat, as emotion flooded it; her husband and brothers were safe.

Moments later Sam and Bomber, Eb and Davie tramped in at the kitchen door, bedraggled but still defiant. There were hugs of relief and tearful reunions in the cramped room. However, the euphoria of their return was soon dispelled when Sam told them that he and Bomber had been charged with police intimidation, and that the others were among those charged with resisting arrest. A subdued silence settled on the room.

'When will you be summonsed?' Samuel Ritson asked his son, voicing the concern of them all.

'A couple of weeks.' Sam let out a heavy sigh. He felt such a turmoil of anger at the police, and guilt towards Louie for the obvious distress this had brought her, that he could hardly look her in the face.

'Sit down, lads,' Fanny urged. 'There's a bowl of soup for you.' Hilda helped her mother serve out the hot broth.

Louie's eyes pricked with tears to see how Sam winced with pain as he lowered himself on to a kitchen chair. His right eye was almost closed with the bruising around it and he had cuts to his right temple. She put a hand out and squeezed his.

'Are you all right, Sam?' she asked shyly.

Embarrassed by the concern, he ignored her question. 'You should be at home resting, not waiting up for me.'

'She would have been if it hadn't been for Minnie Slattery,' his mother

130

complained, using the girl's maiden name with a sneer. 'Fancy making her go out picketing in her condition.'

Sam looked at Louie sharply. 'Is that true? Were you there this morning?' Louie nodded unhappily. 'I've never heard anything so bloody daft in all my life!' he exploded, and stood up. Louie burst into tears.

'Don't upset her. It was my idea,' Minnie told him defiantly. 'Anyways, Sam Ritson, you should be proud of your wife for standing up to the bosses and holding a banner at the pit gates. You're always telling us how we must stand together and fight. Well, that's just what we were doing - me and your Louie and our Margaret - not fighting with our fists and getting arrested, but giving them as good as we got all the same.'

Sam gawped in astonishment at Minnie's outspoken criticism. Bomber looked warily at his mate to see how he would take such brazenness from his wife.

That's right,' Davie laughed suddenly, releasing the tension in the room, 'and the lasses made a better job of it than we did by the look of things. All we succeeded in doing was getting nicked.' He winked at Minnie who returned a saucy look. Louie sniffed and smiled at her brother. Davie grinned back. 'And don't you worry yoursel' about us, pet, they'll not put us away for having a bit of a scrap.' He led Eb and Bomber into the parlour for their supper. Sam's anger deflated.

'I'm sorry, Louie,' he apologised, lowering himself on to the bed beside her, and stroking her hair with quick, self-conscious movements. 'I didn't mean to give you a hard time. It's just this trouble with the bosses. Are you all right, pet?'

'I'm just fine,' Louie assured him. 'All I care about is getting you safely home. Go and get something to eat, then we'll be off, eh?' Sam leant over and kissed her lightly on the top of her head. Louie smiled at her mother as Sam obeyed and followed the others into the front room.

Eleanor spent a fruitless afternoon searching for Eb; there was no sign of him anywhere. She returned to the house and ordered her maid Bridget to draw a hot bath, after which she had supper brought up to her room. Thomas Seward-Scott looked in to see her after dinner and found her sitting on the window-seat gazing listlessly out on to the terrace below. They could hear the laughter of Beatrice and Reginald playing a late game of croquet on the lawn.

'You can't go on blaming Reginald for everything,' her father told her directly. 'He was only doing his best to break this infernal strike.'

'He could have got Beatrice killed,' Eleanor answered accusingly. Her father drew up a chair beside her.

'That's not what makes you so angry though, is it?' he guessed. 'I think you're more concerned for the miners who were injured than your own family. Reginald tells me you've been down to the village and telephoning Dr Joice every hour.'

Eleanor turned and held his look. 'And aren't you concerned for them, Daddy?' she demanded quietly. 'Don't you care what happens to these people if the strike isn't resolved soon?'

'It lies within their hands to solve it,' he answered matter-of-factly. 'We weren't looking for a fight.'

'Reginald was,' his daughter contradicted him roundly, 'and he wants unconditional surrender. We have the resources to sit it out until the miners are starved back to work, isn't that so? Well, that doesn't seem fair to me.'

The coalowner sighed and got to his feet. Why was his elder daughter afflicted with such a wretched dose of conscience? he wondered with irritation. She was obsessed with what was fair rather than what was practicable; just like her departed mother,

Constance, he thought wearily. Thomas wanted his daughter to stand with her own kind, but he suspected she would not. As he stood up, his attention was drawn to a watercolour sketch in the window recess. The unfussy, bold strokes were recognisably a likeness of Eleanor. There was a stark beauty about the simple painting.

'When was this done?' he asked her with interest, momentarily diverted from his brooding thoughts.

'Some months ago,' his daughter answered vaguely, fixing intently on something in the garden below.

'It's good.' Her father smiled. 'It may not be the most flattering portrait, but it captures something of you, my dear. Who is the artist?'

'Oh, an acquaintance of Isobel's.' Eleanor answered lightly, but felt her mouth go dry. 'He's not a real artist, it was just done for fun.'

'He should carry on his art if this is anything to go by.' Thomas was enthusiastic. He glanced around the room and saw paintings of birds and animals done by the same unstylised hand. 'I think you've discovered a new talent,' he said with surprise. 'Not like those awful Vorticists or whatever you call them that glare down on us at breakfast.' Eleanor laughed and turned towards him. Thomas was quick to notice her flushed face. 'I could live with these paintings - don't hide them away up here.'

'I wasn't hiding them.' Eleanor flicked a disinterested hand at them, but her manner was defensive and her father decided not to assuage his curiosity further that evening. There was always a reserve about his elder daughter that he never dared to penetrate. Beatrice and her desires he understood and felt at ease with; Eleanor he loved but would never fathom what drove her. He kissed her on the head and walked over to the door.

As he reached for the brass handle his earlier resolution to lecture her returned. 'You must do what you feel is best,' he told her, 'but I'll not let you put the future security of The Grange and its business in jeopardy, Eleanor, and Reginald is its future. Don't interfere with his handling of the strike.'

Confused, she watched him leave the room. 'I don't know what I'm going to do,' she said out loud to the closing door. Had she given herself away by blushing like a schoolgirl over Eb's modest paintings? If her father pressed her further about this mysterious painter, Eleanor wondered, would she be honest with him?

Until the early hours of the morning, Eleanor read by candlelight, enjoying its dim cosiness that reminded her of holidays spent at her mother's home in the Highlands. She was sure quiet, determined Constance MacKenzie would not have stood idly by while her villagers suffered hardship.

The next morning, after breakfast, Eleanor received a call from Isobel. She told her friend that Hilda had come bearing bad news; Eb had been among those arrested.

'He'll stand trial before the end of May,' Isobel said.

'Does that mean prison?' Eleanor asked, feeling sick inside.

'I doubt they'll be let off with nothing,' Isobel said, 'not with your sister and Reginald having been involved. It'll probably just be a fine in Eb's case. He was only going to Sam's rescue when they bundled him into the van.'

'Thanks for letting me know,' Eleanor answered dully.

Isobel hesitated then made up her mind. 'He's at Greenbrae now if you want to come down and talk to him.' Eleanor's spirits lifted at once at the thought of seeing Eb.

'Yes, I'll do that.' She brightened as she put down the receiver.

On the way to the village she planned how she could pay Eb's fine without him refusing. The shock of hearing about his arrest had jolted her out of her listless confusion. From now on, Eleanor determined, she was going to play a useful role in this dispute, no matter what her father or Reginald had to say.

In the Memorial Hall the following day, an angry crowd of miners were gathered to hear news of the strike and put voice to the rumours that they had been duped by the coalowners. Sam stood on a chair and rapped out his accusations.

'There were strangers planted among us on Monday,' he told them, 'non-union men who took the tainted gold offered by the Seward-Scotts as payment for causing violence.' There were shouts of dismay and threats of revenge. 'I saw a stranger next to me pull a brick from his jacket and deliberately chuck it at the first van. That same man was a police informer, grassing on us union men during the fight -I saw him pointing out our comrade Bomber Bell to the coppers.'

Voices swelled in anger and Johnny Pearson nudged Sam. A stream of policemen were pushing their way into the back of the hall. Sam continued, undaunted.

'The bosses put about the rumour that scab labour was coming into the pit so we would be out in force. They ordered in coppers from outside the area to harass us. They paid their lackeys to start the trouble, so they could arrest our leaders.'

'That's enough,' Superintendent MacGuire shouted from halfway down the hall. 'We're breaking up this meeting.' Jostling began around the uniformed men.

'What gives you the right to try and silence us?' Sam called down at the burly, bewhiskered officer.

'Under the state of emergency, meetings that are likely to cause a breach of the peace are banned. Come on, Sam, I don't want to have to arrest you again.'

'See how the law are in the pockets of the coalowners.' Sam ignored the warning and raised his voice. 'They're too frightened to let us speak. There's a copper been sitting here the last half an hour writing down everything we've been saying.' Sam jerked his thumb contemptuously at a plain-clothes policeman sitting on the end of the third row. The young man, Alfred Turnbull, jumped up nervously and looked to his superior for help as a pitman next to him grabbed his notebook and tore out his notes.

'Right, lads,' MacGuire roared, stung by Sam's implication that he was Seward-Scott's lapdog, 'get everybody out.'

His constables, most of them full-timers drafted in from Durham, began to hustle the listeners from their seats.

'Don't let them bully us!' Sam urged from his chair in blatant defiance of the superintendent. 'If we stand together against the tyranny of the Establishment, we'll win. They're scared of us. MacGuire,' he challenged, 'you're a decent man; don't betray your own kind for the likes of Seward-Scott. His heart's as black and hard as the coal we dig - he doesn't care for you or me or any of us pit folk, can't you see that?'

Around them the atmosphere simmered; Robert MacGuire hesitated in his unwelcome task and for a moment the miners resisted their removal, aware of his irresolution. Sam pressed his advantage.

'The strike is won,' he declared. 'We've shown the solidarity of the working man. Now the Government will be forced to listen to our grievances. This country has been built on the backs of the working class, now it's time we had a share in its prosperity.'

'You're a fool, Sam Ritson.' MacGuire suddenly rounded on him. 'It's your so-called fellow workers who've betrayed you, not the likes of me.'

'What do you mean?' Sam asked him angrily.

'Haven't you heard?' The older man shouted louder so all could hear over the rising noise. 'The TUC have called off the General Strike. It's over, Sam.'

The din of argument ebbed as the words carried across the hall. Sam gaped at him, speechless.

'It's a lie,' Bomber accused the police officer who had once been his football trainer and idol. 'He's just saying that to get us out of here.'

'The TUC would never call off the strike without consulting the miners.' Sam had regained his composure and retaliated quickly.

'It's not a word of a lie,' MacGuire insisted. 'The strike's off. Now I'll give you five minutes to leave this hall or you're under arrest.' He turned on his heel and strode from the room while the meeting broke down in a confusion of argument and denial.

Sam stormed out after the superintendent, with Bomber and Johnny and John Kirkup at his side.

'We'll go to Hawthorn Street,' Sam ordered. 'Iris has a wireless. We'll see if this is true.'

But by the time they had reached the Kirkups' house, the village was buzzing with the rumour that the General Strike was over.

'They've given in,' Jacob Kirkup confirmed the news to his son-in-law, disbelief edging his words. 'Ten days misery and nothing to show for it. What a pointless, pointless sacrifice.' He shook his head sorrowfully. Louie was sitting in the doorway looking pale and shocked, Fanny was silent; Sadie stood in the yard subdued by their pain, twisting a skipping rope in her bony hands.

'The bloody traitors,' Bomber raged at the crackling wireless. 'It was our fight, how dare they call it off when nothing has been won?'

'It's still our fight.' Sam roused himself from the hurt that felt like a winding kick in the stomach. Physical blows he could take, but this numbing sense of betrayal by his own kind could bleed him to death. 'They may have called off the General Strike, but they'll not beat the pitmen into submission so easily.' He thumped the table aggressively.

Jacob Kirkup looked across at the dark, square-jawed man who was now one of his family and admitted a grudging admiration. He disapproved of his son-in-law's atheism and Communist leanings, but Sam was driven by a conviction and sense of justice that was as strong as his own Christian beliefs.

'Striking has never got us anywhere,' Jacob cautioned. 'The forces against us are too strong.'

'Maybes,' Sam answered, his dark eyes fierce, 'but we don't win anything unless we fight our own battles. The TUC aren't going to do it for us, so we must carry on the struggle ourselves.'

'Aye, Sam's right.' Louie spoke up unexpectedly. 'We're on our own now, but we're not beaten.'

Sam swung round in surprise with the others. She was smiling at him, her pale face resigned to further hardship.

'By, my lass has spirit!' Sam beamed at her proudly. He stepped over to the door and grabbed Louie's hand, squeezing it in his own. Nothing more was said between them, but Louie knew the tender look in his brown eyes told her she was loved.

It was John who voiced the uncertainty that hung over them all. 'So what do we do now?'

Chapter Sixteen

During the next week, Sam threw himself into the organisation of relief for the villagers who were feeling the lack of earnings most. Bomber and John were in charge of clearing and chopping dead wood from the dene to provide fuel for the greedy kitchen ranges that were the only means of cooking and boiling up water. Sadie and her friends joined in the dirty game of picking over the spoil heap for cinders, going out with buckets of soapy water to soak the coal dust as it smouldered like a brooding volcano; only then was it cool enough for the children to handle.

After dark, Sam led nightly raids over the pit yard wall to gather the coal strewn around the tracks, dodging the watchmen and roaming policemen. He was fairly certain MacGuire knew of his activities, but as yet had not interfered. Since the clash with the pickets, relations between the pitmen and the local police had grown increasingly strained, and Sam guessed it was only a matter of time before another such incident cut the final strand of civilities between them.

The stolen coal was distributed around the village or sold at the tradesmen's doors of the bigger houses where no questions were asked about its origins. The money raised in this way went to buy food for the relief centre set up in the chapel hall on North Street. This had been Louie's idea.

'Minnie's talking about applying to the parish for money,' she had told Sam one evening, as he was about to depart on a raid. Sam shot her a look of concern. No one went cap in hand to the Board of Guardians and submitted to their humiliating tests unless they were desperate. At the back of everyone's mind lurked the horror of the workhouse in Durham from which there was slim hope of escape once admitted.

'Bomber never told me things were getting that bad,' Sam said.

'They've got nothing left,' Louie continued unhappily, 'and Jack's sickly, but they've got nothing to buy medicines with. I said I'd ask Eb to fetch them something from the allotment, but he's already supplying the Dobsons and the Parkins as well as all of our family.' She did not add that she had already lent Minnie the money they had put by for when the baby came. Sam did not need to know about that yet.

'We can't sit back and see our friends throw themselves on the mercy of the parish,' Sam fretted.

'We could set up a soup kitchen,' Louie suggested decisively, 'like they've done in other villages. At least the worst off can then get one hot meal a day, and their bairns can be fed.'

Sam had agreed and Louie had gone to her father, who'd approached the Reverend Stephen Pinkney at the chapel and arranged the use of the hall as a centre. Every day now, Louie, her mother and Iris, along with Minnie and her sister Margaret, Edie Parkin and the younger Dobson sisters, Susan and Eva, gathered at the chapel to scrub and chop vegetables and make up pans of steaming soup. By the end of the week they were serving up soup and tea to two hundred miners and their families. On their feet all day, the work was exhausting, but at the end of it, Louie could fall asleep as soon as she got into bed, instead of lying awake anxiously thinking of Sam's impending court case. There would be time enough to concern herself about that when the moment came.

The relief centre attracted further volunteers; among them John's girlfriend, Marjory Hewitson, who brought her cheery face and plump giggle to the group of helpers, and Sam's sister Mary, delighted to turn her missionary zeal to good use.

'If you talked less about God and did more of the washing up, we'd get on a lot faster,' Iris complained forthrightly as Mary sermonised over the sink.

'There's good comes out of everything,' Mary continued, undaunted by her sceptical helper.

'I don't see how any good will come from this strike,' Iris grumbled. 'The miners should know when they're beaten and get back to work, I say.' Louie gasped in shock at the disloyal words as she came into the tiny galley with a tray of dirty bowls.

'Don't let our Sam hear you say that,' she cut in reprovingly.

'Well, it's true.' Iris put her hands on her narrow hips and tossed her short auburn curls. 'We can't go on living off soup kitchens for ever. At least if they went back to the pit there'd be some wages coming in - and some's better than none.'

'Don't talk like that.' Louie was scared the others might overhear Iris. It would only confirm their distrust of her as an outsider who did not understand their ways.

'I'll say what I like,' Iris pouted, 'and you'll agree with me once our men have been locked up in Durham gaol. What good will come out of that, eh?' She turned to give Mary a needling look.

'The Lord works in mysterious ways, Iris.' Mary smiled back serenely. 'Look how he's brought us all together here - not thinking of ourselves, but helping the unfortunate poor.'

'We're the unfortunate poor now!' Iris threw down her tea towel and stomped out of the kitchen.

Mary looked round, bewildered at Iris's sudden flash of temper. 'What did I say?' she asked Louie in astonishment. 'I thought we were getting on well.' Louie put a reassuring hand on her sister-in-law's shoulder.

'It's not your fault,' Louie sighed. 'She's just worried about our Davie; you can't blame her really.'

'Does Davie think he's going to gaol?' Mary asked.

Louie laughed shortly. 'I don't think it's occurred to him; he's spending all his time catching rabbits and poaching birds with Tadger Brown. Davie's having the time of his life - he's just a big bairn, that brother of mine.' Louie smiled with affection.

The following week saw the Government proposals to reduce wages and reorganise the coal industry rejected by both the coal owners and the miners' leaders. As warm and sunny May neared its end, the dispute became more entrenched and both sides resigned themselves to a summer of stalemate and increasing hardship. Rumour spread that the Government was planning to import coal from abroad and that a state of emergency would again be declared. Finally the tense waiting ended when Sam and the others received their summonses to attend court in Durham.

'Let me come with you,' Louie pleaded for the umpteenth time as she pressed his best shirt, noticing for the first time how it had begun to fray at the cuffs. Tomorrow her husband would stand as a criminal in the dock wearing this shirt under his brown suit.

'We can't afford to send you by train and I'm not letting you walk all that way with you expecting,' Sam replied firmly. 'And I don't want you getting upset either, so there's an end to it - don't ask me again, Louie.'

Louie took up the shirt and held it to her in silence, frustrated that she could not go. What if Sam was imprisoned? she wondered with rising panic. This could be their last night together for ages. The thought of such loneliness made tears sting her eyes, but she turned away quickly and folded the shirt neatly as she had done scores of times before. 'I've made you up some paste sandwiches - I've been keeping a spare jar for—' She broke off, realising she had been about to say 'a special occasion'.

'Come here.' Sam beckoned her gently and put his arms about her, feeling the bump of their unborn child between them. 'I want you to take good care of yourself,' he whispered in her ear, 'you and the bairn.' Louie nodded speechlessly, tears running down the channels between her round cheeks and button nose. 'It probably won't come to prison,' Sam tried to cheer her, 'but we'll say our goodbyes just in case, eh?'

'I love you, Sam.' Louie choked out the words. Sam gave her an answering hug, wishing he could protect her from the uncertainty of life ahead as his wife, cursing a Fate that had made him a miner.

'Let's go to bed, pet.' He pulled her gently towards the iron bedstead.

For hours they lay awake holding each other, then towards dawn, Sam fell into a fitful doze. But sleep eluded Louie; she lay uncovered in the stuffiness of their tiny room, touching Sam for reassurance and feeling the movements of her restless baby. What dismal future could they offer their first-born? she wondered bleakly.

Against Eb's wishes, Eleanor was determined to attend the court case in Durham. Beatrice had left for London, and was so recovered from her ordeal that she now boasted of her involvement in the General Strike and was dying to tell her friends all about it. Reginald, at last free to travel where he wished, resumed his visits to Waterloo Bridge for tennis and cricket. He was mildly amused by Eleanor's interest in the trials and was only pleased she did not want to accompany him to the Fishers'. Only her father watched her shrewdly and noticed the subtle change in his elder daughter, the decisiveness once more returned to her step, the glint of purpose in her dark eyes.

Eleanor collected Isobel from Greenbrae, as the school had closed for the day, and drove them into the city. They parked near Elvet Bridge and walked the rest of the way to the court. The stark, blind walls of Durham prison loomed overhead like a sleeping bird of prey.

To their amazement, a huge crowd of onlookers had already gathered in front of the building. Isobel looked nervously at her friend, but Eleanor pushed ahead without a second's hesitation. The cordon of police held back the people from the steps to allow the women through. There were a few shouts of derision at the well-dressed ladies in their straw hats and lacy frocks, but Eleanor chose to ignore them.

Inside the courtroom, the visitors' gallery was already packed. The two friends squeezed on to the end of the bench on the back row, trying to appear inconspicuous.

In the heat of the cramped chamber, justice was swiftly dealt out to the stream of miners who came in front of the magistrates, sitting high above them in their sombre black robes. Eleanor recognised the thin-nosed retired banker who led the proceedings. He was a colleague of Reginald's on their local emergency committee and she was under no illusion as to the man's hostility towards the strikers. The first dozen were penalised with petty fines of £3 and £5. Isobel whispered to Eleanor that the union would probably pay up on their behalf. Then it came to the turn of Eb and Davie.

Eleanor watched Eb standing impassively with military erectness before the court, his tall frame filling the dowdy black suit, the stiff white collar cutting into his thick ruddy neck. His blond hair was crudely cropped at the back, his moustache pale against his weathered face. For a moment she glimpsed him objectively as the prosecutor did; a hardened, surly miner who did not flinch under questioning or drop his insolent blue gaze in deference to his superiors. It was only then that she feared for him.

Beside him, Davie appeared scruffily morose, his hair unbrushed and his tie knotted at an angle. Young Alfred Turnbull, who had been in the same class as

Davie at school, gave evidence against him. The court heard how Davie had hit him on the cheek, obstructing the arrest of Samuel Ritson. Davie did not deny it.

The magistrates deliberated. A £50 fine or a month in prison, the retired banker rapped out. There was consternation in the visitors' gallery, as Iris burst into tears and the spectators voiced their incredulity. The central magistrate called for order, threatening to have the gallery cleared at the next disruption. The convicted chose imprisonment and were led away by two policemen.

'They can't possibly afford to pay such a fine,' Eleanor said to Isobel with indignation. 'They have no choice but to go to prison. It's monstrous.'

'Hush,' Isobel cautioned, 'we mustn't draw attention to ourselves.'

Iris, weeping inconsolably, was led past them by a stout man with a nose like the end of a bulbous pipe. Eleanor guessed he must be Ramshaw the publican. They were followed by Fanny and Hilda Kirkup, looking pale with shock. Hilda caught sight of Eleanor at the last minute.

'Oh, miss, what are you doing here?' she cried. Fanny looked blankly at the grand lady clutching a lacquered stick. Recognition dawned as Eleanor spoke.

'I came to see what I could do,' she answered, her dark-brown eyes full of compassion. 'I shall pay their fines,' she insisted to the older woman, concerned at her drawn grey face. Eleanor recalled how handsome she'd been when she'd worked at The Grange.

'Oh, thank you, Miss Eleanor,' Fanny Kirkup said wheezily, with the glimmer of a smile.

'Quiet at the back,' ordered an officer of the court, and Hilda led her mother quickly after Iris.

Eleanor and Isobel stayed on to witness more rough justice meted out to Sam and Bomber. They stood defiant and unrepentant of their actions of resistance against the police. The magistrates pronounced a sentence of two months each, with no option of a fine or appeal. As the stunned miners were led away, the gallery exploded in uproar.

The spectators were bustled from their seats as the police tried to empty the court. Eleanor and Isobel found themselves unceremoniously swept through the door with a tide of pit folk, shoved and pushed towards the main entrance. Word spread faster than they could walk to the crowd waiting outside for news. Howls of protest greeted the verdicts and the demonstrators burst into a noisy rendition of 'The Red Flag' as the accused miners were taken from the courthouse.

Eleanor glimpsed Eb's bald head above the rest and saw Sam give a salute to the crowd before he was swallowed up in a tunnel of dark-blue uniforms.

'We must get out of here,' Isobel said urgently to her friend, but as Eleanor pressed after her, they became parted by the throng of angry miners around them. She found herself pinned against the outside wall without a hope of escape until the crowds were dispersed. The atmosphere was growing more rowdy and menacing, and far from breaking up, the aggrieved miners seemed intent on revenge on the administrators of the law. They bayed for the magistrates and jeered at the policemen who could barely keep order.

A short while later, several police on horseback appeared to the right, followed by reinforcements of constables on foot. Eleanor looked up in alarm at the progress of the horses, thinking how the beasts might rear up in terror at such a din. They could cause a full scale riot. To her relief, the miners began to fall back from the steps of the court building at the approach of the mounted officers. But once a crack had been forced in their ranks, the uniformed men behind charged in with batons, wielding them at the becapped heads of the pitmen. The solid mass of demonstrators scattered and the scene became one of chaos. Eleanor froze in horror at the attack, pressing herself against the cold stone at her back and raising her stick as protection. Even at the height of her suffragist struggles she had not seen such hostility turned against an unruly crowd.

Suddenly she saw a gap open up in front of her and she dashed for safety. Catching her heel on the cobbles, she stumbled and abandoned both shoes, hobbling in her silk stockings until she was round the corner.

Fear and relief welled up and she found herself retching on the pavement. Not since she had been a hot-headed young suffragette, punched by police for throwing eggs at Asquith on a visit to Newcastle, had she experienced such terror. Then, she had been scared rigid by the numbers around her, the stifling press of bodies, the faces of men distorted in hatred as they turned to violence against the protesting women. Today she had witnessed the same heavy-handedness against the miners.

Hatless and shoeless, Eleanor groped her way back to the car, unaware that she was sobbing out loud.

Louie was sitting in the dark of her mother's kitchen, Sadie asleep on her knee and Raymond bedded down in his cot in the parlour, when the bedraggled walkers completed their trek back from Durham. Iris went straight to her sister-in-law and threw her arms about her neck, waking Sadie as she did so.

'They got gaol,' she cried into Louie's shoulder. Sadie started to bawl for her cousin Eb. Louie just felt a coldness creep around her heart, her worst suspicions confirmed.

'How long?' she asked.

'A month for Eb and Davie,' her father replied exhausted. 'Two for Sam and Bomber,' he added, turning away so his daughter could not see how upset he was.

Firelight flickered across Louie's face as she struggled to come to terms with this blow. Even Sam had not thought he would get more than a month. A month she could cope with, but two? Two months stretched away like eternity. What would she live on? What if the baby came a month early and Sam was not there?

'We'll manage.' Fanny answered her unspoken fears, her insides tugging to see the forlorn look on her daughter's face. 'Stay with us tonight. You can sleep with Iris.'

That night, Louie and Iris shared the parlour bed, remembering how they had lain with their men just a day ago. The dark hours seemed endless, but both feigned sleep, not knowing how to comfort the other.

In the morning, Jacob Kirkup went off to the Institute for a morning's quiet reading. The others lingered listlessly over a meagre breakfast of dry toast and tea. Iris began to complain.

'I wish my father could pay Davie's fine,' she said, nibbling on a crust. 'I asked him, but his business has been affected by the strike; he can't afford fifty pounds.'

'It's not a matter of the money.' John stopped his tea-slurping. 'It's a point of principle. A pitman would rather serve time than buy his way out. Sam and the others are not criminals; all they've done wrong is to stand up to the Establishment.'

'Don't talk rubbish,' Iris argued back. 'They'd all be out tomorrow if they had any sense - no one in their right mind wants to spend time in Durham gaol.'

'You don't understand principles, that's your trouble,' John growled back at her.

'Listen to you - Mr High and Mighty - why aren't you there with them if you've got so many principles?' Iris taunted, knowing how John suffered guilt at being the brother who had escaped arrest. He glared back at her with dislike.

Fanny did not have the energy to weather one of their gale-force rows and interrupted quickly. 'Mrs Seward-Scott was at the court yesterday, wasn't she,

Hilda?' She turned to her younger daughter. Hilda was immersed in a book, oblivious to the crackling of tempers in the room.

'What's that, Mam?' She glanced up.

'Mrs Seward-Scott - she said she would pay their fines, didn't she? There might be some hope for Davie and Eb at least.'

'She did say something about it,' Hilda answered cautiously, not wanting to raise too many hopes.

But Iris brightened immediately. 'You should have said so before, Hildy.' She went into the parlour and bathed in cold water. Then, having put on her best cream and brown dress, beige gloves and matching cloche hat with a sprig of artificial flowers, she emerged again, practising a warm smile, her mouth picked out in red lipstick, now rationed for special occasions.

'Come on, Raymond, we've got an errand to run,' she told the boy brightly, sweeping him into her arms.

'Where are you off to?' Louie questioned.

'I'm going to visit the lady at the big house,' she announced, 'and I'm going to get my Davie back.' She clattered out of the back door in her high heels and they heard her tapping down the back lane.

'Good luck to her,' Louie sighed, envious of Iris's nerve at going to approach Mrs Reginald.

'She'll put on a good act, that one,' Fanny commented wryly and coughed into the fire.

'She thinks she's as good as them at the big house anyway,' John added sarcastically. 'I don't know why our Davie married her in the first place.'

Fanny cleared her throat. 'Don't start that again. Hilda, you should be off to Greenbrae - you're late.'

Reluctantly Hilda put down her book, and started to pull on her coat. 'I can't see Eb agreeing to have his fine paid, even if Davie does.'

'Why should the Seward woman want to?' puzzled John. 'That's what I can't understand - she being the missus of the boss an' all.'

Hilda and Louie exchanged glances, but did not speak their suspicions.

'I'm off then, see you tonight.' Hilda rushed for the back door, then hesitated in the doorway. 'Would you like me to come and stay with you for a bit, Louie?' she asked, cocking her head of wispy fair hair on one side.

Louie almost jumped at the offer of company, then realised she was being selfish; Hilda was needed at home. Her mother's cough was worsening and the slightest exertion left her breathless. She should never have attempted the walk into Durham and back yesterday, but she had insisted on being there to support her sons.

'I'll be all right, Hildy.' Louie shook her head. 'But ta anyway.'

'I'm going to live with Louie,' Sadie looked up from where she was squatting on the hearth with a book, 'and I'm going to look after the baby when it comes, aren't I, Louie?'

The women turned to the dark girl in surprise. Sadie was almost eleven yet still small for her age. They kept forgetting how she was growing up too, always sensitive to the emotions around her.

'If you want.' Louie smiled back at her. Sadie nodded vigorously and Louie looked questioningly at her mother. Fanny shrugged, smiling wearily, and with no further ceremony, the young girl became Louie's permanent lodger at Gladstone Terrace.

The supercilious grey-haired butler ordered Iris round to the tradesmen's entrance and kept her waiting for over half an hour. Mrs Dennison, the cook, took pity on Raymond, with his cheeky smile, and gave him milk and a homemade biscuit fresh from the oven. Iris was showing him off to the kitchen staff and prompting him through dog and cat noises when the butler returned.

'Mrs Seward-Scott will see you now in the drawing room,' he intoned, stony-faced. Iris smiled with satisfaction at the manservant and followed him, winking at the cook as she went.

She had expected to be impressed by her surroundings, and her amazement soared as she glimpsed the magnificence of the rooms they passed. Her footsteps echoed on the marble floors, setting off a faint tinkling in the heavily drooping chandeliers overhead. Gilt-framed portraits of men in uniforms and hunting red and women in sumptuous gowns covered the vast walls. There was a general air of quiet industry as maids went about their work. Apart from an army of staff, the house appeared to be deserted.

Iris was shown into a room with massive arched windows and a large recessed marble fireplace. It was light and spacious, although full of furniture and precious ornaments. Chairs, both dainty and upright, deep and cushioned, peppered the room. Glass-fronted cabinets arranged with china vases, elaborate clocks and ornately framed mirrors lined the walls, and beautiful carved and inlaid tables were carelessly strewn with books and magazines. This was more spectacular than any film set, Iris thought in wonder. She had never imagined such wealth existed and yet here it was, on her doorstep. It set off a yearning in her stomach that was more potent than desire for a man. Raymond waddled off in delight at the space before him and Iris had to dash to restrain his enquiring fingers.

The door opened behind her. 'Iris.' Eleanor smiled warmly at the girl. 'You don't mind me calling you by your Christian name, do you?' Iris shook her head.

'Please sit down.' With a slim arm, chinking with outlandish wooden bangles, Eleanor indicated a chair. 'I'm so very sorry about Davie.'

Iris gulped and placed herself gingerly on the edge of a low chair with clawed feet, its seat covered in coral and white striped brocade. She felt shabby in her brown and cream outfit, opposite this sophisticated woman in her short skirt and pale-green silk blouse the colour of ducks' eggs. She plonked Raymond on her knee, acutely aware of his tatty appearance, his blue jumper unravelling at the sleeve. It had been a deliberate ploy to leave him dressed as he was, to provoke sympathy from the lady of the big house, but now she wished she had at least cleaned the grime of the hearth from his hands and face. Raymond soon wriggled off her in annoyance.

'Let him go,' Eleanor said easily. 'He wants to explore.'

They sized each other up for a moment, then Eleanor went on, 'You'll take coffee with me? I'm having some sent along. Or would you prefer tea?'

'Coffee would be grand,' Iris assured her hostess quickly. She had no taste for it, but she loved the rich smell. Besides, she was sick of endless cups of strong, sweet tea, served as the Kirkups liked it.

'Ma'am,' Iris began diffidently, 'Mrs Kirkup said you might be able to pay Davie's fine for him. You'll have guessed that's why I'm here.'

'Yes,' Eleanor nodded, 'I'd be happy to pay his fine - and Eb's too. I intend visiting them this afternoon to offer such payment.' Iris's eyes widened in astonishment that this grand lady would condescend to visit them in gaol.

'That's very good of you, ma'am,' she said. 'But won't it be a bit difficult for you -I mean, your husband being the boss, like?'

Eleanor laughed at her perplexed look and gave a dismissive wave of her hand. 'I do what I like with my money and I go where I please. He doesn't keep me in chains, Iris, like some medieval lord. It's never been like that between us.'

Iris grinned, delighted by the woman's frankness. 'Wish it was like that where I come from - pitmen don't allow their lasses any freedom,' she complained, rolling her eyes heavenwards. 'Not that I've got any money to throw about, even if they did.'

'Are things very difficult at the moment?' Eleanor was suddenly full of concern.

'We're getting by,' Iris said with a sigh, 'just.' She twisted a glove in her hands to give a more pathetic effect; she was beginning to enjoy her role as supplicant.

'I'll give you some money before you leave,' Eleanor reassured her.

'Oh, no, ma'am,' Iris protested, 'I didn't mean . . .'

'I insist,' Eleanor interrupted. 'We don't want young Raymond here getting sick, now do we?' She beckoned at the baby to come to her. To Iris's relief, Raymond put up his arms and allowed himself to be helped on to Eleanor's bony silk-stockinged knees, grabbing her pearl necklace with interest. She could not have primed him better herself. Eleanor seemed to enjoy herself for a few minutes, extracting giggles of appreciation from Raymond at the faces she pulled. Iris found herself warming to the coalowner's wife in a way she had not expected.

'Thanks ever so much for your kindness.' Iris smiled coyly at her benefactress and settled back into her chair in sweet anticipation of coffee served in a thin china cup.

Hearing the thick iron door clang behind her, Eleanor was transported back to her brief grim detention in Newcastle's gaol, after her arrest in 1913. It seemed a lifetime ago. Was she really still the same person as that quick-tempered, intense young woman who had felt no qualms at demonstrating against the male politicians who stood in the way of her enfranchisement? With supreme youthful confidence in her cause, she had submitted to arrest and imprisonment and four days of force-feeding, carried through the fear and pain and humiliation by the conviction that the suffragists would win. She would have served out her month's detention had the authorities not learned of her wealthy connections. Thomas Seward-Scott's daughter had been released after six days and the young, impulsive Eleanor had always been certain of their victory. As she stepped timidly after the prison governor, whose cooperation she had enlisted, she wondered at what stage in her life her courage had ebbed away.

She was shown into a narrow, spartan cell with a table and two wooden chairs. Eleanor shivered in the cold gloominess of the room, edging herself into a seat.

'You must keep the interview brief, madam,' the official told her, and withdrew.

Moments later, Eb was led into the cell and told to sit down. A warder stood on guard at the closed door, an unwanted third presence. They eyed each other wordlessly across the table. Eleanor was taken aback by Eb's shaven head and unshaven appearance and the rough prison clothes that denied individuality. His demeanour was, however, strangely cheerful.

'How are you?' Eleanor began a stilted exchange.

'Champion.' Eb smiled in his bashful way.

'And the others?'

'All champion.' Eb scratched his head, betraying his nervousness at her presence.

'I've promised your family that I'd pay your fine - yours and Davie's,' Eleanor told him. 'Davie will be freed tomorrow, but they tell me you won't accept.' She fixed him with an impatient look. 'Why is that?'

Eb locked his calloused fingers together on the table between them.

'I'm not a fighter, El— Mrs Seward-Scott,' he corrected quickly with a glance at the warder. 'But this is a just cause the pit folk are fighting. That incident on the picket line set me thinking.' He dropped his voice to a low rumble. 'I've been standing on the sidelines pretending the strike has nothing to do with me. After all, I said to myself, I haven't worked at the pit full time for nigh on two years. And I hated it any road. Perhaps it would be better if they closed them all down and the lads of the future like Raymond and Jack wouldn't have to do such dangerous work.'

Eleanor watched his face, struck by the brightness in his vivid blue eyes as he spoke his thoughts carefully. 'But men like Sam showed me that was the coward's way out.' He brought his gaze back to hers. 'No matter how dirty or dangerous, it's the only chance of work the majority in Whitton Grange have. It gives a man pride in himself to be able to graft hard, bring bread to the table, bring his family up right.' He paused to gauge her reaction. When Eleanor did not reply, he continued more aggressively. 'But the past weeks have taught me that the bosses hand us nothing on a plate - not even a living wage for a hard day's graft. So we have to fight for our jobs and our wages, it's as simple as that.' He sat back in his chair and added reflectively, 'Remember what they told us at the end of the War - a land fit for heroes? Well, it was pie in the bloody sky.' His soft voice had become hard-edged.

'So why do you have to remain in prison to be a hero?' Eleanor demanded, short on patience.

'One less mouth to feed at home, isn't it?' Eb joked.

Eleanor stood up with an exasperated sigh. 'Perhaps there are people at home who need you.' She looked pleadingly as she stressed her words. This time Eb smiled wistfully.

'A month will pass over quickly enough,' he replied.

'Not for some.' She said everything in her longing look.

Eb stood up too. 'I'm sorry, I don't mean to hurt anyone.' For a moment he looked at her consideringly, then decided to speak his thoughts. 'There are others you could be helping.'

'Who?' Eleanor took a deep breath and tried to think ahead.

'Louie's soup kitchen badly needs funds,' Eb suggested. 'The lock-out could go on all summer. There are dozens of families already hard up, without enough to eat. It's only going to get worse. Talk to our Louie about it.'

'Yes,' Eleanor brightened at the thought of being occupied and having some slim contact with Eb through his sister, 'I'll do that.'

She turned to the warder and indicated she was ready to leave. She did not want to prolong their parting, or betray the aching emptiness she felt at leaving him behind.

'Goodbye then, Ebenezer,' she said stiffly and held out her hand.

'Goodbye, Mrs Seward-Scott,' he replied and briefly took hold of her gloved hand, pressing it encouragingly. Turning, she felt his blue-eyed gaze follow her movements to the door.

Eleanor kept walking, her mind desperately fixing on the future and not on the man she loved, who chose to remain in this dark, depressing place. Once outside she felt oddly exhilarated to see the fresh green on the trees opposite the prison gates and hear the slow bells of the Cathedral across the river, beckoning the faithful to prayer.

Eb's words stayed with her; he had given her something worthwhile to do. With a touch of the vigour of the young suffragette Eleanor, she stepped purposefully towards her car. Eleanor Seward-Scott was no longer going to stand on the sidelines either, she vowed to herself.

Chapter Seventeen

In the middle of June, Margaret Slattery's feckless husband, Joseph Gallon, disappeared from the village. With the spectre of the workhouse hovering at her shoulder, Margaret threw herself on the mercy of the Board of Guardians. They gave her twelve shillings a week on which she and baby Joe had to exist. No longer able to afford the rent on their cottage, Margaret moved in with her sister Minnie in Gladstone Terrace. Minnie dismissed from her mind what would happen once Bomber was released from gaol at the end of July.

'He was a bad'n any road, your Joseph,' Minnie declared, propped up against Louie's front doorpost. They were watching the children playing in the street, twittering like starlings in the evening sun. Sadie and her friend May had taken Minnie's baby Jack for a push in his pram; his cousin Joe was crawling in the dust in pursuit of a battered metal top. 'I always told you, Margaret - that lad was as useless as a bucket full of dross.'

'He never was a bad'n when I married him,' Margaret insisted, tossing wiry black hair out of her eyes. 'He just couldn't see an end to the strike and us getting back to normal. He'll be back to fetch us once he's found work.'

Minnie snorted in disbelief. 'Work? That lad of yours doesn't know the meaning of work - they're all the same those Gallons - bunch of villains. And to think you chucked in a canny job at the doctor's, all for his sake. What thanks has he ever shown you? None - he just runs off and leaves you in the lurch.'

'Well, where's your husband when you need him?' Margaret bristled defensively. 'Durham gaol, isn't he? So don't go saying the Bells are any better than the Gallons. They're stuck up, but no better.'

'Haway,' Louie interrupted before the argument grew more heated, 'it's not worth falling out about. What's happened has happened and none of us can change anything. We just have to get along as best we can.' She sighed heavily.

Minnie looked sharply at her friend, resting on a kitchen chair in the doorway. Her face was tired and drawn, the girlish plumpness gone from her cheeks and jaw. Louie's bobbed fair hair was lank about her ears and her cotton dress, let out at the waist, was frayed and grubby around the collar and cuffs. Minnie suspected that, with Sam away, Louie was scrimping still further. There was no fire on in her kitchen range, no washing hanging out to air this Monday and no hot meal to return to after working all day at the relief centre.

'You're working too hard,' Minnie told her. 'It's time you had a day off.'

'I'm all right,' Louie answered fretfully. 'Don't fuss.'

'No, Minnie's right.' Margaret quickly dropped the quarrel with her sister. 'You put your feet up tomorrow; we can manage at the chapel without you for a couple of days.'

'But I'm needed,' Louie objected half-heartedly, feeling the fatigue holding her down in her chair like a vice.

'Your first concern is to your baby,' Minnie reminded her. 'It's going to be born serving soup if you don't rest when you can.'

'Aye,' Margaret smiled, 'there are plenty others who can help. You've done enough these past weeks.'

To their surprise, their friend did not protest further. When Sadie and May returned, the sisters plonked Joe into the pram beside a sleeping Jack and wandered off down the street, chatting to neighbours as they made for home. Louie, reluctant to go inside, sat on in the tranquil evening while Sadie contented herself with reading a library book on the step.

It was almost a relief for Louie to be told what to do. Since Sam had been imprisoned she had spent every waking hour working at the centre, cooking and serving, or else begging vegetables from around the houses to help towards the free meals. It helped her to blank out her fearful thoughts of the future and the loneliness she felt without Sam. He had been in Durham gaol for nearly a month now and she had been glad of Sadie's company around the place.

Looking at the dark head of curls bent studiously over her book, Louie smiled to herself. Her young cousin was a sensitive and affectionate companion, growing in confidence and 'bright as a button', as her mother said. Miss Joice had persuaded Jacob and Fanny to allow Sadie to sit the scholarship for the grammar school in Durham. But even if she passed, it was an unattainable prize for Sadie; they could never afford to send her there now that the family had hardly enough to live on. When Hilda had been denied the chance of secondary schooling, Louie had been in agreement. After all, what was the use of all that learning to a pitman's wife? She had thought Hilda strange for wanting to cram her head full of knowledge about foreign countries and long-winded books. But now Louie was not so sure. Perhaps an education for a lass was a good thing. The more she got to know Eleanor Seward-Scott, the more she grudgingly admired the woman, and she was certainly a lady with an education.

Sadie was bright and inquisitive in the way Hilda had been at her age, and Louie felt proud that she had had a large part in nurturing her orphaned cousin. It filled her with sadness that Sadie might have to go into service too. What future was there in Whitton Grange for a young girl? Marry a pitman and face a life of poverty, or be sent far away to skivvy for some rich strangers in the south of England; that was the drab choice. Louie was coming round to the opinion that an education might lift a lass out of such a restricted future.

Louie sighed and mentally scolded herself for such depressing thoughts. Was she not happy enough being married to Sam? It was just the strain of their separation and getting into debt that was colouring her life grey. Somehow they would all get through these bad times; there would be happiness and contentment again, she convinced herself.

The noisy chug of a motor car disturbed her brooding, as a neat green vehicle hove into view round the corner, sending up smoke signals of dust to announce its arrival. As it bounced over the uneven ground Louie recognised it immediately as Eleanor's. Drawn to its shiny grandeur, the children still out playing gathered about the car in excitement, bold fingers reaching out to touch its polished flanks as it parked outside Louie's door.

Louie pulled herself to her feet, proud that such a fuss was going on outside her house and knowing how the neighbours looked on in curiosity. Since the lady at The Grange had shown herself their friend and been active in raising money for the relief of the villagers, suspicion towards Eleanor had ebbed. In open defiance of her husband, she had organised a bazaar at St Cuthbert's to raise funds to feed the children, and Louie knew she had renewed contact with her more radical acquaintances from her suffragette days, to press them to make donations to ease the growing hardship in the valley.

'Good evening, Louie.' Eleanor smiled as she stepped out of the car.

'Evening, Mrs Reginald,' Louie replied, and then felt a flush of panic to think how unwelcoming her home was. There was no fire in the grate or candles to light up the shadowed room. She had nothing to offer Eleanor to eat except some stale bread and a cup of water. Sadie was being fed at the centre now and Louie had given her the last scrapings of jam for tea. She stood unsure in her doorway, and Eleanor guessed her concern.

'I'm sorry to call so late, Louie,' she apologised. 'I won't stay more than a few minutes, I promise. I know you and Sadie will be wanting to retire.' Sadie looked up shyly from her book and moved away from the step. She was still in awe of this formidable lady from the big house at the top of the hill.

'Come in.' Louie beckoned to her visitor. 'I'm sorry I haven't got the kettle on just now.'

'Please don't apologise,' Eleanor answered hastily, feeling embarrassed at Louie's discomfort. 'I really don't need any refreshment - I've just had dinner with friends in Durham.' She went on hastily, guilty at the thought of the leisurely meal she had enjoyed at one of the university colleges. 'I just came with some good news.'

'Oh?' Louie looked at her hopefully. 'We can certainly do with some.' She led Eleanor into her house and they sat on the two horsehair-stuffed chairs that Liza Ritson had given them when her aunt had died earlier in the year. Eleanor ignored the prickling discomfort of the seat against her thin satin dress and leaned forward in the shadows.

'You remember I said I'd approach a London branch of the Women's Guild of Service?' Louie nodded. 'Well, I've had a reply from the secretary of an East End branch. They've agreed to the idea of adopting Whitton Grange.'

Louie's spirits rose. 'So what does that mean, exactly?'

'Well,' Eleanor went on eagerly, 'they're collecting clothes which they'll send on to your Distress Committee - and they've sent an immediate donation of ten pounds to buy food for your kitchen.' Louie clapped her hands together in amazement.

'Ten pounds just like that,' she gasped. 'We could buy some meat - give the bairns a proper meal for once.'

'I'll ask them for shoes and boots too, if they can spare them.' Eleanor was heartened to see Louie's pale face grow animated. 'They may not be needed now, but if the dispute - God forbid - drags on into the autumn they'll come in handy.'

'Aye,' Louie agreed, thinking how John and Davie had taken Sadie out scouring the rail tracks for old tyres with which to mend the men's boots.

'I was wondering, Louie, what do you say to giving the Guild something to raffle?' Eleanor asked. 'Something particular to a mining village that'll be a bit of a novelty.'

Louie screwed her face up in thought. 'I can't think we've got much to give,' she answered doubtfully. Then a thought struck her. 'What about a pitman's lamp? I don't suppose those Londoners have seen one.'

'That's a marvellous idea,' Eleanor replied. 'If you can get hold of one for me, I'll send it on. And if there's anything else I can do, you'll let me know, won't you?' She stood up, not wanting to impose on the tired young woman who, she noticed, was attempting to stifle a yawn. 'I thought Sadie might like these.' She pushed a package across the kitchen table. 'Just a few treats.'

'Thank you, Mrs Reginald,' Louie said gratefully, leaving the packet unopened until her visitor went. 'You shouldn't have bothered.' From the inviting smell, Louie could tell the contents were home-baked.

'It's not much.' Eleanor waved a hand. 'I'd like to give you more, but . . .' She did not know how tactfully to explain that she did not want to tread on Louie's pride in coping without charity.

'You've given us more than enough,' Louie answered stiffly.

'Are your family keeping well?' Eleanor changed the subject as they walked to the open door.

'Well enough, thank you,' Louie answered. 'Davie's hoping to get work up on Stand High Farm picking veg - my Auntie Eva and Uncle Jack live up there. Iris doesn't want him to go' - suddenly Louie found herself unburdening to the older woman - 'thinks he might run off like Margaret's husband. Our Davie's not like that, of course, but there's no use telling that to Iris.'

'She's bound to be concerned for Raymond's sake,' Eleanor commented, 'though I'm sure she's worrying needlessly.' She did not add that perhaps Iris had cause for alarm, given Davie's happy-go-lucky nature.

'Well, anyway,' Louie continued, 'John's working the allotment while Eb's away, and my father helps out occasionally too.'

'You'll be looking forward to seeing your brother soon.' Eleanor breathed in the night air, the ubiquitous whiff of coal fires less pronounced than usual.

'Aye,' Louie smiled, 'Eb'll be out next week.' She glanced at Eleanor's fine-boned face. Was it just the reflection of the dying sun that gave it a certain tinge? 'You must care about him too, Mrs Reginald, what with you visiting him in gaol and that.' Louie did not know where she got the nerve to make such an impertinent remark. Perhaps it was because they were standing on the sandstone doorstep together like equals, chatting as friends.

Eleanor shot her a look, momentarily taken aback, then softly she answered, 'I do care about your brother, Louie.'

The words hung like a spell between them, bewitching them into silence. Eleanor stared out at the rooftops across the street and the ranks of terraced houses that marched away into the sunset. She wondered why she had opened her heart to this young girl from the pit village. Was she very foolish to do so? She did not want to embarrass Eb by her confession, but she could not have lied to Louie.

'You won't do anything to hurt him, miss, will you?' Louie whispered her fear. 'I know it's not my place to say, but our Eb - well - he sometimes takes strange notions - doesn't know his place. He thinks he's a bit different from the rest of us - I think it was something to do with being away in the War, like. He's very deep, our Eb, keeps his feelings hidden, but - well -I know he has a high regard for you, Mrs Reginald. And I don't want to see him hurt; I just thought I'd mention it, seeing how you were being frank with me.' Louie held her breath, hoping she had not gone too far.

Eleanor was mortified by Louie's forthright words. The girl had no right to speak to her like that. It was a matter between herself and Eb. Yet nagging at the back of her mind was the guilty thought that Louie was right; even in her position of power she could offer Eb nothing but frustration and heartache. But she could not bear the truth.

'I merely care about him as a friend,' Eleanor turned to face the other woman and put a briskness into her voice, 'as I care for all your family. It's a part of my duty, that's all; I thought you understood our relationship, Louie. As for Eb, he is man enough to look after himself. He has nothing to fear from me.'

Louie blushed at the reproof. 'No, of course not, miss.' She put an arm about Sadie who was clamped around her waist, turning perplexed dark eyes on each of them in turn. Louie hoped the girl did not understand their discussion.

'I'll call again next week for the lamp.' Eleanor opened her car door. The street was almost deserted now, apart from two boys squatting in the road chatting about motor cars, waiting to see the green vehicle start up and roar away.

'Good night, Mrs Reginald.' Louie waved a hand, and Sadie echoed her farewell. Eleanor returned the gesture and slammed the door shut. With a noisy gurgle from the engine, the car sparked into life and trundled away down the narrow lane.

'Is Miss Eleanor in love with our Eb?' Sadie startled Louie with her question.

'What on earth makes you think that?' her cousin replied sharply.

'I think she is,' Sadie pronounced with a serious nod of her head. 'She goes all funny when she talks about him. And I saw them together in the woods last Christmas, remember?'

'What do you know about such things?' Louie said shortly. 'You mustn't go spreading any rumours, mind. Do you hear me, Sadie?' Louie's look was stern. Sadie glared back crossly at Louie, annoyed at being treated like a child. She was not the bairn they all thought she was and she knew they had been arguing over Eb, not so much in the words said, but in the way they had been spoken.

'I'll not say.' Sadie stuck her nose in the air, haughtily disengaging herself and pushing her way inside. Louie stood looking after her, struck once more by the proof that her young cousin was growing up fast in these hard times.

Eb came home the following week, cheerful and fit, though he had lost his sun-bleached appearance and his shaven head marked him out from the other men. He brought news that Sam and Bomber were in good heart and counting off the days until their release. Eb went straight back to the allotment, reasserting his authority over the small patch of ground, and set to his gardening with renewed vigour. John handed back the job without any protest, though he was less enthusiastic about giving up the privilege of tending the Joices' garden, for at Greenbrae he was pressed to eat dainty sandwiches and homemade scones, a sight that had long since disap-peared from the Kirkup table. But a potential clash between the brothers was averted by the offer of work up on Stand High Farm. Davie and John set off early on a sunny Monday morning to walk the ten miles to the isolated farm up the valley where they were to help pick vegetables.

Louie, meanwhile, continued her work for the Distress Committee, though she found herself slowing down and increasingly exhausted by the weight she carried in her belly. She became used to sudden palpitations and hot flushes that left her breathless, heart hammering as if it would burst from her chest. She chided herself, telling herself she was young and strong, and did her best not to let the others notice her discomfort.

With early July came the ominous news that Baldwin's Government had passed a bill in Parliament allowing the raising of their working hours to eight hours a day. It was a blow to the pitmen, a sign that they were losing ground to the coal owners and that sympathy for their plight was waning. They braced themselves for the next development.

A few days later, Eb went round to Louie's house on a hot Friday afternoon, bringing a head of lettuce and some runner beans for her tea. The small room in Gladstone Terrace was stiflingly hot, even though the front door was ajar to encourage a draught of air. Louie sat awkwardly in a chair by the back door fanning herself with one of Sadie's library books. Her face was flushed and her cotton dress clung damply around her armpits and chest. She could feel the sweat trickling down between her full breasts like a leaky tap.

'Have you seen the notices on the pit gates?' she asked her brother listlessly, too weak to rise from her stupor.

'No, I've just come from the allotment,' Eb called over his shoulder from the small scullery, where he was helping himself to a cup of water. A large fly buzzed drowsily at the disturbance and then flew recklessly into the dangling fly paper, its protest abruptly cut short. Eb downed the water and poured himself another cupful from the jug. 'What's the news?'

'They're going to try and open the pit again,' Louie told him. 'They're offering new contracts - eight-hour day for less wages.'

'Bastards,' Eb muttered, his jaw clenching in anger. 'No one will go back on such terms - they must think we're daft.'

'The notice says they'll guarantee police protection for anyone that wants to return,' Louie answered, a worried frown hovering over her blue eyes. 'There are those desperate enough to think about going back cap in hand. I see them every day at the soup kitchen.'

'Don't worry yourself, Louie,' Eb cajoled his sister. 'The strike here is solid. There's one thing the hewers won't accept and that's an eight-hour day. We fought long and hard for the six-and-a-half-hour shift - it's enough when a man's sweating his guts out in that hole. They can't expect us to work longer for less pay - it's not human.'

But Louie could not shake off the feeling of dread that clutched the back of her neck and left her tense and anxious.

'I wish Sam were here.' She leaned back in her chair and closed her eyes, trying to fight down her fear.

'He will be soon.' Eb looked at his sister in concern. He took hold of her damp hands and squeezed them. 'Why don't you come over to Mam's tonight, eh? You and Sadie. We'll have a singsong round the piano, we haven't done that for ages. Iris has a face as long as a horse with Davie away - you could cheer each other up.'

Louie opened her eyes and smiled fondly at her eldest brother. At times, when he barricaded himself into some inner world and kept them all out, she could not guess his thoughts. But when her spirits were really low, no one could comfort her as Eb could; he seemed to have a gift for saying the right thing at the right time, or just staying quiet when words would only jar.

'I'd like that,' she answered.

A thumping on the front door made her turn round in fright. A figure cast a shadow into the room.

'I'll go.' Eb jumped up immediately. He crossed the room in three strides and pulled open the door. The under-manager, Naylor, was standing there grim-faced, with two other men Eb did not recognise. The official was a short man with thinning brown hair and a blue scar on his forehead that told of his past service underground . Eb knew him for an aggressive, short-tempered man who had worked hard to attain his position of authority at the pit.

'Is Mrs Ritson at home?' he demanded.

'Aye, what do you want with her?' Eb blocked his way.

'I'll speak with her in person,' Naylor ordered.

'What is it, Eb?' Louie rose from her chair and peered past him at the men in her doorway.

'I'm sorry, Mrs Ritson,' Naylor entered and addressed her sternly, 'but I'm giving you notice to quit number sixteen Gladstone Terrace.'

'What?' Louie gasped in disbelief.

'What do you mean?' Eb demanded incredulously.

'The colliery management are repossessing this dwelling. We're giving you three days' notice. Mrs Ritson must be out by Monday.' Louie stood staring at the manager, stunned by his harsh words. She gripped the back of her chair for support.

Eb took a step towards Naylor and clenched his fists threateningly. 'You'd throw a pregnant woman out onto the street?' He shook with rage. 'Have you no shame?'

'We're not throwing anyone out - yet.' Naylor stood his ground. 'The plain fact is Sam Ritson is no longer a desirable tenant - he's a common criminal and troublemaker who no longer works for us, and we don't want his sort at the pit. We don't have anything against Mrs Ritson personally. We know she's from a good family.'

'You can't chuck me out,' Louie whispered, the panic rising inside her at the thought of being made homeless. 'This is our house. It's not much, but it's ours.' She felt hot tears of anger stinging her eyes. 'And the Ritsons are just as decent as the next folk, my Sam included. Are you going to throw the whole of Whitton Grange out on its ear, Mr Naylor? Because Sam's done no more than any self-respecting pitman would do.'

'Sam Ritson has a criminal record,' Naylor repeated defensively, unnerved by the vulnerable look on Louie's face. He hadn't been aware of quite how pregnant the woman was. He continued, 'Besides, the house will be needed by someone who wishes to work.'

'Do you think anyone in the village would see Sam and Louie made homeless and then step in and take Sam's job as well?' Eb asked with scorn.

'Maybe not,' Naylor said coldly, 'but we anticipate labour coming to the pits from elsewhere - men who are not work-shy. We shall accommodate them by any means possible. Now I'm just doing my job - and I'm giving Mrs Ritson plenty of warning.'

'You bastard!' Eb went at him with a raised fist, but one of the other men stepped in and grabbed his arm, twisting it viciously.

'Leave him alone!' Louie screamed, her pulse hammering in her ears like a forge iron. 'Just get out of my house, the lot of you!' The official and his henchmen retreated quickly from the distraught woman, pushing aside children who had gathered in the street at the sound of raised voices.

Louie felt a wave of nausea engulf her body, leaving her giddy. 'Eb, I feel faint.' She reached out for him, and as she toppled forward, her brother ran to catch her. She doubled up as a spasm of pain twisted her insides. Clutching her stomach, Louie allowed Eb to lead her to the bed.

She lay down as Eb went to fetch her a drink of water and felt another cramp knot in her belly. He came back with a damp flannel and pressed it to her brow, then gently tilted her head so she could sip the tepid water. Louie sank back, her head swimming and heart pounding uncomfortably.

'You just rest for a minute,' Eb said with concern, continuing to stroke her forehead with the cloth. Louie closed her eyes and tried to calm herself, pretending that she was beginning to feel better, that the pain was easing off.

Half an hour later she sat up, her face contorted as her body was gripped by another contraction. 'Go and get Mam,' Louie whispered to her brother, 'please, go and get Mam.'

Eb found Sadie in the street and told her to watch by Louie's bedside while he went for his mother. The girl ran in and saw with fright how her cousin panted on the bed and cried out in pain. She wanted to turn and run, but forced herself to hold Louie's hand. She gripped it fiercely, as if by doing so she could prevent her cousin from slipping into unconsciousness.

When Fanny arrived, Sadie's fear mounted at her aunt's troubled face. She peered at Louie's sobbing, contorted visage and felt her burning head.

'I want you to run over to Greenbrae and ask Dr Joice to come,' Fanny instructed Sadie.

Sadie gulped. 'Is Louie going to die?'

'Of course not,' the older woman replied sharply, glancing fearfully at Louie, thankful that she appeared not to have heard. 'Now just do as I say. Quickly!'

Sadie ran blindly for the dene and the houses on the far side, tears blurring her vision. She repeated over and over again that Louie was not going to die, as if the words could act as a charm to protect her favourite cousin. Dr Joice was not at home. A bewildered Isobel Joice tried to calm the distraught girl long enough for her to deliver her message. She called for Hilda, who managed to comprehend that it was Louie who needed the doctor's attention.

'He's over at the Robsons' on Durham Road,' Hilda told Isobel, who had been out all day. 'One of the bairns has whooping cough.'

'Take my bicycle, Hilda,' Isobel determined swiftly. 'Tell Dr Joice to go straight to Gladstone Terrace when he's finished his call.'

'Thanks, miss,' Hilda answered gratefully and tore at her apron, discarding it thoughtlessly on a hall chair.

'You have a glass of milk, Sadie,' her teacher took her by the hand, 'and when you've got your breath back you can run home and tell your aunt that the doctor's on his way.' The girl allowed herself to be led into the large, airy kitchen and took the refreshment without protest.

Evening drew on and Louie was aware of her mother's quiet presence hovering by her bedside. They both knew without speaking that she had gone into labour and the baby was coming early, too early. Louie tried to co-operate with her mother's gentle encouragement, but she felt weak and feverish and could not control her ragged breathing.

Later, she was aware of Hilda being in the room and wondered vaguely where Sadie could be. At some time during the evening, Dr Joice appeared at her bedside and she felt her unspoken fears for the baby intensify. He tried to reassure her in his kindly fashion, but an air of foreboding hung in the sweltering room and none of the usual expectant chatter lightened the heavy silence to ease her worry.

When it grew dark, Dr Joice ordered a lamp to be fetched from the neighbours next door, an elderly couple called Stephenson. Old man Stephenson, whose allotment adjoined Eb's, brought a pail of hot water which his wife had boiled up on their stove. Word leaked anxiously down the street that Louie's baby was on its way. Once Minnie heard, she left Jack sleeping in his cot and came to help.

'Everything'll be fine,' she told her friend with false brightness and took a spell at wiping her brow.

At two in the morning, Louie gave birth to a tiny girl.

'Let me see her,' Louie panted, trying to sit up. 'Is she all right?'

There was a moment of bustling and hushed words between the doctor and Fanny. The baby was wrapped in a sheet and taken over to the kitchen table. The doctor appeared to be examining the bundle. There was no sound. Still Louie waited to hold her daughter.

'What's wrong?' she whispered, the taste in her dry mouth bitter.

'Best not to see it now,' her mother answered inexplicably.

Dr Joice stepped back to the bed and leaned over Louie. 'I'm very sorry, my dear, the baby's stillborn. It came before its time.'

Louie lay back, her closed eyes flooding with scalding tears, disbelief fighting with shock. The unthinkable had happened; her baby had died before it was born. What a cruel paradox.

'I want to see her.' Louie struggled to make herself coherent. Fanny looked uncertainly at the doctor. He seemed at a loss as to what to advise. Minnie stepped forward, picked up the lifeless bundle from the kitchen table and took it to her friend. Louie raised herself up and, with Minnie's help, took the baby awkwardly in her arms.

She saw a small, shiny face with perfectly formed lips and nose, the eyes closed in peaceful repose, as if the baby merely slept. This was the moment she had longed for and, now that it had come, she was overwhelmed with grief that these innocent eyes would never open.

'My bonny lass,' Louie whispered and, bending, kissed her baby goodbye. 'Oh, my bonny, bonny lass.'

Chapter Eighteen

Louie refused to be moved from her home the next day, despite the urgings of her parents and Dr Joice. She said she would remain in her house until the bailiffs came and threw her on to the street. Only Hilda seemed to understand her desire to hold on to the crude roomful of possessions that was her home; the place where she had been happy with Sam, where her daughter had been conceived and born. But no one else wanted to mention the baby in her presence; she had been removed swiftly while Louie was still in a daze of exhaustion, and never referred to again, as if the small scrap of humanity had never been.

At dawn, Eb took the baby away wrapped in a strip of old sheet and went alone to the allotment. Finding a discarded wooden box, he laid the bundle in its makeshift coffin and trudged on up the hill. Against the wishes of the doctor and his mother, Eb was determined to bury the babe himself. He knew if Louie had been well enough to choose, this was what she would have wished.

'She'll only dwell on it.' Fanny had criticised his decision. 'It's best that she tries to forget.' Yet Eb had resisted their warnings, not knowing why it mattered to him so much.

He chose a sheltered spot beside a wall at the top of the Common and began the grim task of carving a miniature grave in the springy turf. He hurried to complete the distasteful job, lowering in the box without ceremony and shovelling the earth back into place. He did not like to think about the contents of the grave as anything he should care about, let alone a part of his own family. He had not even set eyes on Louie's baby.

But as the sun rose higher and streamed into the valley from the east, and the countryside about came awake, Eb was filled with regret for the niece he would never know. Silently, he crouched over the tiny mound of fresh earth for several minutes and prayed for the soul of the dead babe. He prayed for Louie and Sam. Then, with a heavy heart, he turned for home.

Hilda stayed with Louie over the weekend, relieved of her duties from Greenbrae, and Eb brought cinders round from Hawthorn Street to coax the stove into life once more. 'He went and buried the baby up on the Common,' Hilda told her sister, when Eb had gone. 'He said he'd make a cross to mark the place.'

Louie's eyes filled with tears; her brother had never said anything to her and she was overwhelmed by his caring action. Eb had saved her baby from being tossed into an unmarked grave on the edge of the cemetery. She would be able to visit the spot where her baby rested.

'That's good,' she whispered and leaned back on her pillow.

'What was she to be called?' Hilda asked suddenly. Louie looked at her in surprise.

'We hadn't decided.'

'She ought to have a name, Louie,' Hilda insisted.

'Aye.' Louie nodded reflectively. 'I'll give her my name, Louisa. At least I can give her that.'

Her sister smiled approvingly. 'That's nice.'

Louie watched Hilda carry on sewing, unable to express the gratitude she felt towards her thoughtful sister. She had never felt closer to Hilda than at that moment.

'Will you tell Sam what's happened before he gets out?' Hilda asked, glancing up. Louie shook her head weakly.

'He'll learn soon enough,' she answered, and closed her eyes to sleep.

On the Sunday afternoon, Mrs Ritson and her daughters Bel and Mary called to see Louie. Her mother-in-law's ample figure filled the brown horsehair chair as she sniffed into her handkerchief and commiserated.

'I'm that disappointed, Louie,' she told the young woman lying fully dressed on the high bed. 'I was so looking forward—' She broke off and blew her nose vigorously.

'Don't, Mam.' Bel put a hand on her mother's shoulder. She smiled awkwardly at Louie. 'There'll be others, Louie. You'll have better luck next time. This one was just not meant to be. Just think of Johnny's sister - she lost her first baby and now she's got two healthy bairns.'

Louie tried to smile back, but Bel's reassurances stabbed her like clippy hooks. She could not imagine a time when this aching void inside her would close up, or when she would be able to hear the sound of a small child again without it tearing at her heart. Moreover, it pained her to think her daughter would never feel the warmth of Mrs Ritson's bosom or bask in her doting words and cuddles. She would have been such a wonderful grandmother to Louisa.

Hilda moved between them. 'Our Louie's still very tired.' She smiled apologetically at the Ritson women. 'I think we should let her rest now, don't you?'

'Of course.' Mrs Ritson looked at her daughter-in-law with concern, then heaved herself up.

At that moment, Minnie and Margaret came clattering in the back door with their young offspring. Louie froze as she caught sight of baby Joe's round, sun-kissed face and Jack's fluffy red hair.

'We've come to cheer you up,' Minnie called breezily and then stopped at the sight of the Ritson women. 'Oh, I didn't realise you had company.'

'We're just going.' Mrs Ritson sniffed disapprovingly. 'Louie doesn't want visitors just now - especially young ones,' she added pointedly.

'Will you be moving back to Hawthorn Street tomorrow?' Mary asked quickly, having sat mutely for the whole of the visit. 'I think it's a scandal taking your house off you after all that's happened; it's unchristian.'

'I suppose so,' Louie answered tensely, trying not to look at the babies clamped to their mothers' hips. 'Mam said Sam and I could sleep in the kitchen once he returns.'

'You know you could come and stay with us,' Mrs Ritson offered. 'We've got more room than your parents - and there's less of us than all you Kirkups. I think you should get away from this bad street - come and live with us until Sam finds you somewhere else. Don't you agree, Bel?'

'Aye,' Bel smiled, 'that would be grand, and Betty would love it. She's wanting to see you, but I didn't think . . .' Her voice trailed off as she looked uncomfortably at her sister-in-law.

Louie glanced at Hilda for help, unable to argue against the might of the Ritsons. All she knew was that she could not bear to live at such close quarters with baby Betty, a constant reminder of the daughter she could not have. Neither would she be able to revel in their everyday conversations about other people's babies any more; she was excluded from them as if from a club to which she had been denied membership. How could she begin to explain her sensitivity to careless talk? They could not guess at her private agony.

'That's kind of you to offer, Mrs Ritson,' Hilda intervened, 'but it's all been arranged. I'm to move into the servant's room at Greenbrae - and John and Davie are away on the farm just now - so it won't be such a tight squeeze.'

'Very well.' Sam's mother sounded dubious. 'We'll call again soon at your mother's house, Louie,' she assured the girl. Louie summoned up a smile and a croaky 'thank you'.

Mrs Ritson squeezed past the Slattery girls as if they carried something contagious and beckoned her daughters after her. Jack had started to cry fretfully and Minnie was bouncing him up and down to distract him.

'Perhaps we should call in later?' Margaret suggested, aware of Louie's strained expression.

'Aye,' Hilda agreed swiftly, 'Louie needs to sleep now.'

'Ta-ra then, Louie,' Minnie said uncertainly. Louie could hardly reply.

Hilda bustled them out of the room after the Ritsons.

When they had gone Louie burst into uncontrollable tears. Hilda went to her sister and put her arms around her comfortingly and they clung together wordlessly as Louie's grief rang round the small room.

Eb decided to forgo caution and after morning chapel went to seek the help of Isobel Joice.

'I need to speak with Mrs Seward-Scott,' he told her, unable to meet the questioning gaze of the schoolteacher's hazel eyes. 'It's about Louie. The pit management have told her to clear out by tomorrow. And after all she's been through - it's not right. I know she would rather stay in Gladstone Terrace than have to move back in with the family. It's a matter of pride.'

'Yes, of course.' Isobel spoke with quiet concern, horrified at the callousness of the impending eviction. 'I'll get a message to Eleanor. Would you like to meet her here?'

Eb glanced at her gratefully and scratched his head. 'That would be grand.'

Eleanor came the moment she received the message. In the quiet of the doctor's garden, she listened to Eb's story.

'Of course something must be done,' she said at last, snapping off a long-stemmed marguerite in her anger. They stood under the far garden wall, hidden from the house by trailing roses in full bloom around the weathered pergola. 'I had no idea this was going to happen. It's outrageous!'

'Do you think you can stop them?' Eb asked hopefully.

Eleanor looked uncertain. 'I have little influence with my husband now, Eb.' She fixed him with her dark eyes. 'He is furious at what he calls my interfering in his business matters. Reginald won't easily forgive me for helping the Distress Committee - he sees it as siding with the enemy.'

'I'm sorry if things are difficult for you,' Eb replied in a low voice.

'Oh, I don't care what Reginald thinks of me any more,' Eleanor answered stoutly. 'I'm just afraid it weakens my hand when it comes to asking him favours.'

Eb looked glum. 'I don't want you begging to that man on our behalf,' he said with annoyance, 'and I don't want you belittling yourself to him either. I hate the way he treats you.'

Eleanor smiled suddenly and slipped an arm through his. 'That's the first time I've heard you sound jealous over me,' she teased. 'I do believe you care for me after all, Eb Kirkup.' He turned and looked into her eyes.

'Aye, I do care for you,' he mumbled almost incoherently. 'I thought of little else while I was stuck in Durham gaol.' She reached up to him and kissed him on the lips. His arms went around her in an answering embrace. It was the first time they had been intimate since his release from prison, and they kissed each other with a fierce hunger.

Finally pulling apart, Eleanor whispered hoarsely, 'I wish we could have more than just these stolen moments, Eb.' He sighed in reply but said nothing, resting his chin on her soft, short hair. Their arms remained linked about each other, reluctant to relinquish possession.

'Will you go and visit Louie?' he asked her, changing the subject. 'She's so unhappy; it might take her mind off her sorrow to see you. Even if you can't do anything about the house, go and see her,' he urged. Eleanor was touched by his belief that her friendship meant that much to his sister.

'Of course I will,' Eleanor promised him, 'but first I must tackle Reginald.'

It was late on the Sunday evening before Reginald returned from his weekend at Waterloo Bridge. Eleanor waited up for him in the drawing room after her father had retired to bed. By the time her husband had poured himself a nightcap, she had decided what to say.

Stubbing out a scented cigarette, Eleanor turned to confront him. She wore an evening dress of jade and black, the vast gilded mirror above the fireplace reflecting her neat black bob of hair and the bandeau of green satin studded with jet. Around her neck she deliberately wore the Seward family emeralds in their gold setting; she wanted Reginald to be aware of the gesture.

'I heard today that Louie Ritson is to be evicted from her home tomorrow.' Eleanor stared at him frostily. 'Is this true, Reginald?'

He took a gulp of his whisky and crossed his legs in the large armchair. 'I really wouldn't know about such everyday details. It's something Hopkinson never bothers me with.'

'Don't treat me like an idiot, Reggie,' she retorted. 'The order to evict Sam Ritson came from you, didn't it? You've decided to persecute the man, and his wife - my friend - is to be made to suffer too.' Reginald peered into his glass of golden liquid and did not reply. Eleanor's indignation rose. 'Have you any idea how much she has already suffered, Reggie? Did you know that your henchmen's threats precipitated Louie going into labour? Her baby was stillborn just hours after their visit.'

Reginald looked at her in shock. He had forgotten that Ritson's wife was with child. And this sudden attack from his wife after weeks of bored indifference made him nervous. He was overawed by Eleanor's cold beauty in her shimmering black and green attire.

'I'm very sorry to hear it,' Reginald went on the defensive, 'but this strike has forced us to make some hard decisions. It's most unfortunate that Louisa Kirkup is caught up in the middle of this dispute with Ritson. But I tell you, my dear, he is the author of his own misfortune - the man thinks he is above the law in his vendetta against the coalowners.'

'And you've acted totally within the law, haven't you?' Eleanor mocked. 'Some people say you orchestrated that picket violence in order to throw men like Sam Ritson behind bars.'

'You shouldn't listen to such damn lies about your own husband,' Reginald reproved, feeling on safer ground. 'Can I not expect an ounce of loyalty from you, Eleanor?' He sounded hurt.

'This is what you can expect from me, Reginald.' She came towards him, her black eyes fierce with resolution, and her voice steady. 'You will tell Hopkinson and his men that the Ritsons will not be evicted, nor any of the other families whose men have been in prison. Or you can expect me to denounce you as the adulterer that you are.'

155

'How dare you!' Reginald gasped in genuine shock, his handsome face visibly paling at her threat.

'Oh, I dare, Reginald.' Eleanor did not take her eyes from his face. 'Think what the papers will make of such a scandal - a sticky divorce case, reporters flocking to The Grange, to Waterloo Bridge - how utterly shocking for you and your dear friends the Fishers. Because, make no mistake, if you continue to hound the Ritsons I will divorce you, Reggie. And remember, it is through me that you will inherit The Grange and my father's business interests. The law that you so eagerly uphold now protects my inheritance, even though I'm a mere woman.' She smiled at him with unconcealed disdain. 'So if I decide to divorce you for adultery, Reginald, you will lose everything - except the delightful Miss Fisher - though I suspect, if put to the test, your heart is really wedded to The Grange and its money.'

'You bitch,' Reginald cursed her as the seriousness of her words overtook his astonishment. How could she risk her own reputation for these brutish miners and their families? He was astounded by her reckless courage; it was a side of Eleanor he had not seen for years. She had succeeded in terrifying him with her vision of a life without The Grange. This was as much his home as hers; he had grown to manhood here and put all his energies into running its estates well. She would never take it from him; he would have to see to that. For the moment, though, his wife had snatched a surprise victory.

'I shall see Hopkinson first thing tomorrow,' Reginald grudgingly agreed, standing up and draining his drink quickly. He wanted to escape from her triumphant face, the haughty, sculptured Seward features that reminded him he would only ever be a lowly Scott in her eyes. 'Given the unfortunate turn of events at Gladstone Terrace, I shall recommend that Louisa Ritson be allowed to remain there for the foreseeable future.'

'Good,' Eleanor answered, picking up her cigarette case and tapping a Turkish cigarette on the silver lid. Reginald strode from the room without another word and Eleanor sank into the flowered sofa, her heart still pounding nervously. She pulled on her cigarette until she felt calmer. The gold-encased clock on the mantelpiece struck twelve. Eleanor sighed with relief; she had saved Louie from her humiliation just in time. More soberingly, she realised she had made a lifelong enemy of Reginald. Once he might have turned a blind eye to her obsession with 'causes', but now he would never forgive her for threatening to snatch away what he held most dear, The Grange. As she sat in the quiet of the drawing room with only the rhythmic ticking of clocks to keep her company, Eleanor wondered why it was she had been prepared to gamble away her marriage and the security of the privileged society in which she moved, all for the sake of Red Sam Ritson and his young wife.

Reginald kept his word and the following morning instructed his agent to forbid the management to go ahead with their eviction. Until further notice they were to cancel the other planned repossessions too. The coalowner also set Hopkinson on another task; he was to have Eleanor watched and the people she met noted. It was just a hunch, but something Beatrice had once let slip, about Eleanor acting like a lovesick girl, came back to him. He doubted his wife had a lover, but it might be useful to discover with whom she did spend so much of her time mysteriously absent from the house. With that done, he set his mind to the problem of pressing his miners back to work, and the opening of the pits at Whitton Grange.

Louie was heartened by the sudden change in the decision of the pit management to oust her from her home. 'Perhaps there's a peck of goodness in that Naylor after all,' she suggested to Eb when he came to tell her the news.

'Maybes,' Eb answered evasively, thinking it best not to tell his sister of Eleanor's certain intervention in the matter. He wanted to protect Eleanor as much as possible from being the source of village gossip.

'At least Sam can come home to his rightful place,' Louie smiled wanly, 'and not to sharing a crowded house with his in-laws.'

'Aye,' Eb grinned. 'Imagine how pleased Sam would have been celebrating his return in lemonade.' Louie laughed with her brother. It felt strange; she had not found anything to make her smile since losing her baby. The familiar emptiness engulfed her again.

'Oh, poor Sam,' she whispered tearfully, 'coming home to all this.' Eb swung his arm about his sister's shoulders, noticing how thin and fragile her once healthy figure had become. She gave a small cry of pain at the hug and Eb released her quickly. 'I like you cuddling me, Eb,' Louie reassured him. 'It's just so painful - my milk's come in, you see.'

Eb looked at the floor in embarrassment, not knowing what to say. The injuries of mutilated soldiers he could deal with, but the womanly distress that his sister bore left him feeling helpless. 'I'll send Mam over,' he suggested and left quickly.

Later in the day, Fanny and Iris came over and bound up Louie's swollen breasts with old pieces of sheet to give her relief.

'Where's Raymond?' Louie forced herself to ask, knowing she could not avoid the babies of Whitton Grange for ever.

'Sadie's taken him out for a walk,' Iris explained. 'The last thing you want is a bairn crying about the place. When you're ready I'll bring him over to see you, but not before.'

'Thanks, Iris.' Louie squeezed her hand gratefully, surprised by the other woman's sensitivity. The unexpected kindness made her weepy; she no longer seemed to have any control over her feelings.

'I'll stay with our Louie for a bit,' Fanny told Iris. 'You get off home and see what Sadie's up to.'

'Right, Mam.' Iris nodded without protest, Ta-ra, Louie.'

When she had gone, Fanny sat gingerly on the edge of the bed where her daughter lay. 'Did I ever tell you about the bairns I lost?' she began hesitantly. Louie's head shot up in surprise; she shook her head. 'After John was born,' Fanny forced herself to go on, 'I had two daughters in the following two years - one lived a few days, the other lived for three months and died of scarlet fever. That's why there's such a gap in age between our John and our Davie.'

'You never said! Is that why Davie was always so special,' Louie asked with interest, 'you having lost the other two?'

'Maybes.' Her mother shrugged.

'What were they called, Mam?'

'Frances Jane and Jane Frances,' her mother replied, her eyes glistening as she remembered.

'Canny names,' Louie whispered. She was suddenly filled with a desire to ask her mother a thousand questions about these sisters of whom she had never heard. It was so typical of her reserved mother to have kept her personal tragedies to herself. And had her father mourned silently for years too? But Louie did not know how to begin probing, without unearthing her mother's grief, buried for almost as long as their John had been alive.

'I just wanted you to know that I feel for you, Louie pet.' Her mother covered her hand gently. 'I do know what it's like. There're too many of us pitmen's wives who know the pain of losing a bairn.' Louie felt her insides lurch at the sympathetic words. It made such a difference knowing that others shared the same hurt.

'Does it get any better, Mam?' Louie asked desperately.

Fanny remained silent for a moment, struggling with the words that would convey adequately what she felt.

She turned to her daughter, her eyes shiny with tears. 'The pain gets better eventually,' she promised, 'but the memory of the pain stays with you always.'

A week later Louie's milk dried up and she began to go out again, short walks to Hawthorn Street or up to the allotment. She felt drained after each excursion and avoided people she saw in the distance. She did not have the energy to engage in conversation and so skirted the crowded streets of the lower town where children played in their dozens. Until now it had never struck her how many babies there were being pushed around in prams or straddled over mothers' hips. Everyone she knew seemed to have one; Iris, Bel, Margaret, Minnie. Another of Minnie's sisters was expecting and even the minister's wife, Amelia Pinkney, was rumoured to be pregnant with their fifth child.

At times her arms physically ached with emptiness and she would hug them to her body and steel herself to pass an oncoming pram. She could not bear to look at another baby, let alone touch one. Strangely, only Raymond seemed exempt from this aversion. Perhaps it was because he reminded her so much of Davie, with his cheeky grin and spiky hair, that she allowed him to pull himself up on her legs and drew comfort from his brief hugs of affection.

Minnie's Jack was another matter. He was a sickly baby of barely seven months, who seemed to whinge and cry and be at odds with life. Minnie blamed his father's complaining nature and bad temper and ignored his bleating. Louie bit back her comment that Minnie was lucky to hear her baby cry, yet the noise cut through her like a sharp needle.

'It's so boring round here,' Minnie declared one afternoon, sitting at Louie's kitchen table. She was restlessly rocking Jack in his pram, and for once he appeared to be succumbing to the vigorous motion.

Louie carried on peeling carrots for Sadie's tea; simple, mindless household chores seemed the best therapy to occupy her empty hours.

'We've got no money for anything - not even a bag of sweets,' Minnie continued her dirge, 'and Margaret goes on all day about her Joseph and where she thinks he is. It's driving me potty.'

'Bomber'll be back in a couple of weeks,' Louie reminded her.

'Bomber!' Minnie groaned. 'He'll go light when he finds out Margaret and Joe are stopping with us. It'll all be my fault Joseph ran off and left them - he'll probably blame me that the strike's not already settled. I'm responsible for all the troubles of the world as far as Bomber's concerned. And what's he done for me since he got himself nicked? Been about as much use as a chocolate fender! It's been all right for him - three square meals a day in gaol, I bet, while we live off potato stew at the chapel.'

Louie could bear her complaints no longer. 'Listen,' she turned and spoke impatiently, 'why don't you go up to Stand High Farm and see if they're still taking on pickers? It'll get you out of Whitton Grange for a week or so and you'll make a bit of money likely. It'll be hard work, but the bairn could do with some country air.' She jerked her head at the sleeping Jack. 'He's poorly bad staying around these streets - at least there'll be plenty to eat on a farm.'

Minnie's pretty face lit up at the suggestion, her green eyes kindling with life as the idea took hold.

'I don't mind a spot of hard work,' she replied with enthusiasm, 'and I might be able to save a bit of money and put it by for the winter. Our Margaret wouldn't miss us for a couple of weeks.' She rushed and gave her friend a hug. 'Louie, you always think of the answers.'

'As long as you're back when Bomber comes home,' Louie warned.

'Aye.' Minnie shrugged that thought off quickly.

'But will you manage on your own, Louie?' she asked. 'I don't like the thought of leaving you.'

'I'll not be on my own,' Louie pointed out. 'I'll have Sadie for company now that school's nearly finished - and family nearby.'

Minnie scrutinised her friend's pale face, its deep-set blue eyes smudged with fatigue and sadness.

'It might be for the best if Jack isn't around for a bit,' Minnie said quietly. 'It isn't easy for you, is it?'

Louie stopped her chopping and glanced up. 'No,' she admitted. 'Things'll be better when you come back. We'll have Sam and Bomber with us then.'

Shortly afterwards Minnie went home and packed a bagful of possessions for herself and Jack. The following day she set out for Stand High Farm, pushing Jack in his dented black pram.

Four miles up the road, a milk cart stopped and gave her a lift for most of the way, wedging the pram between the heavy metal churns. It was only midday when she reached the farm buildings. The farmer was out, but his wife took Minnie and the baby in and gave them a drink of milk and Minnie a hunk of bread and cheese.

When the farmer came home for his midday meal, he agreed to take Minnie on for a trial week.

'You can sleep in one of the cottages with the other lasses,' Mr Halliday told her. 'There's no running water but the pump's just in the yard. The pay's six shillings a week and your board free.'

Minnie felt like arguing that six shillings was less than Bomber made in one shift, but she smothered her objections.

'What about the bairn?' Mrs Halliday's weathered face crinkled in concern.

'I'll take him in the fields,' Minnie said quickly. 'He'll just sleep in the pram, he's no bother. I'll start tomorrow.' She smiled at the stern-faced farmer.

'You'll start this afternoon,' he contradicted her.

'Jack Kingston the foreman will show you where they're working. You'll find him down the road you came in.'

As Mrs Halliday saw her to the door, Minnie smiled at the farmer's wife, noticing her interest in the baby. 'My bairn's called Jack,' she confided.

'If it rains too hard, you bring him inside—he's got a nasty cough,' Mrs Halliday whispered with a wink. 'My children are all grown up and my three grandbairns live over in Westmorland. You just leave your Jack with me, do you hear?' She gave a short cackle of laughter at the conspiracy and nudged Minnie over the doorstep.

'Ta, Mrs Halliday.' Minnie grinned and went in search of the foreman.

Jack Kingston, a lithe man with large red ears which he kept tugging as he spoke, turned out to be Louie's uncle. As the cheerful man led her to the field gang, Minnie discovered that Davie and John were staying in his cottage with their Auntie Eva, Fanny Kirkup's sister.

'You come round tonight and have a bite of tea with us,' Jack Kingston insisted, 'and you can give us all the news from Whitton.'

All through the hot afternoon, bent double over an endless row of cauliflowers, the thought of an evening at the Kingstons' in Davie Kirkup's company kept up Minnie's spirits. If she was honest, it had been the chance of seeing Davie away from the strictures of the village that had prompted her to come seeking work. More than a few pennies in her pocket, Minnie craved a bit of fun in her drab life of scrimping and going hungry. Davie Kirkup was a kindred spirit, who knew how to laugh and make the cares of the world go away for a while.

That evening, when Minnie had scrubbed the brown dust of the fields from her face and arms, changed into her best dress, still crumpled from being in her bag, and brushed her wavy dark hair, she set off down the road to the foreman's house. Her companions in the cottage made ribald remarks about where she was going dressed up in her finery, but she laughed off their joking. They were hardy women, with thick hands like gnarled wood, who were used to the backbreaking work of the fields, and Minnie was warming to their uninhibited chatter.

She pushed Jack's pram to the front door of the Kingstons' cottage, halfway down the farm track. The baby was asleep by the time they arrived, so she left the pram outside in the warm evening air. In Eva Kingston's cosy kitchen, Minnie tucked into a feast of lamb stew and freshly baked bread, followed by baked apples and strong, hot tea. She could not remember the last time she had eaten so well. The Kirkup boys looked healthy after several weeks on the farm; John's fair skin was tanned a ruddy brown and Davie's lively blue eyes watched her from his sunburnt face, his fair hair bleached as golden hay.

Minnie did not want to dampen the jovial atmosphere, so did not dwell in any detail on Louie's sad news except to tell them that she had lost the baby.

'That poor lass,' Auntie Eva clicked her tongue against her uneven teeth. 'If ever someone deserved a bairn it's young Louie.'

'Is she all right?' Davie asked in concern.

'You know Louie,' Minnie answered brightly. 'Doesn't let her troubles get her down.'

'Aye, she's a strong'un, our Louie.' John nodded and slurped his tea.

'Still, she'll be missing Sam,' Davie said glumly, 'and she was right pleased to be having that bairn.'

'Aye,' Uncle Jack agreed, pulling at his left ear. They fell into contemplation.

Minnie did not want the evening to end in morose thoughts, so she said to John, 'I saw your Marjory before I came away.' His head shot up with interest.

'You did? And how was she?'

'Champion,' Minnie smiled. 'Said she was missing you, like. She's helping at the soup kitchen when she's not at the store.'

Davie nudged his brother so that he spilt his tea. 'Hear that, Marjory's missing you. He's been pining like a sick dog since we left Whitton,' he teased.

'Give over,' John growled back, his face a scalded red.

'Leave the lad alone,' Auntie Eva chided her irrepressible nephew. 'You should be asking after your own wife and bairn.'

Davie gave a bashful laugh and slipped Minnie a look. 'Don't suppose Iris has missed me for a minute, eh?'

Minnie shrugged. 'Don't see her much. Louie said Raymond has cut two more teeth since you've been away, mind.'

'By, that'll be in all the papers,' John mocked, 'News headlines - "Two more teeth for Raymond, when will it stop?"'

Davie gave his brother a hefty push. 'Put it there!' he challenged and thumped his elbow on the table, clenching his hand. John swiftly answered the invitation to arm wrestle by gripping Davie's fist.

'Lads!' Auntie Eva protested. 'Jack, do something about them.' John had Davie's arm down on the table before their uncle could call them to order.

'I beat him every time,' John announced with satisfaction. Minnie laughed at Davie's chagrined look.

'I'm sure our Fanny wouldn't allow such behaviour at her table,' Auntie Eva sighed, with such resignation that Minnie concluded the arm-wrestling must be a regular feature since her nephews had come to stay.

'I don't know how they have the energy after a day picking cauliflowers.' Minnie grinned.

Uncle Jack began fingering his ears, which indicated he was about to speak. 'Best be getting back up the road - you'll need your sleep, lass. The first week nearly kills them,' he told her cheerfully.

'I'll walk you home,' Davie volunteered as Minnie rose, 'Stretch my legs.' He ignored a snort from John, and Minnie did not protest. She thanked her kind hosts and wished them good night. Out in the clear night air, Minnie caught her breath at the myriad of stars spilling across the indigo sky. At home, with the smoke and street lamps, the sky was never so visible, so magical. She breathed in lungfuls of air that tasted of long grass and honeyed flowers.

'Pongs, doesn't it?' Davie shattered her romantic notions of the countryside. 'But you'll get used to it.' Minnie threw back her head and gave in to a fit of the giggles, made worse by trying to suppress the noise in case she woke the baby.

'What's so funny?' Davie laughed bemusedly with her as they continued walking.

'You are,' Minnie answered with mirth.

When they reached the dark flanks of the outbuildings and Minnie's rude quarters, Davie slid a tentative arm about her shoulders. To his surprise she did not shrug him off. In the shadow of the first barn he dared to go further. Pulling Minnie away from the pram, he pushed her against the wall and planted a kiss on her moist lips. She answered his exploration by opening her mouth. Davie felt his excitement soar as if he had just downed a pint in one. He had never kissed Minnie Slattery before, but had often daydreamt of doing so. He could not believe his luck; providence had sent her to him.

A sudden thought of Iris made him reluctantly pull away. 'It's the country air - goes to your head.' Embarrassed, he made light of their embrace.

Minnie giggled, 'Aye, doesn't it.'

'I'll be off then.' Davie stuck his hands in his pockets and stepped backwards.

'See you tomorrow?' Minnie asked with more than a casual question in her husky voice.

'Aye.' Davie could not help a grin.

She turned and pushed the pram across the uneven courtyard towards her cottage. Above the sound of the pram wheels squeaking and bumping over the earth, she could hear Davie Kirkup's light-hearted whistle as he retreated down the track. Minnie guessed she was about to find the amusement for which she had come searching.

Chapter Nineteen

The week before Sam was released, a family dispute arose from an unexpected quarter. Sadie came home triumphantly on the second-last day of school and announced she had won a scholarship to the grammar school in Durham City. Louie was darning her cousin's threadbare stockings by the slowly winking fire in the hearth. For the past two days it had poured with rain, heavy thunderous bursts that turned the dusty back streets into running channels of liquid mud.

'That's grand.' Louie put down her darning and congratulated the girl with a hug. 'You're a clever lass.'

'Jane Pinkney passed as well; and Frank Robson and Tom Gallon - they'll go to the boys' grammar in the town,' Sadie told her with excitement.

'What about May Little?' Louie asked.

'She didn't pass,' Sadie answered dismissively. 'May Little's daft.'

'Sadie!' Louie scolded. 'Don't you go getting a big head all because you passed a few tests. Any road, there's little chance of you being able to go on to secondary school - Mam and Da can't afford to send you.'

Sadie was dashed. 'But it's free, Miss Joice said so!'

'The uniform and the train fares aren't free. How are you going to travel in every day? And you'll need a satchel and a decent pair of shoes—' Louie stopped, seeing the look of acute disappointment on her cousin's face. 'I'm sorry, pet, but these are hard times for us all. We all have to make sacrifices.'

Angry tears spurted into Sadie's dark eyes. 'But I want to go,' she pleaded. 'Please, Louie, let me go!' She buried her head in Louie's lap and sobbed. Her cousin felt a pang of helplessness; she did not want to witness any more unhappiness and yet the problem seemed insoluble.

'It'll be Da's decision,' Louie told her, 'but I'll see if I can put a word in for you, eh?'

'Thanks, Louie.' Sadie sniffed and brightened as her hopes rose again.

That evening, at the Kirkups' house, a row blew up over Sadie's future.

'We've been through all this with our Hildy,' Jacob Kirkup pronounced in his stern pulpit voice. He was polishing his boots through force of habit, although they did not need a clean. 'She's got a good grounding in reading and spelling and sums from Miss Joke - that's all she needs.'

'But, Da,' Louie reasoned, 'she has a head for figures - she can do the housekeeping as well as any of us - and she reads well for her age. It seems a shame not to use the talents God gave her.'

Jacob Kirkup, irked by Louie's persistence, put down the boot he was polishing. 'She'll carry on getting an education until she's fourteen,' he said gruffly, 'like you and Hildy did. It's enough for a lass. Besides, with you married and Hilda out working, Sadie will be a help to your mother.' Louie glanced at Fanny sitting silently by the window, straining her eyes in the poor light as she mended a man's shirt. She needed no reminding that her mother was not in the best of health; the grating cough of last winter had eased to a gentle wheeze, but it lay dormant as a sleeping beast.

'But if Sadie got an education she could get a really good job,' Louie argued. 'There's nothing for her round here, Da.'

'You know we can't afford to send her to Durham,' her father answered impatiently, astonished by his daughter's dissension, 'especially now. Isn't it enough that we've given Sadie a decent home and a loving family?' Louie clamped her lips together, aware that nothing she said would sway her father's mulishness. Sadie kept close to her, her dark eyes fixed in awe on her uncle.

Unexpectedly, Eb stirred from his sketching on the kitchen table. 'I could buy Sadie her uniform,' he offered. They all stared at him.

'With what?' Jacob demanded.

'I could ask the doctor for an advance on my wages,' Eb answered evenly, 'or put in some extra hours at Greenbrae.'

'Oh, Eb, would you?' Sadie piped up in delight.

'Aye, I can ask.' He smiled at the transparent glee on the child's face.

'Thanks, Eb.' Sadie rushed over to him and gave him a peck on his rough cheek.

'But that doesn't solve the problem of the train fares,' Jacob reminded them, agitated by the undermining of his authority.

Iris suddenly entered the debate. 'She could live with my family during the week.' No one had consulted her for an opinion or even thought of it as her business. 'I'm sure my mam would give her bed and board for a bit of help around the house. That way, Sadie would only need to travel in on Monday morning and back on Friday.'

Fanny looked up uncertainly and Jacob seemed quite flummoxed by the suggestion.

'Would you want to live with the Ramshaws, Sadie?' Louie asked, thinking selfishly how much she would miss her company.

'Aye,' the girl nodded vigorously, 'Iris says her sisters have a rocking horse and lots of comics.'

Iris laughed, 'You'd have to put up with my brothers too, you know.'

'B-but, a public house,' Jacob stuttered his objection, 'I can't have my niece living above a pub!'

'The flat is quite separate from the pub,' Iris assured him with an easy smile. 'Different entrances. She need never go near the bar. My family are decent people, Mr Kirkup,' Iris said proudly with a toss of her head.

'Please can I go?' Sadie beseeched her uncle, hopping impatiently onto one foot. Jacob looked at his dark-haired niece, her small face turned to his in supplication, trusting and hopeful. He knew she was bright and quick-witted and from a timid, anxious child, she had flowered before their eyes into a popular, sunny-natured girl, albeit with a flash of Kirkup moodiness and temper. Perhaps for the sake of his long-dead brother George he should allow Sadie the chance none of his own children had had, a grammar school education. As a self-taught lay preacher himself, how could he in all conscience deny Sadie the chance to use her God-given gifts? As he struggled with his prejudices, his family held their breath.

'If Eb really can help out with your uniform and that, and the Ramshaws agree to have you as a lodger,' Jacob at last decreed, 'then I don't hold any objection to you going to the grammar school.'

Sadie screeched in triumph and before her uncle had time to retract, she had flung her arms about his neck as he sat astride a stool with his half-polished boots at his feet.

'Thank you, Uncle Jacob.' She kissed his white-bearded face. 'I'll make you proud of me, I promise.' Jacob looked over to Fanny in the window for her approval and saw her smiling at him with affection.

Eb walked Louie and Sadie home that evening. As Sadie skipped ahead to tell her friend Jane Pinkney the good news, brother and sister walked in companionship, enjoying the freshness of the air, cleared of its dusty mugginess by the last days of rain.

'You're going to ask Mrs Seward-Scott for the money, aren't you?' Louie asked him directly. Eb carried on walking.

'How did you know?' he queried.

'I know there is something going on between the two of you,' Louie answered frankly. 'It worries me, Eb.'

'Don't be worried.' Eb briefly touched her arm. 'We're just friends, that's all.'

'You will be careful?' Louie begged him, as they turned up North Street where the Pinkneys lived. 'You know how folk can talk.'

'I've done nothing to shame anyone,' Eb insisted. 'Now stop nagging me, Louie. I'll be pleased when Sam's back and you've got someone else to fuss over.' She saw from the amusement in his blue eyes that he was teasing.

'So will I.' Louie smiled at him suddenly and hugged his arm.

Another deluge of rain sent the pickers running for cover. Minnie reached the large cowshed before the rain drenched her totally. She was glad Mrs Halliday had repeated her offer to take baby Jack indoors while the unsettled weather lasted. Jack Kingston appeared and told the women they could take their break for dinner early, while the downpour lasted. With grumbles of protest the field gang broke up into twos and threes and found comfortable perches in the hay where they could eat their bait.

Davie, who had been mucking out the byre that morning, found Minnie alone in one of the stalls.

'Morning.' He pushed back his cap and grinned at her. 'You look like a drowned rat,' he teased, noticing how her damp blouse clung to her full body and her curly hair snaked round her cheeks and neck.

'Ta very much,' Minnie retorted. 'You hardly look like Rudolph Valentino yourself - covered in muck.'

Davie laughed and swung himself down beside her. They had not kissed again since that first evening a week ago, but he had enjoyed flirting with Minnie at every opportunity, and his attraction for her was growing. She did not have Iris's piquant good looks, but her face was prettily plump and her green eyes bold and full of mischief.

'There's a canny walk over-by,' Davie told her, cocking his head in the direction of the hills behind the farm. 'Strange rocks. Uncle Jack says there used to be an old hill fort there long ago. You get a canny view from the top.'

'Oh, aye?' Minnie sounded unimpressed. 'And what is there to look at but more hills?' Davie sucked on a piece of straw as if it were a cigarette.

'It's nice and quiet,' he said pointedly and gave her a wink.

'Don't know if I've got the strength for walking after a day at the cauliflowers,' Minnie answered noncommittally and leaned back on her elbows.

Davie was unabashed. 'I'll wait for you up by the old mill. You can't be seen from the farm once you're up there. Meet me there tonight, Minnie,' he pressed.

He leaned close to her but they did not touch. Minnie could see the glisten of fair bristle on his chin, the sinewy strength in his arms where his sleeves were rolled back. She could smell the sourness of his body from his labouring, and the dung on his boots. Yet his earthiness strangely excited her, more than if he had smelt of household soap and starched clean clothes. Life in Whitton Grange seemed so remote from the timelessness of this secluded farm. She hardly thought of Margaret or Louie or even Bomber. The only people real to her at the moment were her companions, the strong-limbed women she lodged with, and handsome Davie Kirkup who was out to court her.

'If the lasses will keep an eye on Jack, I'll come,' Minnie agreed. Davie gave her a chaste peck on her cheek and jumped up with a grin of satisfaction. He sauntered off, whistling, into the rain.

That evening, the rain clouds were furled away like limp rags, leaving the sky a watery, washed-out blue and the breeze fresh. A woman called Sarah agreed to watch over Jack in return for Minnie's promise to procure her some cigarettes. She knew

164

Davie could cadge the odd Woodbine from his uncle, so with the deal struck, she set out for the old mill.

Davie was already waiting in the shadows of the grey stone building with its moss-covered wheel. He took her hand as if they were lovers keeping a tryst and led her up the steep gully behind the mill.

As they scrabbled for a foothold Minnie complained, 'Davie man, I didn't come mountaineerin'.' Davie laughed and pulled her up after him, with surprising force in his slight, muscled body. 'Where's John tonight?' she asked him, gaining her breath again as the moor levelled out.

'Beating my uncle at dominoes,' Davie replied. 'He never knows when to let someone else win. Uncle Jack'll kick us out by the end of the month if he carries on losing, but John won't give an inch. He's a worse loser than the devil.'

Minnie laughed. 'So where did you say you were going?'

'They didn't ask,' Davie said, 'but they'll think I've got a lift down to the Wagon Way, this being Saturday.'

They carried on walking as the sky grew dim overhead and the sun splashed into the hills, sending up waves of rusty orange.

'Here we are,' Davie announced, jumping on to a raised rampart of turf.

'Here we are where?' Minnie asked derisively. 'I thought you said there was a fort or something grand. All I can see is a couple of stones and a lot of sheep muck.' Davie laughed and pulled her unwillingly after him over the ridge and down into a sheltered hollow that was once the dwelling of some long-forgotten tribe. Here the wind did not whip around them as before and Davie spread out his jacket for them to sit on.

'Snug, isn't it?' he questioned.

'Aye.' Minnie breathed her reply, bewitched by the sudden quiet and the heady freshness of the evening air. She pulled her cardigan around her and listened to the faint munching of sheep below the grassy fortifications. 'It's so peaceful,' she whispered.

'Aye, it would drive you mad if you lived out here,' Davie moved close and put his arm about her shoulders, 'but it's just the job for a lad and lass on holiday.'

'Holiday!' Minnie scoffed. 'I don't call picking veg all day long a holiday. Slave labour more like. Look at the state of my hands.' Minnie held them up and studied her cracked and earth-ingrained fingers. Davie took them in his and put them to his lips.

'Bonny hands.' He kissed the palms. Still holding her hands, he nibbled her neck and ear. She smelt of hay and soap and sun-touched skin. 'Give us a kiss, Minnie,' he pleaded.

Minnie lay back on his jacket feeling the moisture from the grass cold on her head. But the ground was only superficially damp, the day's rain unable to quench the thirsty earth after the long, hot, dry spell of previous weeks. She closed her eyes and parted her lips, mesmerised by the tranquillity of their secret hideaway. How many other generations of lovers had lain here as they did now, centuries of courting couples succumbing to their desire amid these stones?

She felt Davie's mouth warm on hers, his hands exploring her body, combing her hair, fumbling with her buttons. Her senses came alive in the open air, as if the wind was stroking her nerve endings. Minnie responded quickly to his caresses which grew more assured and dextrous as their passion rose. For those brief minutes, she emptied her mind of everything and everyone else, giving herself up easily to their unfaithfulness.

Davie's excitement peaked as swiftly as it had stirred. He lay back in the grass, content with his conquest. Minnie Slattery had always caught his interest, like the dreamy-eyed actresses in Sadie's postcard collection. Tonight she was beautiful, full-breasted and soft to the touch. Tomorrow . . . Davie pushed thoughts of tomorrow from his mind. He never thought beyond the moment, no pitman did with life always so uncertain.

'Davie,' Minnie stirred, 'what about —?'

'Don't spoil it,' Davie interrupted her, fearful she would conjure up accusing spectres that he did not want to meet in their hilltop nest. 'Let's just think of ourselves tonight, eh?'

'Give us a kiss then.' Minnie grinned and rolled over on to his prone body.

Slowing to a halt at the junction with the Durham road, Eleanor saw Eb emerge from behind the hedge. She leaned over and swung open the car door.

'Jump in,' she called to him. He gave a nervous look round and then climbed quickly into the green Austin. Eleanor pushed the car into first gear and moved forward, taking the right turn towards Durham. 'Isobel gave me your message.' She broke the silence between them. 'You don't have to tell me what it's about yet, unless you want to.'

'It's Sadie I'm asking you to help.' Eb plunged into his request, embarrassed at having to ask another favour. 'She's won a scholarship to the grammar school.'

'That's marvellous,' Eleanor interrupted with genuine pleasure.

'I've offered to pay for her uniform,' Eb admitted uncomfortably. 'My father wouldn't have considered sending her otherwise.'

'And you'd like me to help with the expense?' Eleanor tried to make it easy for him.

'Aye,' Eb answered gruffly. 'I'll pay you back just as soon as I'm able. It doesn't seem right the lass shouldn't have her chance.' Eleanor smiled to herself, resisting the temptation to remind Eb of his once vehement opposition to Hilda receiving just such an opportunity.

'I quite agree,' she assured him, 'and I'd be delighted to help. You can pay me back if you insist, though I'd be more than happy to let the loan be a gift to Sadie.'

'There's no need for that,' Eb replied proudly. 'It's good of you to lend the money and I'm grateful.' He took off his cap and smoothed his tanned scalp, feeling at a disadvantage sitting in the intimate car with its smells of expensive leather and Eleanor's musky perfume. Even though he was wearing his Sunday suit in preparation for band practice later in the day, he was acutely aware of his own shabbiness and smell of cheap soap.

They continued to chug along in silence for several minutes as the yellow fields of newly cut wheat slid past them. Scarlet poppies daubed the hedgerows like careless splashes of paint and it suddenly occurred to Eb that he did not have the slightest idea where Eleanor was taking him.

'Where are we going?' he asked her nervously.

'Newcastle.' She turned and smiled secretively.

'Why Newcastle?' he questioned in astonishment.

'You'll see.' She looked ahead and curled her cream-gloved fingers firmly around the steering wheel.

'I've got band practice later,' Eb protested half-heartedly. Eleanor ignored the comment.

An hour later, despite fierce objections, Eleanor bought Eb a tasteful green paisley tie. By the time they re-emerged from the discreet shop with its smell of new cloth and polished counters, Eb's face was a thunderous red. Undaunted, Eleanor slipped her arm through his possessively and led him across busy

Northumberland Street into New Bridge Street. At the steps to an impressively large building with Palladian pillars and ostentatious belfry, proclaiming itself the Laing Gallery, she stopped.

'You told me you'd never been inside an art gallery,' she challenged him. 'Well today you will. I just thought you'd feel better in a new tie.'

Eb blushed at the thought of his tattered necktie stuffed in his pocket.

'Stand out less like a sore thumb, you mean?' he accused.

'Look, I don't care what you dress in,' Eleanor replied shortly, 'but we don't want to draw undue attention to ourselves, do we?'

He had to concede Eleanor was right. She was taking a risk as it was being seen in public with a man so obviously not of her class.

'You should have told me we were coming here,' Eb rebuked. 'I could have borrowed John's suit - it's newer than mine.'

'And how would you have explained your appearance to half the village?' Eleanor responded, amused. 'That you were off to town to meet your lover?' Eb blushed at the truth of what she said, strangely excited by the bold intimacy of her words.

'Aye, s'pose not.' He grinned sheepishly and followed her up the steps.

Minutes later, he had forgotten his awkwardness and recent humiliation as he wandered around the high-ceilinged rooms of the gallery, feasting his eyes on the vast selection of paintings. Huge panoramic landscapes, scenes from Tyneside's past, hung in their heavy gilded frames; sombre portraits of local worthies, and naked cherubs in religious friezes adorned the cool rooms. After half an hour, Eleanor found him again.

'It's this exhibition I want you to see.' She hurried him impatiently into a further room. In contrast, the paintings in this smaller exhibition were decidedly modern in style. There was a stark reality to their subjects, harsh lines and brutal contrasts in light and shade and colour. There was nothing pretentious or sentimental about these pictures. Eb was immediately excited by their uncompromising boldness. He stood before a painting of ships in a harbour by an artist called Wadsworth.

'It's good, isn't it?' Eleanor whispered in the quiet of the chamber. There's something hypnotic about the scene - and where have all the fishermen gone? It raises so many questions, don't you think?'

'I wish I could paint like this,' Eb answered enviously.

'You can,' Eleanor encouraged. 'Your style is unfussy too. It's simpler and more natural than these - I like it better - these figures are almost machine-like.'

Eb turned to a self-portrait by another artist. 'His unhappiness is all over his face,' he commented. 'He seems cut off from us.'

'Yes,' Eleanor answered eagerly, 'that's exactly it.' She swept her hand around the room. 'Paintings like these frighten me, if I'm perfectly honest; they show up our alienation, the human cost of our industrialised society.'

Eb found himself agreeing, throwing suggestions and ideas at the paintings as Eleanor did, revelling in seeing such canvases in the flesh and not just in well-thumbed magazines at the library. He found the experience energising; he itched to get back to his paints.

'You should go to night classes, Eb,' Eleanor insisted, 'and develop your talent. A friend of mine, Ruth Spencer, runs an art class in Durham - she gives individual tuition too.'

'How could I possibly afford art classes in Durham?' Eb sighed.

'You know I'd pay for them.' Eleanor's voice was quietly pleading.

'I don't like to be beholden,' Eb objected stubbornly.

'Oh, you're quite impossible!' Eleanor remonstrated.

Their talk was so animated they were unaware of two young women entering the room, until one of them exclaimed, 'Eleanor, fancy meeting you here!'

Eleanor spun round guiltily to see the freckled face of Harriet Swainson, daughter of her father's good friend, beaming at her.

'Harriet,' Eleanor smiled and regained her composure, 'how nice to see you. Are you enjoying the exhibition?'

'Not really,' the girl confessed candidly with a giggle. 'Susie and I were told to fill in an hour until Daddy takes us out to lunch - Susie's an old schoolfriend of mine, by the way.' Harriet hastily introduced her bored-looking friend. Eleanor shook hands with Susie. 'We just came in here for a bit of a lark. Aren't these pictures too, too awful?' Harriet giggled again. 'Won't you join us for lunch?' she asked, suddenly earnest under her pink cloche hat. 'It's ages since Daddy saw you and it would be such fun.'

'I'm afraid we can't stay.' Eleanor quashed the idea firmly. 'We were just on the point of leaving, in fact.' Harriet turned a quizzical brown-eyed gaze on Eleanor's silent companion. 'This is Mr Flanders, an artist friend of mine,' Eleanor improvised quickly. 'He has a train to catch, so you must excuse us.'

Eb nodded stiffly at the two young women in their fresh cotton dresses and beat a hasty retreat behind Eleanor.

'We'll see you soon, I hope,' Harriet called after them. Eleanor waved in acknowledgement. As they disappeared Harriet added to Susie, 'She's a bit of a cool one, used to frighten me to death as a child. Her father owns masses of mines near Durham. I used to have a crush on her husband, Reggie, when I was younger - he's absolutely topping. Daddy says Eleanor's rotten to him though, poor Reggie.'

'Sick-making,' Susie agreed, because that was her favourite expression for everything at the moment.

Harriet giggled suddenly. 'Wonder where she found that artist? Rather good-looking in a common sort of way, don't you think?'

'Didn't look much like an artist to me,' Susie answered scornfully. 'More like a railway porter dressed up for a tea dance.' Harriet dissolved into hysterics at the description.

'Well, Eleanor did say he had a train to catch!' she screeched with mirth. The two friends subsided into giggles and their laughter rang around the hushed gallery until a disapproving attendant wagged a finger at them to stop.

Back out in the bright sunshine, Eleanor hurried Eb into a nearby tea room. She lit up a cigarette despite the sidelong looks of three elderly ladies occupying the table to their right.

'Mr Flanders?' Eb gave way to his amusement and they laughed with the relief of escape. 'What made you say that?'

'It just came into my head.' Eleanor blew smoke at the ceiling. 'Harriet Swainson's parents are very pally with my father - I couldn't take the risk of using your real name - you just never know what might be said.'

Eb's face clouded in worry. 'Will she say anything?'

Eleanor shrugged. 'Harriet is a scatterbrain - she'll probably forget to mention she even saw me, let alone some unknown artist she hardly glanced at.'

Eb accepted her assurances. He did not want their afternoon spoilt by the chance encounter in the gallery. He was enjoying himself more than he could remember, stimulated by his visit to the Laing and the close proximity of the woman he loved. Eleanor ordered tea and they returned to their talk of art and painters, dismissing any lingering thoughts of the garrulous Harriet Swainson.

At the end of the afternoon, Eb took off his new tie and replaced it with his old one, and Eleanor drove him to within half a mile of the village before letting him go.

They arranged to go hiking the following day and Eleanor offered to provide a picnic. A subtle change had seeped into their relationship that day; their friendship was putting down deeper roots, no longer just a manifestation of physical liking and an answer to loneliness. Each increasingly desired the company of the other, like the thirsty allotment plants craving the summer rain.

Louie did not journey to Durham on the day Sam and Bomber were released; instead she went to her mother-in-law's house to help prepare a homecoming meal, while the lodge officials and Sam's friends made a noisy demonstration of solidarity outside the gaol.

Mrs Ritson and Bel bustled around excitedly and Louie ignored their pleas for her to sit and rest, busying herself as much as possible. The food was unspec-tacular; a pot of vegetable soup supplemented by a few fatty ends of bacon Johnny had managed to procure from a butcher friend. There was bread without butter and weak tea, saved for this special occasion. The crowning glory of the meal was a rhubarb pie made by Fanny Kirkup and a tin of peaches which Mary had won at a fund-raising tombola. Liza Ritson calculated there would be enough in the tin to give the men a decent portion each.

'It may not be much,' Mrs Ritson said, her round face glowing from the heat of the stove, 'but at least our Sam'll be eating in freedom.'

'Only the Lord can offer everlasting freedom,' Mary sermonised as she set the table. 'We're all prisoners of our own frailties and only God can set us free from those.' She banged a spoon decisively down on the linen tablecloth.

'Well, I think our Sam'll settle for the freedom he's got today,' Bel commented, 'coming home to Louie and—' She broke off suddenly, reddening at the words left unsaid.

'And all his family,' her mother finished quickly. 'Now less talk of God, our Mary, and more attention to that table. Have you polished the brass candlesticks?'

'Yes,' Mary answered, 'but I don't see why we need candles for tea when it doesn't get dark until nearly ten.'

'We don't have to light them,' her mother replied shortly, 'but they set off the table nicely.'

'We've only got ends to put in them, Mam,' Bel said, rummaging around in the cupboard under the stairs.

'I'll get some from Mr Armstrong,' Mary offered. 'He can take them off my wages.' With a nod from her mother, Mary dashed off to the shop in Mill Terrace where she worked during the week. She caught her employer as he was rolling in his striped canopy above the shop window. It took little persuasion for the bespectacled Mr Armstrong to part with four candles. Mary knew he was generous in allowing his customers to put their tobacco and household goods on credit, and she prayed fervently that the continued lock-out would not bankrupt him and put her out of a job.

By the time she had returned across the village, Sam had arrived home with brother-in-law Johnny and her father. The family in the kitchen appeared strangely subdued, talking in nervous whispers.

'I've got four candles,' Mary announced loudly.

'Shh!' Her mother flapped a plump hand at her youngest. 'Sam's in the parlour with Louie.' Mary looked towards the closed door.

'Why are you all listening then?' Mary asked accusingly.

'We're not.' Her mother spoke at once in a raised voice.

'Get the tea served,' Samuel Ritson ordered brusquely. 'They'll be out any minute.'

By the time Bel and her mother had ladled soup into the first three bowls, the parlour door opened. Sam came out first, forcing his grave face into a smile; Louie's blotchy face and red-rimmed eyes betrayed the fact that she had been weeping. She contributed little to the conversation as the Ritsons talked across the table to each other. Sam told them of his experiences in prison, the monotony and the bad food, the lack of news about the strike. In return, his father told him of the moves at the pit to get men back to work; his mother delighted in bearing the news that Joseph Gallon had deserted one of the Slatterys and that Margaret and child were now living in Bomber's house.

'And that Minnie Slattery hasn't even bothered to come home when her husband comes out of prison,' Mrs Ritson said disapprovingly. 'It's a scandal.'

Mary defended her old classmate. 'She's working up at Stand High to earn some money for her family.'

'Tch!' her mother responded.

'It was my idea that she went.' Louie spoke up for the first time. Mrs Ritson looked at her in surprise, the silence round the table tense. 'She needed to be occupied,' Louie continued, feeling she was somehow on trial. How could she tell them that her main motivation was to remove baby Jack from her sight? 'Minnie'll be back shortly.'

'Aye,' Sam patted her hand, 'of course she will. Now tell me what the Distress Committee has been up to.'

Sam and Louie did not linger after tea. They said their goodbyes and walked home via the dene, talking in snatches about everything but themselves. Louie wanted him to tell her how he felt about their lost baby, but she could not bring herself to ask. The weight of her failure was crushing her chest and blocking the words in her throat.

Fanny Kirkup had taken Sadie back to Hawthorn Street for a few days and the tiny house seemed bleakly empty on their return. They went to bed and lay awake listening to the sounds of men arguing over a game of pitch and toss in the street outside. Louie longed for the physical comfort of Sam's lovemaking, but her womb was still bleeding and he seemed frightened of touching her.

At some time during the night Louie must have fallen asleep, because she awoke in the dark to feel the bed beside her empty.

'Sam?' she called out. There was no reply, so Louie swung herself out of bed. As her eyes grew accustomed to the night she saw that the room was empty and the back door ajar. Louie pulled her bed-shawl around her shoulders and padded barefoot across the peeling linoleum.

She found her husband in his pyjamas leaning against the wall of the back lane. Louie shivered in the chilly damp air.

'You'll catch your death,' she whispered and saw him flinch, startled by her stealthy approach.

'I couldn't sleep,' he answered in a croaking whisper. Louie peered at him in concern and thought she saw his chiselled face damp with tears.

'Sam,' she began.

'Louie!' He suddenly reached for her and smothered her to his chest. She heard his body wrench out a sob. 'I'm sorry, Louie,' he cried, 'I know how much the bairn meant to you.'

Louie let the tears come, clinging to him in their shared grief. She knew it was his way of saying he mourned for their baby too.

'I'll never forgive them for this,' Sam vowed.

'Who Sam?' Louie asked, her head resting on his chest.

'The bosses who are starving us out.' Sam's voice was thick with fury. 'To think they even tried to put you out on the street in your condition. That's why you lost the bairn, and I wasn't here to stop it!'

'Don't, Sam,' Louie was horrified by his hatred. 'Don't blame yourself, don't blame anyone.'

'Someone has to be blamed, Louie,' Sam answered in frustration, 'someone has to!'

'No, Sam.' She cupped her hands around his harrowed face. 'I've been blaming myself since it happened. But your Mary showed me that was pointless. She came and prayed with me one night, Sam, and since then I haven't felt so guilty.'

Sam looked at her strangely as if she was talking in an unknown language. 'Your God didn't stop this happening, did He?' he demanded cruelly.

Louie's hands slipped from his face. 'No,' she admitted quietly, 'and I don't know why He let it happen. All I do know is this; if you let the bitterness take over, it'll destroy you inside like a poison. It'll destroy us both, Sam.'

Chapter Twenty

August came and Louie buried her great hurt in the struggle to help feed her family and neighbours. The numbers at the soup kitchen were growing every day and they desperately needed more funds to buy in basic foodstuffs. Fuel for stoves and fires was almost impossible to come by and on several occasions Eb and Sam had trespassed on to The Grange estate and come back with a barrow-load of wood. It was a common sight to see families picking along the rail track for cinders or combing the dene for dry twigs to keep their stoves alight.

Bomber, nursing his anger at Minnie staying away on the farm a further two weeks, channelled his energies into organising a charity football match. His sister-in-law Margaret persuaded him to let the women take on the men. Hundreds of spectators turned out to see the women dressed in football strips or fancy dress ruthlessly hacking at the ankles of the men, bound together in pairs to put them at a disadvantage. The sums raised were modest but the hilarity of the occasion gave a boost to flagging morale among the pit folk.

Louie had chivvied a morose Iris into taking part. 'It'll stop you thinking about our Davie all the time,' she'd argued.

'I don't think about him all the time,' Iris had replied petulantly, and then with a sigh. 'Do you think he's done a runner like Joseph Gallon? I haven't heard from him in three weeks.' Louie dismissed her own disquiet at her brother's prolonged absence, especially since John had returned without him. She ignored the question and continued her coaxing.

'You're a born performer, Iris, and you'll love it once you're out there in front of the crowds. You'd be doing something good for the village an' all.'

Her moody sister-in-law had been convinced and to the surprise of many, discovered she had a talent for football. She danced around her opponents on nimble slim legs and daringly wore a man's bathing suit along with an old-fashioned floppy straw hat fastened below the chin with a swathe of flowery material. Hilda was dressed as Charlie Chaplin in a baggy pair of her father's trousers and his precious bowler hat. Margaret played in Bomber's football clothes while he drew gleeful cheers dressed in a convict's overalls with a makeshift ball and chain around his leg. The women's team won by ten goals to six in the most unorthodox game ever staged in Whitton Grange Park.

'I really enjoyed myself,' Iris laughed later, 'it's the first time for months I've had a bit of fun.'

Her mother-in-law looked up from her mending, her strained eyes focusing through the gloom. 'You should sign up for that entertainment Reverend Pinkney is organising,' she encouraged. 'Our Eb said he'd play the piano for him.'

'Do you think I should?' Iris sounded excited by the idea, tumbling Raymond on to the rug and tickling him. Unusually, he objected to the rough play, whining in protest.

'Of course you should,' Louie interjected. 'You could sing a few songs with Eb.'

'Aye, I could.' Iris picked up her whingeing son. 'Oh, Raymond, shut up!' She shook him suddenly as her impatience sparked.

'Give him to me,' Louie ordered quietly and held out her arms to the boy.

Iris dumped him into her hold and announced, 'I'm going out. I'll be over at Margaret's if anyone wants me.'

Louie exchanged glances with her mother as Iris swept from the room. She found a stick of rhubarb for Raymond to suck and within minutes he had quietened.

'He's teething again, poor bairn,' Louie diagnosed.

Her mother sighed and put down her needlework. 'Iris is so nervy these days,' she commented softly, 'like tinder ready for the lighting.'

'I wish Davie were home,' Louie answered longingly. Her mother did not reply but Louie knew she spoke for them both.

At Stand High Farm the gang of fieldworkers was about to move on. Sarah, who had become friendly with Minnie, asked her if she wanted to go with them.

'No, I must be going home soon.' Minnie was subdued as she let Jack suckle her breast. Her milk had all but dried up, but she allowed him the comfort of sucking. The young women, their work almost done, were sitting under a hedge, avoiding the sharp-sighted foreman. 'I've a husband who's been in gaol and I haven't seen for nigh on three months.'

'Oh,' Sarah sounded surprised, 'I somehow thought you didn't have a man — you know - you being with Davie . . .' Her words tailed off.

Minnie felt a stab of guilt like indigestion. 'Yes, well, I have,' she answered sharply. They fell silent, allowing the noise of the threshing in the next field and the circling crows to cover the awkward pause. When Sarah saw Davie appear at the far gate and make his way towards them, she sprang up and left them alone.

Davie felt uneasy at the sight of Minnie's baby fastened leech-like to her blue-veined breast. It reminded him that she was a mother and somebody else's wife; not just anybody's, but a friend of Sam and Louie's. In his mind's eye, he recalled Iris nursing Raymond in their bed with a bottle of warm milk; such a homely, intimate act. A hot flush of remorse engulfed him and he turned his eyes away from Minnie's nakedness.

Minnie saw him flinch and pulled Jack from her nipple, quickly buttoning up her blouse. The baby gave a sharp cry of protest. For the first time she felt ill at ease in Davie's presence, aware of his growing coolness towards her.

For two weeks they had revelled in each other's company, coupling in the isolation of their hill fort or recklessly snatching a few moments of heady passion in one of the outhouses, while the work of the farm carried on around them. Their conversations were brief and always light-hearted and seldom did they refer to their families back home. It was as if no one else existed outside their cocooned world on the farm. They had worked hard, eaten well, made vigorous love and slept soundly.

Then John had left for Whitton Grange, arguing with Davie when he refused to go too. Davie's fair-faced brother had been indifferent towards Minnie and turned a disinterested back on their affair. But with his going, the wall of make-believe built around them was breached and the tide of commitments lapped around their feet. They had not gone up the hill for two nights and Minnie could feel Davie's ardour ebbing as his thoughts were pulled towards Whitton Grange.

'There's a wagon going down the valley the day after tomorrow.' Davie spoke to the ripening berries in the hedge. 'It's passing Whitton on the way to Durham.' He picked a pale blackberry and popped it in his mouth. It tasted bitter and he spat it out immediately.

'You haven't finished in the top field yet,' Minnie reminded him. 'Let's wait till Sunday - get a lift with your uncle when he goes to church. I don't mind walking the rest.'

The mention of his uncle or church seemed to irritate Davie. 'You can go later if you like,' he snapped. 'I'm going Friday.'

Minnie reddened at his harsh tone. 'You've changed your tune all of a sudden,' she retaliated. 'Last week you couldn't get enough.' Davie coloured at her crude words, bitten by the truth of what she said. He had gone sniffing after Minnie like a randy animal, with no thought of the consequences. Yet last night he had thrashed sleeplessly in his bed, plagued by thoughts of Iris and Raymond. He had finally fallen asleep only to be confronted by a silent Louie reproaching him at the foot of his bed. The dream had been so real, Davie had called his sister's name as he awoke. But it was unfair to blame his lapse on Minnie, he was frank with himself; he had wanted her and now he would have to be careful not to rouse her quick temper as he ended their liaison. As in all situations he wished to disengage from, Davie thought it best to laugh his way out.

'Listen, pet,' he crouched down on his haunches and gave a disarming smile, 'don't let's fall out about it. We've had a good time, haven't we? It can't go on for ever, but. I've got Iris and you've got Bomber - that's the way it is.'

'But I want you, Davie.' Minnie almost choked with the disappointment rising in her throat; she knew she was about to lose him for good. Jack began to cry again and she jostled him distractedly.

Davie took her hand as if she were a child who needed reassuring. 'I've had a canny time,' he told her. 'You're a bonny lass, I won't deny it. But all this was just a bit of fun, wasn't it? That's what you said when it started - you just wanted a bit of fun.'

Minnie was stung by the reminder of her own words. That was exactly what it had been at the beginning. But some time during those two weeks she had stepped over the line from wanting to needing. She craved Davie Kirkup as if he were the pink sarsaparillas in the sweet jar that she could never afford as a child. To see him now was to be reminded that he was already out of her reach. Nevertheless, she was not going to make a fool of herself over him.

Minnie withdrew her hand from his and stood up with Jack slung on her hip. Looking down on her lover she felt less at a disadvantage.

'The girls are getting a lift to a farm over-by tomorrow,' she said dully. 'I'll go with them and walk home from there.'

Davie nodded, pleased with her acquiescence. 'Aye, best not to be seen together, like.' Minnie looked at him sharply but said nothing. As he stood, Davie added, 'Bet your Bomber'll be looking out for you - after all those lonely nights in the nick.'

It was meant as a casual remark, just something to say, but at the mention of Bomber's name, Minnie's anger was pricked. It burst at Davie like hydrogen gas.

'How dare you throw Bomber in my face, Davie Kirkup?' she shouted. 'Don't go telling me where my place is now you have no further use for me! You men are all the same - you take what you want and throw away what's left. You're a bastard, Davie Kirkup, so you are! Iris Ramshaw's welcome to you!'

Davie watched her, stunned, as her green eyes strafed him furiously and the words exploded like accusing bullets. All at once he was frightened by Minnie's wrath. He backed off, a hand keeping her at bay.

'Don't worry, I'm off,' he answered and turned his back. He marched away quickly and vaulted the gate, leaving her fuming in the deserted field.

'Good riddance!' Minnie bawled at the sky, and the scavenging black crows circling above screamed in accord.

Early one morning, Louie woke to see Sam pulling on his work clothes.

'What are you doing?' she asked sleepily.

'Eb reckons he's found the entrance to the old drift mine,' Sam answered in a whisper so as not to wake Sadie. The girl had been allowed to return and live with them until she started school in September.

The one in the dene?' Louie queried.

'Aye,' Sam nodded, tying the string that held his pit boots together. 'We're going to have a look while it's quiet.'

'Won't it be in a dangerous state?' Louie asked anxiously.

'We won't take any risks.' Sam pecked her cheek. Louie looked at him resignedly, knowing he would go to great risks to provide them with fuel and realising she could do nothing to stop him.

'There's some stotty in the pantry,' Louie whispered. Sam found the stale squat piece of bread and began munching it before he was out of the house.

'Take care,' Louie called quietly as he let himself out of the back door.

The streets were empty as Sam stole through the village, to his ears his boots clanging like a soldier's the more he tried to creep unnoticed. He and John and Eb had decided they should explore the old mine on their own. If there was coal to be gleaned, the police must not know of their activities, so the fewer people who knew, the better. It had been Jacob Kirkup who had made the suggestion, provoked out of his law-abiding stance at the sight of his wife's failing health and his family's daily hunger.

'They say it used to be worked before the deep mines were sunk,' he had told Sam. 'Most of the men around here don't know of its existence - it's been closed a long while.'

'That's right,' Fanny had confirmed. 'I remember my grandfather telling me he worked there when he had a pony. I'd quite forgotten.'

'Can you remember whereabouts it was?' Sam had questioned.

Fanny had shaken her head, then a memory flickered briefly. 'Somewhere in the woods,' she had added tentatively. 'It goes under Whitton Common and the entrance was in the woods.'

A soft, damp mist hung over the dene like net curtains, hiding the trees and stream from view. Eb and John were waiting for him by the railway track that ran parallel to the cindered pathway. At Sam's, suggestion they had agreed to bring Bomber in on their plans. Another two minutes of waiting in the chilly echoing air brought their redheaded friend out of the mist.

'This way,' Eb directed, and they followed him closely. Once they were further away from the village and the dene became more overgrown with brambles and trees, Eb stopped by a high wall. It marked what was locally viewed as the boundary between the common land and the private preserve of the Seward-Scotts. A stark notice was nailed to an overhanging tree, warning the world to keep out. Eb swung himself up on a branch and dropped over the far side of the wall. The others followed.

A few yards away on the forbidden side, a shallow cave mouth gaped at them. The branches of a large honeysuckle hung down obscuring most of the entrance, but someone had recently cleared enough undergrowth to reveal the forgotten drift mine. Beneath the roots and dead foliage it was possible to see where the makeshift tracks had disgorged their truckloads of coal. The markings disappeared into the trees like ghostly footprints from another era.

'How the heck did you find this?' Sam asked with admiration.

Eb omitted to tell them that Eleanor had known of its whereabouts since childhood games of hide and seek with her brother Rupert. 'Had a scout around,' he answered vaguely.

'Gan on then,' Bomber said impatiently and ducked into the opening. Eb hesitated, his dread of underground welling up and threatening to overpower him like mustard gas.

'You stay out and keep guard.' Sam touched his arm briefly and headed after his mate. John followed.

Inside the mouth of the mine, Sam lit his lamp. The walls dripped wet and glistened in the flickering light. Ahead the way appeared to be blocked.

'There's a bit of loose coal lying about,' he told his friends.

'Aye, but the mine's caved in,' Bomber concluded gloomily.

'We can but try,' Sam said doggedly. There's enough here to fill a couple of barrows, then we'll dig a bit further in.'

They went back to the wall where they had left their crude picks and shovels. What hewing they did would be without the aid of any drills or explosives. Eb fetched the barrow they had hidden in the brambles. He had worked out that they could wheel a barrow of coal uphill to where the wall petered out on the brow of the Common and then down through Whitton Woods. It would be a long way round, but the coal was too heavy to lift over the wall, which was anyhow too close to the main path through the dene; they might draw the attention of an observant policeman.

All day the three men worked in the old mine, discarding their jackets and shirts in the sun as they sweated in the confines of the tunnel. Eb wheeled barrowfuls of the mediocre coal up through the trees and deposited it in a heap under an oak tree not far from the allotments, covering the booty with dead branches and brambles. Later in the day, the men heaped the coal into prams and knapsacks and headed for home.

That night the Kirkups and Ritsons enjoyed the heat of a real fire and Louie was able to cook a hot meal of baked potatoes and pea soup, even though the coal was of poor quality. Sam was ravenous after a hard day's work, and Louie rejoiced to see him in such good spirits, fired by their successful grafting.

The next day they struck their way further into the mine, risking the wrath of the hillside in shaking it awake. Bomber was nearly caught by a shower of stones, but, his instinct for danger still intact, managed to roll out of harm. That evening, they had coal to spare for the Kirkups' neighbours, the Parkins, as well as Clara Dobson and her daughters. Bomber took coal home for his parents and a couple of bucketfuls for Minnie's mother. Sam had plans for distributing the illicit coal around the village.

'We'll let a few more lads into the drift,' he said, throwing his pick into the cut they were making. 'There's enough coal here to last us well into the autumn. We'll win this strike yet,' he predicted determinedly.

Word was beginning to spread about this new source of fuel; children were paid in sweets to keep watch along the dene and to take the coal away under the pretence of pushing babies in their prams. Wilfred Parkin and Johnny Pearson came to help, as did Pat, a brother of Minnie's. For a week the working of the old drift mine and the distribution of its treasure went successfully. Then PC Turnbull caught Sadie Kirkup and Frank Robson climbing out of Whitton Woods, a bag of coal at the foot of the wall where they had thrown it.

'Where d'you get that from?' the young policeman demanded suspiciously. Frank's freckled face turned a guilty puce and he froze against the wall where he had dropped. Sadie slithered down after him.

'Get what?' she asked innocently.

That coal, you cheeky lass.' Turnbull pointed aggressively.

'It's nothing to do with us, mister,' Frank insisted.

'You little liar.' The policeman took a threatening step towards the skinny boy, yet he seemed unsure what to do next.

'The wood fairies must have left it.' Sadie stepped between them, giving the constable a fey smile. 'Wasn't that kind of them?'

Alfred Turnbull gawped at her for a moment as if he could not quite believe his own ears. Sadie glanced round and gave Frank a quick nod; the next second they turned on their heels and were fleeing up the lane. The policeman hesitated a fraction too long, reluctant to let them go, yet more interested in collecting the evidence of their theft. He let them escape.

Hauling the shopping bag of coal on to the handlebars of his bicycle, he thought how pleased Superintendent MacGuire would be with his vigilance; the officer dealt toughly with those who stole. The young constable was certain the children were only carrying the coal for others, men who had found some illegal source and were pilfering from the Seward-Scotts. Perhaps Mr Reginald himself would be interested in the discovery and grateful to a conscientious young policeman eager to make his way in the force. PC Turnbull mounted unsteadily with the top-heavy basket and pedalled for the police station.

Eb was taking a break outside the mine opening, sketching on a scrap of old newspaper, when MacGuire appeared with Alfred Turnbull. There was no warning of their coming; the children had gone off to play in the stream and he had been too absorbed in his drawing to hear them approach, truncheons in hand. It was late afternoon and only Sam and John remained inside the mine, oblivious to their ensnarement.

Eb rose cautiously to his feet, dropping his pencil and reaching defensively for his discarded shovel, meeting the policemen with a wary gaze.

'What's going on here, then?' MacGuire demanded stonily, pointing at the mine entrance. The muffled ring of iron on stone disturbed the tranquil peace of the woods. Eb knew he could not bluff his way out of the situation.

'What does it look like?' he answered levelly.

'It looks like trespass and removal of Seward property,' MacGuire thundered back. 'You're facing another prison sentence if you continue your thieving, Eb Kirkup - you of all people!'

'The Seward-Scotts have no use for the dregs in the drift,' Eb countered in a quiet, deliberate voice, appealing to the older man. 'Our families need the fuel. You know how damp the houses get with no fire in the grate - and they've got nothing to cook with unless we get them this coal.'

'We can't turn a blind eye to this sort of carry-on,' Robert MacGuire said uncomfortably.

'Who's in there?' Alfred Turnbull jabbed a thumb towards the drift mine. 'I've heard it's Red Sam Ritson who's the ringleader,' he sneered. 'Nowt but a Bolshie criminal.' Eb gave him a look of disdain; young Turnbull was gaining himself a name as a stirrer of trouble since the picket line clash. Eb gave no answer.

The old superintendent seemed unsure what to do next, but his eager constable was set for confrontation, willing to take on these men who dared to undermine the lock-out.

'Well, if you won't tell us who they are, we'll just have to make them come out,' he said savagely. 'We'll knock a few pit props away and see how they like it.'

As he stepped forward, Eb thrust himself between the policeman and the drift opening. Turnbull was all of his height but he was no match for Eb's brawny strength. Eb pushed the shovel against the young man's uniformed chest.

'Go any nearer that pit and I'll kill you,' he threatened in a low voice full of fury.

Alfred Turnbull turned red with indignation. 'Do you hear that, sir?' He called for his superior's intervention. 'Kirkup's threatening assault. That's another charge we'll get him on. Didn't you get long enough in gaol last time, eh?' he taunted.

'That's enough, Alfred,' MacGuire ordered, aware of the pent-up violence in Eb's taut arms. He believed at that moment the war-scarred miner would go to any lengths to protect his friends inside the drift. 'We'll give you ten minutes to clear out of here and stay out of here,' he continued bullishly. 'I never want to see anyone this side of the dene wall again. The next person I find trespassing will swing for it. Do you understand?' he growled.

Eb said nothing, but stepped back and relaxed the grip on his spade.

'You're not going to let them get away with it?' Turnbull gasped in disbelief at his own humiliation.

'Belt up and follow me,' MacGuire snapped at the belligerent young man. 'I want to hear no more about this.'

With that, the superintendent strode from the woodland clearing, his face tight with anger; anger at his constable's behaviour, at the pitman's contemptuous defiance, and at this bitter strike that was rending his community apart. It sickened him that he had to threaten Eb Kirkup, a war veteran who had gained the Military Medal for bravery, for grubbing on Seward land for a handful of coal.

Alfred Turnbull threw a look of loathing towards Eb as he reluctantly withdrew, kicking a heap of clothes discarded by the hewers into the adjacent stream in a last spiteful gesture. Eb watched them leave with relief. It was a blow to their fight for survival that their working of the drift mine had been uncovered, but he was thankful that MacGuire had decided to be lenient with them on this occasion. He did not trust young Turnbull, though, and foresaw further trouble from the quarrelsome policeman. Grimly, he turned and braced himself to enter the claustrophobic mine to alert Sam and John to the bad news.

That night Davie came home. Whistling, he sauntered through the back door to find 28 Hawthorn Street deserted. Dashed by the lack of welcome he knocked on Edie Parkin's door to discover the whereabouts of his family.

'They're all at the entertainment,' Edie told him, 'for the Relief Fund. Been practising all week - heard them through the wall. I'd have gone, but Mr Parkin's bad with his chest and—'

'Iris is there then?' Davie asked impatiently, cutting the neighbour short.

'Aye, she's singing in it, didn't you know?' Edie answered with a direct look.

'No, how could I?' Davie replied rather crossly. 'Where's it on at, Mrs Parkin?'

'Chapel hall.' Edie crossed her arms and Davie noticed how the skin wrinkled loose about her wrists. He thanked her and took off out of the yard gate. 'Grand to see you back,' Edie called after him. 'Not before time, mind you.'

By the time Davie reached the hall in North Street the show was into its second half. Pushing his way into the spartan, crowded room with the audience squeezed on to every available bench and chair, he saw the end of Sadie's dance with May Little and Jane Pinkney. They were dressed in a bizarre combination of Oriental kimonos and Sunday School hats and shoes, but the applause from the spectators was enthusiastic.

As they left the stage, beaming, Eb came on with Iris. Davie felt his stomach lurch at the sight of his wife dressed in an expensive fringed frock of black and jade and a fetching green band around her gleaming auburn hair. She was thinner than he had remembered, but her face was suffused with excitement, her red-painted lips parting in a generous smile at the gasps of appreciation from the audience. Davie felt his insides aching at her elfin beauty.

'Mammy!' a small voice cried from the left of the hall and Davie glanced over to see Raymond standing on Louie's knee and pointing joyously at his mother up on the big wide stage. Fanny and Jacob sat either side of them, with Sam, Hilda,

John and Marjory Hewitson squashed on to the end of the row. For a moment, Davie felt shut out, like a tramp in the cold watching a cosy family scene through a closed window. Then Eb struck up on the piano and Davie's attention was once more riveted on the singer before him.

Iris sang a couple of popular songs and then a string of traditional favourites, the audience cheering and whistling for more. She revelled in their adoration, intoxicated by the attention and the sound of her own voice filling the tightly packed hall. She had shaken with nerves right up until the moment she opened her mouth to sing. But Eb had given her arm an encouraging squeeze as they left the shelter of the wings and she had felt his quiet calm infect her body as she took the deep breaths before her performance.

For an encore she belted out 'The Lambton Worm' and Davie's favourite, 'Cushy Butterfield', wondering fleetingly where her truant husband might be.

As she took her final bows, she dragged Eb from his stool and made him accept the applause too. Scanning the rows in front, Iris saw Eleanor Seward-Scott smiling up at them. To perform in front of such a lady made her feel like a professional singer, dressed as she was in one of Eleanor's gowns, borrowed for the occasion. Iris was sure that for the rest of her life she would never forget this heady moment of dominating the stage in the dowdy hall; she felt powerful, sensual, loved and famous all at the same time.

As Iris and Eb left the stage to make way for Frank Robson's jokes and the Reverend Pinkney's violin, Davie felt a stab of envy at seeing his vivacious wife, so obviously happy in his absence, disappearing on the arm of his older brother. It seemed an age before the end of the show when all the performers shuffled on stage like a disorganised flock to take their final bows. Children spilled into the aisles and up on to the stage before the minister could finish the evening with a prayer. He shouted his blessing over the chatter of schoolfriends and the wail of tired babies.

Iris and Eb muscled their way off stage and over to the Kirkups, while Davie fought his way further into the hall against the retreating crowd. His family were chatting excitedly together as if he did not exist, until at last John spotted him climbing over a bench to reach them.

'Look who's finally decided to show his face,' he grunted.

'Davie!' his mother cried with delight and held out her arms to kiss him. Her youngest son warmed at the affectionate greeting and gave her a hug. Raymond looked puzzled and then pointed interestedly at his father.

'Hello, bonny lad.' Davie swept him from Louie's hold and kissed him gladly. 'By, have I missed you, son.' Louie kissed her brother on the cheek.

'We've missed you too,' she told him.

'Aye, pet.' Davie gave her a hug with his free arm. 'I'm sorry about - you know - the baby . . .'

'Aye.' Louie nodded and took Raymond back, then quickly changed the subject. 'Aren't you going to congratulate Iris on her singing, or did you miss it?'

Davie turned to his wife. She was watching him with considering green eyes. They were dramatically outlined in black liner, her cheeks flushed pink with energy, her red mouth moist in a tentative half-smile.

'Anybody want to introduce us?' she quipped. 'I don't think I've had the pleasure.'

Hilda smirked and Marjory giggled nervously, wondering if she was about to witness a famous Iris and Davie flare-up. But Davie was contrite and grinned in reply.

'Can I walk you home?' He stepped forward and offered Iris his arm.

'You can.' She kept her voice prim and slipped an arm through her husband's. The others fell in behind, relieved that the dramatics had been left behind on stage.

Outside in the dark Davie slipped an arm around Iris's waist. 'You were champion up there,' he told her. 'I was that proud of you, bonny lass.'

Iris smiled, pleased at the compliment. Unexpectedly she kissed him on the lips as they walked along. 'I'm glad you've come home, Davie,' she murmured. 'I've been a right misery without you - everyone will tell you.' Davie felt guilt clutch at his insides.

'I've missed you too, pet.' He squeezed her waist. 'I'll not be going away again.'

'Good,' Iris smiled and slipped her arm around his back,' 'cos I don't intend letting you out of my sight.'

Chapter Twenty-One

As August waned so did the resolve of some of the pitmen. The miners' leaders could wrest no concessions from the inflexible mine owners. Instead, the management at the Whitton Grange pits were actively seeking men who were desperate enough to return to work at a reduced wage. To counter their pressure, Sam and Johnny Pearson walked from village to village the length of the valley urging union members to stand together and uphold the strike. Sam would leap up at unofficial meetings, held in the back rooms of pubs and halls to avoid the attentions of the local police, and argue that to give up now would be suicide for their communities.

'We have sacrificed too much to give in to the bullying of the bosses,' he rallied the worried men. 'Our families can't have gone through all this suffering for nothing - we mustn't let them down now.'

But rumours were fluttering down the dusty streets that some men were considering a return to work. There was tension in the groups gathering on the street corners, a suspicion of one's neighbour that kept conversations guarded.

Raymond fell ill with a stomach complaint that manifested itself in three days of violent sickness and diarrhoea, leaving him weak and fractious. In desperation Iris announced that she was leaving and taking her baby son to her parents in Durham until he was better.

'He needs proper feeding,' she told Davie defensively. 'Dr Joice said he's ill because of his bad diet.'

'I can get him what he needs,' Davie answered desperately.

'With what?' Iris rounded on him.

'I'll steal if I have to,' Davie replied lamely.

'And land yourself in prison again?' Iris scoffed. 'A fat lot of use you'd be to us then.'

'I don't want you to go away to Durham again.' Davie's thin face pleaded with her forlornly. 'You said you wanted us to be together from now on.'

Iris sighed and sat down on their bed in the parlour, a half-packed bag at her feet. 'I do want us to be together,' she said more calmly. 'If only you'd let me speak to Mrs Seward-Scott -'

'No!' Davie was adamant. He scratched his bristly head in agitation. 'We're not going begging to her again - I'll not be beholden.'

'Well, if you won't take her money, the only other choice is to go back to work, can't you see that, Davie?' Iris pleaded.

'Don't ask me to do that, Iris,' Davie answered shocked. 'I'll not betray my family.'

'We're your family now, Davie,' Iris shouted back, 'and I'll not see Raymond starve to death!' She stood up and continued throwing clothes into the canvas bag.

She left later that morning, pawning her cameo brooch on the way to the station to pay for the train fare into Durham.

Her mother, delighted to see her grandson, fussed over the sickly child. 'We'll make you right as rain, little pet,' she crooned over the small boy. Iris's brothers and sisters, pleased to see their married sibling, plagued her with questions about Sadie, curious to discover more about the young girl who was shortly coming to live with them.

In the evenings, Iris helped out in the pub. Business was slack and the publican had had to lay off his two barmaids, but he was glad of Iris's company. Some nights the regular patrons would persuade Ramshaw's pretty daughter to sing at the piano in the back room, and her lively renditions of traditional local songs became so popular that the Market Inn soon boasted a reputation for entertainment, attracting others to come to sing or play the piano in the smoky intimacy of the snug. The portly Ramshaw was pleased with his eldest daughter for swelling the numbers of drinkers in his bar, and by her second week home he had begun to advertise her performances in the local newspaper.

One evening, a group of travelling players came in to refresh themselves after a show in a nearby hall. After hearing Iris sing, a wiry middle-aged man with grey hair sprouting from his cheekbones and a bluish tinge to his shaven chin approached the young woman. She half recognised his darting hooded eyes.

'Name's Barnfather,' he put out his hand. Iris shook it with an enquiring smile. 'Friends call me Barny.'

'We've met before,' Iris smiled at the small, energetic man before her.

'Whitley Bay,' Barny replied, 'couple of years back - talent contest - you won. Your voice has come on since then - lovely singer.' He rattled out his praise in short, quick sentences.

'Ta very much.' Iris grinned with pleasure. 'I remember you now. You were working the beaches with Columbine and Pierrot, weren't you?'

'Still am,' Barny laughed, croaky as a crow. 'Town halls, palaces, pier ends - any place that'll take us.' He jerked his head towards his companions. 'Come and have a drink with us.'

'I wish I could, but I'm serving here,' Iris explained. 'This is my dad's pub.'

Barny whistled through nicotined teeth. 'What a waste - you should be singing for a living. We're looking for a singer and tap-dancer to take Lavinia's place.'

'What happened to Lavinia?' Iris asked, amused and flattered by his offer.

'Ran off with a Latvian tailor,' Barny remarked. 'Said he always had her in stitches!' Iris laughed, unsure if this was the truth or just a joke from Barny's comic routine.

'Sorry, I'm the stay-at-home kind,' Iris answered wistfully.

'Well, if you ever get the urge,' Barny winked, 'let me know.' As he turned away he thought to add, 'The Laughing Duck, Scarborough - they always know where I am - you can leave a message there.'

'How long are you in town?' Iris asked on impulse.

'End of the week,' Barny told her.

'I'll come and see you if I get a night off,' Iris promised with a smile. A night of entertainment away from all her cares would be just the tonic she needed.

'Say you're a friend of Barny's - they'll let you in free,' the man assured her. 'Come backstage afterwards - meet the troupe - smell the greasepaint - show you the ropes,' he offered. Iris nodded as her attention was called by two becapped customers. She returned to serving drinks.

It was a still day in early September, the kind when summer lingers on in mellow sunshine and yellow fields shorn of wheat. A smell of dewy grass and ripening briars hung in the woods as Eb made his way up to the Common to meet Eleanor. He had a notebook of watercolours to show her, scenes of the countryside they had explored together over the past two months. Despite the hunger and misery surrounding him in the village below, this summer had been liberating for Eb. He had found his love for the squire's wife growing and strengthening. Eleanor had shared her friendship and quiet passion and given him a new-found confidence in himself. Above all she had convinced him of his ability to paint; out of the wreckage of his post-war existence had sprung this creativity that was gradually redeeming his life.

Eleanor was wearing hiking shoes and a purple skirt and matching short-sleeved blouse. Apart from a silver brooch, her appearance lacked adornment. Her short, dark hair was uncovered and the summer sun had toasted her pale face to a healthy tan. Eb thought how girlish and unsophisticated she seemed stretching out eagerly to meet him.

'Let's walk for a bit.' She smiled and took his hand unselfconsciously. They hiked across the Common and headed west, avoiding any pockets of habitation. For two hours they walked and talked, listened and were silent, enjoying the pale azure of the sky and the balmy, breathless air around them. At a dip in the hillside they scrambled down to a stream hidden by mossy banks and drank thirstily of the icy bubbling water. Throwing down her knapsack, Eleanor sank behind a screen of gorse bushes and unpacked the picnic. Mrs Dennison had made up a flask of hot coffee, salmon and mayonnaise sandwiches and chocolate cake. The amiable cook never questioned why her mistress had taken to eating lunch out in the open so much over the summer months. Eleanor watched with satisfaction as Eb tucked in enthusiastically.

'Let me see these paintings then,' Eleanor said as the last of the sandwiches was devoured. Eb grinned and, reaching into his discarded jacket, pulled out the notebook from inside the patched lining. He spread the pictures over the grass. Eleanor picked them up in turn, nodding and making small grunts of approval.

'This is my favourite.' She held up a vivid sunset of violent purples and phosphorous yellow battling over the familiar outlines of Whitton Common. 'It reminds me of when we first used to meet and watch the sun setting.'

'Aye, I often think of those times too,' Eb admitted. 'Sometimes I wonder what—' He stopped his musings abruptly.

'Wonder what?' Eleanor probed, watching the struggle going on in his vital blue eyes.

'What I'd have done if I hadn't met you,' he added in a low mumble.

'Meaning?' Eleanor asked softly. Eb held her look directly.

'I was dead inside, Eleanor,' he answered. 'In Flanders I died a hundred times over.' She waited as he found the words for which he searched. 'But with you I'm living again - inside - I'm happy. I know it sounds daft, with all the strife going on around us.' He dropped his gaze in embarrassment.

'No it doesn't.' Eleanor leaned towards him and clutched his hands. 'It's the way I feel too.' She continued reflectively, 'At first I thought I was drawn to you because you reminded me of my brother Rupert - you were an echo of the past. But it didn't take me long to realise I wanted you for yourself - I fell in love with *you*, Eb. Believe me, I tried not to - it seemed such a hopeless situation - the lady at the manor and the lowly collier and all that nonsense!' Her laugh was self-deprecatory. 'But here we are against all the odds.'

'You put it much better than I can,' Eb told her with a smile, 'but you speak for us both.' Gripping her hands tight, he pulled her close to him and brushed her face with his lips. Eleanor's mouth parted and they came together in an eager kiss.

Slipping back on to the tufted heath, the spiky gorse providing a discreet screen, they gave in to the passion they had kept in check for so long. Seared with longing, the two of them gave vent to their feelings under the impassive cloudless sky. Eleanor wept with delight at Eb's caressings, her body waking up from its long winter of neglect and rejection. In his arms she whispered her love to the surrounding insects and curious skylark, craving the final intimacy with this strong-limbed man.

Eb lay back trembling from the force of their lovemaking and gently kissed Eleanor's forehead. 'What now?' he wondered aloud.

Eleanor leaned into his firm shoulder. 'We talk about nature, read poetry and make love again,' she replied dreamily.

Eb laughed and let his fingers stroke her arm where he held her. 'Which first?' he demanded. She raised her lips to his once more in reply.

Later, Eleanor pulled on her blouse as a breeze stole down from the hilltops and cooled their zeal for each other. She propped herself against Eb's supine body.

'I want to read you a poem,' she told him. 'It's the last one that Rupert wrote as far as I know.' Eb watched her reach into the knapsack and unfold a fragile piece of paper covered in leaping handwriting. 'I've always been unsure whether to let you hear it,' she confessed, 'but now I want you to.'

Eb closed his eyes and basked in the temperate sun and the quiet emotion of Eleanor's clear voice as she recited Rupert's final poem, 'The Hungry Hills'. He listened to the nostalgic thoughts of a homesick boy far from home, dreaming about the glories of the countryside around Whitton Grange as Eb himself had done all those years ago. When Eleanor had finished, they remained wrapped in the silence of her dead brother's haunting words.

Finally Eb said, 'How quickly men grow old in war. It seems your brother knew he was going to die and yet he accepted it.'

He sat up, wishing to shake off the suddenly subdued mood that gripped them. Eleanor had tears on her cheeks. He brushed them away with his rough-skinned hands.

'The words always make me feel so guilty,' Eleanor whispered. 'Rupert should have lived to enjoy all this.' She swept the vista with her hands.

'At least he knew of such a place,' Eb comforted. He squeezed her slim shoulder. 'These are our hills now, Eleanor,' he added throatily. 'They're for the living.'

They reached for each other in a tender kiss, for a while longer shutting out the creeping, anxious thoughts of what lay beyond that moment.

Louie took great care in folding Sadie's new school blouse and skirt into the modest parcel she was packing for her journey into Durham. She ran her fingers over the shiny satchel Eb had bought and held it to her nose to breathe in the expensive odour of new leather. How she would miss the chattering and affectionate girl who had helped make her life bearable since her baby's death. Sadie was already at Hawthorn Street having a meagre farewell breakfast before Louie walked her to the Durham Road. Davie had volunteered to take their young cousin into Durham, Sam having arranged for them to cadge a lift into town with Mr Armstrong, the shopkeeper in Mill Terrace.

Sam would not be there himself. He was organising a picket at the gates of the Eleanor and Beatrice pits, which had opened for business. A dozen men had returned to work that week amid a storm of protest and abuse from their former workmates. The solid ranks of resistance had been breached and the fight was threatening to turn in on itself. Louie shuddered at the implications of the blacklegs' action, listening with bitterness to the unaccustomed clank of the pithead gear once more in motion at the top of the street.

Unexpectedly Minnie appeared in the doorway. The cut lip and black eye that Bomber had given her on her return from the farm had almost healed. A yellowish hue stained her left brow-bone above her lacklustre green eyes. Louie had found her friend strangely subdued these past weeks, as if her husband's violent temper at her truancy had extinguished her natural spark. It distressed her that Bomber had sunk to physical violence against Minnie, but Sam had told her not to interfere between husband and wife.

'Need a hand with anything?' Minnie asked without enthusiasm.

'No ta,' Louie responded briskly, to hide the sick emptiness she felt inside. 'I'm nearly done.' She folded the flaps of a grocery box around the sheets and clothing Sadie was taking with her, and tied the parcel up with string. 'Davie'll be here any minute to carry this lot.'

'Will he?' Minnie asked with too studied an indifference.

Louie glanced up quickly, a vague uneasiness worrying at the back of her mind. Minnie's face, recently the colour of tallow, was growing pink at the mention of her brother's name.

'Aye.' Louie scrutinised the other woman's face. Minnie's unguarded look betrayed her eagerness. 'Where's Jack?' Louie asked pointedly.

'With Margaret,' her friend answered quickly. 'I'll walk down the village with you and Davie.'

'What happened at Stand High Farm between you?' Louie asked abruptly. Minnie suddenly crumpled on to a kitchen chair, her head sagging like a marionette's.

Realisation came to Louie as if a blindfold had been loosened from her eyes. She could read Minnie's face all too well and it was guilt-ridden; yet she clearly could not deny herself this chance of a brief moment in Davie's company. Louie had known her schoolfriend had always admired her elder brother, but surely she was wrong in thinking something illicit had happened between them while they had been away from Whitton? Louie grew hot at the thought that she had virtually thrown them together in her desire to get Minnie and Jack out of her sight while she came to terms with her grief. She waited to hear Minnie's denial, but none came.

'It just happened,' Minnie replied, and burst into tears. Louie felt as if her stomach was weighted with stone. She could not go to her friend or offer comfort.

'Oh, Minnie!' Louie breathed out her disappointment. 'How could you?'

'I'm that unhappy about it,' Minnie tried to explain, 'but I still love him.'

Louie's disbelief gave way to anger. 'Get yourself home this minute, Minnie Bell, back to your husband and your bairn,' she ordered. 'I don't want you here when Davie comes, do you hear?'

The harshness of Louie's words seemed to jolt Minnie out of her self-pity. She stood up and wiped her nose on her sleeve. 'I didn't expect you to understand.' Minnie tossed her head. 'You don't know what it's like being married to a man who knocks you around. Your Sam's Mister Perfect.' She threw Louie a bitter look. 'Well, for just a few weeks I had a bit of fun too, and I don't regret a minute of it.'

Louie turned her back and said nothing more, deliberately continuing with her packing. She heard Minnie leave. Calming herself, she untied her apron and hung it on the back of the door. She combed her hair, fixed on her hat and buttoned up her cardigan. Minutes later Davie tramped in at the back door; Louie did not know if he had passed Minnie on the way or if words had been exchanged.

Tight-lipped and still fuming about Minnie's revelation, she answered Davie's banter with curt instructions and a frosty look. Davie attributed his sister's tense behaviour to her unhappiness at parting with Sadie.

'She'll be back on Friday,' he teased. 'You would think the lass was going off to Australia to look at your long face.' Davie gave Louie a quick hug. She brushed him off.

'Mind you bring Iris and Raymond back with you,' she answered shortly.

'They'll have to come home.' Davie was optimistic. 'There'll not be room for them at the Ramshaws' once Sadie's there.'

'Good,' Louie replied and marched out of the house. Davie shook his head, baffled by his sister's sudden concern for Iris. Still, it pleased him to think Louie missed his wife and son too, and he visibly brightened at the pleasant thought of seeing them again.

Reginald called at Hopkinson's house on his way home from a day's riding at Waterloo Bridge. His agent, who lived in the largest of the solid brick houses whose gardens straddled the dene, had indicated there was something of importance he wished to discuss. A bachelor who lived with his sister, Hopkinson had a propensity for brown paint; the doors, windowsills and skirting boards were daubed in a uniform chocolate brown, with faded cream and green wallpaper from another era. Reginald was ushered by a housemaid into the drawing room where his agent was hovering among the potted plants and heavy mahogany furniture. The room smelt of polish and a faint odour of gas from the unlit lamps.

'This had better be urgent,' Reginald told the grey-faced man bluntly. 'I've declined dinner at Fisher's to come here.'

Hopkinson drew his shoulders up stiffly. 'I merely wanted to report on that matter you asked me to look into,' he answered in his dry, clipped voice, 'that matter about Mrs Seward-Scott's companions.' Reginald's eyes lit up with interest. Before continuing, his host paused to pour them both a whisky from a cut-glass decanter. Reginald took a glass and swigged greedily at the strong liquid.

'Well then?' he asked impatiently.

Hopkinson sucked in his thin cheeks and sipped at his own drink. 'Mrs Seward-Scott is rumoured to be friendly with the Kirkup family—'

'I know that,' Reginald interrupted brusquely. 'She's made no secret of it, for God's sake.'

'Particularly friendly with a certain Ebenezer Kirkup,' Hopkinson went on, unruffled by his employer's rudeness, 'the eldest son.'

Reginald took a more considered sip of his whisky. 'Go on,' he ordered.

'Ebenezer is a war hero - stretcher-bearer in the Fifteenth - decorated for pulling an officer from a crater under persistent enemy fire—'

'I don't need a history of the man,' Reginald said testily. 'What is his relationship with my wife?'

Hopkinson coughed uneasily. 'There may be nothing in it,' he cautioned, 'but they have been seen walking together over the Common.' He hesitated. 'Mrs Seward-Scott has also given him lifts in her motor car.'

Reginald's brow furrowed in annoyance. 'Does he work for us?' he snapped.

'No,' his agent replied. 'He has been out of full-time employment for a couple of years - took a scunner to working underground after the war.'

'Probably just one of Eleanor's lame ducks,' Reginald grunted.

'He tends Dr Joice's garden from time to time,' the older man remarked.

'Does he?' the mine owner said with a tightening of his jaw. 'So no doubt Isobel Joice knows of this liaison.' He finished his drink quickly. 'I want them watched continually,' Reginald determined, 'and I want to know as much about this failed miner as there is to know. I'll not have him making a fool of my wife.'

Hopkinson looked at him unhappily. 'Would it not be better to hire someone more suited to the job of detective?' he asked peevishly. 'I find the whole thing rather -' He floundered for an acceptable word.

'Distasteful?' Reginald supplied it.

'Well - yes.' The agent coughed.

'I trust you,' his employer answered frankly, 'and I know that what is discussed between us is quite confidential. Do as I ask, and you'll be well rewarded.' He picked up his hat, discarded on the green velvet sofa. 'In the meantime, we keep our suspicions to ourselves, is that understood?'

Hopkinson nodded grimly and placed his half-finished whisky on a side table as he showed the tall mine owner to the door. He found such matters as marital intrigue and infidelity quite incomprehensible; they merely muddied the clear waters of commerce and business endeavour. Still, Reginald Seward-Scott was his paymaster and if he wished to pin the accusation of adultery on his haughty wife, then he, Hopkinson, would strive to find him the evidence.

Iris had persuaded her father to let her go to the Saturday matinee of Barny's touring players, and, for the first time in ages, she sat in a dimmed auditorium, albeit on a hard hall chair, and watched the magic of a theatrical performance. She gasped at the dancers, cried at the crooner's sentimental songs, howled at Barny's jokes and clapped the magician. For two hours she left behind the dreary world outside the half-empty hall, forgot the pub and her family, forgot the troubles of Whitton Grange, even emptied her head of Davie and Raymond.

So afterwards, when she was about to seek out her new acquaintances backstage, it was a shock to find Davie barging his way across the hall to meet her.

'What are you doing here?' she asked, momentarily taken aback.

'I've brought Sadie in. I might have guessed you'd have left the bairn to come and watch a bunch of second-rate actors,' Davie grumbled.

'They were very good,' Iris defended them body, 'and it's the first time I've had a minute to myself all week. I'm entitled to an hour off, aren't I? If I'm not serving pints, I'm changing and washing nappies or skivvying for my mam. The past two weeks haven't exactly been a holiday.'

'Well, you needn't worry about the bar any longer.' Davie took hold of her hand fiercely. 'You're coming home with me - you and the bairn. I'm not having my wife working for anyone. You belong back in Whitton with me.' Iris gawped at him; she had never heard Davie so riled over her before. People making for the exit were casting interested glances at the impending row.

'Don't boss me around,' Iris blazed back. 'You're hurting my hand.' At that moment Barny approached them up the aisle, his face still caked in lurid make-up.

'Giving you trouble is he?' the small comic asked. 'No need for harsh words, young man. Go quietly - there's a good lad.'

'And who the hell are you?' Davie rounded on the odd little man.

'Barnfather's the name - Barny to my friends.' He smiled an exaggerated red and white grimace.

'Well, Barnfather,' Davie shouted, 'you can go and—'

'Davie, shut up!' Iris cut off her husband's obscenities. 'I'm sorry, Barny, this is my husband. We can settle our own arguments, ta all the same.'

'There's nothing to argue about,' Davie answered aggressively. 'Iris is coming home with me now.'

He had not meant to lose his temper with his wife, but the disappointment of not finding her at home, compounded by his annoyance at seeing her watching the entertainment with rapture on her slim, pretty face, had lit the slow fuse to his anger. He was filled with a dread of the power of these actors to cast their spell over Iris and lead her away from him forever.

Iris struggled out of his hold. 'No, Davie, this time I'm not coming home - not as long as we've no home of our own and no money and no food. I'm not going to bed at night with an empty stomach again - I'm not prepared to see Raymond running around with no shoes on. I want a proper home of my own. I want a new dress without patches in it, I want money to go to the pictures once in a while. I want a husband who's in work, Davie!'

Davie and Barny stared at her passionate face in awe.

'I want all those things too,' Davie insisted, his anger blown over as soon as it had come. 'We'll have all you want once the strike is over and they're taking lads on at the pit again.'

'They're taking lads on now,' Iris reminded him pointedly, 'and they're offering a fortnight's bonus on top of normal wages for those who'll work - I've read it in the paper.'

'I couldn't scab,' Davie answered miserably. Lately, Tadger Brown had been whispering of such temptation, but Davie had closed his ears. Iris looked at him hopelessly.

'It's either that or I don't come home, Davie,' she said flatly. 'Barny's offered to take me on - and I'll go if you won't give us the home me and Raymond deserve.'

Davie was shocked by her words. He knew he had failed her as a husband; they had nothing of their own, not even a bed; any money he had come by had gone on beer and Woodbines and pitch and toss with his mates. He had even lain with another woman that summer while Iris worked in Louie's soup kitchen and sang on stage to raise money for his people. Remorse twisted his insides like a knife.

Barny looked from Davie to Iris, unembarrassed, as if watching a gripping play in whose outcome he was mildly interested.

'Just shove off, will you?' Davie turned on him with exasperation. Barny winked at Iris.

'If you need me,' he said with a cock of his head, 'backstage.' He left them alone.

'Iris,' Davie began, his mind in a turmoil of indecision, 'if I go back down the pit, they'd give us a hard time of it - folk wouldn't speak to us.'

Iris saw him wavering and pressed her advantage. 'I'll stand by you whatever they say,' she promised, 'and I don't care what they call me as long as my bairn is clothed and fed properly and we have a home of our own.'

Davie drew courage from the determined look in his wife's eyes. Life might be rough for a bit, he thought, but things would calm down eventually as more and more of them returned to work. Only fanatics like Sam Ritson thought they could still win the strike; most of the pitmen knew they were in the last throes of defeat. It was a matter of being practical and thinking of the future, like Iris was. Whatever happened he would still have her and Raymond.

With that thought to console him, Davie sighed heavily. 'All right, bonny lass, I'll go and see Naylor on Monday.'

'Promise?' Iris held his gaze suspiciously.

Davie's face relaxed into its familiar grin. 'Aye, I promise.'

They walked out of the hall into the September sun, arm in arm, oblivious to the storm they were about to create.

Chapter Twenty-Two

'I'll not let you do it!' Jacob Kirkup thundered at his youngest son. 'No son of mine will betray his own kind as a scab, do you hear me?'

'I don't have any choice.' Davie's slim face scowled. 'Me and Iris have discussed it over and over.'

'And why didn't you talk to your own family about it first?' his father glowered at him accusingly.

'It's a matter for Davie and me,' Iris piped up, annoyed at the way she was being ignored. 'He's doing it for me and the bairn - it's nothing to do with you, Mr Kirkup.'

Her tall, bearded father-in-law turned and gave her a dismissive look. 'As long as my son lives under my roof, whatever he does concerns me.' Iris gave a humph of frustration. Louie exchanged wary glances with her mother, who sat motionless in her chair, hands gripped in her lap.

Davie thrust his hands in his trouser pockets and went on the offensive. 'You don't believe in the strike either. It's got us nothing but empty bellies and empty pockets. Look at Mam.' Davie nodded at his listless mother. 'She's not eaten a decent meal for weeks.' Fanny looked at him unhappily, silently pleading for her favourite son to stop his rebellion.

'Don't you tell me your mother's bad health is my fault.' Jacob trembled with rage. His fingers itched at his broad leather belt as if he would use it against Davie as he'd done when his son was a boy.

'I'm saying nothing,' Davie answered petulantly and spat into the reeking fireplace. He leaned against the mantelpiece, his back to his hostile family.

'Don't waste your breath talking to a waster like him,' John vilified his brother. 'He's always thought of himself and no one else.' The brothers exchanged hostile looks.

'That's not true.' Iris crossed the kitchen and stood by her husband. 'Davie's thinking of me and Raymond.'

John laughed derisively. 'Ask him how much he was thinking of you up at Stand High Farm.'

'Don't, John.' Louie threw her brother a furious look.

'What do you mean by that?' Iris demanded.

But she got no reply. Their arguing was cut short by Sam walking in, shaking the rain from his upturned collar. Louie shivered from the damp draught he brought in with the open door. The room fell silent as Sam and Davie considered each other.

'I hear you've been to speak to Naylor this morning.' Sam's voice was calm.

'Aye,' Davie replied sullenly. 'What's it to do with you?'

'Sit down, son.' Sam indicated the chair Iris had just vacated. No one else challenged Sam's authority and Davie reluctantly sat down. Still standing, Sam leaned both fists on the table and fixed his brother-in-law with an intense look. 'I can understand your reasons for wanting to give in to Seward-Scott,' he began quietly. 'He's made life tough for all of us. Don't you think I want to get back to work too? My Louie has suffered more than most from this lock-out and sometimes I've been near to breaking myself.'

Davie glanced up at Sam in surprise; he could not imagine this pitman leader ever having doubts about anything.

'We've lost the fight, Sam man.' Davie flinched under his brother-in-law's dark gaze.

'No, we haven't, not by a long way.' Sam raised his voice. 'As long as we all stick together, we can't lose.' His fists clenched white as he spoke. 'The bosses are trying to break us down, district by district - split our ranks. Can't you see, Davie?'

189

he reasoned passionately. 'As a union man you must abide by our lodge decisions. We've voted to stay out on strike and that means all of us. Whatever we do we must have unity - when it's time to go back we'll all go back together.'

'But we're not united,' Davie argued. 'There're lads already back at the pit.'

'Just a handful out of hundreds of pitmen.' Sam jabbed the bare table top with a forefinger. 'We'll persuade them they've made the wrong decision.'

Louie felt a stirring of unease at the menace in her husband's voice and the steely set of his face. Her anger at Davie's selfishness was tinged with fear for his safety.

Davie hung his head, overwhelmed by his family's censure and Sam's lecturing. He did not feel strong enough to resist them all. Perhaps Sam was right and he should wait a while longer. Iris saw the indecision in her husband's boyish face and was riled by his weakness.

'Are you going to let Sam Ritson tell you what to do?' she ridiculed. 'Have you no mind of your own?'

Davie bit his lip, goaded by her disdain. He would not be humiliated in front of Iris just to please Louie's Bolshie husband. Sam might starve for his principles, but his own needs were much simpler. Davie pushed back his chair.

'Aye, I've a mind of my own. As far as I can see, unity and lodge votes have got us nowhere,' he answered back. 'I don't understand what all this hardship has been for - unless it's to give clever men like you a name for themselves.' Davie's small chin jutted out at Sam in defiance.

'Davie!' Louie remonstrated, but he ignored his sister's shocked face.

'Well, I'm not a clever man,' he glared at them all, 'I'm a hungry man with a hungry wife and bairn - and I'll provide for them any way I can.' He turned to Iris. 'I start next week as a hewer, with three shillings a day bonus on top of wages for the first fortnight.'

Iris's face broke into a smile of relief; she flung her arms around his neck and boldly kissed his mouth in front of the others. Louie felt a sick dread in the pit of her stomach at the finality of Davie's words. Sam thumped the table in disgust.

'Oh, son.' Jacob Kirkup's expression was pained; he looked up to the ceiling. 'What have I done to deserve a lad who'll betray his people for a bag of silver?'

'I'll not speak to you again, Judas.' John glared at his brother with hatred.

'That'll be no miss,' Davie snapped back.

'Stop it lads!' Fanny unexpectedly broke her silence and pulled herself to a standing position. 'This is still your father's house and we all have to get by under the same roof. I'll have no more shouting in my kitchen.' Her dark-ringed eyes blazed and Louie could see her mother's malnourished hands shaking as she faced Davie. 'I think what you're about to do is wrong, though God knows when I hear Raymond coughing I can understand why you're doing it. But whatever happens,' she turned now to John, 'he's my son and he's your brother and I'll not have him hounded out by your sharp tongue.' The Kirkup men fell into a sullen silence at her critical words.

Sam, who had not taken his eyes from Davie's belligerent face, called to his wife. 'Come on, Louie, we'll not stay while there's a scab amongst us.'

Louie hesitated, seeing the shimmer of tears in her mother's eyes. Then she stood up and walked over to Sam, lifting her coat off a nail in the back of the door.

'Call again soon, Louie pet,' her mother said.

'Aye, I will,' Louie agreed quietly, loath to leave her mother alone with her warring family.

Sam briskly ushered her out, but stopped long enough to deliver his final message. 'Cross that picket line, Davie Kirkup,' he warned, 'and you'll be a leper in Whitton Grange till the day you die.'

On a chilly morning in late September, Davie went back to the pit. He was among a small group of young men, including Tadger Brown, who were lured by the prospect of a hewer's job. No longer would they have to shift heavy tubs of coal around the pit, risking being run over by a wagon or trampled on by a nervous pony. As hewers they were now the elite of the pitmen, grafting at the coalface like their older brothers and fathers had done.

'We would've had to wait another ten years to get a job like this,' Tadger commented brightly, his breath suspended in a cloud before him in the covered van that was transporting them to the pit. 'They're the daft ones, not us.'

Davie lifted a flap of canvas and peered out of the van, but it was too dark to see more than the shadow of houses about them. Around him he could hear the crunch of boots; several dozen policemen had been drafted in to protect the fifteen men in the van.

'They've stopped my union benefits.' A voice at the end of the bench spoke up nervously. The vehicle lumbered on, jolting over the rough lanes towards the pit gates.

'Let's start our own thrift fund,' another suggested. 'Give our families a bit of insurance - shilling a week, say?'

There was a general murmur of agreement, then they fell silent again. Davie scrutinised the man opposite him, the one who had suggested the insurance fund. Under his large cap, his face was angular, with a thin moustache. Davie realised he had never seen the man before.

'You're not from round here, then?' Davie enquired.

'No,' the other man shook his head, 'I'm from t'other side of Durham.'

'Why d'you come here?' Davie was intrigued.

'I was the only man wanted work in my village.' He sounded more defensive. 'It wasn't safe for me and the missus, so they moved us here.' There was no reply from his companions so he added bitterly, 'I had four bairns to support - until the baby died last month. I'll dig coal for any bugger before I see another of my bairns die.'

The silence was no longer awkward as they felt drawn to each other in their common plight. The van laboured up the final stretch to the pit. Suddenly shouting broke out ahead.

'Pickets,' Tadger muttered apprehensively.

Moments later, the canvas protection around them was pelted with stones. They heard the scuffling of a crowd just feet away from where they huddled.

'Scabs! Scabs!' the chant went up. 'Let us at the bastards!' The abuse went on incessantly as the van crawled and sputtered its way to the gates. Davie could feel the force of bodies jostling the wagon and for a few minutes he thought they were going to be overturned. Then came the sound of their uniformed protectors smacking into the demonstrators with their truncheons. He wondered if Sam and John were among the pickets. Well, it was their own daft fault if they were, he thought savagely; they were the ones causing the division between the pitmen, not him.

'Don't worry, you get used to it,' the stranger assured him. 'Just think of your family until you're safe inside that pit.'

Davie forced a cheerful smile. 'That's the first time I've heard someone call a pit safe,' he joked.

'Safe as houses, the Eleanor and Beatrice,' the man laughed.

The van surged forward, nearly throwing the men off their makeshift seats.

The gates clanged shut behind them and the noise of the pickets' obscenities subsided. Inside the yard the men disembarked in a chatter of relief and made their way to the winding house.

Running the gauntlet of angry pickets became a twice-daily event, at the beginning and end of Davie's shift. He closed his eyes and ears to the bitter frustration of the union men who harangued him from the other side of the van walls. Each day he was herded with the other blacklegs like shamed criminals into the anonymous van that the pit management had hired to bring them to work. Each day, scores of policemen were there to provide a safe passage through the angry demonstrators lining the road to the pit.

'We know who you are,' they shouted, 'and we know where you live.'

But at the end of the fortnight, Davie took home his first pay packet for many months. He sent Iris out to the store and she came back with bacon ends for a substantial broth, jam and butter, tea, cocoa and tinned fruit. With the milk they could now afford she made semolina pudding for Raymond with a generous dollop of jam. Sadie, who was home from school for the weekend, helped her stagger back with bags of flour, sugar and eggs for Fanny to do her longed-for baking. The fire was stoked up with the coal Davie earned as part of his wages and the small kitchen was once again bathed in firelight and the smell of warm bread.

Yet for Jacob and Fanny their delight at the sight of Raymond and Sadie cramming their mouths with the welcome food was blighted by their guilt at sharing such bounty. At the thought of their hungry neighbours, each mouthful felt stodgy and indigestible. Sam and Louie stayed away and declined tea with them that Saturday and John refused to eat Iris's food, taking himself off to Marjory Hewitson's family for his meals.

Eb seemed devoid of appetite too, and Hilda curtailed her afternoon off and returned to Greenbrae on the pretext that the Joices were entertaining that evening and needed her help. Jacob rebuffed his wife when she offered him a second cup of tea and hastened out to spend the evening at the Institute working on his sermon for the following day.

Only Iris seemed undaunted by the strained atmosphere around her. After she and Sadie had cleared away the plates and washed up, she instructed Davie to bring in the tin bath from its hook in the yard and fill it with steaming-hot water from the boiling pot. With Raymond put to bed and Davie away to the pub, she undressed behind the clotheshorse and steeped herself in the warm water. For half an hour she lathered herself with her new bar of Lux soap and luxuriated in the steamy warmth of the kitchen, singing musical hits to herself. On the other side of the screen of clothes Fanny sat sewing on buttons with the thread her daughter-in-law had bought, while Sadie, engrossed in some homework at the kitchen table, sucked a pencil under the phosphorous glow of a paraffin lamp.

This is the life, Iris smiled to herself, eyes closed in a half stupor. Her stomach was full, her skin clean and smelling of soap, and her bones warm. She hummed cheerfully and thought erotic thoughts in anticipation of Davie's return from the pub. He would be in a good humour; she was mellow and ready for love.

Suddenly the cosy calm was shattered by a deafening crash and the violent splintering of glass, as a brick came hurtling into the peaceful kitchen. Iris screamed in shock as she floundered for her towel. Fanny gasped and dropped her mending.

'Sadie, get under the table!' her aunt ordered, fearful of a further attack. The slight girl slid off her chair and cowered under the solid table. The offending brick lay inches away, having ripped a hole in the thin linoleum as it landed. Reaching out to touch it, Sadie realised her hand was bleeding, though the sight of her own blood did not alarm her. She crouched there, heart hammering, as the women took charge. Iris, wrapped in her towel, leapt over to the window and pulled the flimsy curtain across the gaping teeth of glass. She heard someone running away but it was too dark to make out the assailant's face.

'Mind your feet,' Fanny warned, but Iris already felt her soles smarting as broken fragments of glass pierced her skin.

'What the bloody hell do they think they're playing at?' she shouted in fright.

'Watch your language,' Fanny reprimanded.

'They could have killed one of us.' Iris was indignant. 'Are you all right, Sadie?' She peered under the table. The frightened girl nodded.

'You can come out now, pet,' Fanny coaxed. 'They won't be back.' Cautiously, her dark-haired niece emerged from her sanctuary.

'I'll go and check on Raymond,' Iris said. 'To think, it could have been the parlour window —' She shuddered.

'You get the brush and pan, Sadie, and we'll get the floor swept up before there's any more harm done.'

As the young girl moved towards the cupboard, Fanny noticed she was hurt.

'Let me take a look at that,' she demanded. She tutted at the wound in the skinny hand. 'Why didn't you say you were bleeding, lass?' she remonstrated. 'Let's get this washed and bandaged up first.' She felt sick and faint as she tended to Sadie's cuts and then saw to the splinters in Iris's feet. How could anyone contemplate attacking innocent women sitting in the quiet of their own home? she wondered, scandalised. But looking at Iris's wincing face as she daubed her lacerated feet, Fanny knew it had only been a matter of time before the bitter anger of the village was turned against them for harbouring a blackleg. Her own beloved Davie, a traitor to his people, had brought that brick hurtling through their window. A wave of humiliation flooded over her at the thought of how the Kirkups were now despised.

When Jacob returned he went white with fury as Fanny told him of the attack on his home and family. It was a subdued Davie who took his father's lecturing that night, the pleasant fuzz of inebriation evaporating quickly in the cold shock of what had taken place.

'I'll ask Naylor to house us somewhere else,' Davie suggested resignedly.

'You don't have to give in to the threats of troublemakers,' his father answered more leniently. 'They were just bad lads - no union men would have done this.'

'They'll come back again,' Davie sighed, 'and I've brought you and Mam enough trouble as it is.'

'If you packed in your job at the pit, we'd all be able to live here safely,' his father growled.

'No,' Davie replied stubbornly, 'there's no going back now. Iris and I'll move out just as soon as we can.' He got up quickly and shut himself in the parlour before the tears in his mother's eyes spilled over.

The pit management found Davie a dilapidated house in Whitton Station, a half-mile from Whitton Grange. The only other person who knew them there was Davie's new workmate, Alfred Hutchinson, the stranger from East Durham. He and his wife Molly and their three remaining children lived two doors away in Station Lane. Davie and Iris's house consisted of a downstairs kitchen-cum-parlour and an upstairs bedroom. It had been vacant for some time. The rooms were inches thick with coal dust and grime and they had to share the earthen closet with three other families, but Iris set to work with vigour, cleaning and scrubbing her new home. Molly offered to mind Raymond while her new neighbour tackled the dirt, fetching her cups of tea at regular intervals. Iris gulped them down thankfully, her throat and eyes irritated by the ubiquitous dust.

By the time Davie returned home on their first day in their new house, Iris had it passably clean, with a cheery fire crackling in the grate and the kitchen decorated with her few treasured possessions: a white linen tablecloth with D and I embroidered on to the corner, two china spaniels, and photographs of film stars which she'd torn from magazines and pinned around the room.

'I don't mind having my tea with Mary Pickford,' Davie teased, 'but Ramon Novarro puts me right off my bacon and eggs.'

'That's from The Prisoner of Zenda, don't you remember?' Iris sounded put out.

'I remember what happened after.' Davie grinned and slipped his arms around her waist, pecking her neck. Iris giggled. 'Why don't you show me how you've arranged the bedroom?' Davie suggested.

'I'll have to put Raymond to bed first,' Iris answered.

'Molly'll have him for a bit,' Davie persisted, nibbling her ear.

'All right then,' Iris smiled in agreement.

Shortly afterwards they lay together upstairs in the creaking bed they had exchanged for a half-ton of coal. The room was devoid of other furniture, save an old washstand with a cracked pink flowered bowl and jug standing on its marble top. Iris's three dresses and Davie's suit hung behind the door.

'It's grand to have our own place at last.' Iris sighed contentedly, 'We can do what we want now without half your family looking on in disapproval.'

'Aye.' Davie kissed her head as she lay on his shoulder. 'Things'll be just champion from now on.'

'No more John calling you worse than muck,' Iris added.

'No more sermons from Sam,' Davie laughed.

'Just us two - and Raymond,' Iris said softly.

'Aye, just us,' Davie echoed. Both of them fell silent in their own thoughts, as a line of trucks trundled noisily past their window.

October finished in a flurry of wet gales, with the valley turning from burnished gold to wintry browns. The trees of Whitton Woods were shedding their leaves in preparation for a long sleep, nature bedding down under their roots. Eleanor learned from Eb that the villagers were plodding on in their half-starved state, waiting for the inevitable end to the protracted lockout. Few thought they would gain anything from their sacrifice, but fewer still had taken the easy way out of their penury and returned to the pit.

Two-thirds of the families in Whitton Grange were relying on the soup kitchen at the chapel to feed their children. Eleanor had made anonymous donations for the helpers to buy food and she had gone to London on two occasions to speak to gatherings of radical women in order to keep alive sympathy for the miners' cause and to raise funds. Reginald had been livid with her for her open defiance towards him and her father. Perhaps to placate them, she had agreed to hold a party to celebrate Reginald's thirty-seventh birthday, and, as it fell on the second day in November, between Hallowe'en and Guy Fawkes Night, it was decided to make it a fancy dress ball with bonfire and fireworks.

That night the stars shone in a cold, inky-black sky as if specially lit for the occasion. As the scores of guests arrived from around the county and disgorged from their chauffeur-driven cars in bizarre costumes, a huge bonfire was set alight in a specially built surround beyond the terrace.

Clasping drinks of hot whisky punch, the revellers gasped and cheered as fireworks shot off into the sky, showering them with coloured flashes of light. There were shrieks from some of the younger guests, led by Beatrice, as louder fireworks were set off along the terrace just in front of the spectators.

'This is absolutely thrilling!' screamed Harriet Swainson as another bang ricocheted around the grounds.

'Give me another drink, darling.' Rose Fisher beckoned over the tight-lipped butler, Laws, and exchanged an empty glass for a full one from his tray.

'Look, the guy's caught fire!' Libby Fisher, dressed in Turkish harem pants and veil, pointed excitedly. Eleanor saw Reginald standing close to her on the terrace, illuminated by the lights from the house and the glow from the bonfire. She glanced from them to the blazing guy, impaled on its stake. Someone had tied a muffler around its neck and jammed a cap on its head. Eleanor had not noticed until now how alike the effigy was to a miner.

'Bravo!' cried Reginald, fired by the punch. 'I could think of a few men I'd like to see up there!' His guests responded with laughter.

'One of your Bolshies perhaps?' Swainson the ship owner suggested.

'Rather,' agreed Reginald.

'Burn the bally lot, I say,' Libby added loudly, slopping punch on to the flagstones as she gestured towards Whitton Grange.

Eleanor turned and retreated to the house before her simmering rage could erupt at the jeering, insensitive faces paying court to her husband.

Food was served in the dining room and a band played in the ballroom until the early hours of the morning. Beatrice, unrestrained in Sandy's absence, called for more daring dances and then insisted on the younger guests ducking for apples in the ornamental pond on the terrace. Several fell in or were pushed and had to be given dry clothes.

Breakfast was served at four in the morning. Eleanor escaped to the conservatory where she found Isobel and the art teacher, Ruth Spencer. She sat down exhausted, lighting up a cigarette. 'A quiet corner at last,' she breathed.

Before either of her friends had time to answer, Harriet Swainson appeared with Beatrice and half a dozen others.

'Can we join you?' Harriet asked, plonking herself down on a wicker chair. The others were vocal in their recounting of the evening's events as they cleared their plates of kedgeree and toast.

'How is your artist friend?' Harriet suddenly asked Eleanor. Eleanor started in astonishment.

'What friend?' she countered, withdrawing behind a veil of smoke.

'That - gentleman you introduced Susie and me to at the Laing Gallery,' Harriet reminded her. 'Mr Saunders or something. Surely you recall our meeting? It's the last time I saw you before this evening.'

'Oh, yes.' Eleanor tried to sound nonchalant. 'That was Mr Flanders.'

'Flanders?' Ruth Spencer queried with interest. 'I don't know the name. Is he a new find of yours, Eleanor?' the art teacher enquired.

'He's a modern artist,' Harriet interrupted, triumphant at being able to talk knowledgeably about art. 'At least he was studying those ghastly cube-shaped paintings in the gallery. Isn't that so, Eleanor?'

'Yes,' Eleanor answered feebly, feeling a flush of panic rushing to her cheeks. She lit another cigarette from the burning end in her holder. 'He's an amateur, Ruth.' She recovered her poise. 'That's why you won't have heard of him.'

'Not so amateur,' her father interjected from behind; Eleanor turned and saw him standing in the doorway with Reginald. Her insides lurched with fear. 'I've seen pictures by this mysterious artist in Eleanor's room - he did an excellent portrait of you, didn't he, my dear?'

Eleanor drew hard on her cigarette and managed a smile.

'I'd be interested to see it,' Ruth said, unaware of her friend's predicament.

'We all would.' Reginald eyed his wife keenly. 'You've never told me about him, Eleanor. Where does this Mr Flanders do his painting?' She knew then that Reginald had overheard the whole conversation. Dragging her face into a smile and inwardly cursing the talkative Harriet, she gave an indifferent shrug.

'In Darlington, I believe,' she fabricated quickly. 'That's where he's from, anyway. Isobel introduced me to him - he's a teacher - isn't that so, Isobel?' She hardly dared look at her friend's face, but Isobel was the only person who could pull her free of the trap which Reginald was about to snap shut.

'That's right,' Isobel replied calmly. 'Mr Flanders enjoys painting as a hobby - Eleanor was kind enough to show him around the Laing for me as I had to return home early. We'd all been through to Newcastle for the day together.' She met Reginald's hostile look with serene hazel eyes; Eleanor shot her a grateful glance.

'I always knew you were a dark one, Isobel,' Beatrice laughed. 'How bohemian of you to have an artist friend.' She stood up, her dyed blonde hair frizzing around her face after her earlier ducking in the pond. 'Come on everyone, let's have a last fling on the dance floor.'

'What a ripping idea.' Harriet clapped her hands in agreement and followed, pulling up a tired-looking Egyptian king from his seat. Eleanor relaxed as she saw Reginald retreat from the conservatory too, leaving the three friends alone.

'Thank you,' she murmured to Isobel. For a moment the friends all looked at each other. Ruth Spencer broke the silence.

'Anybody like to tell me what's going on?' she asked bemusedly.

Iris opened the door cautiously. To her amazement she found Louie standing on the step, a basket balanced on her arm. None of Davie's family had been near them since their move to Whitton Station, over a month ago. She had called once with Raymond to see Fanny but had had to leave swiftly when John came in with Marjory.

'Is Davie in?' Louie asked awkwardly.

'Yes, come in.' Iris smiled cheerfully. 'He's kipping upstairs before he goes—' She broke off suddenly, embarrassed to mention his work.

'I won't disturb him then,' Louie answered stiffly and stepped backwards, suddenly doubtful about her rash decision to visit her outcast brother.

'Don't be daft.' Iris took her arm. 'Come inside - I've been longing to see you and hear news of everyone.' She nodded her head for Louie to follow her.

Louie obeyed, curious to see how Iris had arranged her new home. She gasped to see a large sideboard and upright chairs which matched the central table. Two new solid, square-armed easy chairs filled the area in front of the fire. The furnishings were plain and severe in Louie's opinion, but they aped the ultra-modern fashions she had seen in catalogues. Brightly flowered curtains hung at the window and there were freshly made biscuits on the table. Her blue eyes widened and she felt the saliva collecting in her mouth.

'It's all on tick.' Iris laughed at Louie's envious appraisal of the room. 'It'll be years before we pay this lot off - but you've got to live for today, haven't you?' Louie made no comment. 'Haway and sit down.' Iris pushed her into one of the spacious new armchairs. 'I'll make a pot of tea and go and tell Davie you're here. Raymond's having a nap too - he'll be cock-a-hoop to see his Auntie Louie again.'

Louie's face relaxed; she did not like to admit that it was Raymond she most wished to see. A month of adhering to Sam's ban on visits to Davie's house had driven her nearly frantic with wondering how her brother and nephew were. To her surprise she was even glad to see Iris once more. Whatever part she had played in this split within the family, Iris had been a strong support to Louie over the summer. With her jokes and forthright comments at the soup kitchen, and her singing, she had kept her sister-in-law's blue moods at bay. Louie hated to admit how much she missed them all, how dreary life was without them, Sam constantly absent at meetings and the others listless with hunger and too much time on their hands.

Iris warmed the teapot and disappeared upstairs. Louie got up and made the tea. Unable to resist the biscuits before her, she crammed one into her mouth as Iris reappeared with Raymond.

'Look who's here to see you.' She held the boy towards his aunt. Immediately he spread his arms out for Louie to take him, which she responded to at once.

'I've missed you, little pet.' Louie hugged the auburn-haired boy and kissed his button nose. 'Tell Auntie Louie what you've been up to, eh?' She sat him on her knee and began a vigorous bouncing game.

Raymond squealed in delight. He began a babble of nonsensical conversation.

'Have another biscuit,' Iris grinned. 'Molly made them - she's my new neighbour. Got three kids of her own - had four, but her baby died in August. That's why they moved here - husband's working down the Eleanor, he's a marra of Davie's.'

Louie looked up, her eyes filling with unexpected tears; it took so little to remind her how deeply she still felt the loss of her baby.

'I'm sorry for her,' she answered quietly.

'You might like to meet her,' Iris suggested.

'Maybes.' Louie shrugged noncommittally.

Suddenly she yearned to confide in Iris her worry that she had not fallen pregnant, the gnawing fear that she might never carry another baby. Sam, she knew, would not talk about it and pride would never let her discuss her worries with her mother or Hilda, but Iris was worldly-wise, she might put Louie's mind at rest.

But as she struggled to find the words, Davie came thumping down the stairs. He burst into the room, his hair tousled and his eyes still bleary.

'Louie,' he grinned at her with pleasure, 'it's grand to see you.' He came across the room and kissed her bashfully. 'By, you look skinny,' he exclaimed. 'Get something down you. Iris - fetch our Louie a sandwich.'

'I didn't come for food,' Louie said proudly.

'Don't be daft,' Davie interrupted.

'You'll stay and have tea with us, won't you?' Iris insisted too.

'No, I'll have to get back soon - Sam doesn't know I'm here,' Louie explained. 'I'll have to be home before he is.'

'Still rallying the troops, is he?' Davie teased.

'Aye.' Louie looked at him sharply. 'The strike's not finished yet.'

'I give it another couple of weeks,' Davie predicted. 'No man'll stick it out till Christmas.'

'Stop talking about the strike.' Iris was impatient. 'I want to hear all the gossip.'

'Not much to tell,' Louie sighed. 'There's nothing going on these days - except at The Grange. Did you see the fireworks the other night?'

'Yes,' Iris nodded, as she made a cheese sandwich for her guest, 'lit up the sky for miles around. Saw the guests leaving the next morning when Davie was going to work - by, they know how to enjoy themselves up there!'

'More money than sense,' Louie commented caustically.

'Mam all right?' Davie asked casually, his tone belying the concern he felt.

'Cough's bad again,' Louie reported. 'Dr Joice was out the other day. Says it won't improve while she's living in a damp house with no fire.'

'She doesn't have to!' Davie thumped the table in frustration.

'She's loyal to Da,' Louie sparked back. 'She'd never force him back to the pit because of her health.' The three of them fell into an uneasy silence.

'How's Sam then?' Iris tried to break the tension.

'Hardly see him.' Louie's pale face betrayed her unhappiness. 'He's on a one-man crusade to keep the men together - speaks wherever he can dodge the police. Even Bomber can't be bothered to help him now the cold weather's set in,' she added bitterly.

'Too busy knocking Minnie around, I bet.' Iris did not conceal her distaste. Louie shot her a cautious look.

'No, not recently,' she answered, looking beyond the chattering Raymond to her brother. He did not meet her gaze, but seemed intent on something by his feet. 'Minnie's pregnant again - Bomber's pleased.'

'By, those Slatterys breed like rabbits!' Iris cried. 'I bet Bomber's thinking hard about going back to work now. Might have him as a marra soon, Davie.' She looked at her husband.

'Aye,' Davie mumbled. 'Now are you going to get my tea ready?' He seemed keen to change the subject. Louie watched his expression, but it betrayed no feeling. It had occurred to her before now that Davie might be the father of Minnie's unborn child. She wondered if he pondered the likelihood too.

'Just goes to show you never know what goes on between husband and wife behind closed doors.' Iris continued to talk as she checked the pie in the round-doored oven. 'Bomber and Minnie, I mean - always at each other's throat in public,' she laughed. 'You pit folk are a strange lot.'

Behind Iris's back, Davie met the enquiring eyes of his sister. For a moment Louie saw the guilt that clung to her brother like a shadow. She glanced away in disappointment and turned her attention to her chattering nephew.

Chapter Twenty-Three

By the end of November the miners' leaders began to cave into pressure from the owners to capitulate on their terms. In the Midlands, the national newspapers gleefully reported, large numbers of miners were returning to work. Deals were being struck locally. In the face of the crumbling strike, the Durham lodges stood almost alone, still voting against the Government's proposals that would ensure them the most meagre wages and conditions.

The Durham owners set up a negotiating committee, with Reginald Seward-Scott as its chairman, with full powers to work out a district settlement. To Sam's disgust, his father Samuel Ritson and members of the Durham Association met with the owners on three occasions. Minimum wages would be paid until February; coal and rent would no longer be considered as extras but as part of wages. After a long wrangle in which Seward-Scott put up vehement objections, the hewers were to be allowed a seven-and-a-half-hour shift, while the other miners worked an eight-hour day plus an hour's winding. It was little consolation to the dispirited men.

'You've given them everything they want!' Sam railed at his father.

'No one's to be victimised,' his father defended lamely. 'They won't hold it against you lads who took action during the stoppage. The likes of you and Bomber will get your jobs back.'

'Aye, your father made sure of that.' Liza Ritson nodded her grey head, her once plump face sagging at the jowls like an old bloodhound.

'And you believe them?' Sam said contemptuously.

'They gave their word,' Samuel replied stoutly.

Sam shook his head in disbelief. 'The word of Seward-Scott is as empty as that grate.' He stabbed a finger at the ash-filled range. He left abruptly, leaving behind a family subdued and resentful at his accusing words.

At the end of the month there was a further ballot. Locally the vote was still to prolong the strike, but throughout the region they did not get the two-thirds majority needed to continue their action. Sam fumed as the press pilloried the Durham miners as Communist agitators. Finally, on the 4th December, the Durham Association instructed their members to return to work; all the other coalfields had already surrendered to the combined might of the owners, the Government, the press, and hunger.

Louie sat huddled in her coat and gloves by the light of a guttering candle as Sam told her the inevitable - the strike was over. Tomorrow, pitmen would be queuing up for work at the manager's office.

'I'll not go begging for my job back,' Sam said bitterly.

Louie glanced at her husband, haggard, tired and hollow-cheeked in the distorting candlelight. He looked old, as if time had drawn a mask of lines and shadows across his once handsome square-jawed face. Louie shivered, pressing her hands between her legs for warmth. She felt chilled to the marrow.

'You've done more than anyone for this village,' Louie said wearily, 'but the fighting's over, Sam. We need your job at the pit.' She thought silently of the mountain of credit they owed at the store, of their pawned silver tea service of which she had been so proud, of the fear of eviction that still hung over them if Sam was not re-employed at the Eleanor.

But Sam appeared not to hear. He continued fretfully, 'Bomber voted to return to work, can you believe it? A marra of mine and he stabs me in the back like that!'

'You can't blame him,' Louie reasoned, 'with Minnie pregnant and wee Jack always poorly - they're desperate.' She bit back the words 'just like us'.

'I'll not speak to him,' Sam declared stubbornly.

Louie sighed with impatience, yet she did not have the strength to argue back. As things were going, there would be no one to whom they could speak. All around them, people had betrayed Sam's cause, found wanting when their strength of purpose was tested beyond endurance. Few men with craving bellies upheld the passionate convictions of her iron-willed husband, and often she found it hard to measure up to his exacting standards. He did not know about her secret visits to Davie and Iris, and she would never tell him. She felt edgy with guilt at going behind Sam's back, and yet resentful that she could not visit her brother openly and was denied her nephew's cheerful company.

'I'm going over to Mam's.' Louie rose, hugging herself against the cold.

Sam watched her silently as she brushed past him, nearly extinguishing the spluttering candle. He wanted to reach out and stop her, hold her tall, frail body to his, but he could not bring himself to do so. His heart was so full of venomous thoughts against those who had made his people suffer, his disappointment at the futile strike so acute, that he could not take comfort in his wife's presence. Her blue eyes were accusing; she wished him to humble his pride and go back cap in hand to the bosses. Well, pride was all he had left, and Sam Ritson would not trade it in for a reduced wage. He would wait until they sent for him. Louie went, stony-faced, knowing nothing she could say would change Sam's mind.

The following week saw half of Whitton Grange return to work. Men came back from shifts underground with grim stories of the worsened conditions below. They were working up to their waists in water in one of the seams. But Christmas was approaching, and the pitmen accepted what work and wages they were given. Jacob and John Kirkup were taken back and Samuel Ritson and his son-in-law Johnny Pearson were also hired as face workers. A week before Christmas, Bomber approached the under-manager and asked for a job.

Minnie came rushing into Louie's house in floods of tears. When her friend had finally calmed her down, she gathered from Minnie the awful news that there was no work for Bomber at the Eleanor or Beatrice.

'Naylor said there was no need for him just now - not enough work,' Minnie sobbed.

'That's rubbish!' Louie cried. 'They're still taking on strangers from outside the village.'

'They won't have Bomber.' Minnie hid her face in her hands.

'Don't worry,' Louie tried to comfort her distraught friend, 'I'll see if Sam can have a word.' Minnie looked up at her in disbelief.

'You don't understand.' Her tear-streaked face tensed in misery, 'If they won't take Bomber back, there's not a chance they'll have Sam. Don't you see that?'

Eleanor returned from Christmas shopping in Durham and a pleasant lunch with Ruth Spencer. As a consequence of the November party she had shown Ruth some of Eb's paintings and Ruth had expressed her keenness to have Eb as a student in her class.

Eleanor had laughed and said she was still trying to persuade Eb to meet her art teacher friend.

'He's naturally suspicious of those in authority,' Eleanor had joked, 'especially those who want to tell him what to do.'

'I'm quite intrigued to meet this - friend - of yours,' Ruth had answered with a wry smile, pushing back wisps of red hair that had sprung loose from their pins.

'I'll bring him before Christmas,' Eleanor had promised.

'You'll be far too busy organising Beatrice's wedding, surely?' Ruth had replied. 'Isobel tells me you've been landed with most of the arrangements.'

'Yes.' Eleanor had betrayed her lack of enthusiasm with a heavy sigh. 'Sandy's leave has been brought forward - his regiment is leaving for Malta in January and Beatrice wants to go with him. It's all a bit of a rush - but who can blame them - they want to be together.'

Peters, the young footman, carried Eleanor's parcels into the house while his mistress discarded her fur coat and hat and ordered tea to be brought to her upstairs drawing room. The hallway was filled with the scent of pine from the huge Christmas tree stretching away up the stairwell. Eleanor could not help feeling a childish thrill at the sight of the gaudy baubles and tinsel catching in the electric light, as the day darkened swiftly behind her. Beatrice would be home in a couple of days for the holiday festivities, then there would be all the chaotic excitement of her New Year wedding and a house full of guests. Eleanor did not like to think beyond her sister's marriage to when The Grange would echo emptily to her solitary footsteps.

For a short time she could turn her mind from the unhappiness of Whitton Grange and the destitution that lapped at their door. Perhaps she could infect Eb with some of the gaiety of Christmas; he was so preoccupied by the plight of the pitmen since the ending of the strike, he had little enthusiasm for painting. What nagged at her mind most, though, was his subtle change towards her now that the miners had returned to work. It was as if the boundaries that separated them had been redrawn, she was once more the lady of the big house and not a comrade in arms. They had not been alone together for a couple of weeks and the yearning for her lover was burrowing inside her like a frantic animal.

To halt her broodings, Eleanor curled up on a sofa amid cream and green cushions, in front of a crackling fire, and absorbed herself in a book until tea arrived. When someone knocked at her door and entered, she did not look up.

'Put the tray on the table please, Bridget,' Eleanor instructed.

There was a formal cough and she glanced up to see Reginald advancing towards her, already dressed in evening wear, his wavy hair groomed and shiny. Eleanor's heart sank at the stern expression on his face; she was not in the mood for one of his lectures.

'You're dressed for dinner early.' She smiled to disconcert her husband.

'I'm going to a concert in Newcastle,' he answered brusquely. 'I won't be back tonight.' Eleanor was now used to Reginald being matter of fact about his deliberate staying away from home. She suspected half the county talked about his affair with Libby Fisher.

'Enjoy your evening then.' She dismissed him and concentrated hard on the book in her lap.

'There's a matter I want cleared up with you first.' Reginald ignored her rebuff and strode to the fireside. He planted his feet firmly on the Persian hearth rug. 'You will never again threaten me with divorce - or attempt to interfere in the business of the mines. If the management chooses to dispense with the services of various pitmen - such as Red Ritson - you will refrain from meddling in such decisions. Is that quite clear?' Eleanor looked up at him in astonishment. Why on earth was he being so aggressive with her now?

'And how will you stop me?' she asked, keeping her voice level, though the steely set of his face made her nervous.

'I will expose your grubby little liaison with Ebenezer Kirkup,' Reginald answered triumphantly. 'I have compiled a dossier on you, Eleanor, which makes interesting if distasteful reading. If anyone issues divorce proceedings it will be me. The next time you attempt to undermine my authority, I'll have all the Kirkups thrown out of their jobs.'

'You disgust me!' Eleanor hissed, her chest and throat tight with shock.

'You are the disgusting one, my dear.' His impassive brown eyes were scornful. 'You have brought shame to the name of Seward-Scott with your sordid little affair. I have a list of dates and places where you have been seen together which I would not hesitate to show to your father or anyone else if you dare to cross me again. Imagine how this invalid miner of yours would be shunned by his own community if they knew about his adulterous relationship with you.'

Reginald was pleased with the stunned look on his wife's face; he had played his trump card and beaten her this time. Hopkinson had done an excellent job in recruiting young Constable Turnbull to do a spot of spying on Eleanor. The policeman had proved an eager detective, seeming to relish the opportunity of bringing evidence against Ebenezer Kirkup. At some future date, Reginald would make sure PC Turnbull was well rewarded. He would be more use than the feisty old MacGuire.

'I have nothing to say to you,' Eleanor answered him more calmly than she felt, 'except to say I refuse to be threatened by your odious accusations.'

Reginald laughed mirthlessly. 'The choice is yours. I know everything that is worth knowing about your lover,' he almost spat out the word, 'and I really don't care how you find your amusement, Eleanor, except when it affects my business.'

'Our business,' Eleanor reminded him crossly.

'No.' He stepped away from the fire. 'As far as the property of the mines is concerned, they are my business - I am your father's heir in that respect - it's all been signed over to me. And the mines are the lifeblood of The Grange, remember that - without them this place would be bankrupt.'

'That's outrageous,' Eleanor retorted. 'Father wouldn't do such a thing without my knowledge.'

Reginald looked at her in triumph. 'Oh, but he has. Your father is too good a man of business to allow your selfishness to jeopardise the future of The Grange. He doesn't want you interfering in his business interests any more than I do.'

'It's a betrayal,' Eleanor spluttered furiously.

'You're the betrayer,' Reginald said with contempt. 'You've gone against your own kind and I'll never forgive you for that.'

Eleanor looked away from him, sickened by her father's part in Reginald's scheming and at the way her husband had hunted and cornered her over Eb. He had sought out her vulnerability and struck like an adder. She knew he would not hesitate in poisoning Eb's life too. It maddened her to think she was powerless to protect him or his family.

'Get out,' Eleanor shouted, her anger igniting. 'Go to your whore!'

They glared at each other in hatred. Reginald turned abruptly and marched to the door. He glanced back before reaching for the brass handle.

'I've not the faintest idea what I ever saw in you, Eleanor,' he told her coldly. 'Everything about you sickens me.' He closed the door behind him.

Eleanor stood up and reached for her cigarette case. It took intense concentration for her to stop shaking long enough to light a cigarette and suck the smoke into her nostrils. She took three deep inhalations, then crossed to the window.

Bridget came in with the tea, but Eleanor did not notice, so the maid left it unpoured on the table and withdrew. A few minutes later, Eleanor saw Sandford bring the Bentley round to the front entrance and open the door for her husband. The chauffeur-driven car left with a crunch of wheels on the frosty driveway. She saw all these things and yet felt nothing, as if she was watching a rather boring play from the upper circle.

The Bentley's headlamps illuminated a group of children making their way up the drive and then dumped them into darkness again. Eleanor's numb brain could not work out what they were doing there, until moments later when they gathered round the front steps. She made out the figure of Reverend Hodgson towering above his miniature flock.

Suddenly the frosty evening was filled with the quavering singing of dozens of voices. Eleanor threw up the sash window to hear the carols more clearly. The cold air bit at her face and neck, but she welcomed its rawness on her skin. Familiar, comforting phrases about shepherds and silent nights drifted up to her like balm to her torn nerves.

She listened for several minutes as the children, muffled and becapped against the cold, sang lustily through their repertoire. Eleanor felt humbled that these villagers, who had suffered so much hardship and had so little to their name, could comfort her battered heart with their amateur carol singing. Here they were, with all the resilience and optimism of youth, rebuking her self-pity. All at once she longed to be with them.

'Wait while I come down!' she called to the vicar, as they paused between carols. She would take them into the kitchen and get Mrs Dennison to fill them up with mince pies and cake and hot drinks. She was still the lady of The Grange and she would do what she liked in her own home, no matter what her callous husband said.

Stubbing out her second cigarette, she turned resolutely to the door and hurried out to her motley group of visitors.

Two days before Christmas, Sam and Bomber were served with eviction orders. Men from the next village who had jobs at the Whitton Grange pits were to have their accommodation. Eb and John went round to help Sam and Louie transport their possessions back to Hawthorn Street on an open cart they had borrowed from the cheerful ice cream vendor Dimarco.

'I'll not give them the pleasure of throwing me out on the street,' Sam told his brothers-in-law, as Louie packed her kitchenware into two large boxes. Her best linen had already been taken round to her parents' house with a suitcase of clothes. Through the window she watched Eb and Sam haul their gate-legged table on to the cart. Three kitchen chairs were piled around, their splintered legs stuck in the air. Across the street neighbours stood at their doors and watched the move, their breath puffing in the cold air like pipe smoke as they muttered to each other.

Eb returned. 'What about the bed?' he asked bashfully.

'We'll have to leave it,' Sam answered shortly.

'There's no room at Mam's,' Louie added. It was a symbol of their marriage, yet stripped of its homely covers and standing in the empty, chilly room it was no more than an old rusty bed. Louie turned away and picked the kettle off the dead stove, determined not to be sentimental about their going. Why cry over a cramped dark room like this? She had never thought of it as a permanent home for them anyway.

Without stopping for a last glance round, Louie marched out of the back door, her small chin jutting in the air. Sam followed, a mat rolled up under his arm, and slammed the door behind him. They walked proudly beside the cart as Eb and John took the long handles and pulled it behind them.

Minnie ran out of her front doorway.

'Louie!' she wailed and burst into tears. Louie hugged her friend awkwardly. They had not spoken much since Sam and Bomber had fallen out over the return to work. The men paused but looked away.

'We won't be neighbours but we'll still see each other,' Louie promised.

'It's Jack's first birthday on Boxing Day and what does he get?' Minnie cried. 'Not even a roof over his head!'

'You're going to Bomber's parents, aren't you?'

'Aye,' Minnie tossed her unkempt curls from her face, 'not that they'll make me feel welcome. They'd sooner wipe their feet on a Slattery.'

'At least they're speaking to you at last. Just be thankful they're standing by you,' Louie said resignedly. 'What about Margaret and the bairn?'

'She's gone back to Mam's,' Minnie replied dejectedly.

'Haway, Minnie,' Louie chided, 'cheer up your miserable face. There'll be work to be found at one of the other pits round about after Christmas.'

'Pigs'll fly,' Minnie retorted, wiping her nose on her sleeve.

'Come on, Louie,' Sam called impatiently.

'I'll call round to see you,' Louie promised and squeezed her friend's arm quickly. She ran to catch up with the cart as it trundled and shook down the rough lane. Glancing back, she saw a runny-nosed Jack clinging on to his mother's dress, whining. Louie waved.

'I couldn't stop him,' Eleanor told Eb on Christmas Eve. 'He threatened to dismiss all your family if I interfered.'

After the carol service at St Cuthbert's parish church she had gone straight to Greenbrae to seek him out. Isobel, having told her Eb would be there receiving his Christmas parcel, left them alone in the large warm kitchen.

'So he knows about us then?' Eb asked quietly. Eleanor nodded. Eb gave out a long sigh. 'What are you going to do?' Ha met her worried gaze as he spoke.

'I don't know.' Eleanor shrugged. 'I'm frightened of what he might try to do to you - or your family.' Eb's blue eyes considered her disconcertingly, as if they found her wanting.

She got up abruptly from her chair. 'What can I do?' she demanded desperately.

'You must give me up,' Eb told her, his look unflinching. Eleanor started at his brutal words. His jaw was set, his fists clenched on his knees.

'I -I can't,' Eleanor stammered. 'I'll not be bullied and blackmailed by my husband. Don't ask me not to see you, Eb.'

He sprang to his feet, belying the calm of moments before. 'I can't ask anything of you,' he rasped. 'I've only ever been able to take what you've offered, Eleanor.' He turned blazing eyes on her. 'I'm not your husband. You've never really belonged to me!'

Eleanor supported herself on the scrubbed table as the tirade hit her. She had never seen such anger in him before.

'You speak of me as if I were something to possess,' she said in a trembling voice. 'I've given freely of my love - I've cared for you, Eb, as I've cared for no one else in my life. I'm Reginald's wife in name only.' Her dark eyes filled with unsummoned tears. 'Is my love not enough for you?'

Eb swung away from her, biting hard on his earth-ingrained hand. For a moment there was silence, except for the rhythmic ticking of a large black clock next to the larder door.

When he answered her plea, his voice was empty of anger.

'Your husband will use me against you. As long as we continue to see each other he has a hold over both of us - and over my family. Perhaps if we end our friendship he will stop persecuting Sam and Louie.'

Eleanor bowed her head under the weight of his reasoning. Eb seemed to know the kind of man her husband was.

'You're right, of course,' she whispered, fiddling with a mother-of-pearl button on her dress.

Eb turned and came towards her, but Eleanor froze at the thought of him touching her in comfort. If she allowed him to hold and kiss her goodbye she would never have the strength to let him go.

'No, Eb,' she warded him off with her hands, 'we've made our decision.'

He stopped, unsure, his face suffused with sadness. Then the door behind them swung open and Hilda came bursting in, long arms protruding from a too-short coat as they gripped a basketful of last-minute groceries.

'By, it's parky out there,' she exclaimed, then stopped at the sight of her brother and Eleanor Seward-Scott. They stood apart like chiselled statues. 'Sorry, miss,' Hilda apologised hastily, 'I didn't realise you were here.'

Eleanor took a grip on her emotions and managed a smile.

'That's perfectly all right, Hilda. I was leaving anyway. I just called in with a Christmas box for you and your family - Eb can carry it home.'

'Thank you, miss,' Hilda answered brightly, 'that's very kind of you. Isn't it, Eb?' Hilda saw her brother struggling to look pleased. He managed a nod; Hilda felt annoyed at his rudeness.

'Well, I'll go and join Miss Joice in the drawing room,' Eleanor announced. 'Goodbye, Hilda, goodbye, Eb.' She met his look briefly and saw the pain.

When her brother did not reply, Hilda gave a cheerful farewell for both of them. 'Have a happy Christmas, miss, and thanks again for the present.' Eleanor left the kitchen and immediately Hilda pulled the string on the wrapped box on the table. Delving into its contents she found a large ham, tins of fruit, conserves, pickles and chestnuts.

'This'll make Mam's Christmas dinner,' Hilda declared. 'We were just going to have soup.' She glanced at her brother, who still stood looking at the kitchen door. 'What in the wide world's wrong with you?' she asked, although she guessed something momentous had just taken place. 'It's Miss Eleanor, isn't it?' Hilda answered her own question. 'Have you fallen out?'

Eb turned and looked helplessly at his sister. 'Oh, Hildy,' he sighed, 'give us a hug, will you?'

Without further interrogation, Hilda rushed to her eldest brother and flung her arms around his neck like she used to when he came home on leave from the War and she was still a spelk of a girl.

'You've always got your family, you know,' Hilda assured him. Eb gave an answering squeeze.

Chapter Twenty-Four

During the following week, Eleanor immersed herself in preparations for Beatrice and Sandy's wedding, which was set for the eighth of January. Christmas passed in an uneasy truce between herself and Reginald. Her father chose to ignore her anger towards him for siding with Reginald over control of the mines and attempted to jolly his elder daughter with a ride on New Year's Day. Despite her hurt, Eleanor relished the chance to escape for the day and canter across the brown moors following The Grange hunt. The chase did not hold the same thrill for her as it did her father or husband, but she delighted in the cold polar-blue sky above and the glinting white frost that never thawed from the north-facing briars and hedgerows.

At the end of the day she came home exhausted, declined an after-dinner game of bridge and, for the first time in over a week, slept soundly. Sandy joined them on the fifth of January, with his parents, Colonel and Mrs Mackintosh, and by the sixth Beatrice had worked herself up into a frenzy of excitement.

'Just two more days to go, Eleanor,' she cried ecstatically, 'then I'll be Mrs Alexander Mackintosh!' They were walking out of St Cuthbert's having discussed the flower arrangements with Mrs Hodgson and their own head gardener.

'It'll be a wonderful way to start the New Year.' Eleanor squeezed her sister's arm affectionately. 'Let's hope it'll be a happier one than last year.'

'Oh, don't be such a grump,' Beatrice complained. 'It wasn't such a bad time. Even that boring old strike had its moments - you should have tried driving one of those vans - what a lark!'

Eleanor withdrew her arm, astonished by her sister's lack of sensitivity. 'It was no lark for the miners and their famines,' she retorted.

'Oh, who cares?' Beatrice pouted. 'They've got their jobs back now, so they can't complain. I thought you'd be thankful it's all over - Reggie's in a much better mood these days.'

'Not with me.'

Beatrice scrutinised her elder sister. 'Are you still having an affair with your mystery man?' she asked bluntly.

'No, that's all over,' Eleanor snapped, and walked briskly to the car.

'Then what you need is a new lover,' Beatrice decreed without a blush. 'Play Reggie at his own game.'

Eleanor laughed shortly. 'Hardly the thoughts that should be going through the head of a prospective bride.'

'Oh, Sandy and I are different - we're young and madly in love. There's no question of darling Sandy being unfaithful to me.'

Eleanor was silenced by Beatrice's youthful arrogance and tactlessness. A moment ago she had been tempted to confide in her sister about her future plans, the ones she was wrestling with each sleepless night in her huge empty black and white bedroom. But Beatrice was so blind to anything beyond her own limited social world, she would not comprehend Eleanor's ideas. Climbing into the back of the Bentley with her sister chattering about her bridesmaids' dresses, Eleanor realised the depth of the chasm yawning between them. She herself had once belonged to a world of debutantes and formal parties, high fashion and *Tatler* gossip, but none of that interested her now.

Out of the car window she watched four parishioners hanging out flags above the lych gate and bedecking the bare trees around the small country church with bunting. It had been decreed that the local children would have a holiday from school in celebration of Beatrice's marriage and Eleanor knew there would be a large crowd, drawn by curiosity and excitement, hoping to catch a glimpse of the grand wedding. But how many of the pit folk resented the flaunting of such wealth and happiness in the midst of their misery? She imagined how Eb would take himself off to his allotment for the day, turning his back on the conspicuous celebrations and shunning the cap-doffing to the daughter of the landlord. At that moment Eleanor felt helplessly alone.

The other house guests arrived on the eve of the wedding: Beatrice's friend Sukie who was chief bridesmaid; Charlie Ventnor and his new wife; Will Bryce; two MacKenzie aunts and uncles and seven cousins (three of whom were to be bridesmaids and one a pageboy); two schoolfriends of Beatrice from Cheltenham Ladies' College; and Sandy's two brothers. Reginald's parents, Henry and Alice Scott, now retired to Wimbledon after thirty-two years in the Indian Civil Service, were taking tea in the drawing room when the sisters returned. Henry, a first cousin of Thomas Seward-Scott, was a quiet, stooped man with only a few strands of hair left on a pink scalp, his face and hands stained with brown sunspots. Alice sat straight-backed in her chintz-covered chair with all the stern authority of a memsahib overseeing her household.

How she would shudder at the moral lapses of her son and daughter-in-law if she knew about them, Eleanor thought drily as she brushed her mother-in-law's cheek with a kiss, thankful that she only saw the Scotts on rare family occasions such as this.

'Eleanor, you look too thin,' portly Alice Scott scolded predictably. Eleanor knew she was a disappointment to her mother-in-law, championing causes instead of producing the next generation of Seward-Scotts.

'Have some more Christmas cake,' Eleanor smiled, turning away. She shook hands with her father-in-law; he had never been one for kissing unless his natural shyness had been loosened by a couple of gimlets. The MacKenzies were different, and Eleanor was swamped by embraces from her Scottish cousins.

Will Bryce detached himself from a group by the fire and came to join Eleanor in the recessed window. He kissed her cheek.

'I think you look swell,' he teased, 'thin but swell.'

Eleanor laughed and felt grateful for his attention. As they talked about trivial things, she remembered how amusing Will could be. He had cultivated a slim moustache since their last meeting, which gave his genial face a raffish appearance.

After dinner, there was open house for neighbours and wedding guests to meet for drinks and dancing until midnight. Just before then, Sandy and his brothers would leave for a hotel in Durham, so as not to bring bad luck by seeing the bride on her wedding day before the ceremony. The Mackintoshes were adamant the tradition should be adhered to.

Sandy's stocky brothers, Roderick and James, struck up the pipes at eleven and filled the ballroom with a deafening blast of music. Sandy grabbed Beatrice and whirled her around the dance floor to the spirited jigs, and soon the glass-domed room was a sea of kilted revellers twirling partners in sparkling evening gowns and headdresses.

Will forced Eleanor on to the gleaming dance floor. They spun around in a fast polka until their heads reeled and Eleanor felt the American's grip tighten around her waist. He did not disengage himself immediately the dancing stopped.

Champagne was brought in on silver trays for all the guests and a round of toasts made to the forthcoming wedding. Soon after, Sandy and his entourage of Highlanders left, and Eleanor chased Beatrice and Sukie to bed.

'I'll not sleep,' Beatrice protested.

'You will,' Eleanor insisted. 'You must have all your strength for tomorrow.'

Knowing that Will was waiting for a moment to find her alone, Eleanor feigned tiredness and escaped to her bedroom. She found his persistence flattering, but to give him expectations of becoming her lover would only be to use him as a means to smother her longing for Eb. Aching as the emptiness inside her was at the thought of not seeing Eb, she could not treat Will so carelessly.

The morning of the wedding passed in a flurry of activity and last-minute preparations. As breakfast was cleared away in the dining room, an army of servants set about erecting trestle tables in the ballroom to accommodate the vast number of guests. On top of the starched linen were set polished silver cutlery and ornate candelabras, thin-stemmed glasses and the best gold-edged family china for the wedding feast that the kitchen staff had been preparing all week. Huge arrangements of flowers came in from the hothouses and added fresh splashes of colour now that the festive holly and Christmas decorations had been dismantled. The ballroom sparkled in the soft wintry light that emanated from the opaque roof. Fires that had been banked down over night were stoked up, coal scuttles refilled and dozens of bottles of wine and champagne brought up from the cellars. Outside, the gardeners festooned the entrance way and pillars with Union flags, banners depicting the Seward raven and a St Andrew's flag in honour of Sandy's family.

The house reverberated to the orders of the butler, housekeeper and cook and the feverish chatter of guests passing on the stairs or congregating in the drawing room.

At eleven, Bridget helped Eleanor dress in her outfit of coral and green, fastened down the back with tiny pearl buttons. To go with it she had a matching wraparound coat and pearl-studded cap that she would put on at the last minute. She went to help Beatrice dress.

'You look wonderful,' she gasped in genuine admiration, catching her sister's reflection in the long mirror. The body of Beatrice's dress was of plain satin, hanging loosely over her curved form and gathered at the hips. Over this was an outer dress of intricate lace matching the long train that fell away from her lacy headdress. Strings of pearls hung over her breasts and the dress was raised at the front to show her slim ankles clad in white silk stockings, and her satin shoes.

'Do you think so?' Beatrice smiled with nervous red lips, the blonde curls of her hair stuck firmly around her flushed forehead and cheeks. Her green eyes shone impishly, as if she had been drinking.

'Mother would have been so proud.' Eleanor felt the emotion bottle her throat. She went impulsively to Beatrice and hugged her.

'Mind my veil,' her sister complained.

Sukie came in from the adjoining room in a flowing pink dress and a low-brimmed cloche hat. 'We're all ready, Bea,' she grinned. She was followed by a chattering horde of pink satin bridesmaids, their dark hair enhanced by white flowers.

'Where's Archibald?' Beatrice demanded crossly. Sukie looked around for the missing pageboy.

'Probably run off with other boys,' Sukie shrugged. Eleanor thought her sister was about to burst into tears. Below could be heard the smooth thrum of car engines as the house guests set off for the church.

'I'll find him, you go on downstairs - Daddy'll be waiting,' she said, taking charge.

The kilted Archibald was found clambering along an outside window ledge, the bouquets of flowers were distributed and the whole entourage helped into the two waiting cars and an open carriage. Beatrice had insisted on being driven to St

Cuthbert's in the magnificently polished blue Seward landau. Eleanor had persuaded her not to demand that the tenants pull her down the hill to church as had been the custom in the last century. Eleanor had called the custom positively feudal and her sister had reluctantly settled for two horses instead.

All the staff turned out at the front door to see Miss Beatrice off to church on the arm of a proudly beaming Thomas Seward-Scott, his face the colour of his red buttonhole. Eleanor watched them detachedly for an instant, reflecting that it was an aeon ago that she had left with her father for her own wedding in the ancient medieval church on the edge of the village. Younger than Beatrice, she had taken the step into marriage with hardly a second thought. Silently she wished her sister a happier partnership than she had achieved.

Then she stepped into the final car where Reginald and Sukie were waiting and watched The Grange and its waving retainers disappear as the car swung away down the drive.

'I can't be bothered.' Louie resisted Hilda's attempts to drag her down the village to see the bride arrive. Hilda had the day off work as the Joices would be attending the reception, and she was eager to participate in the fun.

'Oh, come on, Louie,' she pleaded, 'you know you want to see Miss Beatrice's dress.'

All at once, Fanny was convulsed by coughing and her daughters looked at her anxiously, momentarily distracted from their arguing.

'I remember going to see Miss Eleanor married,' Fanny Kirkup reminisced as she cleared her throat. 'She was a beauty in those days.'

'Please, Louie,' Sadie added her weight to winning round her cousin, 'there's tea and cake in the church hall afterwards.'

Louie grunted. 'They wouldn't give us a crumb during the lock-out.'

'Go on, pet,' her mother intervened unexpectedly, 'you deserve a day off. You said Sam won't be home until tea time - he'll not know.'

Louie glanced at her mother in surprise; the older woman understood her so well. Sam had chosen the day of the coal owners' festivities to tramp down the valley to seek work in a neighbouring pit belonging to a different coal company. It was his unspoken protest at what he saw as the sickening extravagance of the Seward-Scott wedding. 'Salt in our wounds,' he had complained to Louie. 'All that money spent on a silly spoilt lass instead of paying us decent wages - it's a bloody disgrace!'

Louie had agreed, so to go now and participate in the revelries seemed disloyal to Sam. Still, she so longed for a dash of spice in the grey drudgery of her life and it would all be over long before Sam returned. He probably wouldn't question her anyway. He was so wrapped up in his own shroud of bitterness, he no longer seemed to care what she did.

'All right,' she grudgingly agreed. Sadie clapped her hands and Hilda dashed to get Louie's coat and hat.

'I want to hear all the details, mind,' Fanny croaked.

'Aye, Mam,' Louie promised, unable to hide a smile.

As they headed out of the door, Hilda gabbled excitedly. 'Miss Joice said the bride's dress came from Paris,' she announced, proud of her knowledge.

'And Paris is the capital of France,' Sadie said, thinking it important to demonstrate her newly acquired wisdom.

'Fancy going all that way for a dress,' Louie remarked as the younger girls bustled her into the lane to join the other women and children making their way to St Cuthbert's.

In the end, Louie was glad she had gone. For a couple of hours she forgot her worries about Sam's unemployment, the debts they owed and their creeping estrangement, and feasted her eyes on the spectacular sight of the wedding party. The road around the church was thronged with villagers all pressing for a view of the bride. Following Sadie, who managed to wriggle her way to the side of the road, opposite the lych gate, they commanded a good view of the arriving guests. Those who had been waiting all morning stamped their feet to keep warm.

As the stream of cars purred to a halt under the naked black trees, there were gasps at the elegant society women who filed past as if the villagers were not there, and nudges and giggles at the kilted Scots who swaggered confidently into the church amid the sombre morning dress of the Englishmen. When Beatrice alighted from her carriage with her father, a loud cheer went up from the assembled onlookers and Louie felt a lump form in her throat at the young woman's pretty flushed face. Whatever the gap between them, she recognised the happy anticipation of a bride-to-be and, for that instant, secretly wished Miss Beatrice well.

When the newly wedded couple emerged from the church under the raised swords of the groom's Highland soldiers, treacherous tears of emotion spilled on to Louie's cheeks. She quickly wiped them away before anyone noticed.

Hilda had no such inhibitions. 'Isn't she beautiful?' she cried, her nose running and her face awash with tears. The crowd cheered afresh and called out good wishes to the beaming Beatrice and her handsome uniformed husband. Some threw extravagant handfuls of rice at them to bring luck. Louie marvelled at the generous and spontaneous response of the Whitton Grange people; Sam, she knew, would have been mystified by the whole scene.

'How do you think she manages?' Sadie asked seriously.

'Manages what?' Louie was startled out of her reverie.

'To go to the toilet with that long train?'

Hilda and Louie burst out laughing at the sight of Sadie's winsome face puckered in concern.

'I don't know, pet.' Louie threw an arm about her bony shoulders and hugged the girl to her.

'Posh folk don't go to the toilet,' Hilda winked at her sister, 'do they, Louie?'

Sadie had shot her an astonished look before it dawned on her that she was being teased. She set her lips in a disapproving pout until her cousins coaxed her mood away with the reminder of cake in the parish hall. Minnie and Margaret waved to them on their way in and they joined up and pushed their way inside, chattering all the while. Minnie was already looking heavily pregnant under her tight coat.

Elbowing their way to the far tables, they were greeted with platefuls of sandwiches, cake and scones. Sadie's mouth was soon silenced by the delicious food, and Minnie too tucked in enthusiastically.

'There's a bit of space over there,' Louie indicated to her friend. 'You can sit down on the bench, Minnie. You should be resting instead of being on your feet all this time,' she fussed.

On their way over, Louie bumped into Iris and Raymond.

'Wasn't it romantic, Louie?' her sister-in-law exclaimed as Raymond held up his arms for his aunt.

'Aye,' Louie agreed, kissing her nephew warmly, though Minnie regarded the auburn-haired girl warily. They had not spoken to each other since Iris and Davie had gone to live in Whitton Station, though Margaret had kept in touch with Iris and passed on occasional snippets of news to her sister.

'By, you're looking big.' Iris gave Minnie a onceover glance. 'When's it due?'

'April,' Minnie answered through a mouthful of cake. Her green eyes looked resentfully at Iris's slim figure.

'Good luck to you,' the Durham girl laughed. 'You won't get me making that mistake again - one bairn's enough trouble.'

'You're no trouble are you, pet?' Louie let Raymond's fingers explore her mouth.

'How is Davie?' Minnie asked provocatively, annoyed by Iris's scornful words. She ignored Louie's warning glance.

'Why d'you ask?' Iris shot the dark-haired girl a suspicious look.

'No reasons,' Minnie answered, licking her fingertips with a smacking noise. 'Eeh, we had such a laugh on the farm last summer.'

'He's just grand,' Iris replied testily and turned back to Louie. 'You haven't been to see us since before Christmas - Davie's missing you.'

'I've been that busy,' Louie mumbled, prickled with guilt.

'You mean Sam won't let you visit,' Iris said forthrightly.

'Well, he's around all day just now, seeing as they'd rather have scabs at the pit instead of good union men like my Sam,' Louie said defensively.

'Davie's not blacklegging any more,' Iris retorted. 'The strike's over, Louie, can't you just let bygones be bygones? He's so longing to see his family again, though he won't admit it.'

'You've got a nerve,' Minnie butted in, 'after what Sam and Bomber have been through! Of course Louie can't forgive you for what you've done. Davie would never have broken the strike unless you'd forced him to, though I can't see what you've got that's so special,' she scoffed.

'Minnie, be quiet!' Louie remonstrated, aware of curious glances from the people round about.

'And what makes you such an authority on my Davie?' Iris glared at her opponent.

'Don't say another word,' Louie warned her friend. 'Here, Iris,' she handed Raymond back to his mother, 'it's time we were off. Tell Davie we're not ready to see him back home yet - it's too soon - there's too much bad feeling.' The boy gave a howl of protest at the abrupt rejection. 'I'll come and see you again soon, pet.' Louie tried to placate her crying nephew.

'Don't put yourself out,' Iris said caustically. 'I'll just tell our Davie his sister's too high and mighty to speak to him any more. I knew Sam Ritson was too stubborn to forgive, but I never thought you would be, Louie.'

Stung, Louie turned from the flushed, accusing face of her sister-in-law and grabbed Sadie's hand. The young girl had been watching them in silent perplexity and was reluctant to leave Iris so soon. Louie knew that her cousin was growing fond of Iris's family, with whom she lodged during the week, and it made her feel more ashamed at the harsh words just spoken. If only Minnie had not tried to stir things up between them. She had not meant to argue.

Louie pushed her way out into the bright, cold sunshine, dragging a protesting Sadie behind her.

'She's always been too big for her boots, that one,' Minnie declared as they trooped back into the village. Louie pressed her lips together and did not reply. Already she was feeling remorse at leaving Iris and Raymond so rudely, and the bad words that had been uttered rang in her head like relentless tolling bells. After all, Iris and Davie had few enough friends in this village without her turning her back on them as well.

'I wanted to stay with Iris,' Sadie said grumpily. 'Why did you shout at her, Louie?' For a few steps, Louie did not answer but increased her pace.

'I'll take you to see her next week,' Louie promised impatiently. 'But don't you breathe a word of it to Sam, do you hear?'

During the long, lavish lunch, Eleanor allowed herself to drink too much wine. She gave in to the hazy relaxed state that it induced and the afternoon seemed to melt away like the magnificent iced sorbets. Once the speeches and banquet were over, Beatrice disappeared with a gaggle of friends to change into her going-away outfit and prepare to leave with Sandy. They were to spend a brief honeymoon in Scotland before sailing with the regiment for Malta.

Eleanor slipped after them, wishing to get her sister on her own just one last time. She felt suddenly overwhelmed by the finality of today. Her young sister was leaving as wife to an army captain and from now on her visits home would be rare. No matter how infuriating Beatrice could be at times, Eleanor would always feel a protective tenderness towards her.

But Beatrice remained surrounded by her lively friends while she changed, and Eleanor sat on the edge of the bed listening to their laughter and ribald remarks about the night to come.

Only as they descended the stairs to the hallway, where the guests were gathering to wave them away, did Eleanor slip an arm through Beatrice's and whisper, 'I hate to admit how much I'll miss you. This house'll be deadly quiet without you and your friends, Bea.'

Beatrice smiled, pleased at her sister's confession. 'I thought you'd be thankful to have it all to yourself - plenty of time to read those ghastly books and entertain your blue-stocking pals,' she joked.

Eleanor smiled ruefully and kept back the words she had been tempted to say. Beatrice would hear about her plans soon enough and she did not intend to spoil her day in any way.

They kissed on the steps and Beatrice hugged her father warmly. Before stepping into the waiting car, she tossed her bouquet into the crowd of well-wishers where it was caught by a delighted Harriet Swainson. The car pulled away with a rattle of tin cans tied to its back fender, amid a roar of goodbyes and frantic waving from the guests. That's the end then, Eleanor thought to herself, a strange emptiness opening up inside; the end of our family life together.

Instead of following the others inside for tea, Eleanor crept off in the direction of the water garden. In the growing dark she could make out the partially frozen lake, its thin film of ice covered by the footprints of tiny birds. She shivered and hugged her arms around her body, allowing the silence of the late winter afternoon to soothe her after the cacophony of noise at the reception.

Dry twigs cracked behind her and Eleanor swung round to see Will sauntering down the path. She turned back to watch the pale-gold light dim across the water.

'Sad?' Will asked, his breath like steam in the icy air. Eleanor nodded. 'I didn't think you and your baby sister were close.'

'Perhaps not recently,' Eleanor admitted, 'but I still care for Beatrice. It's the end of an era for our family - Rupert, then mother, now Beatrice gone. Just me and father - and he's more interested in business and following his own pursuits. We've grown apart too.' Eleanor hated the self-pity in her words, but it eased her loneliness to speak them aloud.

'And there's Reginald,' Will added softly. He slipped out his cigarette case and offered it to Eleanor. She took a cigarette and waited for him to light it before she answered.

'I'm going to leave him,' she said, blowing smoke at the glimmering lake.

Will jerked round in surprise. 'You mean divorce Reggie?'

'I mean separate - if he wants a divorce he can have one. No doubt the strident Miss Fisher will press him to do so.'

'But Reggie won't give up The Grange - the business,' Will commented.

'No,' Eleanor replied calmly. 'I will.'

Will whistled in disbelief at the indigo sky. 'You'd give up your family home - all this - just to get away from your husband? Boy, you must really hate that guy!' He watched the end of her cigarette glow as she drew on it.

'I don't think I do hate him,' Eleanor mused. 'Sometimes I feel sorry for him. He's so immersed in making money out of other people - that's all he seems to live for - he's lost sight of the important things in life - love, friendship, that sort of thing.'

'What will you do?' Will ground his cigarette underfoot. Eleanor did the same.

'I have various plans,' she answered vaguely. Suddenly, Will stepped towards her and took hold of her thin arms.

'Come away with me, Eleanor,' he suggested enthusiastically. 'We'll travel round Europe - have a ball. I've friends in the south of France we could stay with for the winter - Antibes - it's all the rage.'

Eleanor smiled at his eagerness, flattered that this debonair American should want her company. She shook her head. 'At least not yet, Will,' she said gently. 'Though I find the offer tempting.'

'There's still someone else, isn't there?' Will's face showed disappointment as his hands dropped to his side.

'I don't know,' Eleanor whispered doubtfully. 'I just know that I have to give him one last chance.'

Throughout the weekend Iris brooded over Minnie's insinuations about Davie. They reinforced something John had implied during a past argument about Davie's behaviour at Stand High Farm. Nevertheless, it infuriated her that the Slattery girl should make remarks about her husband as if she had some claim to him. It had been Davie's decision, as much as hers, to go back to work and Minnie had no right to treat her as an outcast. She obviously influenced Louie's mind on the matter too, else why had her sister-in-law's visits become more infrequent? Was it possible that she would never be accepted as part of this close-knit community? At first she had thought that it would just take time, but here she was, two and a half years later, very much an outsider. Only Margaret Gallon, Minnie's sister, and her neighbour Molly Hutchinson, a stranger to the village herself, could be numbered among her friends. Though it was Louie's warm, unshowy friendship that she hankered after the most.

Iris vented her hurt feelings on Davie. On Monday, as he tucked into an early breakfast before going on the morning shift, she tackled him.

'I saw Minnie Bell at the wedding,' Iris said frostily, flicking roughly through a magazine. 'She was asking especially after you.'

Davie continued methodically eating his bacon and fried bread, head down, though a tinge of colour crept into his fair jaw. 'Oh?'

'Yes.' Iris warmed to her theme. 'Says she's six months pregnant, though she looks more to me.' She tossed the well-thumbed magazine on to the floor and uncrossed her legs. Davie scraped the last of the grease from his knife and licked the fork clean. Pushing the plate away from him he grinned uncertainly.

'Made you broody, did it? Wanting another bairn, I bet? Well, that's fine by me - we can practise any time.' Iris leapt to her feet, startling Raymond who was kneeling in the hearth in his pyjamas, playing with some old farm animals of Sadie's.

'That's not what I meant at all,' she answered crossly, pulling her dressing gown tightly around her. 'I want to know what really happened between the pair of you on that farm. And don't give me that butter-wouldn't-melt-in-your-mouth look, Davie Kirkup, she as good as said there'd been some carry-on.'

Davie stood up agitatedly, his face a guilty crimson. 'You shouldn't listen to the likes of Minnie - she's got too much imagination for her own good.'

'Well, you should know,' Iris said sarcastically.

'Listen, there's nothing between me and Minnie Bell, all right? You're the only one I care for, Iris, always have done and always will.' Davie took a step round the table and grabbed her hand. He tried to kiss her but she shook him off. Sensing their disagreement, Raymond climbed to his feet with a whimper and grabbed his mother's dressing gown.

'Is she having your baby?' Iris demanded, hazel eyes narrowed in suspicion.

Davie went on the defensive. 'I'll not be questioned like a criminal by my own wife!' He turned away and reached for his jacket on the back of his chair.

'And I'll not let you go till you answer me.' Iris blocked his way to the door.

'I'll be late for work,' Davie said aggressively. 'Out of my way.'

'It's true then,' Iris shouted as he pushed his way past. 'While I worked myself ragged in that soup kitchen you were having it away with Minnie Bell!' Raymond began to cry and ran after his father. Davie stopped him at the door and ruffled his auburn hair distractedly.

'Look, you're upsetting the bairn.'

'What about upsetting me?' Iris blazed.

'You've got it all wrong, Iris lass.' Davie floundered under her accusing gaze.

'I don't think so. You've made me a laughing stock. I bet half of Whitton's talking about it!'

Davie wanted to say he was sorry, but the words lodged in his throat; Iris's scorn was more than he could bear. He bent and kissed Raymond on the head and disengaged the small boy's grip on his legs.

'I'll see you later.' He glanced up briefly at Iris and left quickly, shamed by her raw hurt. Tonight he would make it up to her, show her she was the only woman for whom he had ever really cared. His wife's temper was as violent and brief as a firework. A spot of loving and she would forgive him, Davie assured himself. Still, looking back up the dark street, he was disappointed not to see Iris waving him away as usual. The door was closed and no curtain was lifted at the lighted window to betray a change of heart. He tramped on regardless to meet his friend Alfred Hutchinson, though today his sulky mouth could not form into a cheerful whistle.

Iris shook with the upset of the past few minutes and the realisation of her husband's infidelity. She was furious, sick with the knowledge that their romance had been marred by his selfishness. How could he have done this to her? She grabbed Raymond into a rough hug until he wriggled to be free.

'Don't you turn out like your father,' Iris warned the uncomprehending boy passionately. 'Don't you ever!'

Half an hour later, as she spilled out her story to Molly, she felt the anger easing to disappointment.

'It happens more than you think,' said the philosophical Molly. 'Life's not like the flicks you know.'

'But I thought Davie loved me,' Iris answered bitterly.

'He does,' Molly assured her, 'everyone can see that. He just didn't expect you to find out. To Davie it was a summer fling.'

Iris grunted. 'I know where I'd like to fling Minnie Bell.'

Molly laughed and poured Iris another cup of tea.

Davie entered the pit gates with Alfred, his nostrils filling with the smell of tarred fences and engine grease, and they picked their way across the debris-strewn yard, dimly illuminated by light from the solid pit buildings. His friend was discussing the merits of their Saturday football game; they had formed a new team, from men who had worked during the strike, and had travelled into Durham for the match.

'Tadger's a useful player - if he didn't drink so much on a Friday night,' Alfred maintained.

Passing the forge and the redbrick telephone exchange, they took the iron steps up the pit bank. Davie wondered if he should call in to see his mother on the way home from work. If he could be sure of Sam Ritson being out, he was tempted to do so. It was time they put a stop to this stand-off between them; life was too short and he knew his mother would accept him no matter what he did. Today he was going to put things right with his family and his wife. All at once he was optimistic.

'Are you still half asleep?' Alfred complained. 'You haven't listened to a word I've said.'

'Sorry,' Davie grinned and patted his neighbour on the back, 'I was just thinking.'

'Don't, it's bad for you,' Alfred joked over the noise of the engine house. They passed the screens and entered the winding room just as the hooter blew for the change of shift. Squeezing into the cage, Davie found himself crouched next to his former neighbour, Wilfred Parkin. The boy was now a putter working on the same flat as Davie.

'Morning,' Davie greeted him cheerfully. Wilfred looked at him sleepily and grunted an acknowledgement. It was all Davie could get out of the plump-faced young man; before the strike they would have passed the time disputing football until they reached the deputy's kist. At least the lad did not refuse to work with him, unlike members of his own family.

As they wound down the shaft to the bottom, the other cage passed them on its way up. For an instant, in the glare of light through the mesh, Davie was sure he saw his father ascending to the pit bank. His white-bearded face was expressionless, yet recognition flashed in the red-ringed blue eyes. Davie wanted to laugh at the sight; it reminded him of pictures in the children's Bible stories he used to see at Sunday School. His father was a stern-faced prophet disappearing into the heavens; the irreverent thought amused him. I'll go and see the old bugger on my way home, Davie determined.

The deputy, Cummings was waiting at his desk.

'I've checked the flat half an hour ago. Bit gassy in-bye, so gan canny,' he instructed. The men continued down the tunnel, splashing through water up to their calves.

'Bit gassy,' Davie snorted. 'There's enough gas in the Victoria seam to light St James's Park.'

Twenty minutes later they were crawling on all fours along the face. With the unspoken co-operation of men who work well together, the hewers set about their task of kerving the rock with their picks. For several hours Davie lay on his side in the foul-smelling tunnel and hewed. They stopped for their bait mid-shift and took a welcome break.

'That new deputy's giving me a suntan - the amount of times he's been along here and shone a light in my face,' Davie grumbled.

'Someone had better tell him we work at our own pace,' Alfred suggested.

'We're ready to fire her anyways,' Davie said, getting up off his haunches, 'then Wilfred can get cracking on filling his tubs. All right, son?' He nodded at the wheezing boy. 'You sound like your dad's bellows,' he laughed.

'Just feel a bit queer,' Wilfred said, snapping shut his tin of half-eaten sandwiches.

'Aye, I've got a headache this morning too,' Alfred sympathised.

'Too much beer yesterday, I say,' Davie teased, not wanting to admit the fusty air was making him feel sick.

Alfred drilled a hole near the top of the face and filled it with black powder from the tin strapped to his shoulder. With the shot eased gently in place, he tamped the end of the hole with clay and pricked it with a copper pricker to leave a tiny opening for the fuse.

A few minutes later he called, 'Ready, everyone back!'

The men in the surrounding stalls moved to a safe distance. Alfred lit the fuse and scrabbled backwards.

There was a hiss, a pop and then a massive, deafening bang as the explosive went off, igniting gas from the surrounding rock. Davie was thrown back by the force of the blast, knocking his head against an empty truck. For a moment he lay stunned, wondering where he was. Then there was an ominous rumble in the walls about them and the ceiling where they had been working moments before gave way in a torrent of stones. Davie's lamp snuffed out and he blinked as the darkness blinded him.

He heard a man scream out as the treacherous rocks caught him. The cramped tunnel filled quickly with suffocating dust, and, with the instinct for survival electrifying him into action, Davie crawled in the dark in the direction of the shaft bottom. Miraculously the way seemed unblocked. Retching, his eyes stinging,

Davie clamped his cap over his mouth to prevent the evil dust from snatching away his breath.

He gasped in horror as he found himself crawling over the lifeless body of a young putter, and panic gripped him as he struggled to escape from the tunnel. There was hardly any air to breathe; it was as if a giant vacuum had sucked the life out of the seam. A deathly silence descended and no one answered his muffled calls. The walls seemed to press in around him in the blackness, crushing his chest and lungs.

All at once he was aware of movement beneath one of the disabled trucks, turned on its side by the force of the explosion.

'Help me,' a voice wailed, 'please help!'

'Wilfred?' Davie called through his cap.

'I'm trapped under the tub, Davie man, help me,' the boy sobbed.

Davie hesitated. Instinct told him he had merely minutes left in which to get out before the lack of oxygen overcame him. If he stopped now to help the luckless Wilfred it might mean the end of both of them.

Fleetingly he conjured up a picture of Iris's saucy face, and wished with all his heart that he was safe above ground with her now. He stuffed his cap further into his mouth and turned to reach out for Wilfred.

'You push and I'll pull.' He gave calm, muffled instructions to the terrified putter. As he became more light-headed, his vision more blurred, the empty tub began to move, rocking back on to the rails.

Davie gulped for air, aware that the tunnel was growing lighter. Someone's coming to pull us out, he thought, sinking back with relief. Closing his eyes he could see himself above ground, smelling the sweet air. He was walking along a riverbank with Iris holding his hand and smiling. Ridiculous, of course, because he was stuck in a black hole with Wilfred Parkin. He wanted to ask Wilfred if he recalled the time he had let Parkin's pig loose in the street. Perhaps the lad was too young to remember. In a minute he would ask him, when he had got his breath back. He could feel Wilfred tugging on his arm, yet there was no need to hurry. He just needed to rest for a moment.

That morning, Louie saw Sam off to his new job. Her husband had been taken on at a pit near Ushaw Moor known locally as the Cathedral because of its tall twin shafts. The under-manager had been a childhood friend of Samuel Ritson's and had looked sympathetically on the plight of Samuel's son. He could offer only the position of part-time stoneman, but it was a start and Sam seemed pleased to be working again.

'Gives a man his self-respect,' he had told Louie as she kissed him goodbye on the doorstep. It would take him over an hour to walk to the pit, for there was no money for train fares. 'It may mean a move to Ushaw Moor, Louie,' Sam had warned, 'if the job becomes full-time. But we'll see.'

Louie had said nothing to this, hoping silently that they would not have to leave Whitton Grange. She could not imagine living anywhere else. It was a tough existence at times, but it was her home and these were her people. They would never get another colliery house as long as Sam was barred from working at the Eleanor or Beatrice, but one day they might be able to afford to rent one of the new whitewashed council houses. She felt a flicker of optimism now that he had found work at last.

With Sam gone, Louie set about the usual Monday morning task of washing. With a certain flicker of pride she noticed that theirs was the first wash-house in the street to be lit up, that she had the first fire crackling under the washing pot. The water was boiling and the first round of washing was being possed in the tub before the rest of the family had had breakfast.

'Don't forget your clean handkerchiefs,' she reminded Sadie as she packed her bag for the week. Louie now had to do all Sadie's washing on a Saturday when she returned from Durham so that she could have clean underwear and blouses ready for her departure on Monday. The girl was reading a book at the table as she finished her boiled egg and toast.

'Hurry up,' Louie nagged, 'you'll miss your train.'

'Can't I stay until Uncle Jacob gets in?' Sadie pleaded.

'No,' Fanny answered firmly, stripping the sheets from the pull-out bed Sadie used at weekends. 'He'll be tired and wanting his bath. You'll see him soon enough.'

Sadie gathered up her books and stuffed them into her satchel.

'I'll walk you down to the station if you like,' Eb volunteered.

'Oh, yes please,' Sadie answered happily and pulled on her coat. She loved it when one of her relations saw her off on the train; it made her feel important in front of the other pupils. Frank Robson and Tom Gallon would not dare pull her hair if Eb was there to protect her.

'Let me do your buttons up,' Louie fussed as she fastened Sadie's coat. 'You'll catch your death out there this morning. Now give me a kiss and be off,' she ordered.

Sadie gave her an affectionate kiss and hug, then did the same for Fanny. Not that her aunt was as cuddly these days; her arms and hands felt as brittle as winter twigs, and hugging her always set off her sandpaper cough.

'See you on Friday!' Sadie called cheerfully as she left. She skipped down Hawthorn Street trying to keep up with Eb's long strides. Her tall cousin was quieter than ever these days. Sadie attempted to draw him into conversation.

'I haven't seen any of your paintings recently.'

'Haven't done any,' Eb confessed.

'I don't do any drawing at school,' Sadie grumbled. 'I have to do needlework instead.'

Eb snorted. 'And you don't like needlework?'

'I hate it,' Sadie was adamant, 'and Miss English tells me off for licking the thread and making it dirty.' Eb laughed softly.

Sadie suddenly brightened. 'Would you teach me drawing? I'd love to make pictures like yours.' Eb felt a twinge of gratitude to his young cousin for her request.

'If you'd like that,' he agreed.

'Of course I would,' Sadie answered and slipped her hand into his.

They arrived at Whitton Station with ten minutes to spare.

'Can we go and see Iris and Raymond?' Sadie asked shyly.

'Don't think there's time.' Eb was reluctant.

'Iris and Louie had a row last week at Miss Beatrice's wedding,' Sadie confided. 'Iris wanted to know why Louie had stopped visiting them.'

'Louie's been seeing Iris and Davie?' Eb asked in surprise.

'Yes, but you mustn't tell Sam, or I'll get a hiding from Louie.' Eb smiled to himself to think of his sister challenging Sam's authority and making secret trips to see her brother. How like Louie not to let a point of principle stand in the way of her loyalty to her own flesh and blood. He felt ashamed of his own reluctance to see Davie or Iris; he had stayed out of the way and avoided taking a stance on the issue. By doing so he knew he was perpetuating the bitterness and division that cut the community like open weeping wounds.

Eb gave in. 'If we're quick we can say hello to Iris.'

To Sadie's disappointment there was no one at home, but then she remembered Iris's neighbours, the Hutchinsons, and, sure enough, Iris and Raymond were there. Eb sensed a certain tenseness and assumed it was coolness towards him.

Sadie seemed uninhibited by the atmosphere. 'Have you any messages for your family?' she asked Iris, heaving Raymond to his feet and attempting to carry him around.

'Just send my love.' Iris waved a hand. 'I might come through to Durham and see them soon.'

'They'd like that.' Sadie smiled and dumped Raymond among Molly's children. 'Is Davie at work?'

'Aye,' Iris answered shortly.

Eb gave her a considering look. 'Everything all right?' he enquired.

Iris sighed. 'Had a bit of a barny before he left,' she admitted. 'You probably know what it's about.' She gave him a suspicious look. Eb had no idea, and said so.

'Oh, it doesn't matter then,' Iris sighed. 'It's nothing we can't work out between ourselves.'

There was no time for the cup of tea that the fair-haired Molly offered. Eb was glad that Iris had found a pleasant friend to keep her company; Molly appeared sympathetic and had a kind face that smiled easily.

'I'll call again,' he promised Iris awkwardly. That's if you'd like me to. I don't intend to turn my back on Davie anymore.'

'He'll be glad about that,' Iris smiled, 'and I'd like to see you too.'

They dashed back to the station and Eb bundled Sadie on board into a noisy carriage of friends. She waved from the window as the train hissed and started to move, and Eb turned for home.

It was mid-morning and Louie was blueing the shirts to give them extra brightness when Eb walked into the yard.

'She got safely away,' he told her before she could ask. Louie nodded with satisfaction. 'We saw Iris,' he continued. Louie stopped moving the shirt around in the dyed water. 'I said I'd call again. I know you've been visiting too.'

'She shouldn't have said,' Louie answered tersely.

'I'm glad you have,' Eb reassured his sister. 'Whatever he's done, Davie is still our brother and we shouldn't cut him off.'

'Was Davie there?' Louie looked up hopefully, pushing hair out of her eyes.

Eb never replied, because at that moment the quiet humdrum of the morning was shattered by three short, ominous blasts from the pit hooter. Eb and Louie looked at each other in concern.

'It's not time for the change of shift,' Louie said unnecessarily. Eb went to the gate and looked up the lane. Through the flags of washing he could see other anxious faces appear, sleeves rolled up and red-raw hands on hips, all chores abandoned. Questions and rumour rippled down the street like semaphore.

'I'll go and see,' Eb told Louie and raced out of the back yard. He was joined by others desperate to know the cause of the warning siren. Ten minutes later he reached the pit gates among a throng of troubled pitmen.

'There's been an explosion in the Eleanor,' a deputy greeted them, 'the Victoria seam - there's a blockage - a dozen men unaccounted for.' Without thinking, Eb volunteered to go below with the rescue party. He knew from Iris that Davie would be down there and he could not desert his brother now. Fighting the panic that gripped his stomach and throat, he crouched in the cage with the other rescuers and felt the old familiar fear as he dropped into the pit.

Four hours later, Louie and her mother were still standing waiting with the other women in the back lane. Jacob and John had gone to seek news. All they knew was that there had been an accident and that there were men trapped and missing down the Eleanor. Washing flapped listlessly in the chilly breeze, a mournful backdrop that reminded Louie of winding sheets. Edie Parkin was sobbing quietly into Clara Dobson's shoulder. Her Wilfred had not come out.

Louie made tea and brought it out to her neighbours. Another half an hour passed and then there was a commotion at the top of the street. A crowd appeared leading a stretcher being carried by four men. Edie Parkin rushed towards them. Louie heard her screech her son's name and saw her fall on the stretcher. Her heart sank. But when Edie turned around she was smiling, gushing tears of relief. As they drew closer to home and the neighbours thronged about, Louie could see the white strain of pain on Wilfred's face. Both legs were bound in makeshift bandages, but he was alive.

'He's fine,' one of the men called out. 'Doctor's seen him. He's a lucky lad.' The man shook his head sombrely.

Two men detached themselves from the group who had escorted the young putter home.

'I'm afraid we've bad news, Mrs Kirkup,' one of them muttered, pulling off his cap. 'It's your Davie.'

'Davie?' Fanny repeated with incomprehension. Louie felt her insides jerk at her brother's name.

'They've managed to rescue his body - they're bringing him home now. There's nothing more they could have done. I'm sorry.' Fanny gave a soft moan.

'Not my Davie? My poor baby.' She bowed her head. Louie watched her mother crumple under the shocking news and reached out to support her. She could not believe the man's words; she had not wanted to contemplate that Davie might be down there.

'They're bringing him here. Should I fetch his widow?' the pitman offered. Widow; the word stung Louie. He meant Iris, of course. Pretty, vivacious Iris was now a widow. Was it possible?

'If you would,' Louie heard herself reply calmly. 'She lives in Whitton Station.'

'Aye,' the man nodded, 'there's another hewer from there been killed. Alfred Hutchinson, they called him, marra of Davie's.'

Louie shuddered at the words, thinking of his wife Molly and her three children, oblivious to the tragedy. Iris had persuaded her to meet Molly on one visit and she had warmed to the woman immediately. They had talked about their lost babies and Louie had marvelled at the woman's kindness and strength. But surely no one was strong enough to bear this too?

As the pitman left, Louie heard the rumble of the covered stretcher cart as it creaked down the street. She hardly dared to look at the death wagon, as the children callously called it. Walking beside it were her father, John and another man blackened in coal dust. It was only as they arrived at the gate that Louie recognised the harrowed face of Eb under the black grime.

Together the men lifted the stretcher from the cart and carried the body into the house. Louie helped her mother through the door behind them, watching her brothers lay Davie's soiled, limp corpse on the long draining board. All her life, Louie had seen her mother keep the washboard scrubbed and clean, clear of all dishes, in preparation for the unmentionable. 'Just in case,' Fanny had once said, and the young Louie had accepted the ritual. Now the spectre that haunted every pitwoman had been visited on their home.

Louie found herself ordering John to fetch water from the pump and boil it up on the fire. Overcoming her fear of touching her dead brother, she began gently to remove his clothes. Her mother took them from her, unable to take her eyes from her son. Together they silently set about the grisly job of cleaning him. Louie marvelled at how there were no marks of violence on Davie's sinewy body. He looked as if he lay sleeping on the cold draining board, peaceful and untroubled, as she had seen him so many times before.

'Eb found him.' Jacob talked to them softly. 'Deputy says he risked his life to pull Davie out. They wanted to block off the flat in case of another fall, but Ebenezer insisted on going in.'

Louie glanced round for her eldest brother but he had gone back outside. She knew what a supreme effort it must have been for him to enter that pit. For the first time, tears stung her eyes and she blinked them away quickly.

'I saw Davie this morning,' her father continued reflectively.

'Davie?' she asked astonished. 'You saw our Davie?'

Jacob nodded. 'We passed each other in the shaft.'

'So you didn't speak.' Louie's voice was desolate.

'No, but he was smiling,' her father whispered hoarsely. Louie's throat constricted with a dry sob. She turned back to bathing her brother's body.

'My Davie was born smiling,' Fanny added softly and bent to kiss her son.

By the time Iris arrived, distraught and tear-stained, they had transferred Davie to the parlour. His body was wrapped and laid on the bed and the curtains were drawn. Tomorrow they would tie black ribbon to the bedstead and place his coffin on a trestle ready for the visiting.

Iris rent the air with a scream when she saw her husband stiff on the bed where they had slept. She flung herself at him and covered his cold grey face with kisses. Louie, horrified by her hysterical grief, tried to pull her away but Iris went on shouting something incomprehensible about Davie, as if he were somehow to blame for his own death.

'He saved Wilfred's life,' Louie tried to tell her through the screaming. 'If it hadn't been for Davie, Wilfred would be dead too - he said so - Da's been to see him.'

'He should have saved himself.' Iris ranted, her eyes wild in her stricken face. 'What about me and Raymond? It was me he loved - me! It was his fault we argued. Davie! Davie!' she cried at the lifeless pitman. Then she covered him with kisses again and told him she loved him.

Eventually Fanny and Louie managed to coax Iris out of the parlour and sat her by the fire. Louie was glad that John had taken Raymond next door and he did not have to witness his mother's hysteria. Iris sat shaking in her chair but the uncontrolled sobbing had ceased.

'Try and drink something,' Louie said kindly, offering her sister-in-law a cup of stewed tea. Iris shook her head. She seemed to be struggling to say something.

'I-I didn't say goodbye, Louie,' she whispered. Louie placed a comforting arm around her shoulders.

'None of us did,' she answered, gripped with remorse. 'We all feel bad about not speaking to him. It was wrong and now we'll never have the chance to make amends.' Tears trickled down Louie's face.

'No,' Iris said more urgently, gripping Louie's free hand, 'I didn't wave him off when he went to work this morning. You once told me always to see your man off to the pit - in case you never see him again.' Iris broke off with renewed weeping.

'Don't blame yourself now,' Louie comforted. 'Davie knew you loved him.'

'I've been a bad pitman's wife, haven't I, Louie?' Iris sniffed. 'I should have said goodbye. He never saw me say goodbye!'

Louie put her arms around Iris and hugged her tight, unable to answer her question.

Chapter Twenty-Six

The following day the pits closed as a mark of respect for the men who had died. Five had lost their lives; Davie and Alfred, a stoneman named Trewick and two young putters barely seventeen years old.

At 28 Hawthorn Terrace there was open house for relations and friends to visit and take one last look at Davie lying on the trestle in the parlour. Men who had not spoken to him since his blacklegging came and expressed their condolences to his parents and widow. Iris, who had exhausted herself with weeping and railing on the day of the accident, had withdrawn into a tense, morose silence. She hardly uttered a word to anyone. Louie found herself having to cope with Raymond as well as make the arrangements for the funeral wake. She clothed herself in a protective numbness and found relief in keeping busy.

It had been decided by the families and the local churchmen who represented them to hold a joint burial service at the cemetery. So the Methodist minister, Stephen Pinkney, liaised with Reverend Hodgson, the vicar of St Cuthbert's, over the arrangements for burying the dead. There was no need to send round callers inviting neighbours to the funeral, everyone in Whitton Grange knew the service was to be on Saturday.

Aunt Eva and Uncle Jack travelled down from Stand High Farm on the Friday night.

'Fanny!' Eva flew into her sister's arms. 'Poor Fanny. Such a canny lad! I'm that choked.'

Louie watched her mother anxiously for signs of strain, but her face was set and her answer stoical.

'We all miss him,' she agreed quietly with her sister, 'but Iris needs your sympathy most.' Eva glanced through the open parlour door at the listless figure sitting hunched in the gloom. 'She's not moved from his side all day,' Fanny whispered. 'The lass is still in shock. Louie and I don't know what to do.'

'I'll have a word.' Eva squeezed her sister's frail arm and without taking off her thick coat went and sat with Iris.

From time to time, Louie could hear her voice speaking gently to the immobile Iris as if to a child. What she said Louie could not make out, but she saw Iris turn to Davie's aunt and ask her a question and then nod before resuming her vigil.

That night, Louie lay awake in the upstairs bed next to Sam, her aunt and uncle on the other side of the partition. She could not sleep and she longed to talk to Sam about Davie, but they had had no opportunity to be alone together since his death. Sam had been shocked by the news, but had said little.

What was he feeling, Louie wondered? Did the lump of guilt that weighed in her stomach give Sam unease too? There had been no sign of any personal remorse on her husband's part at having severed all contact with Davie. How had she let him dictate to her about not seeing her own brother, Louie thought angrily? But as she tossed restlessly, turning her back to Sam, she knew that she was merely trying to shift her own burden of guilt onto him. Only when she recalled her few infrequent clandestine visits to Whitton Station did she achieve a degree of peace of mind.

The morning of Davie's funeral dawned grey and cold. A raw east wind blew down the valley, causing draughts to blow under every uneven door and rattling the ill-fitting windows of the colliery terraces. The Kirkup men dressed in their sombre dark suits, black armbands and stiff white collars and sat about the kitchen saying little. Sam had left early that morning for the Cathedral pit, in spite of Louie's reproachful looks.

'It's my first week,' Sam had defended himself sternly. 'I'll lose this job if I don't turn in.'

'You could have explained it was family,' Louie had answered spiritedly. 'Everyone has a right to bury their dead.' Sam had not replied. Instead he had left in his work clothes, with his bait tin and bottle in Eb's old army knapsack, without embracing his wife.

Louie, seething inside at Sam's decision, pressed her lips firmly together, ignoring the wary glances of her family, and set about helping Aunt Eva and Hilda prepare a modest spread of sandwiches and scones for the mourners who would return to Hawthorn Street after the burial. Sadie occupied Raymond's attention with a game of snakes and ladders which he did not understand, while Fanny helped Iris dress in the parlour.

As she spread butter thinly across the bread, Louie's gaze kept flicking across to the closed door of the front room. Why were they taking so long? What could they be saying?

'Here's the undertaker,' Eb told them as he stooped and rubbed the condensation from the window behind the thin curtain.

'Better knock,' Aunt Eva nodded to Louie. Her niece crossed to the parlour and gave a timid tap on the door before entering. Iris stood by the large dresser, in a plain black dress of her mother-in-law's and black wool stockings. Her pale face was translucent above the widow's clothes, her auburn hair pulled back by grips. She wore no make-up, giving her a girlish appearance. Far too young to be widowed, Louie thought with a stab, regretting the terse words she had exchanged with her own husband that morning.

'Mr MacGregor's here,' Louie said gently. Her mother nodded and stood up; she was already wearing her coat and hat.

'Come on, Iris pet,' Fanny said to her daughter-in-law. Iris was clinging protectively to the closed coffin, which was covered in bunches of greenery and winter jasmine from neighbours and an elaborate spray of hothouse flowers from the Seward-Scotts that had arrived the previous day. Together Louie and her mother moved towards Iris and steered her away.

MacGregor and two of his men, joiners at the pit, came in to carry the coffin out to the waiting funeral carriage. Louie felt sick at the thought of her brother departing for the last time from the house where they had grown up together. How could so much energy and love of life and joking be snuffed out so brutally? she wondered bitterly. Where was Davie, her laughing, affectionate brother now? Stemming her thoughts, she helped Iris put on her coat and hat, to which Hilda's dextrous hands had added a piece of black gauze for a veil.

At that moment, Jacob Kirkup halted the men.

'He can't leave without a prayer,' he ordered in his vibrant voice. MacGregor's helpers placed the coffin on the floor where the lay preacher indicated, and the family gathered around wordlessly.

Louie squeezed her eyes shut, partly to prevent the tears escaping, as her father gave a short extempore prayer for Davie's life. For the first time ever she heard his strong voice praise her brother for his joy of life and the friendship he had shown to others. She knew it took great courage for her reticent parent to bare his heart at such a painful time, but it was a relief to hear him. It would help mend the rift between her father and Iris, and already the awful tension of the morning was dissolving as they stood side by side in silent unity.

'Greater love hath no man than to lay down his life for others,' Jacob quoted.

'Now we commend our brother Davie into your care, O Lord. Amen.'

'Amen,' Louie choked with the others.

'We'll sing a hymn as Davie leaves for his eternal home,' Jacob encouraged his family and began a robust singing.

'Onward goes the pilgrim band,
Singing songs of expectation,
Marching to the promised land!'

Louie gripped Iris's hand as they sang and although her sister-in-law did not know the words to join in, she felt an answering squeeze.

They were about to set off from the house behind the coffin, still singing, just as Iris's family arrived. The Ramshaws seemed quite taken aback by the rousing noise emanating from behind the curtained windows. Iris rushed forward and greeted them in a flood of words and tears and embracing. Louie was thankful portly Mr Ramshaw and his talkative wife had managed not to be late. The boys, Tom and Percy, and their sisters, Nora and Jean, pressed around their eldest sibling and supported her out of the door.

For the first time in four days, Louie heard Iris answer questions and consoling words with a degree of her old spark. Her face streamed with tears as she clung on to her mother and was supported by her father on the other side as they stepped into the crowded street.

'Keep Raymond indoors,' Louie called to Sadie. 'No point in him seeing his mother this upset.' The small boy seemed oblivious to the grief-stricken atmosphere around him and was enjoying the singing until he saw everyone leave the room. As Louie closed the door behind her, Raymond ran to it, battering and howling in protest, and Sadie rushed to restrain him.

'Mammy and Auntie Louie will be back soon,' the young girl assured him, hugging him to her. 'Look, we'll watch from the window.' Raymond allowed himself to be carried into the parlour and they peeked out of the curtains, even though it made Sadie shiver to step into that room of death.

'There's Mammy,' she jollied the baby, pointing at a black figure surrounded on all sides by family and neighbours. 'Raymond wave.'

'Daddy?' the small boy queried, turning to his cousin with a puzzled look. 'Daddy ta-ta?'

'Yes, Daddy ta-ta,' Sadie answered hoarsely, repeating the babyish words that Raymond used to call when his father left for work. She let the curtain fall and took Raymond back into the kitchen.

Eleanor had never seen a crowd like it. A swathe of behatted mourners, grim-faced and virtually silent, stretched as far as the eye could see. She parked the car outside St Cuthbert's because the way up to the public cemetery was choked with the slow tide of villagers edging their way to the Memorial Park. The park had been created in remembrance of an earlier pit explosion when fifteen men had been killed. It had happened before the war, when Eleanor was away at a suffragist rally, and she had not been aware of the intensity of the tragedy.

But now she knew one of the miners involved; Davie Kirkup, whom she had first met when Will nearly ran him over one summer night that seemed so long ago. Through Davie she had met Louie, a sensible and brave miner's daughter whom she counted as a friend - and she had met Eb. Eleanor's heart twisted in pain to think how the Kirkups were suffering now. She had wanted to rush and see them as soon as Hopkinson brought news of the disaster, but her wish not to intrude on their grief had made her hesitate. All week she had stayed away. How she longed to put her arms around Eb so they could comfort one another.

But she stood utterly alone now, outside the church where Beatrice and Sandy had been married just a week ago. Eleanor was sure she could recall seeing chestnut-haired Iris grinning by the lych gate in a green velvet hat, holding up her baby to see the grand people who rustled by them in their fancy clothes. Eleanor's own problems paled into insignificance when she thought of Davie's young widow and child without their breadwinner. What would they do now? she pondered as she waited for the Joices to join her. Hopkinson had said there was another woman even worse off, a Mrs Hutchinson who was left with three young children.

Eleanor had demanded to know what would be done for them. Reginald had answered coldly that there would be provision for the widows and families involved. Kirkup and Hutchinson had been paying into a new insurance fund and Trewick's family would be cared for by his union.

'Fortunately the other two were just boys with no families to support,' Reginald had added, then flushed under the outraged glare of his wife.

'So as long as they're young and unmarried they're expendable?' Eleanor had seethed. 'Such comforting sentiments for the families who've lost them.'

'That's not what I meant,' Reginald had retorted and ordered her out of his study so he could discuss further with his agent the situation at the damaged pit. Eleanor had stormed from the room, shaking with indignation, quite forgetting that the reason she had sought Reginald in the first place was to tell him she wanted a separation.

Pulling her fur collar about her slim neck, so it met the back of her black hat, she watched Isobel and her father emerge out of the dene towards her. Reginald had thought it inappropriate for either himself or Eleanor to attend the funeral; after all it was a private affair for the bereaved mining families. Eleanor snorted to think of her husband's excuses as she saw hundreds of people lining the road to see the passing funeral cortege.

'Isobel.' She kissed her friend on the cheek. Dr Joice gave Eleanor a hug; no more words were necessary. They walked down the lane and fell in behind a family crossing the green to the park. Joining the orderly throng at the tall iron gates, Eleanor looked back down the village. A low hum of noise carried on the wind and her eyes watered in the icy air.

Far down the hill, snaking its way through the respectful mourners came the procession of carriages, the first three horse-drawn, the last two motorised. Before them marched the colliery band, their brass instruments glinting dully under a grey shrouded sky. Eleanor strained to see if Eb was playing, but they were too far off to discern any faces. Blasts of music rose and died as the wind snatched the notes and tossed them up to the clouds. There was a hushed tenseness as they waited.

Isobel slipped an arm through her friend's as the cortege drew nearer. By now it was possible to make out the figures beside the carriages and the magnificent horses crowned with black plumes, their drivers hanging on to top hats in the stiff breeze. The band swept past and Eleanor saw Eb frowning in concentration under his military-style cap, then other heads got in the way of her view.

'They're the Trewicks,' Isobel murmured and nodded at the first party; two women surrounded by children of differing ages and a host of relations about them. Eleanor did not know which one was the widow, for both central figures were bowed in grief.

Following them were the coffins and families of the dead boys. There was a gap of several yards and then came the first motorised hearse. No one walked beside it, but Eleanor glimpsed a young, pale-faced woman sitting in the front, two children either side and another one on her knee.

225

'The Hutchinsons?' she whispered. Isobel nodded.

'They're strangers here - her daughter Lily is at our school. She gets picked on because her father was a scab,' the teacher explained in a hushed voice.

'How dreadful.' Eleanor's pity for the lone woman and her wide-eyed children increased. But it was the sight of the final group of mourners that really wrung her heart. Behind the carriage bearing the wreath-covered coffin stumbled Iris, gripped on either side by her parents. There were several muffled children who could have been members of her family, and among them the Kirkups, the tall distinguished lay preacher and his frail grey-faced wife who no longer resembled the maid Eleanor had known in her childhood. John walked between Hilda and Louie, the threesome arm in arm for support, while behind came another couple whom Eleanor did not recognise. They moved together as if bound by some invisible web, a family in complete unity in their loss. Louie's comely face was haggard with distress and Eleanor wondered fleetingly why Sam Ritson was not at her side.

As the last of the procession moved through the gates the crowd fell in behind in a solid phalanx of support. Eleanor was struck by the solemn dignity of the whole procession, the eerie silence of a thousand souls gathered to bury their dead. Whatever the divisions wrought by the strike, today all were equal in their sadness and no one withheld their sympathy.

Eleanor and the Joices moved with the procession of followers through the park to the neatly laid-out cemetery. The headstones looked drab with no shaft of sunlight to illuminate the gold lettering on the more elaborate graves. Being the depth of winter, the mounds of earth were unadorned with flowers or shrubs to console the visitors; not even a sparkling hoarfrost clothed the bleakness. Behind them stood the massive black pitheads of the Eleanor and Beatrice and their hump-backs of slag, aloof and oblivious to the destruction they caused.

The churchmen were assembled at the gaping graves and Reverend Hodgson announced the first hymn. The band struck up 'O God, Our Help in Ages Past' and all about the pit folk raised their voices in song. So fervent was the singing that the crowd drowned out the musicians. Eventually, those who sang further away lagged a line behind so that the words seemed to echo around the sparse field.

Unexpectedly, Eleanor succumbed to tears at the moving refrain, 'Time like an ever-rolling stream, Bears all its sons away . . .' It made her think of the occasions she had sung these words at memorial services on the eleventh of each November for her brother Rupert. How many ghosts of friends did Eb conjure up as he played the hymn? she wondered.

The singing died away and Stephen Pinkney gave a reading, his strong preacher's voice ringing out over the hushed assembly. Both he and the vicar said prayers and Reverend Hodgson gave a short sermon that Eleanor could hardly catch in the contrary wind. There was a further hymn and then the coffins were laid one by one in the waiting graves.

'Dust to dust, ashes to ashes,' the minister said over Davie's box as the dull thud of earth could be heard hitting the wood. Eleanor saw Iris visibly shrink, and an agonised wail went up as if from a wounded animal. All around the gravesides women were sobbing and children crying inconsolably, while the men stood bowed and tight-faced, fighting to keep their emotions under control.

It seemed to take an age for each coffin to be lowered out of sight and their church leader deliver the final rites. Eleanor thought she would faint from the biting cold and the palpable distress of all around her. If she had not been penned in by the crowd, she would have turned and fled from the misery.

At last the ceremony was over. The mourners were guided away from the grim pits and the gravediggers set to work filling in the mounds of dark soil. One last time, the band spurred the onlookers forward with stout music and the spectators fell back to let them through. This time Eleanor was standing on the side Eb was playing and, as he passed, their eyes held each other for an instant before he was gone. Eleanor thought he registered surprise at seeing her there among the villagers. She had no opportunity to follow him, for by the time the families had shuffled after the players, the crowd broke up and she found herself jostled away from the funeral party.

'Father wishes to call on the Kirkups for a few minutes,' Isobel told her as they inched their way out of the cemetery. 'You could go and wait at Greenbrae until we return - unless you'd like to come too?' she added cautiously. Eleanor hesitated.

'Should I?' she asked, unsure.

'Iris would appreciate it, I'm certain,' Isobel encouraged. 'You've been kind to her and Davie - she likes you.'

'But won't I embarrass - after all that's happened - I'm a Seward-Scott in their eyes?'

'You're not Reginald.' Isobel gave a ghost of a smile. 'Come on, we'll be brief.'

Eleanor was secretly thankful at her friend's persuasion and her spirits lifted as they made their way across the village. Turning into Hawthorn Street, they had no difficulty in finding the Kirkups' house with its throng of callers spilling out into the street.

People stepped aside and conversation dried up as the important visitors arrived. Eleanor felt awkward at their cool deference towards her and for a moment wished she had not come.

'Miss Eleanor!' Louie cried in surprise on seeing her enter with the doctor and schoolteacher. 'How kind of you to call.'

'I won't stay long.' Eleanor flushed at the young woman's generous greeting. 'I just wanted to say how very sorry I am about Davie -'

'You'll stay for a cup of tea,' Louie insisted, fussing around them. 'Iris is through in the front room if you'd like a word.'

Eleanor nodded and moved round the table. Entering the parlour, she saw Davie's widow sitting on a high-backed chair by a cheery fire, surrounded by family. The subdued talk was punctuated by chatter and occasional bursts of laughter from her brothers and sisters and Sadie who were all playing a board game in the corner of the room.

'Mrs Seward-Scott.' Iris's wan face brightened in a smile at the sight of the unexpected guest.

'Iris,' Eleanor went to her and gripped both her hands in hers, 'I'm so sorry.'

'I'm pleased you came,' Iris brushed aside the condolence. 'Davie thought the world of you. He was pleased as punch at the way you befriended us.'

'I did nothing really.' Eleanor gulped in embarrassment. 'I was fond of you both - am fond. You will let me know if there's anything I can do, won't you? And I mean anything.'

'Thank you, miss.' Iris smiled with pleasure and her hazel eyes filled up with tears. Eleanor withdrew quickly and left her with her family.

Accepting Louie's cup of tea, she took it out into the yard and waited for her friends. It was a relief to escape the stifling fug in the small house and the press of bodies in the over-furnished parlour. Out here the raw air soon cooled her flushed face and no one else appeared to have sought refuge in the dank yard. Sipping her tea, Eleanor saw Eb trudge in from the lane, his cap removed and his fair face tinged blue with the cold.

He stopped still on seeing her, but soon recovered his composure, aware that others might be watching.

'Mrs Seward-Scott.' He nodded respectfully and, stepping nearer, thanked her for calling as if she were just an ordinary neighbour.

'How are you, Eb?' Eleanor kept her voice low and even.

'As well as can be expected,' he replied guardedly.

Eleanor glanced round to make sure no one could overhear. 'I know this is not the time or place, but I do need to speak to you.'

'I don't think that's a good idea,' Eb said, looking the other way.

'Please, Eb,' she beseeched.

His jaw clenched and then he gave a grudging, 'Very well. Meet me at the allotment before dark - I'll try and get away.' Not waiting for her assent, Eb turned and disappeared into the house. To Eleanor's relief, Isobel and her father emerged at the same time and indicated it was time to leave.

'They're all being remarkably brave about things,' Isobel commented as they let themselves out of the back gate.

'It's part of being a pitman,' her father replied. 'They're the most resilient men I know.'

Isobel gave him one of her forthright looks. 'I was thinking of the women, Papa.'

'Isobel's right,' Eleanor agreed. They're the ones who have to cope with keeping the family together.'

'Of course,' Dr Joice acquiesced hastily. 'My daughter is constantly reminding me which is the stronger sex.' Father and daughter smiled at each other in sudden amusement and Eleanor felt a twinge of regret that she had allowed herself to grow so apart from her own father.

Louie was washing up the final teacups when Sam came in from the darkness outside. Iris was resting upstairs, her parents were in the parlour with the children and her brothers had gone out on separate errands. Water was boiling on the fire for Sam's bath and there was bacon ready to cook for his tea. For the first time that day the kitchen was a haven of peace, but Louie dreaded the time when there was nothing left with which to occupy herself.

Sam approached her at the scullery sink and pecked her lightly on the cheek.

'Water's boiling,' Louie said without looking at him.

'I called in at Mrs Trewick's,' Sam told her, 'wanted to make sure everything was in order for her insurance payout.'

'That was good of you.' Louie could not keep the sarcasm out of her voice. She brushed past him and busied herself with carving a thick slice of bread for frying.

'How's Iris?' Sam asked, hovering next to her, aware of his wife's hostility.

'Fine time to ask now.' Louie suddenly turned on him angrily. 'Well, she's tired out after that funeral - we all are - it's been one of the saddest days of my life. I'll never forget it - all those people there, but not you - you weren't there to support us. I'll never forget that either, Sam! Couldn't you have swallowed your precious pride for just one day?'

Sam gaped at his wife. Her young face was shadowed in fatigue, her blue eyes narrowed in fury. He felt ashamed at having caused her extra unhappiness; his quarrel had been with Davie not with the woman he loved above all else. He had been meaning to keep silent about his movements that day, but he could not compound Louie's grief for the sake of his own dignity. Sam forced himself to be humble.

'I'm sorry, pet.' He stepped towards her. 'I should've been with you today - for your sake if not for Davie's.' Louie remained rigidly silent. 'I was halfway to Ushaw when I realised my mistake.'

'What's done is done,' Louie replied dismissively and continued to snip the bacon.

'So I came back,' Sam persisted. 'I was too late to leave from the house with you, but I followed in the crowd. I saw your brother buried, Louie,' Sam said quietly. 'I paid my respects like the rest of them.'

Louie turned to look into his face, her mouth opening in astonishment. For the first time she saw Sam properly; there was no grime on his face or neck; he had not been down the pit that day. She dropped the scissors and reached out for her husband. Their arms went about each other in a fierce hug.

'I'm so glad,' Louie cried into his shoulder. 'I didn't want any bad feeling to come between us, Sam, over our Davie.'

'It won't,' Sam promised. 'I know we've had it rough this past year, Louie, but we'll manage, and I'm proud of the way you've been strong for your family since Davie died.'

'I don't feel strong,' Louie confessed with a sniff. 'I miss him that much.'

Sam stroked her fair hair clumsily. 'Aye,' he whispered, 'I know you do.' Only inwardly could Sam admit that he missed the lad too.

It was almost dark by the time Eb reached the allotment; what dismal light the day had shed was draining quickly out of the sky. Eleanor was waiting for him. Without a word they entered the hut and Eb lit a candle stub, placing it high on a shelf to cast its glow further. Eleanor decided to get straight to the point.

'I'm leaving Reginald,' she announced. 'I'm leaving The Grange.' Eb started at the news, peering in the dimness to see if she was jesting. Her slim face was quite composed. A thousand questions burst into his mind but he did not know where to begin, so instead he allowed her to continue.

'With Beatrice gone and Reginald and my father more away from home than here, I feel I'm carrying out some silly charade - pretending to be the lady of the manor.' She gave a self-deprecatory laugh. 'The Grange no longer feels like home - it's just a place of memories for me. My life there is pointless and shallow - has been for ages. I want to do something worthwhile for once! Oh, doesn't that sound pompous?'

'No.' Eb found his voice. 'What do you intend to do?'

'I shall move to Durham where I have friends who won't care about the scandal. I also want to set up a birth control clinic - here in the village. It's something I've talked about doing for a long time but never done anything about. Well, now I've discussed it with Dr Joice and he is prepared to help me.'

Eb gave out a soft whistle. 'You're serious, aren't you?'

'Of course I am,' Eleanor responded sharply.

'Does your husband know of your plans?'

Eleanor nodded. 'We discussed it this afternoon. He wasn't even upset,' she said with a touch of chagrin, 'treated it like one of his business arrangements. Reginald is simply relieved I'm not going to fight over the estate - I'll have quite enough to live on for my needs.' Eleanor stopped, aware that her reduced wealth would still be beyond the aspirations of a miner.

'And he's just letting you go without a fight - after all his spying and threats and blackmailing?' Eb sounded amazed.

'Yes,' Eleanor answered with a shrug of resignation. 'The threats were only to prevent me meddling in his business. I haven't been of use to my husband for a long time - only my money interests him. In a couple of years we can quietly divorce after the furore of my desertion has died down. He will bask in the sympathy of the county and be free to marry Libby Fisher who will oblige him with his longed-for heir. That's the only other thing Reginald cares about.' Eleanor's tone was matter of fact, but as she lit a cigarette from the wavering candle her hands shook.

'And you, Eleanor?' Eb asked quietly. 'Do you plan to remarry?'

'I've had an offer from an American tycoon already.' She laughed and then at once regretted her flippancy. 'I told him it depended on you.'

Eb shifted uneasily on to his other leg, his arms crossed defensively against his chest. 'How can I fit into your plans?' he growled.

'By coming to live with me in Durham. There's nothing to stop us being together now,' Eleanor urged. 'You can concentrate on your painting - have lessons with Ruth Spencer - you don't have to worry about the financial side of things, I'll take care of that.'

'Be a kept man, you mean?' Eb's face betrayed his disapproval. 'I can hear them laughing now - Eb Kirkup, the Seward woman's fancy man.'

Eleanor was offended by his harsh laughter. 'What does it matter what other people think of us? You've always spurned convention. Why should it concern you if we live off my private income while you paint? All the great artists have had their patrons.'

Eb glared at her. 'Still Lady Bountiful.' He shook his head. 'I would always be beholden to you, don't you see? I'm not like your husband; I've never wanted your money, Eleanor, and I don't want it now.'

'You're impossible!' She dropped her cigarette and stamped on the glowing end. 'At last we have a chance to be together and you throw it back in my face. I've a good mind to accept the American's offer - I can see you no longer love me the way I love you!'

'That's not what I said,' Eb countered, removing his cap and running a hand agitatedly over his head. 'I do still care for you. But this is all too sudden - I can't think straight, what with Davie just buried!' He took a deep breath and continued more calmly. 'My family needs me now, Eleanor, more than you do. Davie's death has brought us all closer. If I left to live with you they would never understand. As far as my parents would be concerned, you would still be Mrs Reginald Seward-Scott and your place should be with your husband. They would probably never speak to me again - I'd be betraying my own kind in their eyes. It's too soon after Davie's death for them to lose another son.'

Eleanor bit her lip. 'How long do I have to wait for you, Eb?'

He looked at her unhappily. 'Best not to wait,' he answered and reached for the door. He pulled it open and the sudden blast of wind snuffed out the candle, leaving the hut in pitch blackness. Eleanor hurried past Eb, glad that he could not see the bitter tears of disappointment flooding her eyes.

Chapter Twenty-Seven

Eleanor found a house in the cobbled Bailey, a stone's throw from the quiet Cathedral quadrangle in the heart of Durham. It had a narrow secluded garden which overhung the sluggish River Wear and was close to two colleges. She enjoyed being woken by peals of bells on a Sunday morning and watching the students dawdling along the ancient street to their lectures during the week. Bridget her maid had moved with her as housekeeper, and she had engaged Molly Hutchinson as cook. The young widow had jumped at the chance of being in Durham close to her own people at the village of Pity Me. She arranged for her sister to look after the children during the day and was allowed every other weekend off to be with them.

For the first time in years, Eleanor relished her freedom to come and go as she pleased, entertain her friends in the cosy charm of her comfortable sitting room and not have to keep up stilted appearances for either Reginald or her father. Thomas Seward-Scott occasionally called if he was in the town and kept her informed of county gossip. Otherwise she had no contact with The Grange. She was no longer included in weekend house parties at the country houses of former friends, or invited out with the Swainsons; Reginald had circulated a rumour that her behaviour had grown increasingly bizarre until it had put an unacceptable strain on their marriage. 'And she refused to give me children,' Eleanor could hear him saying stoically. 'That's all I ever asked of Eleanor.' In a wave of sympathy the ladies of the county were falling over themselves to entertain him. It made Eleanor laugh to think of the quiet, respectable life she now lived being portrayed in animated dinner conversations as 'quite mad'.

By chance she had once overheard Rose Fisher gossiping about her in a Durham tea shop. 'Of course there was another man involved.' Rose spoke with a jangle of bracelets in the hushed upstairs salon. 'Reggie would never be so disloyal as to admit it,' she continued, red lips pursed in satisfaction at the scandalised look on her friend's face, 'but Libby said there was one all the same.' Eleanor felt herself blushing puce at the realisation that she was the subject of their salacious talk. She froze on the stairs, just out of view of the women.

'Naturally we were all agog to discover who the lover was - but she kept that one to herself, didn't she?' Rose looked disapproving.

'Such a cold fish,' the other woman murmured. 'Who would have thought -'

'Of course, I think it was that American, Bryce. She always allowed him to flirt with her in front of poor Reggie. The joke is that Bryce ditched her as soon as she made her move. Out in the cold - just like that. Burnt her bridges, poor old girl.'

Eleanor wanted to laugh out loud at their speculations; they could not have been more wrong about the reasons behind her separation from Reginald. Tempted to turn and run from their wagging tongues, Eleanor steeled herself and mounted the final steps into the tea room. She walked straight up to Rose Fisher and greeted her warmly, relishing the woman's embarrassed confusion.

'I'm waiting for a friend.' Eleanor smiled. 'Perhaps I could sit with you until she comes?'

'Sorry, darling,' Rose managed a look of regret, 'I really can't stay. It's been lovely to see you.' The two women stood up quickly, gathering their bags and umbrellas as if they had just received a distress signal.

'Another time then?' Eleanor suggested calmly.

'Yes, of course.' Rose's painted face grimaced in a smile.

'Regards to Libby.' Eleanor could not resist flinging a parting shot. Rose and her friend fled downstairs without a backward glance. Eleanor had still been smiling over the incident when Ruth Spencer came to join her. She did not care that she was ostracised from county 'society', Eleanor realised with a new clarity; it was a relief to throw off its constraints and petty snobberies.

The clinic, however, was not proving to be such an instant success. In March she opened premises in South Street, opposite the Memorial Hall, which could not have been more central for the population of Whitton Grange. Word soon spread about the birth control clinic, but for the first month only three women came for advice. One day Minnie Bell puffed her way cautiously upstairs to the stark waiting room. Eleanor immediately ushered her into a private room with a narrow dormer window and a hissing gas fire and helped lower the heavily pregnant visitor into a comfortable armchair.

Minnie refused a cup of tea. 'I'm right off it just now.' They sat awkwardly eyeing each other, Minnie looking stranded and ill at ease in the deep seat.

'I'll have to go in a minute to collect the bairn,' Minnie told her.

'What is it you've come to ask about, Mrs Bell?'

Minnie blushed furiously and looked down at her huge bump. 'I would have thought it was obvious. I don't want this to happen again, miss,' she admitted. 'It's my second in two years and we can't afford to feed the first one. You'll think I'm daft being so ignorant about things, but no one ever tells you. The only thing I know is from that film you once showed at the hall, but I didn't have the nerve to ask any questions. The thing is I don't know how—you know . . .' Her voice trailed off.

Glad that Minnie had plunged in bravely and expressed her worries, Eleanor began to outline the various options for Minnie to consider once her baby was weaned. She talked about it in such a matter-of-fact way - as if they were discussing shopping - that Minnie began to relax and ask questions. At the end of half an hour, she was smiling with relief.

"Course I shouldn't be here,' she laughed. 'Mam would go light if she knew. Not that she disapproves of what you're doing, but she'd make me confess to Father Monahan. He says it's against God's will for us to stop having babies - but then he doesn't have to have them, does he?'

Eleanor smiled with her, warming to Minnie's open, animated manner. 'I wondered why so few women had come to see me or Dr Joice,' she said.

'I've only come 'cos it's dark outside and no one saw me come in,' Minnie told her. 'But there's plenty of lasses are desperate not to get pregnant.'

'What would you suggest I do to reach them?' Eleanor asked, crossing her legs in front of the fire. Minnie sucked in her cheeks thoughtfully.

'You could make it more inviting - more social like. Tea and biscuits and a film like you had in the hall that time - that would get people along. And if you had advice on how to keep the bairns healthy too, then the priest can hardly complain if the likes of us come along, can he?'

'You mean somewhere for young mothers to meet with their babies?'

'Aye.' Minnie's green eyes grew animated. 'There's nowhere else except in folk's houses. Then we could have a bit of chat - share our problems - have a moan about the men!' Minnie laughed.

'That's an excellent idea. Thank you, Mrs Bell.' Eleanor smiled. 'You've helped me more than I've helped you today.'

Minnie smiled, feeling important. 'The name's Minnie,' she said as she left.

Iris saw the light still on in Eleanor's clinic, so pushed open the downstairs door and hurried in from the damp March drizzle. As she did so, she heard the heavy footsteps of someone descending the narrow stairs and waited in the hall to let them pass. In the dim gaslight it took several seconds to recognise the swollen girth of Minnie Bell, her pale face and dark hair obscured by an unfashionable large-brimmed hat. Iris's first emotion was of horror at being confronted by Davie's pregnant lover. This soon gave way to a perverse satisfaction in seeing how ungainly and dowdy she looked in a shapeless brown coat that would not meet over her belly, and with her pallid face blemished by a rash over her chin.

Minnie gasped and stopped as she recognised the neat figure in the velvet hat, her red lips shining under the gas lamp.

'Iris!'

Iris nodded but did not reply. Minnie continued to descend, holding tightly to the banister.

'Have you come to see Mrs Seward-Scott?' Minnie asked nervously.

'Obviously,' Iris answered scornfully. 'Looks like you've left it a bit late.'

Minnie's face went a blotchy red. 'I'm sorry, Iris,' she answered meekly. 'I know it doesn't change anything to say so - but I'm really sorry about Davie.'

Iris did not know whether she was referring to her husband's death or Minnie's part in his infidelity. She had often daydreamt about meeting Minnie Bell and giving her a mouthful of abuse or slapping her cheeky face. If Minnie had said anything galling, like she had loved Davie too, Iris would not have hesitated in pulling her down the last flight of stairs. Yet now, as she looked at the young woman before her, weighed down by her cumbersome burden, Iris admitted to a feeling of pity.

'None of us can change what's happened,' she replied stonily. 'Now are you going to let me up those stairs or not?'

'Sorry,' Minnie repeated in a fluster and hurried down the last steps. Iris tensed as they came near to touching in the hallway. She watched frostily as Minnie hesitated, then spoke.

'He never loved me,' Minnie looked at Iris boldly, 'I know that now. You and Raymond were everything to Davie. I just thought I should say that.'

Iris felt her insides clench at the words. She swallowed hard to prevent the tears that welled up in her throat. Minnie turned and walked towards the door; Iris mounted the first step. Something made her call over her shoulder, before Minnie was halfway out of the door.

'Take care of that baby, won't you?'

Minnie glanced back in surprise. 'Aye - I will,' she stammered in confusion. But Iris's erect back was already turned, her high-heeled shoes tapping up the linoleum-covered stairs.

Eleanor was taken aback to see Iris walk into the clinic just as she was preparing to leave.

'I can come another time,' Iris suggested hurriedly, clutching her coat about her.

'No, stay,' Eleanor insisted. 'I've been thinking about you a lot.'

'Surprised to see me here though?' Iris smiled ironically.

Eleanor laughed. 'Yes, I suppose I am a bit. But pleased none the less. Do sit down.'

Iris sat upright on the edge of the large armchair opposite the fire. Eleanor disappeared for a minute behind a wooden partition which separated off a small galley and poured out two cups of coffee from a pot on the stove. Returning, she offered one to Iris.

'I thought you'd prefer coffee.'

Iris smiled, touched that Eleanor should have remembered her tastes. She took a sip and placed the cup carefully back on its saucer.

'I haven't come for advice,' Iris began, 'but you did say if there was something you could do to help, I was to ask.' She looked composedly at Eleanor's concerned face.

'I did.' Eleanor nodded.

'Well, I was wondering if you wouldn't mind lending me a bit of money.' Iris rattled through her request. 'Just a loan, mind, I'll pay you back when I can.'

'How much do you need?' Eleanor asked.

Iris took a deep breath. 'About twenty pounds.'

'I don't mean to pry, Iris,' Eleanor considered her, 'but what do you intend spending—'

'Oh, I'll tell you that,' Iris interrupted, keen to share her secret. 'I've decided to leave Whitton Grange. There's nothing here for me now that Davie's gone. I've never liked the place much - it was Davie that I came here for.' She cleared her throat and went on quickly. 'The Kirkups have been canny and taken me and Raymond back in with them, but we can't live there for ever. I need to find a job, then I can give Raymond a home of our own.'

Eleanor nodded in understanding. 'Will you look for something in Durham? Of course I'm willing to lend you some money while you find your feet, that goes without saying. But perhaps I could help secure you a position as a housekeeper or something?'

Iris shook her head vigorously. 'No, I'd be useless at that. You see, there's only one thing I'm any good at, and that's singing.' Iris lifted her chin proudly. 'I want to have a go on the stage.' She looked at Eleanor, wary of ridicule, but saw none in the older woman's face.

'That's very brave of you, Iris,' Eleanor commented, 'and certainly you have the talent. But where would you start?'

'I know a man called Barnfather - travels with a company who do music hall. There's a pub in Scarborough where I can get news of his whereabouts - I've sent a letter. He'll give me a job if I can find him.' Iris's slim face was determined.

'But what about Raymond?' Eleanor voiced her concern. 'He's still just a baby - it would be very difficult travelling alone with him, wouldn't it?'

'Yes,' Iris sighed, 'I wouldn't be able to take him with me - not at first. I'd wait till I got something regular, then come back for him. The money would help keep him while I'm gone.'

Eleanor saw the strain on the young woman's face as she spoke. It was obvious what a painful decision it was to leave her son, her only child and her most tangible link with Davie.

'You seem to have it all worked out. Your mother would look after him for you in the mean time, I suppose?' Eleanor asked.

'No.' Iris's eyes glistened brightly in the electric light. 'I've asked Louie to care for him, she's his godmother. Raymond thinks the world of his Auntie Louie - and Louie would make the best mam for him I know.'

Two weeks later, on a blustery April morning when the dene rustled with yellow-headed daffodils, Iris packed her bag to leave. Word had come from the Scarborough publican that Barnfather's players were in Manchester for the week, so that was where she was heading. The previous Saturday, John had announced his engagement to Marjory Hewitson, and the parlour at 28 Hawthorn Street had resounded to Eb's lively piano playing and Iris's singing. There had not been such a happy family occasion since Davie and Iris had left the house on bad terms in the dying weeks of the strike.

It was an emotional evening, with everyone silently thinking of the missing Davie who always enjoyed a good singsong and would urge his wife to repeat her whole repertoire of traditional songs. Louie struggled to keep her sorrow to herself as she joined in John and Marjory's celebration. They sat close to each other on the small horsehair sofa, red-faced and beaming after the special tea that Louie and her mother had made. Louie could not remember John being so relaxed and talkative, as he took Marjory's plump hand in his own and called requests to Eb.

Her eldest brother was as quiet as usual, though Eb gave his wistful smile from time to time and occasionally shared a joke with Hilda, who was turning the music for him. Louie had to admit she was relieved that his liaison with Miss Eleanor had come to nothing. It was scandal enough that the mine owner's wife had left her husband, and Louie was thankful her brother did not appear to be involved.

Louie felt grateful now towards Eb and the rest of her family for giving her parents something to be cheerful about after the loss of their youngest son. Her father was joining in the singing in his deep bass voice, while her mother sat by the fire with her sewing, joining in snatches of song and smiling over at Marjory with approval. The cheerful Hewitson girl was just the daughter-in-law her mother longed for, Louie thought. They shared an interest in embroidery; Marjory's family had been in the village for as long as the Kirkups; she was helpful and competent in the home and put up with John's bouts of temper. In addition she was not over-pretty; Marjory had a pleasant, round-cheeked face, framed in soft brown curls, and an infectious giggle which made Fanny want to join in the joke.

'Have another piece of Louie's jam sponge,' Fanny pressed Marjory to indulge. Louie smiled with satisfaction when her future sister-in-law did not refuse. She would be so much easier to get on with than the temperamental Iris.

Yet watching Iris's animated face, sparkling with life after painful months of grief, Louie felt a flood of affection for her sister-in-law. She could not look at Iris without being reminded of her favourite brother Davie, and she dreaded the moment when they would have to say goodbye. Louie was thrilled that Iris had entrusted Raymond into her care. She loved the boy as her own and having him to care for made her feel less wretched about her inability to conceive again. So she had done her best to muffle her parents' criticism of Iris for abandoning her son to go on the stage.

'It's unnatural,' Jacob had blustered behind Iris's back.

'What would Davie have said?' Fanny had asked accusingly.

'He'd have wanted Iris to be happy,' Louie had argued, 'and she's doing this for Raymond's sake in the long run. She's promised she'll come back for him.'

'She won't go,' Fanny assured herself. 'When she thinks it through, she'll change her mind.'

But Iris did not. Louie methodically cleared the breakfast dishes as Iris fetched her possessions and stuffed them haphazardly into her case. Sadie was off school for the Easter holidays and was distracting Raymond with a story about dragons that she was making up as she went along. Hilda had come over the previous evening from Greenbrae to say goodbye and John had said a gruff farewell and pecked her on the cheek before going on shift that morning. Only Eb had elected to accompany Iris to the station.

Jacob sat studying the Bible as if he were reading it for the first time, while Fanny hovered over Iris's packing until her daughter-in-law snapped at her to stop fussing.

'I'll take Raymond for a walk now, shall I?' Louie asked quickly. It had been arranged that the boy should not see his mother leave.

'Yes,' Iris answered distractedly. 'I'm nearly ready.'

'Come on, Raymond,' Louie called and held out her hand. 'We'll go and get Uncle Sam's tobacco from the shop.' The small boy got obediently to his feet and Louie dressed him in a coat and hat.

'Dragon smoke baccy, Sadie?' he asked his cousin.

Sadie nodded. 'All dragons smoke. You go and buy some baccy for the dragon.'

'Sadie come too,' Raymond insisted. Louie and Sadie stood either side of him holding on to his proffered hands. Louie hesitated as Iris regarded her son nervously.

'Give Mammy a kiss,' Louie ordered suddenly, unable to bear the thought of Iris leaving without touching Raymond again. Iris stood granite-like on the clippy mat. Raymond trotted over and put up his arms, and Iris picked him up and squeezed him tightly for a moment. The room seemed to hold its breath, but seconds later he wriggled to be free, impatient to carry out his errand. Iris fiercely kissed his auburn hair.

'You be good for Auntie Louie, won't you?' she mumbled hoarsely.

'Of course he will.' Louie smiled at Iris and blinked back the tears that stung her eyes. Ta-ra then.' She turned away hurriedly and added softly, 'Take care of yourself.'

'Ta-ra, Louie,' Iris replied mechanically, not taking her eyes off the small figure clinging happily to his aunt and cousin. They disappeared out of the door and Iris resisted the urge to run after them and hug Raymond to her again. If he had made a fuss about leaving her, she might have relented and stayed, even at this late hour.

But why should he? He thought he was merely going to Armstrong's the tobacconists and that she would be at home on his return. Would Raymond at two years of age realise that his mother had left him? she wondered guiltily.

Swiftly she pulled on her coat, arranged her hat in the parlour mirror and checked that half of Eleanor's money was safely tucked into a pocket sewn into the lining of her coat. The other ten pounds she had given to Fanny to keep for Raymond, as Louie had refused to take it. There were stilted goodbyes to her parents-in-law as Eb picked up her case. She longed to tell Fanny and Jacob how much their friendship to her had meant over the past weeks, but the words clogged in her throat and she could only hug them silently.

Tramping through the village, Iris viewed her surroundings as if in a film. Familiar streets flicked past, well-known shops that had taken her business; Lake's the haberdashers, the fish and chip shop, the grand co-operative building in South Street with its treasures in drapery. Dimarco's ice cream cart trundled by with a wave from the cheerful boy who pulled it; he must have recognised her face from the many times she had pressed Davie into buying her a delicious homemade ice.

As they passed Eleanor's clinic, Iris wondered what was going through Eb's mind. She knew from a conversation she had overheard between Louie and Hilda that her brother-in-law and the lady from The Grange had been close friends. All at once she wanted to break the sad silence between them.

'Miss Eleanor lent me the money, you know,' Iris said. 'I couldn't be doing this without her help.'

Eb glanced at her from under his cap, but said nothing. They continued past the Memorial Hall and turned on to the Durham Road.

'She's a real lady, Miss Eleanor,' Iris persisted. 'She's been a good friend to us all.'

'Aye,' Eb agreed grudgingly, 'but there's more to friendship than charity.'

'Is that all you think it is?' Iris answered scornfully. 'Well, I see it as more than that - Miss Eleanor's been kindness itself to me and Davie. She didn't have to give me anything - she's not the boss's wife any more. The trouble with you pitmen is your stupid pride - you can't see real friendship when it stares you in the face. Sam's just the same - still not talking to Bomber over nothing.'

'Why are you going on about Mrs Seward-Scott to me?' Eb asked testily. Iris shot him a knowing look.

'You know very well why. Because she cares about you,' she answered boldly. 'She was asking after you when I went to see her. You can call me interfering, but I think you're daft for giving her up. If you want something in life you should grab on to it - and not give tuppence-halfpenny for what other people think.'

Iris saw Eb's jaw colour and his face grow stormy, so she dropped the subject. They marched on round the corner where the new redbrick Catholic church stood.

'Don't want to bump into that Minnie Bell again,' Iris complained, ducking her head.

'I thought you were friends with her sister?' Eb was glad of the shift in conversation.

'Margaret's canny enough,' Iris pouted, 'but that Minnie's nothing but a troublemaker. You know it's Davie's bairn she's having?'

Eb rounded on her, astounded. 'Never!'

'Aye,' Iris sneered, 'my Davie. Sowing oats up at Stand High Farm last summer, he was. That's why I don't want to be around when she has the baby - I don't wish her any harm, I just don't want to know anything about it.'

Eb suddenly swung an arm around her shoulder. 'Sorry, pet,' he said kindly. 'You've had a rough time of it.' He let out a long sigh as they walked close together. 'I don't blame you for leaving, you know. There's a world out there waiting for you - people brought up in Whitton sometimes think there's nowhere else worth bothering about, but that's not true. Make sure you find what you're looking for, Iris.'

They reached Whitton Station as the train pulled in, so there was no prolonged leave-taking. Iris kissed Eb warmly on the mouth.

'You're a good'n,' she smiled. 'Look after yourself as well as the others though, won't you?' Eb smiled in reply and helped her on to the train.

Iris watched the dismal station and her former dwelling in Station Lane shunt out of view, with Eb raising his cap and waving her away. She felt a clash of feelings; regret at leaving the place she had made her home, bittersweet longing for Raymond's chattering voice, fear at the unknown ahead, a dull ache for Davie.

Yet sitting back in the scratchy seat watching the newly ploughed fields slipping out of sight, Iris felt a stirring of relief. A small flame of freedom lit deep inside her and quickened to excitement at the momentous step she had taken. For the first time in her life, she was going to pursue her dream of a career in front of the footlights. Who could now say that it was only a dream?

Chapter Twenty-Eight

The night before the Big Meeting, Louie sat on the doorstep mending a tear in Sam's shirt. The frayed cotton defied the surgery that Louie applied, but it would have to do. The warm July evening had brought neighbours to their back gates and the children into the streets, making the most of their parents' liberal mood in allowing them out so late. It was at moments like this that Louie came nearest to contentment, listening to her mother and Marjory discussing plans for the wedding, feeling mellow and young in the balmy evening air and watching Raymond asleep on Sadie's knee, his bonny face untroubled by cares.

They had received only two postcards in over three months from Iris; one from Skegness and the other from Swansea. They told little of her itinerant life except to say she was working with a man called Barny and she hoped to see them soon. Raymond had long stopped asking when his mother was coming back and lately had slipped into calling Louie 'Mammy'. She grew closer to him as the weeks went by, surprising even herself with the depth of love she felt for another woman's child. He filled her hours, his chatter and liveliness giving her endless pleasure, assuaging her despair at being childless. If only Sam would take as much interest in the small boy, she thought sadly, instead of begrudging Raymond his place in their home. As it was, Sam ignored them both these days, Louie thought bitterly, preferring the company of the Lodge committee to his own family. Louie blocked out the thought of what would happen should Iris return and claim her son. Sam, however, did not; it had been the reason for several of their arguments this summer.

'You're too fond of that lad,' Sam had complained when he'd come home exhausted one evening. Louie had suggested taking Raymond for a walk in the park before bed.

'It's a good job somebody is,' Louie had sparked back. 'He's lost his dad and his mam isn't hurrying back for him.'

'So just remember you're not his mam.'

'Why don't you show him more affection?' Louie had hissed, trying not to let their dispute carry downstairs to members of her family. Sam's coolness towards the boy continued to rankle with her.

'He's not my son,' Sam had replied harshly.

'Well, he might be the nearest you get to one,' Louie had retorted.

'What do you mean by that?' He had looked at her sternly.

'I mean you never spend any time at home,' Louie had accused. 'And it's not just because you have to work over at Ushaw. When you do have time to spare you prefer to spend it at your blessed meetings. It's not like being married any more, Sam,' Louie had said desperately. 'Ever since we had to leave Gladstone Terrace, it's like we've been living apart!'

Sam had stormed out of the bedroom and stayed away all evening. It marked the worst wrangle of their marriage and Louie pushed it from her mind as best she could. When her mother had tried to find out what was wrong, Louie had put up her defences. If Sam and she had problems they would solve them by themselves; she would not discuss their unhappiness with anyone else.

More than anything, Louie had been hurt by Sam's lack of acknowledgement of the anniversary of their baby's death. On the 6th July, Louie had gone with Hilda to visit Louisa's grave on the Common and had placed there a modest posy of flowers picked from Eb's garden. The sisters had prayed and hugged and cried together and Louie had felt a great lifting of the unseen burden she carried. Yet Sam had made no mention of their shared loss and had stayed away from home most of the day. Louie found that hard to forgive.

As she put down her mending and strolled to the gate on this July evening, the thought of Sam's un-approachability, his swings in mood, cast a blight over her excitement at the holiday about to start. There had not been a Big Meeting for two years and she was determined to snatch and enjoy this gift of a day off from household routines. Sam could spend the outing with his friends in the lodge, processing and getting drunk, but she would have her fun too.

Minnie strolled by, pushing a pram, with Bomber carrying Jack on his shoulders. They crossed the street when Louie hailed them.

'How's little Nancy?' Louie asked and peered into the sturdy old pram.

'Sleeping like a top,' Minnie answered with a grin. Louie was thankful that Minnie's baby, who had been born three days after Iris departed, showed no resemblance to her brother. She had a sprout of dark hair like her mother and a round face like a Slattery.

'She's no bother, this one,' Bomber said with pride. 'You're Daddy's little lass, aren't you?'

Louie flicked a look at her friend, but Minnie studiously avoided her gaze. Was it possible that Bomber had no suspicions about Nancy's origins? she wondered. She hoped for her friend's sake that the truth would for ever lie buried with her brother. Certainly Minnie and Bomber appeared to be getting on better with each other since Nancy's arrival. Even the fact that Bomber still had no proper employment did not seem to be straining their marriage unduly at the moment. He filled in his time knocking on doors and offering to do odd jobs. If only Sam could put in a word for his old marra at the Cathedral pit, she thought with frustration. But no, the two former friends continued to shun each other's company. Why had she married such a stubborn, unbending man as Sam Ritson?

'Sam out?' Minnie enquired.

'Aye,' Louie sighed, 'lodge meetin'.'

'Must be cosy - union meetings,' Bomber sneered, 'all workers together. Why can't they do more for them that're out of work instead of sitting around on their backsides?'

'Don't start your complaining,' Minnie reprimanded. 'It's nothing to do with Louie.'

Louie ignored the hostile criticism and leaned over to stroke baby Nancy's cheek. 'She's as bonny as they come.' Louie smiled wistfully at Minnie. 'See you on the train tomorrow?'

'Aye,' Minnie answered, wheeling the pram around. 'If we get separated I'll meet you under our banner at the racecourse.'

Louie nodded and dragged herself away from the street scene. Picking the sleeping Raymond out of Sadie's arms she whispered, 'Bedtime, little pet, we've a long day tomorrow.'

Eb left the Cathedral after the service and peeled off from the rest of the band making their way back to the pubs in the town or their families in the tea tents by the riverside. His head still vibrated with the power of their music and the echoing grandeur of the ancient abbey. It had been an emotional moment parading into the church with the Whitton Grange banner draped in black ribbon to mark the death of Davie and his comrades in the January explosion. He imagined how Davie would have laughed at their sober sombreness, while his ghost preferred to celebrate in a bar in the town.

Impulsively Eb turned into a pub in Sadler Street and ordered a beer in the narrow crowded room. Listening to the lively conversation of the pitmen, reliving the disputes of last year's strike and putting the world to rights, Eb raised his glass silently to Davie. He downed the beer in two long draughts and handed back his glass.

The street outside was strangely empty, the crowds of pit folk having quickly dispersed and gone to seek amusement. Eb wandered aimlessly up the cobbled lane, undecided what to do next. He could turn and start back to the station or just walk around Durham's medieval streets for a while longer . . .

Eleanor almost did not answer the ring at the bell. She was happily curled up on a swinging garden seat with a book, alone as Bridget and Molly had the day off for the Gala. It was probably high jinks from some young village children ringing all the bells in the street; no one would fight their way through the crowds on Miners' Gala day to visit her. The bell rang again and reluctantly Eleanor obeyed its call.

'Eb?' She stood nonplussed on the doorstep at the sight of the pitman in his band uniform, instrument tucked under his arm. She had not seen or heard of him in months. In fact she had grown resigned to the idea of never seeing Eb Kirkup again.

'I was passing by.' Eb said, scratching his head.

'How did you know where to find me?' Eleanor asked in surprise.

'Iris said - Molly must have told her. Or perhaps it was Hildy.' Eb blushed in confusion. 'Do you mind me calling?'

'Of course not.' Eleanor recovered her composure and stood aside to let him pass. 'Please come in. I was in the garden. You'll take a glass of lemonade?' Eb nodded quickly, overawed by her formality.

He followed her through the narrow hallway lined with books, into a neat dining room arrayed with polished silver and out through open French windows into the secluded garden. Eleanor silently poured a tall tumbler of fresh lemonade and handed it to him.

'Lovely garden,' Eb commented, taking the drink.

'Yes,' Eleanor agreed, standing half turned from him.

'Are you well?' he asked between gulps.

'Very,' she replied, quite tongue-tied.

'I hear the clinic's going well.' Eb struggled to converse. 'I must say it surprised me.'

'Oh?' Eleanor eyed him. 'Didn't you think I was serious?'

Eb flinched under her challenging gaze. 'Perhaps not.' He was candid. He finished his drink quickly.

Eleanor felt dashed by his words. 'I thought you at least would have wanted me to do something for the village - after all the hatred and futility of the past year. And don't look at me like that, Eb Kirkup,' she challenged, 'it wasn't just some grand gesture to make me feel good. The women of Whitton need the support of the clinic, but I also need to be usefully occupied.' Eleanor reached back and sat on the swing seat. 'For the first time in many years, I feel I'm doing something worthwhile with my life - I wake in the morning feeling there's a purpose to it all - just like I did when I fought for women's suffrage. Oh, there are people who used to count themselves as friends who think I've thrown my life away; they think by leaving Reginald and The Grange I've got nothing left of worth.' Eleanor laughed softly. 'Giving them up was a small price to pay for the freedom I have now - for peace of mind.'

She watched Eb put down his glass and study the intricate pattern of the wrought-iron table.

'I've misjudged you, Eleanor,' he admitted quietly. 'I admire you for what you've done, your achievements at the clinic, your courage in leaving your husband. There are plenty of folk in the village don't approve of you now, but not me.' He looked up cautiously. 'I'm ashamed of how I've behaved towards you - how I gave you no help or encouragement when you needed it most.'

'You had your own problems,' Eleanor answered kindly. 'I was selfish expecting you to drop everything and be at my beck and call. It was better this way. I've learnt how to stand on my own feet alone. Now I don't expect too much from anybody.'

Eb gave her a strange look from his vivid blue eyes. 'You'll never know how much I wanted to go with you,' he said in a low voice.

Eleanor's heart lurched at his confession, yet she could not reply. She knew Eb must have found it difficult to come to her today and she saw now how he wrestled with his feelings. If he still wanted her, it would have to come from him; never again would she behave as if she had rights over Eb. Much as she desired him, she had proved to herself that she could live without him. Still, she waited, holding her breath, as the slow bells of the Cathedral began their late afternoon toll.

Eb fixed on a rose bush framing the back of Eleanor's head and spoke to it. 'I would have come before today, but I didn't know what I'd say after the way we parted. I expected to hear you'd married that American or something - didn't think you'd want to see me.' He gave a wary smile. 'I've thought of you such a lot, Eleanor.'

'Come and sit beside me,' Eleanor told him gently. Eb hesitated then lowered himself on to the faded cushion on the swing. The frame creaked as his weight set it in motion. 'What are you trying to tell me, Eb?'

This time he regarded her directly. 'I want to be with you, Eleanor, if that's what you still want. Is it too late . . . ?'

Eleanor leaned over and touched his cheek with her hand. 'No,' she whispered, 'it's not too late.'

They reached out for each other and held one another tightly. Eb clung to Eleanor and she closed her eyes, enjoying the warmth and strength of his embrace.

'I've missed you,' he whispered into her hair, 'but I was afraid of loving you too much. I thought life would be simpler if I forgot all about loving you - but that was impossible. These past months have been pointless without you, Eleanor, I've not been able to settle to anything - not even painting.' He gave a wry smile.

Eleanor felt a surge of longing for Eb that she had suppressed for an age. She pulled back to look into his face and saw it mirroring her own tenderness.

'Oh Eb, I love you,' she smiled back, 'but I had to hear it from you first.' They drew together and kissed fiercely in their relief. Afterwards their kisses grew more lingering and intimate, as the realisation dawned on them both that they had all the time in the world.

They talked long into the evening. At one point Eleanor asked, 'What about your family?'

Eb shrugged. 'They won't like it, having their son causing tongues to wag in the village. Maybe they'll come round to it in time,' he added doubtfully.

'I don't want to cause a rift between you.'

'I want to marry you, Eleanor,' Eb said determinedly, 'when you divorce your husband. If that's not good enough for my family then that's the way it will have to be. I can't be without you again. Hildy and Louie will see it my way.'

Eleanor kissed him affectionately. 'Even if you're a kept man?' she teased.

'I intend to pay my way with my painting - when I've learnt my craft,' Eb answered defensively. Eleanor did not like to disillusion him with stories of how poverty-stricken most full-time painters were. It was enough that he wished to be with her and that together they could nurture his talent.

'Then that's settled,' Eleanor smiled contentedly, lying back in his arms.

The following day, Eb returned home to collect his possessions and announce his intentions to his family.

Eb's parents took the news worse than he had expected. As he packed his clothing and paints into an old kitbag, they railed at him for his foolishness and the sin he would be committing.

'She's a married woman,' Fanny wheezed at her eldest child. 'What could you be thinking of? How long has this affair been going on? You'll be the death of your poor old mother!' she cried. Louie tried to calm her, without success.

'Look how you've upset her,' she chided her brother when they were alone for a moment upstairs. 'I knew nothing good would come of this.'

'She's a fine woman,' Eb insisted. 'She doesn't deserve their criticism or scorn. She's done a lot for this village - for our family. It was thanks to her that you weren't evicted from Gladstone Terrace when Sam was in gaol, didn't you know that?'

'No,' Louie blushed at the news, 'I didn't. But,' she argued, 'no matter what she's done for us, in their eyes she's still married.'

'Only in name,' Eb answered, folding up the tie Eleanor had bought him the previous summer. 'Her husband treats his animals with more respect than he ever gave Eleanor. No one criticises his long-standing infidelity to her.'

'I don't know about such things,' Louie answered uncomfortably. 'What the posh folk get up to is their business not ours.'

Eb snorted at the hypocrisy.

'And how long do you think her infatuation with you will last?' Louie demanded desperately. 'A month, a year, two years, before she tires of you too?'

Eb swung round and glared at his sister. 'Is that all you think we mean to each other - a passing fancy?'

'Well, isn't it?' Louie demanded. 'I just worry for you.'

'That's not what really bothers you, Louie,' Eb answered grimly. 'Isn't it more to do with her being the boss's wife and me working class? That's what all this fuss is about. You're worried about what Sam will say to his comrades when they hear his brother-in-law's taken up with someone from the wrong class.' Louie went puce at the words, astonished by the barely suppressed rage in her placid eldest brother. 'Well, you're all just as bad as them at the big house, with your prejudices and snobberies. I've bowed to it for too long. Now I've got a chance of being happy with the woman I love and I'm going to take it!'

'How dare you insult your own family like that?' Louie was close to tears. 'Mam's right - you've always thought yourself above the rest of us. You're not fit to call yourself a Kirkup!'

Even as she threw the accusations at him, Louie felt a churning regret. But the words were out and the air between them was poisoned like the foulness in a gassy pit. Eb winced at her outburst, his blue eyes full of fury, but he uttered not a word more. Louie followed him downstairs, cursing herself for having antagonised him and destroyed any last chance of changing his mind.

Eb picked up his cap and jacket from the back of the chair. Sadie and Raymond watched him in awe from the corner of the hearth, where their play was suspended.

'I'll be off then,' Eb announced. 'I'll call in and see Hildy on the way.'

His parents stared back at him wordlessly. John, the only one attempting to eat his dinner, studied his bowl of broth. Louie stood rooted to the floor, her face ashen.

'Goodbye, Mam.' Eb approached his mother and tried to kiss her cheek, but she turned it aside. 'Da.' He nodded at his father.

'Unless you see the error of your way,' Jacob pronounced, 'and apologise for the shame you've brought on your parents, you'll not step over my doorstep again.'

Eb seemed visibly shocked by the harsh finality of his father's decree, but he did not argue. As he hastened to the door, he touched Louie's shoulder in farewell. She could not be disloyal to her parents and show weakness now, so she gave him no goodbye kiss.

Unexpectedly, Sam stepped forward and lifted the kitbag on to Eb's shoulder. He had taken no part in the row that had raged all morning and he felt pity for his old comrade. Eb had stood by him in the past and even gone to prison for his sake and he would not cold-shoulder him now.

'Good luck, Eb,' he grunted at his brother-in-law. 'Be true to what you believe in.' Sam stuck out his hand and gripped Eb's firmly.

'Thanks, Sam,' Eb answered gratefully, with a ghost of a smile. Then he was swinging out of the door and out of their lives for good.

Louie stared after him, unable to comprehend the abruptness of her brother's going. Behind her she could hear her mother beginning to sob.

'See to your Mam,' Sam ordered Louie. 'I'm going to get some kip before my shift.'

Hilda could only spare a few minutes from her duties at Greenbrae. She listened intently to what Eb told her.

'I've told Miss Joice that I'll come back and do the garden from time to time. John's going to take over the allotment.'

'So why are you pulling such a long face?' Hilda asked, her head on one side.

Eb sighed. 'It's Louie.' He voiced his concern. 'I expected Mam and Da to be upset - it's come as a complete shock and I know it's hard for them to understand. But Louie - I've hurt her feelings badly. I don't want to be cut off from her too.'

'She'll come round,' Hilda comforted. 'Louie can't bear a grudge for long - it's not in her nature.'

'Will you tell her I'm sorry?' Eb asked.

'Aye,' Hilda promised.

'You're a grand lass.' Eb smiled in relief at his younger sister and gave her a hug. 'And you'll come and visit us, won't you?'

'Of course I will,' Hilda grinned. 'I've only read through half of Miss Eleanor's books, I'll be calling on you for a few years yet.'

She kissed her brother goodbye and hurried inside as a bell summonsed her to an upstairs room. Eb marched away from Greenbrae, through the foliage-choked dene and out of the village on the road leading to Durham. Although he could hear the familiar clanking and hiss from the pits, spitting their farewell behind him, he did not look back.

Chapter Twenty-Nine

John and Marjory were married in the Wesleyan Chapel on North Street in October. To Louie's pleasure, Sam was best man and Sadie a bridesmaid alongside Marjory's sister Beth. It was a happy occasion with a chance to get together with friends and neighbours outside the chapel and later at the Hewitsons' home in Holly Street. The Ritsons were invited and Louie enjoyed a natter with Sam's sisters, Mary and Bel.

'Hasn't Raymond come on?' Bel exclaimed as if he were Louie's own, and Louie basked in the admiration. 'He's full of life, your Raymond.'

They watched him playing in the yard with Bel's daughter Betty, squabbling over a ball. Betty was bigger and held on to the ball, giving up interest in the prize immediately Raymond conceded defeat and wandered off.

'It's nice to see your Aunt Eva and Uncle Jack here,' Bel said pleasantly. 'I haven't seen them since—' Abruptly she broke off and coloured furiously. Louie knew Sam's sister had suddenly remembered that the last occasion to bring them to Whitton had been Davie's funeral.

'Aye, it is nice,' Louie answered quickly, 'especially for Mam. She hardly gets out these days with her bad chest and it's company for her.'

'Perhaps she'd like to come to one of our meetings?' Mary piped up enthusiastically. Louie had heard Mary was now a member of the Baptist Church on East Street. 'We have a magnificent speaker visiting us next month. Pastor Graham says he can slay people with the Holy Spirit. He could cure your mother,' Mary suggested eagerly.

'I'll mention it to her,' Louie smiled, wishing she felt half Mary's uncomplicated conviction. Privately she believed that her mother's ailments went deeper than a bronchial chest; there was a sickness of spirit that plagued and gripped her in a grey depression. Today she alternately smiled and wept, overcome with happiness for John and Marjory and regret that the last of her sons was leaving home. Yet Louie knew that what gnawed at her mother's spirit the most was her sense of bereavement for Eb as well as her beloved Davie. Eb was absent from the family gathering; he hadn't been invited to the wedding. Louie knew John would have asked him, but he would not go against his parents' wishes. She too longed to be reconciled with her eldest brother, but she knew contact with him would be seen as disloyal to her parents.

Waving John and his new wife away from the Hewitsons', Louie was engulfed in sadness. They would be living only three streets away in Daniel Terrace, but it might as well have been in the next county for all she would see of her brother. There would be no more Saturday evenings around the piano without Eb to play it, or Iris to lead the singing.

How had her closely bound family fallen apart so rapidly? Louie wondered forlornly. Her father stalked the house like a fretful visitor, increasingly content to spend his evenings at the Institute or his free afternoons walking up on Highfell. Once in an argument with Hilda he had said that both Davie and Eb had betrayed him; now he never mentioned either son. Yet Louie saw the haunted look of doubt trouble his face when he prayed in chapel and she was unsure what his inner thoughts were. Like a true Kirkup he kept his feelings to himself.

Tomorrow there would be only her parents, herself, Raymond and Sam left in the house at Hawthorn Street that had once burst to overflowing with family and friends. Was she frightened of being alone with Sam? she wondered. They carried on the appearance of a harmonious couple, but they did not share their hopes or fears as once they had done.

Two or three times Louie had caught Sam playing with Raymond, making him figures out of his pipe cleaners or knocking a ball against the yard wall. But he had quickly busied himself with something else when he saw his wife watching and he seemed oblivious to the young boy's adoration. Raymond yearned for his Uncle Sam's attention, but to little avail.

Louie suspected Sam looked at Raymond and saw Davie, the brother who had committed the ultimate betrayal and sold his labour while his comrades starved. It seemed so unfair that a small boy should be saddled with his dead father's shortcomings, but deep down Louie understood the acute hurt that Sam had suffered. Whether she could forgive it for blighting her own marriage was another matter.

Still, she thought resignedly, there would be Sadie home at weekends and Hilda on her nights off and the lively chattering Raymond. At least, Louie smiled to herself, she had Raymond.

One afternoon in December, Sam was returning home from working down the valley when he saw an ambulance roaring out of the village. It spluttered past him along the Durham Road, billowing fumes as he jumped into the ditch to get out of its way. Briskening his pace, he saw a group of villagers gathered about the corner of Railway Terrace, opposite the rail tracks running alongside the leafless dene. Darkness was descending quickly, but he could just make out the anxious stance of the bystanders.

'What's happened?' Sam asked, approaching the group.

'Been an accident on the tracks,' a man told him.

'A young bairn's been knocked over,' a small woman added worriedly, 'crossing the line when a truck hit him. Just a laddie no more than three. It's a crying shame.'

Sam felt a wrenching pull in his guts at the news, yet he could not understand the source of his unease.

'It was a lad?' he asked.

'Aye,' she nodded.

'Whose lad?' he demanded.

She shrugged. 'From up the village. Bonny bairn with red hair. Don't know the family.'

Sam breathed in sharply as if he had been winded. He refused to believe what his instincts were telling him. A boy with red hair, a three-year-old. Raymond was big enough to be taken for three.

'Is he dead?' Sam forced himself to ask.

'Not when he left in the ambulance,' the man interjected. 'Mind you, he was in a bad way, poor wee lad.'

Sam did not stay to hear any more. He took off up the hill towards Hawthorn Street at a sprint, ignoring the tiredness of his limbs after a day's work and a long walk home.

Turning into the street he could see the open back door throwing light on to the darkening lane. There was a huddle of neighbours gathered in the yard. It was true then, Sam thought, feeling sick; the news had reached Louie and her parents; friends were gathering to be with them.

He clattered through the gate and pushed his way through the visitors. He could see Louie half inside the house, her face shadowed by the light thrown out behind her.

'Louie!' Sam gasped and reached forward to grab her.

'Sam?' Louie queried in astonishment. 'What's wrong?'

For a moment he hesitated, confused by her bemused look.

'Where's Raymond?' he croaked.

'He's here,' Louie answered, nonplussed. Sam glanced beyond her and saw the boy kneeling beside Sadie on a kitchen chair, playing with his 'stick men' as he called Sam's pipe cleaners. Raymond looked round enquiringly at Sam's voice and his face lit up in a happy grin at the sight of his uncle.

'Look, Sam!' He held up a wiry figure for approval. A wave of relief washed over Sam at the domestic scene and his exhausted legs almost gave way as his weakness shook him. Without hesitation, he went over and threw his arms around his nephew, gripping him tightly to his filthy jacket.

'Sam,' Louie reprimanded, 'he's just had a bath and you'll make him black.'

Self-consciously Sam let go and turned round, feeling foolish. He caught sight of his sister Mary and her friends peering in curiously at the back door.

'Mary's here to sing carols for Mam,' Louie explained, seeing Sam's confusion. 'You're just in time to hear them.'

'Oh.' Sam's head sagged as he plonked himself down on the chair next to Raymond.

'Are you all right?' Louie asked in concern. 'You haven't been drinking, have you?' she asked more suspiciously.

'No.' Sam laughed shortly. 'I'll tell you later.'

In came the carol singers, while Louie poured her husband a cup of rejuvenating tea. Raymond wheedled his way on to his uncle's lap during the singing, but no protests were made about the coal grime on his nightclothes.

Later, when they were upstairs in bed, Sam told Louie what he had seen and heard on his return home.

'The poor parents,' Louie whispered so as not to wake Raymond or Sadie beyond the curtain, 'what must they be feeling now?'

'Aye,' Sam sighed, 'I feel guilty thinking about it. For a minute I was just so thankful it was someone else's bairn when I saw Raymond safe.' Louie edged nearer his side and slipped a hand tentatively on to his bare chest.

'You do love him, don't you?'

Sam gulped, 'Aye,' almost inaudibly.

'I'm glad,' Louie said softly and kissed his cheek. 'I thought I'd lost you. You've been so different this past year. I want my old Sam back.'

She heard him snort quietly in the dark. 'I can't promise I'll be any different to live with, Louie,' he answered honestly. 'We've all been changed by what's gone on. There are certain things I can't forgive - will never forgive! The way the bosses treated us, the way we were betrayed. The bairn we lost,' he added hoarsely, 'all alone in that tiny grave.'

Louie felt a spasm at his words. Because he never mentioned their baby, she had not known he ever thought about her. As far as she knew Sam had never been to visit Louisa's solitary grave on the Common where Eb had buried her. But his words suggested otherwise. They lay in silence for a while, then Sam continued quietly.

'But I do know that I'd never have got through any of it without you, Louie. I'm not good at saying what I feel,' he growled, 'but I love you, pet. I know it sometimes seems like I don't.'

'Oh, Sam.' Louie nestled into him tenderly. She pulled his jaw towards her and kissed his mouth.

'I've seen how much you love that bairn,' Sam rolled on to his side and faced her, 'and if we can't have one of our own, I'll be a father to this one.'

Louie wanted to weep at Sam's loving words. As he leaned over to embrace her, the tears came.

'What's wrong?' he asked startled. 'I thought that's what you wanted?'

'Aye, it is.' Louie tried to control her crying. 'But it may be too late.' Louie took a deep breath. 'Sadie brought news today from Durham.'

'Go on,' Sam said stiffly.

'The Ramshaws have heard from Iris. She's touring in a pantomime. She'll be in Durham for Christmas.'

A week later, a letter arrived from Iris requesting that she have Raymond for Christmas at her parents' house. 'I'll come and fetch him on Christmas Eve after the show,' her childish writing told them. What was to happen after the holiday when Iris moved on was not explained. Louie tried hard to hide her disappointment that the boy would not be with them for the special festival and immersed herself in seasonal rituals, baking mince pies, and cutting out paper streamers and hanging them about the house. The look of excitement on Raymond's face as they decorated the parlour made her heart ache.

In the end, Sam decided it would be best if they dispensed with the waiting and took Raymond into Durham to meet his mother. They sent word via the Ramshaws that they were coming.

'We could see the pantomime and have a look round the shops - you'd like that, wouldn't you?' he asked Louie, falsely cheerful.

They boarded the morning train on Christmas Eve. Sam had come off the night shift three hours before and had grabbed a couple of hours of fitful sleep. Louie clutched a small bagful of her nephew's clothes and their present to him of two metal soldiers which she had spotted at a bazaar and spent precious housekeeping money to procure. Raymond was bursting with excitement at the treats in store; a ride on the train, fish and chips for dinner and something called a pantomime which he was told all children enjoy.

'And you'll see your mammy,' Louie told him with a grimace of a smile, 'and stay with her for Christmas. Aren't you a lucky lad?'

'But you're my mammy,' Raymond answered with a perplexed little frown. Louie and Sam exchanged wary glances, but said nothing more. However, later they found their appetites had deserted them when they unwrapped the fish they were sharing and the bags of chips. Raymond tucked enthusiastically into his, though, smearing his small mouth and fingers with delicious grease.

The Durham shops were festively bedecked with holly and baubles, and the cries of the busy market-stall traders mixed with a Salvation Army band bringing Christmas cheer to the passers-by. Even Louie could not help her spirits lifting with the anticipation and joyfulness she saw around her. Durham was looking like a scene from a Christmas card, with a sugar covering of snow on the noble town buildings.

They filed into the packed church hall where Barnfather's company was performing Cinderella. Iris was playing Prince Charming, and Louie's heart lurched to see how attractive her slim, vivacious sister-in-law appeared in her dashing costume. As the magic of the show took hold of its audience, Louie forgot for a time why they were there, giving herself up to the pleasure of the singing and the romantic story. Raymond screamed with delight at the Ugly Sisters, but grew bored at the singing and love story. He seesawed restlessly from Sam's knee to Louie's, and Louie felt a stirring of unease when Raymond did not appear to recognise his mother.

'Watch Mammy now,' Louie bade the child, but he just laughed as if she was teasing him.

Afterwards, with leaden hearts, his aunt and uncle took Raymond by the hand and led him backstage to see Iris. She came out of a tiny room, her face bizarrely accentuated by stage make-up. She was still in costume, though her auburn hair was freed from its wig and curling about her pretty face.

'Raymond!' she cried at the overawed boy and threw her arms around him. Raymond gave out a yelp of panic and struggled to loosen her hold on him.

'Mammy,' he blubbered and held out his arms to Louie. She was flustered with embarrassment.

'Don't be daft, give your mammy a kiss, Raymond,' she instructed, but the boy howled the louder until Iris released him in indignation.

'I'm sorry, Iris,' Louie gabbled, 'he'll come round, he's just not used to seeing you -'

'It's all right.' Iris brushed her excuses aside. 'Of course I seem like a stranger to him at the moment. He'll get used to me soon.'

'Aye,' Sam nodded. 'It was a canny show.'

'Good,' Iris put on a smile, 'I'm glad you enjoyed it.'

'So you're getting plenty of work?' Louie asked tensely, as Raymond held tightly on to her hand.

'Yes.' Iris brightened. 'It's hard work, and the pay's up and down, but I love it.'

'I'm glad you're happy,' Louie smiled back, more at ease. To break the awkwardness, Iris showed them around backstage and introduced them to the fast-talking Barny.

'Pleased to meet you - you're a nice kiddie.' He bent and pinched Raymond's cheek, which sent him behind Louie's skirt again. 'No harm meant. He'll get used to me. He'll have to!' Barny grinned and disappeared.

'What does he mean by that?' Louie felt her heart begin to hammer nervously. 'You'll be moving on soon, won't you?'

'Yes,' Iris began, fixing her sister-in-law with a determined look, 'and I've decided to take Raymond with me. I'm earning enough to support us both and I want him back.' She stretched out a hand and ruffled her son's hair. 'You've no idea how much Mammy's missed you, pet.'

Louie's body turned shivery-cold. 'But you can't!' she cried.

'Louie.' Sam put a warning hand on her arm, which she shook off.

'I mean, we - we haven't brought all his things with us. I need more warning than this - to pack - it's too sudden . . . ' Her voice dried up with fear.

'We don't work tomorrow,' Iris continued resolutely. 'I'll get Barny to run me through to Whitton and fetch Raymond's belongings. I'll bring Raymond with me too,' Iris smiled reassuringly, 'so you can see him again before we go. That fair enough?'

'Of course,' Sam agreed for both of them. 'He's your bairn after all. We'll say goodbye then and be off, won't we, Louie?' Louie could say nothing; she had lost all power of speech and movement. She just stared at Raymond, unable to comprehend that she was about to lose him forever.

Iris bent down and kissed her son's head. 'I've got so much planned for us to do,' she promised him. 'We're going to have a grand time, me and you, see the world together.'

'Well, ta-ta, Raymond.' Sam tried to keep his voice even. 'We'll see you tomorrow. Let go his hand, Louie.'

Louie forced herself to disengage the boy's limpet hold. She crouched down to his level and gave him a kiss. From somewhere her voice came. 'You go to your mammy, she's going to take care of you now. Auntie Louie will see you very soon.'

Raymond's face crumpled in dismay at her words and he threw himself at her legs and clung on tightly. Iris reached out for him and seized his arms.

'Come on, baby,' she spoke coaxingly, 'Mammy wants a big kiss and cuddle.'

'No!' Raymond howled in protest at the half-familiar woman dragging him from Louie. 'Mammy! Mammy!' he continued to scream as Louie backed away in distress.

'Come on,' Sam insisted grimly. 'He'll be fine once we've gone.'

Louie fought down the sob in her throat. 'Tomorrow, Raymond, I'll see you tomorrow.'

'Just go!' Iris ordered desperately. She had the boy in a grip while he kicked and struggled to be free, his horror at seeing Louie depart transparent on his thin face. He yelled for her again above Iris's nervous placating voice. It was more than Louie could bear.

'What did you expect,' she accused miserably stopping in her tracks, 'that he'd come running to you with open arms after the way you left him?'

'Stop it,' Sam hissed and pulled at his wife's arm. 'You're making things worse.'

'We're the ones who've cared for him,' Louie could not stop herself. 'You can't blame him for loving us.'

'I'm his mother,' Iris shouted in fury, her patience snapping. 'You've turned him against me. I blame you for this, Louie!'

'Out of here *now*.' Sam seized Louie by the arm and pushed her down the corridor to the side entrance. Raymond's screams and Iris's efforts to control her son chased them from the hall.

For a full five minutes Louie buried herself in Sam's arms and wept uncontrollably as the townsfolk of Durham hurried by in the crisp gloom of late afternoon. In spite of the curious looks from passers-by, Sam held his wife closely, patting her back and murmuring comforting words which she hardly heard. Eventually, grief gave way to a listless numbness and Louie wiped her swollen eyes and red nose.

'We've over an hour before the next train,' Sam said glumly.

'I can't look round the shops now,' Louie sighed heavily, 'not without . . .'

Sam hesitated and cleared his throat. 'There is something else we could do,' he began tentatively. Louie met his unsure look. 'Call on Eb and Mrs Seward-Scott if you like?'

Suddenly the thought of seeing her quiet brother again seemed the only right action to take. Eb would understand how distraught she was at losing Raymond to Iris; Eb, who had been brave and compassionate enough to bury her baby Louisa, who had always been there to turn to when she was low. How had she not thought of the idea herself? Her parents need never know that they had called on him and 'the Seward woman', as they referred to Eleanor now. Yet she was plagued with doubt. It was nearly half a year since they had parted on bad terms and they had not seen each other since, in spite of Hilda's attempts to get Louie to visit Eb when he worked at Greenbrae.

'What if he doesn't want to see us?' Louie asked anxiously.

'We won't know unless we try,' Sam said drily. Louie looked gratefully at her husband; she was astonished by his sensitivity. He was prepared to swallow his pride and visit Eleanor just so that she could see Eb. Although she knew Sam could never see Eleanor as anything but a member of a despised privileged class, he did not understand Fanny and Jacob's moral objections to Eb's decision to be with her. In this instance, Louie knew, it had been her own pride and stubbornness that were at fault.

'They live in the Bailey,' Louie said, and, attempting a smile, linked her arm through Sam's.

Lights shone out welcomingly from the narrow house and with the curtains drawn back, Louie could see a beautiful sitting room centred around a roaring fire. Her heart pounded fearfully as Bridget opened the door.

'Is Mrs Seward-Scott at home?' Louie asked meekly. 'Or-er-Mr Kirkup?'

'Yes, ma'am,' the young woman answered. 'Please come in. Who should I say's calling?'

'Louie Ritson - Mr and Mrs Ritson,' Louie stammered, impressed that the housekeeper showed no disdain at finding them on the doorstep in their shabby finery. She was obviously used to a wide variety of callers.

Eleanor quickly appeared and greeted them with hands outstretched, making no comment on Louie's harrowed, blotchy face.

'How wonderful to see you,' she cried with pleasure. 'Bridget, take their coats. You'll stay for tea, won't you?'

'Thank you,' Louie accepted, thinking how well the other woman looked. Her face, always as delicate as bone china, had filled out around the jaw line and her prominent cheeks glowed pink in the bright electric light. Her black hair, once severely shorn, had grown to cover her ears and gleamed with a soft sheen. She moved in a calm, relaxed way and Louie was gladdened to think Eb made her happy. They followed her into the cosy sitting room, and Louie was grateful to Eleanor for her lack of reproach or questions as to their sudden appearance.

'Have you been doing your Christmas shopping?' Eleanor asked. 'I'm so glad you called, Eb talks about you such a lot.' Louie met her considering gaze, but saw a look of encouragement, not criticism.

'Is he here?' Louie asked breathlessly.

'Yes, he's in his studio. I'll take you up there now if you like. Sam and I can start tea without you.'

Louie nodded and Eleanor led the way up to a back room looking out over the darkened garden. A man in a casual green jumper was sitting at a sloping table, bent over some sketches, under the glare of an electric lamp.

Eleanor had closed the door on them before Eb looked round.

'Louie?' he questioned in amazement. 'Louie!'

'Eb,' Louie replied, rooted to the floor as she stared at her brother. He had grown a red-tinged beard that was closely cropped and made his moustache look bushy. His clothes looked comfortable if scruffy, paint splashes daubed on his sleeves and trousers. It was the first time she had seen him out of his pit clothes or Sunday best and for an instant he appeared a stranger.

Seconds later, Eb leapt to his feet and strode across to meet her. He threw his arms around her shoulders and she felt herself returning the hug. They laughed embarrassedly, with tears in their eyes.

'I've longed to see you,' Louie confessed.

'So have I.' Eb steered her over to the table and pushed her into a chair. He sat down opposite. 'I never wanted us to fall out, Louie. How are Mam and Da?'

'Champion,' Louie lied; she would not have him blame himself further for the torture her parents inflicted on themselves.

'And you, Louie? How are you and Sam?'

'We're canny too. Sam's downstairs waiting to see you.' Louie tried to put on a brave face, staring hard at his pictures. 'Your painting's going well then? Hildy tells me you've sold some already. Are you happy living here?' Louie genuinely wanted to know if Eb had made the right decision.

'Very.' Eb smiled back contentedly. 'I love my work - and I love Eleanor. We plan to marry as soon as she's free from Reginald. I hope you'll come to the wedding.'

'Maybes,' Louie answered, knowing it was a gentle dig at the way he had been excluded from John's marriage celebrations. She dragged her gaze back from the drawings to meet his. 'Iris is back.'

Eb nodded seriously. 'I know; she's been to see us. She said she'd come for Raymond.'

Louie's chin sank on to her chest and she burst into tears. At once Eb's arms were about her again, comforting her.

'She's taking him away from me,' Louie sobbed. 'I can't bear it.'

'You must and you will,' he encouraged. 'You're as strong as they come.'

'But I love Raymond,' Louie sobbed. 'He's become our son. I never thought I could love another bairn after - Louisa.' She said the name softly. She knew she could speak her daughter's name to Eb without fear of embarrassment.

'I know, but he's Iris's son,' Eb reminded her gently, 'and she loves him too.'

'Aye,' Louie admitted unhappily, 'I know she does.'

Eb continued to cradle his sister in his arms. 'One day,' he said tenderly, 'you'll have a family of your own, God willing.'

'But it might never happen,' Louie answered fearfully. 'I might not be able -'

'Eleanor thought the same until recently,' Eb whispered into her hair. Louie drew back and regarded him quizzically. What was her brother trying to say?

'Miss Eleanor?' Louie breathed in sharply.

'Yes, she's going to have our child,' Eb told her gently. 'She thought she was barren, but God has been good to us.'

Louie was jolted at the news, and she felt a pang of envy. She stared into Eb's tender, loving face and felt ashamed.

Hugging him back she whispered, 'I'm happy for you. Oh, Eb, you'll make a canny father, I've always thought it.'

'Thank you, Louie.' Eb smiled back gratefully. 'I hoped you'd understand.'

Downstairs, Eleanor poured Sam a second cup of tea. The noise was like a waterfall in the edgy silence between them. The polite exchange of pleasantries had dried up several minutes ago.

Eleanor lit up a cigarette, then seemed to change her mind and quickly stubbed it out again. She knew Sam did not altogether trust her, ever since the time she had arranged for Reginald to see him. What had transpired at that meeting Eleanor would never know, but she suspected that her husband had tried to coerce or bribe this hard-faced pitman.

'I know you're not enjoying this, Sam,' she decided to be direct, 'but I do appreciate your bringing Louie to see her brother. It will mean a great deal to him.'

'It was Louie's decision,' Sam answered stiffly.

'But no doubt you had a hand in it,' Eleanor murmured. They fell into silence again while Eleanor stood up and threw another log on the fire. Sam resisted the urge to help her stoke it up.

'You're still working at the Cathedral, I hear?'

'Aye, how do you know that?' Sam asked suspiciously.

Eleanor decided not to give Hilda as the source in case it got back to her parents that Hilda was visiting them. She ignored the question.

'The travelling must be tedious for you. I wish I still had some influence at The Grange pits, but I'm afraid I don't.' She smiled ruefully.

'I wouldn't accept any favours if you did,' Sam retorted quickly, and then flushed to think he had secured his present job because of his father's friendship with the under-manager.

'No, I'm sorry, I didn't mean it like that,' Eleanor apologised, at once seeing how she antagonised him. She glanced at the door hoping Louie would reappear and release the tension in the room.

'I think you're doing a grand job with the clinic,' Sam suddenly announced. Eleanor gawped at him in surprise. 'Not that I know much about what goes on,' he added bashfully, 'but I've heard the women talking. They speak of you highly - the younger lasses at any rate.'

'Thank you for saying so,' Eleanor said delightedly. 'It's really been a pleasure getting to know some of the girls better.'

Sam gave her a quizzical look. 'Surprised to find we're quite human?' he could not resist saying.

Eleanor coloured, but held his dark-eyed gaze. 'I've never doubted it,' she answered quietly, 'even if my family have at times treated you otherwise.' Sam had no reply, so she went on, 'I've been impressed by their cheerfulness and resilience after all they've put up with - continue to put up with.'

'They're Durham people,' Sam stated proudly. 'That's the way we are.'

Eleanor was glad that the wall of suspicion was being chipped away between them; perhaps now Sam Ritson would open up to her and talk about things that mattered to him. This radical interested her and his reticence only tantalised; she was sure they had more in common than he would like to admit. Eleanor opened her mouth to speak when the sitting room door opened and Louie walked in, her arm linked through Eb's. She saw with relief that both were smiling.

Christmas morning was a bittersweet experience for Louie and Sam. They watched Sadie tearing open her meagre presents with glee. There was a musical box, a second-hand book, a pencil and an orange. Louie wondered distractedly if Raymond was playing with his new toy soldiers or whether they were already discarded as he joined in the play with Iris's brothers and sisters. The waiting for him to arrive was unbearable, yet she dreaded the time of his coming because it marked the final leave-taking.

Louie served up a special breakfast of bacon and eggs and then they trouped off to chapel for the Christmas service. John and Marjory were there and many of their neighbours. Louie prayed for a miracle.

Perhaps Iris would not come for Raymond's possessions; perhaps she would leave with her actors and Sam and Louie would journey triumphantly into Durham to collect her precious nephew and bring him home. Then she chided herself for such selfish thoughts. Raymond was Iris's son; he was all Iris had in the world. How could she begrudge her sister-in-law what was rightfully hers? On the way home, they called into Clara Dobson's house for the traditional cake and ginger wine, and it was midday by the time they turned into Hawthorn Street.

Louie's heart plummeted to see a strange van parked outside the house. Barny was sitting behind the wheel and waved to them as they passed.

Steeling herself for the ordeal ahead, Louie entered the house briskly, leaving Sam to follow behind with her father and Sadie. Fanny Kirkup, who had declared herself too ill to walk to chapel, was sitting tensely in the kitchen, waiting with Iris and Raymond. As soon as the boy saw Louie he rushed across and flung up his arms to be hugged.

'Soldiers, Mammy!' he cried, clutching his presents in either hand.

'Happy Christmas, pet.' Louie kissed him. 'Happy Christmas, Iris,' she greeted her sister-in-law bravely.

Iris stood up. 'I want a word, Louie,' she said, almost severely, 'alone.'

'In the parlour then?' Louie suggested, her heart pounding fearfully. Raymond began to protest as Louie put him down, but Sam and Jacob appeared through the door at that moment and he ran to his uncle.

'Close the door,' Iris ordered quickly. Louie glanced at Fanny's anxious face beyond the door and then obeyed.

'I've been thinking things through since yesterday,' Iris began brusquely. 'It's going to be hard taking Raymond away from you.' Louie gulped, her mouth painfully dry.

'I'm sorry about the way I spoke.' Louie was contrite. 'I was just a bit upset.'

'I know,' Iris said tightly, 'and Raymond was too.'

'He's too young to understand.' Louie tried to find an excuse. 'Soon it'll be me he won't remember,' she joked painfully.

'Maybe.' Iris fiddled with the large buttons on her orange and black dress. She looked up at Louie and her voice became businesslike. 'There's no problem keeping him while I travel - there are girls in the cast who can help out. And I can give him just as much love as you,' she said defiantly. She stared at Louie with glittering hazel eyes. 'But I saw how much you and Sam have come to mean to Raymond. I was kidding myself he would accept me straight back as his mam. It hurts me that he doesn't.'

The two women looked at each other helplessly. Iris's voice dropped. 'But you can give Raymond the home that he wants as well as your love. Who would have thought he'd be such a happy bairn after all he's been through - with his dad dying and that? It's thanks to you and Sam, Louie, that he is.'

Iris turned and looked out of the window. 'If you'd agree to carry on looking after him,' her voice wavered, 'I'd like you to bring him up.'

Louie thought she had misheard. Yet Iris was watching her now for her opinion. Feeling her heart swelling with joy at the request, she rushed at Iris and flung her arms about her.

'Of course I'll agree,' she cried. 'I love that lad like my own.'

'Yes,' Iris closed her eyes against tears as she hugged the other woman, 'I know you do.'

They heard Raymond's insistent voice beyond the door and the men's attempts to pacify him. He started to rattle the stiff doorknob. Iris drew away.

'Promise me you'll talk about me to Raymond once in a while,' she asked, 'and about his father?'

'I promise,' Louie smiled tearfully. 'He'll grow up knowing who his real mam and dad are, and how much you love him.'

'I'll write - and visit when I'm in the area, of course.' Iris sniffed and struggled to compose her face.

'Of course.' Louie squeezed her hand. 'Come when you can.'

Iris glanced at her reflection in the parlour mirror and wiped a smudge of eyeliner with her handkerchief. 'Barny's waiting to get back to Durham.' She spoke more briskly. 'I'll get the bairn's bag from the van and then go.'

'Stay for a mince pie - you and Barny,' Louie insisted.

'No ta, Louie.' Iris's strained face was unguarded for a second. 'I'll just say a quick goodbye to Raymond.'

They emerged from the parlour to five pairs of enquiring eyes. Louie explained Iris's decision quickly and the joyful relief in the warm kitchen was palpable. Iris bent down and kissed Fanny on the cheek. Louie could see her mother's eyes shining with tears and knew how much it would lift her spirits to have the boy around each day.

'Look after yourself, pet,' the frail older woman urged, 'and we'll take good care of your bairn.'

Iris smiled distractedly as she buttoned up her coat. In one swift movement she whisked Raymond off his feet in a sudden embrace before the boy could protest.

'I'll be back soon, bonny lad, with a sackful of presents for my favourite boy,' she promised, kissing him roundly on his small mouth.

To Louie's relief he did not object. Iris handed her son over to Sam and they followed her out of the door.

In the quiet street, Iris swung round and faced Louie. They regarded each other silently for a moment, each recalling a hundred small memories they shared, would always share, no matter how far apart.

'Merry Christmas Louie.' Iris smiled wistfully. Louie nodded, unable to speak or adequately express her gratitude. She could only guess at the empty loneliness the other woman must be feeling at that instant. She knew how others would accuse Iris of selfishness in leaving her son behind, but Louie would defend her. Only the most generous love could enable the Durham girl to turn now and leave without her small boy. Louie took Raymond's bag from Iris and clutched it to her.

The van sparked into life and chugged down the icy street, Sam and Louie waving it away. Louie smiled happily at her husband still holding their nephew. She breathed in the cold air in joyful gulps.

'What a wonderful Christmas present you've given us,' she whispered to the pale-blue sky and went to put her arms around the grinning pair who stood before her.

THE HUNGRY HILLS is the first in the Durham Mining Trilogy. The second is THE DARKENING SKIES. With the vivid backdrop of Whitton Grange strained by the tensions of the Second World War and the fate of their Italian community, THE DARKENING SKIES is a vibrant and moving story of conflicting loyalties, passions and cultures.

Praise for THE DARKENING SKIES:

'A moving and well written tale, The Darkening Skies continues the story of the people who live in the fictitious mining community of Whitton Grange. Janet convincingly portrays the rising tide of hate that engulfs the village...There is a good deal of worry, misery and poverty. But there is also courage, warmth, and, above all hope.' **The Newcastle Journal**

'This rich slice of pit-town life shows a world which is all but forgotten.'
Northern Echo

'I have just finished reading the fantastic novel 'The Darkening Skies' and I must say that I found your novel impossible to put down. You have written a story about prejudice, hatred and passion and you've managed to make me chuckle as well as shed a tear. You clearly are one of the genre's best writers. I hope that you keep producing more great books.'
J.D.B. - Malta.

***

Praise for NEVER STAND ALONE (the last in The Durham Trilogy):

'A gritty, heartrending and impassioned drama' **Newcastle Journal**

'A tough, compelling and ultimately satisfying novel ... another classy, irresistible read'
Sunderland Echo

'She pulls no punches, tells it like it is and taps directly into your emotions. Excellent'
Northern Echo

'The gritty, unforgettable story of families torn apart by the conflict that divided a nation...a powerful story'
World Books

Janet welcomes comments and feedback on her stories. If you would like to do so, you can contact her through her website: www.janetmacleodtrotter.com

Lightning Source UK Ltd.
Milton Keynes UK
UKOW030216241111

182609UK00002B/10/P